Caesar Ascending – The Han

By R.W. Peake

Also by R.W Peake

Marching With Caesar® – Birth of the 10th
Marching With Caesar – Conquest of Gaul
Marching With Caesar – Civil War
Marching With Caesar – Antony and Cleopatra, Parts I & II
Marching With Caesar – Rise of Augustus
Marching With Caesar – Last Campaign
Marching With Caesar – Rebellion
Marching With Caesar – A New Era
Marching With Caesar – Pax Romana
Marching With Caesar – Fraternitas
Marching With Caesar – Vengeance
Marching With Caesar – Rise of Germanicus
Marching With Caesar – Revolt of the Legions
Marching With Caesar – Avenging Varus, Part I
Marching With Caesar – Avenging Varus Part II
Caesar Triumphant
Caesar Ascending – Invasion of Parthia
Caesar Ascending – Conquest of Parthia
Caesar Ascending – Pandya
Caesar Ascending – The Ganges
Caesar Ascending – The Han

Critical praise for the Marching with Caesar series:

Marching With Caesar-Antony and Cleopatra: Part I-Antony
"Peake has become a master of depicting Roman military life and action, and in this latest novel he proves adept at evoking the subtleties of his characters, often with an understated humour and surprising pathos. Very highly recommended."

Marching With Caesar-Civil War
"Fans of the author will be delighted that Peake's writing has gone from strength to strength in this, the second volume...Peake manages to portray Pullus and all his fellow soldiers with a marvelous feeling of reality quite apart from the star historical name... There's history here, and character, and action enough for three novels, and all of it can be enjoyed even if readers haven't seen the first volume yet. Very highly recommended."
~The Historical Novel Society

"The hinge of history pivoted on the career of Julius Caesar, as Rome's Republic became an Empire, but the muscle to swing that gateway came from soldiers like Titus Pullus. What an amazing story from a student now become the master of historical fiction at its best."
~Professor Frank Holt, University of Houston

Caesar Ascending – The Han by R.W. Peake

Copyright © 2021 by R.W. Peake

All rights reserved. This book or any portion thereof may not be reproduced or used in any manner whatsoever without the express written permission of the publisher except for the use of brief quotations in a book review.
Cover Artwork by Michael Perry from *Imperial Chinese Armies* by CJ Peers, © Osprey Publishing, part of Bloomsbury
Cover Design by Laura Prevost
Cover Design Copyright © 2021 R. W. Peake
Maps © Google Earth®
All Rights Reserved

Foreword

Considering that I just released *Caesar Ascending-The Ganges* on August 18th, this will be short and sweet, but I also want to use this moment to start with an apology to both my editor Beth Lynne, and to my cover artist Laura Prevost, neither of whom I mentioned last time. I have no excuse other than I'm getting old, but as always, I couldn't have done this without their help, and I am especially thankful to Beth, considering that I have dragged her across the known world and forced her to become more familiar with so much of the ancient world than she probably ever wanted. And it really, really helps that Laura is able to actually understand what is going on in my head when I describe the layout of a cover to her.

This marks the last purely original story of the *Caesar Ascending* series; as I mentioned in *Ganges*, what will follow *The Han* will be the Second Edition of *Caesar Triumphant*, in two parts, which I intend on releasing by the end of the year. When I do, it will close a chapter in my career as a storyteller where I wasn't bound by the historical record, and while I currently don't have any plans for more alternative history, I confess that, for the most part, I enjoyed the process of putting myself in Caesar's *caligae* and thinking, "What would I do if I was Caesar?" when it came to accomplishing this endeavor. I emphasize "for the most part," but I blame myself for the aggravation and the sleepless nights, based on my obsessive-compulsive need to do whatever I could to make the implausible seem at least somewhat plausible.

Could Caesar and his army have traversed the known world in a decade? Probably not...but before Alexander invaded India, it was impossible for a Macedonian King to do so. Before Magellan (or to be accurate, de Magalhães) circumnavigated the globe, it was impossible. By and large, just about everything that we've done has been thought to be impossible at some point, if only by some people. That, at least, is my story, and I'm sticking to it.

And with that, my awesome readers, I hope you enjoy *Caesar Ascending-The Han.*

Semper Fidelis
R.W. Peake
September 17, 2021

Historical Notes

With every mile Caesar's army moves east, the challenge for me as both an author and someone whose knowledge of the East in general and ancient China in particular is...skimpy, is trying to decide what information is crucial to the story and what's something that's nice to know but doesn't provide the reader with meaningful context.

And, as with the kingdoms of southern India, there was *so* much to learn, but in one sense, I was fortunate because of how well-documented the ancient history of China is, going back even before the era that coincides with *Caesar Ascending*, that of the early Han Dynasty. For the most part, the members of Emperor Yuan's court were real individuals, and while Zhang Meng is my invention, his grandfather Zhang Qian existed, and as I say in the story, was one of the great explorers of his age, responsible for learning more about the western reaches of the Silk Road. General Gan existed, but General Xao and all the other officers are my creation. It's also true that the island of Zhuya (modern day Hainan) was abandoned by Emperor Yuan because of the cost involved in maintaining a presence on the island, and it's also true that the island became something of a refuge for disaffected members of Yuan's military, and that there was significant friction between the native *Li* (who still comprise a sizable ethnic minority on the island) and the Han. If there was an active rebellion by military officers on the island, it's a happy accident; it just seemed likely to me that if you have a bunch of pissed-off warriors all together on an island, it's not much of a stretch to think they might rebel, especially when Yuan already had his hands full. The rebellion of Zhizhi Chanyu and the *Xiongnu*, and the time period in which it took place, is also historically accurate; however, it was part of a much larger, far more complex situation, and let me say up front that I only skimmed the surface of that conflict, using it only for the purposes of my story.

As far as the organization of the Chinese military, as well documented as the time period was, I found it a challenge to pin down exactly when the organizational components I used were in use by the Han Dynasty, which is understandable given that it lasted about four centuries. It's entirely possible (in fact, I think it's likely) that the *Tu-wei-fu* and *Sui* I use are from the later Han Dynasty in the First and Second Centuries CE. I also want to stress that my comparisons; that a *Tu-wei-fu* was the rough equivalent of a Legion is *very* rough, and the truth is that I think it's more like a Cohort than a Legion. Where I'm on a bit of firmer ground is with the *Sui* and the *Hou*; the *Sui*, which consisted of eleven men, is a section, and with seven *Sui,* a *Hou* is close to a Century. Each *Sui* was commanded by a *Sui-Chang* (or Ducanus, although as long-time readers know I use the term Sergeant, for reasons I explained back in my very first book and which, to this point, a total of one reader has objected to), while a *Hou* was commanded by a *Hou-Chang*, which leaves the *Hou-Kuan*, which I decided to use as essentially a Primus Pilus of the *Tu-wei-fu*.

Now that I've explained how I've organized the Han, I want to explain the breakdown between what would be considered the standard infantry of the ancient world, the spearmen, and the missile troops. In almost every account that I read, there was commentary on how the Han employed missile troops to a greater degree than rival militaries of their age, and how it was the crossbow that was the missile weapon they relied on the most for their missile troops who weren't mounted. Several centuries before the crossbow became the scourge of European warfare, the Han crossbow provided the same advantages; a flatter trajectory that made aiming easier, and conversely made it more difficult for a defender to track its flight, which in turn required less skill to operate. Another factor in its ubiquity was that, during this period of time, there were issues with the quality of iron available to the Han, and the Han crossbow only required one piece of iron in the trigger, a piece where quality wasn't as important as it would be for a sword or even a spear blade. It was this issue with iron that also reduced the number of *liren*, or swordsmen in my conception of a Han *Tu-wei-fu*, so that there are four *Sui* of *Qiangmao*, or spearmen; four *Sui* of *Qiangnu*, or crossbowmen, and two *Sui* of *liren*.

Along with the crossbowmen and the challenge I believe they would provide Pullus and his comrades, there is the men who wield the *ji*, or as it's more commonly known, the halberd. And yes, I'm aware that there was a wide variety of pole weapons used by the Han that would qualify as a *ji*, but I decided on the type that's featured on the cover of the book, for the simple reason that I believe that it would be more dangerous to face. The style of *ji* with a single curved spur off of the main blade would be effective for hooking the top of a shield and pulling it towards the attacker, or using it to shove the defender backward, but with this crescent piece of iron attached just below the spear blade, an attacker has those capabilities, and the ability to trap his opponent's blade, whether it was a sword or spear. Having the Han work in pairs, with one warrior wielding a conventional spear and the other the *ji* is my own invention as well, based on nothing more than my own inner warrior geek trying to think of the best way to employ these weapons. My emphasis on both the crossbow and the *ji* is simply the continuation of the challenges that Caesar and his army would face as they march eastward and encounter new weapons and tactics, and how the Romans would defeat them. I'm fairly certain by this point that the readers of the series have picked up on a theme, and that is my belief in and admiration of what I consider to be the greatest asset the Romans possessed, and that was their adaptability, and it's become a natural process for me as I tell this story to think about how Caesar and his men would defeat some new enemy and their new weapons.

Of all of the new cultures that have become part of this story, I'm acutely aware that, of all of them, the people I call the Khmer are probably the skimpiest in terms of detail; perhaps the fact that the Khmer Empire didn't appear for more than a millennium but I use that name anyway gives an indication of the difficulty I ran into trying to get a better understanding of the people who occupied what is now part of Thailand, Cambodia, and Vietnam. For those of you more conversant with this culture during antiquity, I apologize for giving them short shrift, as it were. The city of Angkor Wat existed, of course, but again, I could find no information that indicated whether it was known by that name in the First Century BCE, so my compromise was to simply call it Angkor instead of the full name.

I have decided to include maps, not only of the assaults on both Hanou (modern day Haikou) and Yazhou (modern day Sanya), but Caesar and the army's route, starting from the western side of the Mon (Malay) Peninsula, along with the fleet's voyage to Ke Van (modern day Vinh, Vietnam).

When I release the Second Edition of *Caesar Triumphant*, I will be including the maps documenting the entire route, starting from Caesar's jumping off point into Parthia, with each locality that plays an important part of the story.

Table of Contents

Chapter One 1

Chapter Two 45

Chapter Three 88

Chapter Four 129

Chapter Five 180

Chapter Six 230

Chapter Seven 273

Chapter Eight 326

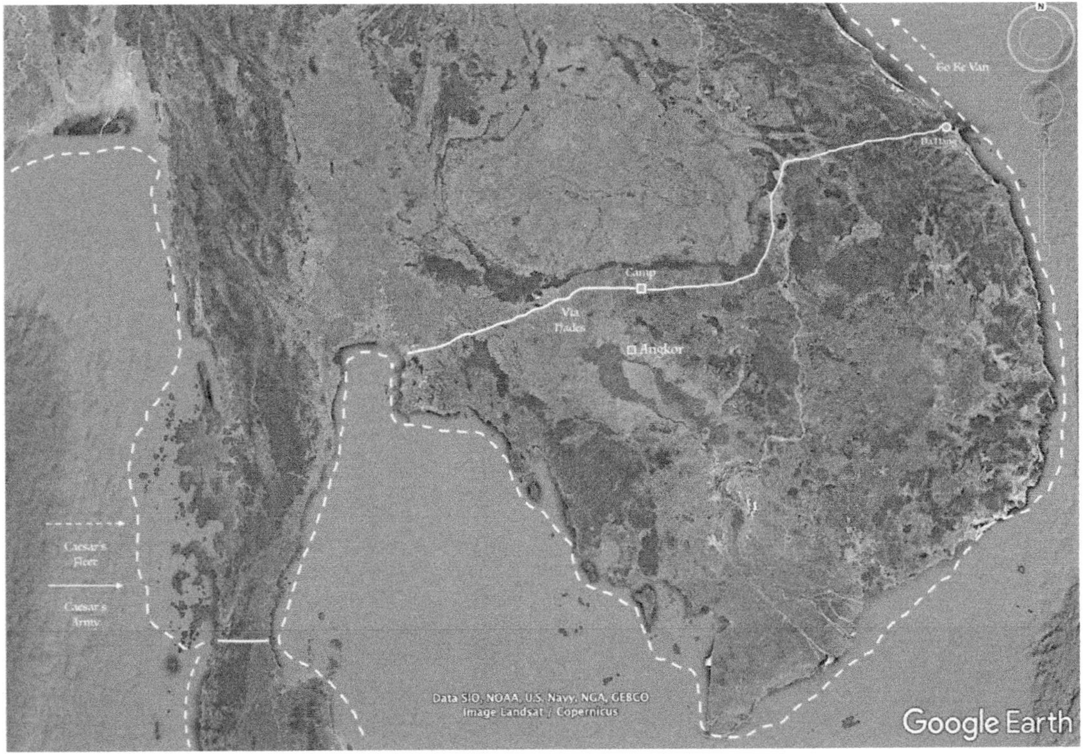
Caesar's Fleet
Caesar's Army
Camp
Angkor
Data SIO, NOAA, U.S. Navy, NGA, GEBCO
Image Landsat / Copernicus
Google Earth

Chapter One

Seven years, thought Titus Pullus. Seven long years.

"Seven years? What are you talking about?"

Quintus Balbus' words startled Pullus, making him realize that he had spoken aloud and it forced him to explain, "We've been at this for more than seven years." Pausing, Pullus added awkwardly, "That's a...long time."

"You're just realizing that now?" Balbus snorted, then nudged Scribonius. "I think Titus has finally gone soft in the head."

"After listening to you for that long, I'm just surprised it hasn't happened sooner," Scribonius scoffed.

"Better than you nattering on about your ponce Greek philosophers," Balbus retorted. "Besides, how many times have you read all those scrolls?"

"Too many to count." Scribonius sighed. "I tried to learn Sanskrit, but we weren't in India long enough to spend time on it. The Mon and Khmer didn't have any written language at all, and now that we're here in Han territory, there's no way I can decipher any of their chicken scratches. Although," he admitted, "from what I learned from Juán, their writing actually makes sense, because instead of using letters to form a word, they use a character that represents the word itself."

"That's not the only thing you've learned from her," Balbus gave Scribonius his version of a smirk, and he was rewarded by the reddening of Scribonius' face, amusing even Pullus, who had been staring morosely into the bowl of rice that had been seasoned with the dwindling supply of Indian peppers and spices that he had come to love, although more because it reminded him of the first time he had tasted them years before in Bharuch, sitting at the table of a queen with whom he was already falling in love.

"He has you there." Pullus laughed. "Old Long knew what he was doing when he introduced one of his daughters to you."

"Be quiet, and that's not how it happened," Scribonius grumbled, but said nothing else, preferring to copy Pullus and concentrate on his food.

Normally an intensely private person, Scribonius had confided to Pullus that he had begun a relationship with Juán, thanks in great part to Barhinder Gotra, who, as Diocles had suspected, had a facility for languages that, while he would never say as much, overshadowed Achaemenes, and rivaled Caesar himself in his facility for languages. The fact that they were there at all was nothing short of a miracle, and was a topic of intense debate among the rankers. Now, on this island that the Han called Zhuya, what mattered was that it was currently a permanent camp for the ever-decreasing number of Romans who comprised Caesar's army, although the Legions remained near full strength. Nearly two years had elapsed since their time on the Khmer peninsula, the previous year's nightmare of difficult terrain now behind them. Like every other Roman marching for Caesar, Scribonius thought he had been prepared for what the people of India called a *jangla,* since that had been a feature of their entire time in India, but nothing could have prepared him and his comrades for the nightmare that had come from Caesar's decision to send his army across the large peninsula that, for a second time, Caesar had decided to march across while his fleet sailed around. While Scribonius wouldn't have described it as commonplace, Caesar, and by extension, his men, were at least accustomed to the very Roman method of making certain that the shortest distance between two points was a straight line. Not for the first time, Scribonius considered what might have transpired had Caesar not learned that there was a waterborne counterpart to the Silk Road and chosen to take that instead of the harsh, arduous route that traveled through what the natives called the Hindu Kush. Nobody, not even Alexander, could have envisioned all that the men of Rome, and now, several other kingdoms, had accomplished, but to Scribonius, Caesar's greatest achievement had been somehow investing his men with, if not the same, at least a similar passion to traverse the known world. It certainly hadn't been easy; when Caesar had ordered that, rather than sail down the long but narrow peninsula where the Mon people lived, they traverse the thirty-five miles that was the narrowest part of the peninsula, it had taken them almost a month, and that was only after he, once again, managed to prevent the mutiny of his entire army, at the huge camp on an island in the middle of the southernmost of the five mouths of the Ganges that was called the Mega by the Gangaridae. The Mon hadn't been the obstacle; of the myriad people that Scribonius and his fellow Romans had encountered to that point, these people were abidingly peaceful, and rather than descend on their column in an attempt to stop the white-skinned invaders, they had seemed more bemused than anything, content to watch them struggle as they hacked a path from west to east. The Romans had been forced to negotiate the low but rugged mountains that ran down the middle of the peninsula like a spine, whereupon they were forced to wait another month before the Roman fleet was spotted sailing north after navigating around the southern tip of the peninsula under the command of the Legate Tiberius Claudius Nero. Using the maps created by Volusenus on the pioneering voyage that Caesar had sent him on when they had finally reached the Ganges that was born of desperation, a distance of what was estimated as being more than two thousand miles...each way, taking seven months. What Scribonius and his friend, along with the other Primi Pili, determined was that it was this sign of the gods' favor that kept the men under control to that point. So much had transpired before and since then, Scribonius thought sadly, but then Juán came into his mind, and he visibly brightened at the thought of her.

"Why are you smiling like an idiot?" Pullus asked irritably. "Until we hear back from the Han, we're going to sit here and rot."

"The gods forbid that Titus Pullus might not have anyone to kill for the next few months," Scribonius retorted, eliciting a chorus of snickers, but rather than Balbus, Pullus chose the fourth member at the table.

"So, how do you like being Optio in a front-line Cohort?

Lentulus says you haven't fucked anything up...yet."

Porcinus had expected this from his uncle, and if he was being honest, he was still having trouble adjusting to the idea that he had been promoted to Optio of the Second Century of the Fourth Cohort, and it was even stranger to him than it was to his uncle. The fact that it had been Caesar himself who had approved the promotion, something of a rarity that the general commanding the entire army had gotten involved, made Porcinus suspicious that his uncle had prevailed on Caesar to elevate him to the posting. However, Porcinus also was aware that winning the Civic Crown not once, having been awarded the most prized decoration the first time for saving his Pilus Prior Scribonius at Bharuch, and now twice, had certainly helped his case. That it hadn't been at the hands of an enemy combatant but one of the tigers that, during their time on what they now knew was the Khmer Peninsula, had proven to be a threat to any unwary man who walked even a short distance from the security provided by the army was one thing; that it had been Asinius Pollio's life, when one of the striped beasts had taken advantage of Pollio's curiosity when the Legate left the column that was hacking its way across the large peninsula to examine a stone idol erected in a clearing was what made Porcinus' efforts worthy of attention by Caesar. From Porcinus' perspective, which he kept to himself even from his uncle, it had simply been a matter of being in the right place at the right time because he too had stepped away from the column, where he had been marching as the Optio in the Sixth Century of the Tenth Cohort, to relieve himself. It had been Pollio's horse suddenly bursting through the thick and tangled leafy undergrowth in an obvious panic that first alerted Porcinus, and he was forced to throw himself out of the way as the animal galloped past, eyes so wide with fright that Porcinus would remember later that he saw the white, although it was the Legate's shout for help that got him moving without any thought.

Instinctively following the path Pollio's horse had made as it crushed the smaller vegetation in its flight, Porcinus did think to draw his *gladius,* but he wasn't wearing armor, and the foliage was so thick that he didn't have a clear view aside from a flashing glimpse of orange, black, and white, while he heard both the beast roaring with what turned out to be frustration mingled with the panicked neighing of the horse and Pollio's continued shouts. It was, Porcinus would reflect later, something he would have otherwise done differently, charging headlong into a small clearing containing what was a startlingly lifelike but massive stone carving of a head, upon which Pollio was perched, holding on with one hand while flailing with his own *spatha*, the longer cavalry sword, with the other. At the base of the carving was the tiger, snarling in frustration as it sat on its haunches to use its massive front paws to swipe at the blade as it whistled past its head. When he emerged into the clearing, rather than stop to assess matters he had run headlong at the turned back of the tiger, but while in that moment he was unaware that he was bellowing at the top of his lungs, the tiger clearly heard, spun about, and in one smooth motion, leapt at this new threat. The fact that he was generally aware of what had happened next was due only to Pollio, who witnessed it all, because for Porcinus, everything was a blur, where he was seemingly enveloped in a world composed only of orange, black, and white, with a stench in his nostrils unlike anything he had ever smelled before. It was the sound, however, that Porcinus would remember the rest of his days, a snarling, ferocious noise that completely overwhelmed his auditory sense in a manner similar to his vision, but one that immediately changed to a low, breathy moan that was eerily human, at least in the moment. What remained with Porcinus wasn't as much the sight and sound of being attacked by a tiger; it was the sensations of being crushed under the dead weight of the massive animal, the searing pain coming from his upper back and left shoulder, and the sudden sticky, wet warmth that doused his lower body. It had taken four men, who arrived just heartbeats later, to pull the corpse of the animal off of Porcinus, but he didn't rise immediately, staring up at the green canopy as he suddenly realized that he had never really taken the time to notice just how many shades of green there were in this part of the world. Pollio was unharmed, having leapt off of his horse onto the broad, flat head of the stone carving that, under other circumstances, would have been yet another object of wonder and interest to the Romans. Instead, what was undoubtedly some sort of native idol of some sort, albeit with vastly different facial features than anything they had seen before, barely rated a glance as the entire progress of the army, as excruciatingly slow as it was, came to a stop. By the time Caesar arrived at the gallop with some of his bodyguards, Porcinus was sitting up as a *medicus* inspected his back through the shreds of his ruined and bloody tunic, while a small crowd, including Pollio, had gathered around the dead animal.

"Porcinus here saved my bacon, Caesar," Pollio had said, whereupon Porcinus heard for the first of what would be many, many times, about how, reacting instinctively, Porcinus thrust his left arm out as if he was carrying a shield, while executing the thrust the Romans called the first position.

The animal's own momentum and its massive weight had done the rest; this, at least, was how Porcinus viewed it, and his immediate concern, which was borne out, was how his uncle would react.

"What were you thinking?"

The only reason Pullus' question wasn't delivered at full volume was because of where they were, in the hospital tent, which, as it had been from almost the beginning of this part of the campaign beyond India and the Mon Peninsula, hacking their way across the large peninsula on what the men had taken to calling the Via Hades, was full of men whose fever had become serious, but Porcinus wasn't fooled, knowing he would have been wincing from the pain to his ears just as much as he was from the wounds.

Perhaps because of his long exposure to his original Centurion Scribonius, Porcinus had learned the best defense was to remain calm, which he was now when he replied mildly, "That a Legate is worth more to this army than me?"

Porcinus was rewarded by the look of consternation on his uncle's face as Pullus struggled to find what he considered an appropriate response instead of blurting out the truth, that as far as his uncle was concerned, he was the one man in this army, save for Caesar himself, and perhaps Scribonius and Balbus, who was the most important to him.

"Well," he said with a grudging humor, "when you put it

that way, I suppose it's hard to argue."

Over the ensuing two weeks, Pullus would have cause to rethink his position because, as Porcinus had been warned was likely, the long, deep furrows that ran from below his left shoulder blade up and over his clavicle became corrupt, although the single puncture wound on his upper bicep remained clean, and Porcinus had hovered between life and death as the Pandyan healer that was now part of Caesar's retinue worked tirelessly to keep him alive. It had been a miserable experience for Porcinus, suspended in one of the hammocks in the almost eight dozen wagons that were now required to carry men who hadn't fallen to an enemy blade or arrow, but to a foul vapor, or a bite from one of the seemingly millions of different bugs that carried with it some form of exotic illness that were a daily feature of this world. Nevertheless, he had survived the ordeal, healing slowly, and now he bore the scars with a secret pride; normally, having scars on a Roman's back was a mark of shame since it was because of either a striping or they had turned their back in battle, but these were different. His promotion to Optio had come two months after the incident, during the period of time they had stopped in the middle of the peninsula to wait out the monsoon season, but at the insistence of his uncle, Porcinus had been relegated to serving as Optio in the Sixth Century of the Tenth Cohort, the more traditional path for men being promoted. He had been resentful at first, if only because by this point there were perhaps three Romans per section, with the rest of the higher numbered Cohorts of the third line composed of a mishmash of Parthians, Pandyan, and a handful of Bharuchian, with a sprinkling of men who had been vague about their origins but who had been deemed worthy of enlisting, most of them found in the Greek colony of Palaesimundum on Taprobane. Early on during his time with the Fifth, Porcinus had shied away from performing what was essentially a ritual that had been passed down through the centuries, of spending part of the night circulating around the fires of each section, albeit only because he couldn't understand what was being said. It had been the *Aquilifer* of his Century, Lucius Petronius, who had offered him some advice.

"When we started moving Romans up to plump up the first line Cohorts and took on the Parthians, I wasn't happy about it. But," he admitted, "I was wrong to think they didn't have what it takes to be under the standard. We only got a handful of men from Bharuch, but they were Macedonian trained and are some hard bastards, and we have enough boys who speak Greek that it wasn't as hard. Then, we plumped up with Pandyans, and I felt the same way as I did about the Parthians, although not for as long. They," he said with obvious pride, "are good men, Optio. And, once you learn enough of their words, they'll accept you much faster."

"I don't have the time to learn Parthian, then Sanskrit, then Tamil!" Porcinus protested.

"I didn't say you have to learn how to speak it fluently," Petronius told him patiently. "What matters is the effort. Once they see you making the effort, Optio, then you'll see a different side to them."

Somewhat to his embarrassment, Porcinus quickly learned that Petronius had been absolutely correct; within a matter of a couple of months, and with the help of Barhinder, he had learned enough to carry on a rudimentary conversation in four different tongues. Most importantly, when he showed up outside a section tent, and addressed a Parthian ranker in his tongue, or a Pandyan, the rankers showed him mercy by switching to Latin, although it was a kind of Latin that would have made a man like Marcus Tullius Cicero pull out what was left of his hair. In reality, it was a mishmash of languages, dialects, and colloquialisms that would gradually turn into something of its own language, but originally spoken only by a few thousand men, scattered over the Legions of Caesar's army, although it would spread from there, through the women, then children of these men. During their time on Zhuya and after they had conquered the island, when he was informed by his uncle that, when Princeps Prior Lentulus' Optio had succumbed to a fever, Lentulus had personally requested Porcinus to move into the dead man's spot, Porcinus had almost said no because of his reluctance to leave the men of the Sixth of the Tenth. Only when Pullus had growled that it wasn't really a request had he relented, but he still occasionally dropped by his old Century, just as he did with his original home in the First of the Second, thinking that he was unique in this when the truth was that almost every man who had been elevated into the Optionate did the same thing, at least at first.

Aside from his personal successes, however, that period of time when Caesar's army had carved a path through the lands occupied by the people known as the Khmers, who unlike the Mon people of the first narrow peninsula they had cut across as their fleet took the longer sea route, were anything but peaceful, and it had been a torment for the army as a whole, culminating in what was the third attempted mutiny of the army, when a substantial number of the Romans in the Legions, including some Centurions, had finally had enough of Caesar's dream, his *real* dream that he had first shared with his army in their huge camp at the mouth of the Ganges the year before. That had been the site of the second mutiny, back when the idea of returning to Rome had still been what seemed to be an achievable dream. As Caesar had planned, they had reached the Ganges in what was the fifth year of the campaign, only after helping the young Pandyan king Nedunj, first of his name, to subdue and ultimately annex their hereditary enemy, the Chola, who occupied the eastern half of the lower part of India. It had been accomplished by a combination of guile, treachery, and a reliance on the impetuous nature of the Crown Prince of the Chola Empire, Prince Divakar, who, in direct violation of his father, King Karikala, had violated the terms of a negotiated settlement that gave Caesar and his army a guarantee of safe passage through their lands.

The overland route that Caesar chose to use had been carefully selected, although not for the stated reasons that he had given to his Primi Pili to disseminate to their Legions. Superficially, negotiating the narrow pass in the line of mountains that effectively served as the border between the Pandyan and Cholan Empires was the quickest route for Caesar's half of the army to reach the eastern coast of southern India, because in a manner similar to their advance on Bharuch from Pattala two years earlier, Caesar had divided his army, but this time, it was Legate Pollio and the 5th, 6th, 8th, 28th, and 30th who used the fleet, although their departure from Muziris only occurred after Caesar and the 10th, 12th, 15th, 21st, 22nd, and 25th Legions departed from Karoura, where they marched with King Nedunj and his army. The guile in the plan that had actually been suggested by the young Pandyan king, although it was modified by Caesar, relied on Nedunj's intimate knowledge of his Cholan enemy, particularly Divakar, who, during a period of time when Nedunj's father Puddapandyan and King Karikala had attempted to settle their differences diplomatically, had been a guest of the Pandyan king for almost a year, which in turn was reciprocated when young prince Nedunj had accompanied Divakar back to the Cholan capital of Uraiyur, where he spent the same interval of time. Over the course of those two years, Nedunj, displaying the acumen that had initially impressed Caesar, had observed Divakar not through the eyes of a playmate, albeit of royal blood, but as a future king would evaluate a future adversary.

Integral to the Roman-Pandyan plan was Nedunj's knowledge of Divakar, and his conviction that, despite his father's wishes, the headstrong Crown Prince would view Caesar's army as an invader and would behave accordingly. Under the guise of merely escorting Caesar's part of the army to the border befitting a kingdom that had been awarded Friend and Ally status by Caesar, in his role as Dictator for Life of the Roman Republic, the combined host reached the narrow pass, where Nedunj and his force were marching just ahead of the huge baggage train, and with the 10th in the vanguard. On the surface, it was an unremarkable event; the fact that Nedunj had attached himself and his hundred elephants, all of them armored and crewed, along with his infantry and horse cavalry immediately behind the last Legion but in front of the Roman baggage train was a deliberate provocation, knowing that Divakar would have scouts on the Pandyan side of the border watching from the cover of the forest on the slopes of the mountains that surrounded the road who would report that the Pandyans were part of this foreign army and not simply following it. And, exactly as Nedunj had assured Caesar, Divakar, who had asserted his authority as both Crown Prince and the commander of the Southern Army of the Chola, had arrayed his forces in the same forest but on the Cholan side of the border, prepared for battle. More importantly, Nedunj's prediction that Divakar would be unable to restrain himself and order an attack and would do so using his own elephants was proven accurate. However, what Nedunj had *not* anticipated was that Divakar would spring his trap fatally early, while the 10th was laboring up the steepest, narrowest part of the pass, thereby reducing his attack to a narrow front only five elephants across. With all of his other faults, Nedunj had been honest with Caesar when he told the Roman that when Divakar attacked, they could be certain that the Crown Prince would be leading from the front, and this was borne out, Divakar riding the elephant in the center of the rank of beasts who at least did have the advantage of attacking downhill. It also meant that, because Pullus and the 10th were prepared for it, and using the tactics they had developed over the winter, the two-man teams responsible for employing the deadly but volatile jars of naphtha, which the teams carried in net bags suspended from their person and their *furca*, turned the five animals and the men riding them into blazing torches of burning flesh. What transpired after that was something that the Romans had become accustomed to, the sight of more than a hundred armored elephants panicking and, displaying an agility that they still found surprising even after witnessing it on two other occasions, turning about to stampede through the ranks of their human comrades in the Cholan infantry who had swept down from their position on the southern slope of the pass, then scattering the Cholan horse cavalry.

It was a battle that reminded men like Pullus and those other veterans who had been there of Thapsus, when Scipio's elephants had turned into the deadliest weapon for which Caesar and his men could have dreamed. With the Cholan's attempted ambush, Nedunj dropped any pretext of peaceful intentions by moving to the head of the column, albeit with a fair amount of difficulty as his Roman allies were forced to scramble out of the way, to go in pursuit of the shattered enemy, catching up with them when one of the surviving officers of noble rank tried to rally and consolidate the Cholan forces. Aside from the initial contact, Caesar's men didn't participate in the ensuing slaughter, and while Nedunj's horse cavalry ran down the panicked and fleeing Cholan spearmen, the Pandyan king and his corps of elephants and their crews engaged in the kind of combat that, prior to the arrival of Rome in the form of Caesar, had represented the ultimate combat power in the Indian part of the known world for several centuries. By the end of the day, the Southern Army of the Chola Empire essentially no longer existed, with less than thirty elephants remaining, many of them injured, while those considered suitable were subsumed into the Pandyan force. More importantly, within a span of heartbeats after Divakar initiated his disastrous attack, a rider was galloping southwest, heading for Muziris and carrying the orders to Pollio to immediately set sail, their destination Taprobane, which had been claimed by Chola and was garrisoned with troops, although this island had been the bone of contention between Pandya and Chola for decades. Recognizing the island's strategic importance to his larger goals, Caesar had deemed that it must be under Roman control, albeit through Pandya, King Nedunj being perfectly happy to add the island to his domains in exchange for a lifetime permission for the Romans to maintain a supply base, using the Greek trading colony of Palaesimundum, located a short distance upriver from the strait between island and mainland. As it turned out, the overwhelming force hadn't been necessary; the Cholan garrison at Palaesimundum had been poorly led, and they were completely unprepared for the sight of Roman ships arriving at the small complex of docks and warehouses shortly after daylight, with those soldiers who survived the onslaught in chains by the end of the noon watch. There was another Cholan force on the island located on the cape that jutted out several miles on the northern end, where what constituted the Cholan navy in the form of a handful of *biremes* patrolled the narrow strait that was almost connected by a series of smaller islands. This took Pollio's Legions another two days to reduce, so that a week to the day after Pollio and his part of the army departed from Muziris, Taprobane was completely under Roman control, whereupon the Legion *immunes* were put to work, using their unskilled comrades as the labor to construct what would essentially be a copy of the Parthian port of

Caesarea, rendering the former Greek colony unrecognizable, which took another two weeks.

Meanwhile, Caesar and Nedunj hadn't dawdled, spending only a day after the death of Divakar encamped, and that was only to discuss the next steps. At that moment, neither of them were aware that they now had an ally, in the form of the highest ranking Cholan noble to survive the debacle of the day before, Senganan his name, and he was a senior councilor to his King Karikala. His presence with Divakar had been an attempt by his father to try to keep the Crown Prince under a semblance of control, the failure of which Senganan acknowledged to his King on his arrival back at Madoura, where the king was waiting for his son's return. Fortunately for Senganan, while Karikala had loved his oldest son, he had already come to the conclusion that the wrong son was Crown Prince, so that in some ways, Divakar's death solved a problem he would have had to confront at some point in the future. As events transpired, however, that forgiveness didn't extend to the Romans, one in particular, because in another example of what his men would call Caesar's Luck, and most importantly for the combined fortunes of Romans and Pandyans, Senganan had witnessed the barbarian Romans' use of naphtha, and the ease with which what Senganan, like all of his contemporaries in India, had previously considered an almost unconquerable force literally heartbeats before, was destroyed. It had begun when a giant barbarian with a white-crested helmet ordered a line of men forward working in pairs, changing Senganan's world by flinging smoking jars that erupted in sticky flame, but Senganan witnessing that event ultimately worked in their favor, when he took it upon himself to seek a truce with the Romans to try and salvage something of the previous agreement, where Karikala had provisionally agreed to allow the Romans safe passage through his kingdom. Senganan had returned to Madoura with little hope that he would be allowed to live long enough to explain himself to Karikala, but to his surprise, he hadn't been executed, and he went on to advise his King to seek a meeting with Caesar before deciding whether to resist the Romans. The result was Senganan returning from Madoura to meet the advancing army, and under Karikala's authority, informing Caesar that the King had learned that his son the Crown Prince had initiated an unprovoked attack, and that the agreement for safe passage still held.

The march to Madoura took three days, Senganan unaware that this was a leisurely pace for the Romans, but it was a crucial period of time because it gave the Cholan noble, who was treated as an honored guest and afforded his own tent and body slave, although Senganan knew perfectly well the slave was spying on him, to see firsthand what made these Romans so formidable. Yes, the naphtha weapon that they employed, which Senganan had heard of and knew came from Parthia, was certainly part of it, but what he saw in the form of the ordered lines of tents, the uniformity, and more than anything, the manner in which the men of Caesar's Legions behaved and the way they responded to their Centurions left a deep impression on Senganan. The result was that by the time they came within sight of the walls of Madoura, Senganan was determined to convince Karikala to follow the lead of their mortal enemy, the Pandya, in forming an alliance with the invaders. It wasn't totally because Senganan was intimidated; he found to his surprise that he liked Caesar a great deal, and he actually believed the Roman when he assured Senganan that his only remaining desire was to reach the Ganges. That Caesar's purpose in doing so was to assault and take the fabled city of Palibothra wasn't Senganan's, or the Cholans' concern; that kingdom could have been on the other side of the world, their actions having absolutely no impact on the Chola. Their concerns centered on the Pandya to their west and the Andhra to their north, and Senganan was acutely aware that if he couldn't convince Karikala to agree to an alliance but the king still allowed the Romans to continue their progress northward, it was entirely possible that the young, vigorous King of the Andhra, Satakarni, second of his name, would see the value in such an agreement. This would isolate the Chola, who would then be surrounded by the two strongest rivals to their power in southern India, supported by these foreign invaders who had conquered Parthia, Pattala, and Bharuch, and inflicted enough damage on the Pandyans that King Nedunj sought an accommodation with them.

No, it was more than just possessing this evil substance, of which they seemed to have an ample supply judging from the number of wagons, all of them painted with a large red circle, that was part of the most massive baggage train Senganan had ever seen. And, at first, it appeared that Karikala intended on following his counsel, allowing the Roman army to make camp five miles south of Madoura under the pretext of an official meeting between the King and Caesar. It was during their first meeting that the Roman Caesar had, with a casualness that even Senganan found infuriating, informed Karikala that, not only was the Roman army twice the size of what the Cholans had been allowed to see, the other half had landed on the island they called Taprobane but the people of southern India called Ravana. In Caesar's telling, while their intentions had been peaceful, with the only goal being improving the old Greek trading post at Palaesimundum, the commander of the Chola garrison had launched an unprovoked attack on the Romans that forced them to defend themselves. That it resulted in the eradication of any Chola presence on the island was, in Caesar's telling, an unfortunate accident, but he also had made it clear to Karikala that he wouldn't be handing control of the small forts at the trading post and on the northernmost tip of the island back to Chola. Reeling from the shock of the double blows of losing his son and a strategically important island, Karikala had listlessly agreed to allow the Romans to continue their northward journey, whereupon the combined forces of Rome and Pandya, along with the remnant of the Southern Army that had fled to Madoura, made the fifty-mile journey north to the Chola capital of Uraiyur, where Caesar and his army made another camp, although this one was within sight of the walls of the city, where the two parties settled down to wait in an uneasy truce.

The events that transpired after the Romans' arrival outside Uraiyur was caused by a spontaneous comment that Senganan had made to Karikala immediately after the first meeting between Caesar and his officers, which had included the Primi Pili, and the king and his senior council outside Madoura, whereupon Titus Pullus suddenly found himself the target of a vengeful king who, as Senganan decided in the aftermath, was grieving for his dead son more deeply than he had let on. Although this also ended up ultimately working in Caesar's favor, Pullus wasn't particularly appreciative or happy about a barbarian king sending four pairs of men, salvaged from the large pit in the ground inside Uraiyur that served as a prison into the Roman camp to murder him, but as Scribonius had already pointed out by this time, it was hardly surprising; even from a distance, Titus Pullus was a distinctive figure, and Senganan had been in a position to witness and correctly guess that it had been Pullus who issued the orders to his men that culminated in Prince Divakar's fiery death. On the part of Lord Senganan, he didn't have any ulterior motive in mentioning this to his King as they returned to Madoura after he had seen the giant Roman on the day of Divakar's death when Senganan had returned under the Indian version of a flag of truce. It was only in retrospect that he realized he should have anticipated linking the Roman to Divakar's death might evoke a reaction, particularly given the horrific manner of his son's demise. Karikala's knowledge of Pullus' role had culminated with the Chola king making his agreement to the terms presented to him by Caesar and King Nedunj contingent on one nonnegotiable condition, and that was the death of Titus Pullus. Otherwise, he assured his two adversaries, he would commit to bringing ultimate destruction, to Cholan, Pandyan, and Roman, even as he acknowledged that it would be a futile enterprise. For a brief span of time, Pullus considered himself a dead man when viewing the situation pragmatically, but while he was willing to offer himself as sacrifice, Caesar wasn't, and Caesar's counterproposal for a duel between Pullus and a champion selected by the Cholan king was, grudgingly, accepted. What transpired was not only a brief combat between Pullus and Prashant, the commander of Karikala's royal bodyguard, it added to the legend of Titus Pullus; more crucially, watching Prashant slain within a matter of heartbeats, and with what to the Cholan king was an ease that displayed the huge Roman's utter contempt for his foe, not only effectively ended the chances of Karikala acceding to the terms, but ensured his obsession with avenging his son, thereby giving his enemies the very pretext for the war that at least one of them in King Nedunj, had wanted all along.

The result of this second attempt in the camp was another failure, with three of the four pairs of men barely penetrating the earthen wall, while one man of the last pair actually made it to Pullus' tent. He was stopped by Barhinder Gotra, who just happened to rouse himself from his spot against the back wall of the outer office for a reason he would never be able to explain to check on his master, who was sleeping soundly on his cot. Reacting without thinking, Barhinder threw himself at the Cholan who had just entered through a slit in the tent, the Bharuch youth armed only with the dagger he had snatched from Diocles' desk that the Greek clerk had only recently begun to keep close to hand, strongly suspecting that the Cholan king would make another attempt. Pullus emerged unscathed, while Barhinder sustained a serious wound that took several weeks to heal, but the youth would realize relatively quickly that, by earning this scar he would carry for the rest of his life, he received something of far more value, the trust and protection of the Roman he had once hated with the passion that only the young possess. In a larger sense, it also provided the pretext Nedunj, and Caesar, needed, enabling them to execute the plan that they had actually begun forming during their time in Karoura, culminating in an assault on Uraiyur after Karikala refused to agree to accept the terms offered by the Roman and Pandyan leaders. And, to Karikala's credit, he had seen through the fiction that Chola would be what the Romans called a client, with a limited set of rights, but would instead be an outright vassal kingdom controlled by their hereditary enemy, the Pandya. Nevertheless, his councilors, Senganan included, had urged him to make an accommodation, arguing that one never knew what the future held, and this could prove to be a temporary condition, imposed only as long as the Romans were in India. Certainly, they had argued, the Romans would ultimately return back to their part of the world once their leader Caesar had achieved what Senganan had correctly guessed was his burning ambition to supplant Alexander as the greatest general in history. At the time, it had seemed a reasonable assumption, but it hadn't swayed Karikala, and when it became obvious that the Chola king was willing to sacrifice every man, woman, and child inside the capital of Uraiyur, the nobles took matters into their own hands, with Lord Venkata slaying the warrior Yogesh, who had assumed command of the royal bodyguard after Prashant's death, and Senganan driving his sword into Karikala's body, even as their city was burning and enemy troops, exclusively Pandyan and led by King Nedunj, were literally fighting in the entrance to the Cholan king's throne room. The conditions for the assault itself had been part of the agreement between Nedunj and Caesar; the only aid the Romans provided was in the form of their artillery, using a supply of their precious naphtha, relegating Pullus and his comrades to being spectators as a young king fulfilled an ambition stretching back generations on the part of every Pandyan king, the conquest of Chola.

With affairs in Uraiyur settled, and with Caesar holding the two surviving sons of Karikala, Princes Kumaran and Karthikeyan, hostage, with Senganan as their *de facto* guardian, the Romans departed, leaving King Nedunj to achieve the final submission of the last remaining army of the Chola, the Northern Army commanded by Kavirathan, Karikala's younger brother. The young Pandyan king proved equal to the challenge, thereby securing all of southern India, while Taprobane remained as what would become the last outpost in what was the longest chain of supply bases in the known world that, ultimately, stretched from Rome, down the peninsula of Italia to Brundisium, across Our Sea, to the twin cities of Ctesiphon and Seleucia, then to the capital of the Roman province Parthia Inferior at Susa, with the Western portion culminating at the now four year-old port town of Caesarea, at the mouth of the Euphrates. From there, the old Alexandrian depots of Harmozeia and Barbaricum had been resurrected and revitalized, with the terminus for the northern, and heavily Greek influenced kingdoms of India, at Bharuch, where a widowed queen was secretly raising the son of one of Caesar's Centurions, with the city serving as a conduit for the goods produced in the Indian interior, while also supplanting Pattala as the preferred waypoint on both the overland and waterborne

Silk Road. In recognition of its importance, while it didn't keep a Praetor after Publius Ventidius was summoned to the Ganges, and was administered as a client kingdom, it became the home of the 6th Legion, commanded by Marcus Junius Felix, who Caesar had sent by using the overland route from the Andhra kingdom, which followed the headwaters of the Narmada. The 14th Legion, under the command of Primus Pilus Gnaeus Figulus, who had proven to be crucial to the efforts of Gaius Octavius when the young Praetor had assaulted Ecbatana, had been dispatched to Bharuch from Parthia under Caesar's orders. Once Caesar concluded his negotiations with the Andhra king Satakarni, which included sending a guide, the 14th had been the first Roman Legion to make the overland trek that ended in Kantakosylla, where they were met by part of the fleet that had brought the 6th from the Ganges, who retraced the 14th's route back to Bharuch, while the 14th used those ships to unite with the rest of Caesar's army, still in their Ganges camp. On the southwest coast of the vast country known as India, Muziris became the next waypoint, but Caesar's decision to detach his 22nd Legion when the reunited army was still in the Andhra kingdom and preparing to traverse the final five hundred miles to the mouth of the Ganges, sending them back to the Friend and Ally of Rome Pandyan kingdom, was based in what Caesar considered alarming signs of King Nedunj reconsidering his kingdom's relationship with Rome. That Primus Pilus Crispus and his men were also sent back with a not insubstantial portion of their precious supply of the weapon that had proven so terribly effective against their enemies was a reminder to Nedunj that, at least to this point during their time on Zhuya in what was now the seventh year of this extraordinary campaign, he had heeded.

It had been in the Andhra kingdom, meeting with their king Satakarni, the second of his name and about a decade older than his fellow king Nedunj, that Caesar was first confronted by the fact that culminated in the second mutiny of his army. The exact whereabouts of Palibothra on the Ganges had been a matter of mystery to the Romans, and it was only with hindsight that Caesar determined that he had been deliberately, if not misled, then kept in the dark by his ostensible allies, starting with King Peithon of Pattala. With the Pattalan king, Caesar was willing to grant that the misunderstanding might have resulted in the fact that, while the Pattalans, who were directly descended from the Macedonians in Alexander's army, their citadel even being constructed by Alexander's most trusted and beloved general, Hephaestion, spoke Greek, it was in a dialect that might have been understandable three centuries earlier, but was extremely difficult for modern Greek speakers like Caesar to understand. The same couldn't be said for Queen Hyppolita of Bharuch; her Greek was flawless, but again, there was a possibility that, being a woman, King Abhiraka had never involved her in any discussions about the exact location of the fabled city. It was Nedunj, however, who Caesar felt certain had withheld the crucial information that, rather than being a matter of perhaps a hundred miles up the Ganges, the city was almost four hundred miles inland. This, in and of itself, might not have been an insurmountable problem, but from Satakarni, he also learned that, perhaps for the only time, the city of Palibothra was every bit as powerful and wealthy as the rankers had made it out to be. Satakarni had informed Caesar that the city was supposed to be about nine miles long and five miles wide, in the shape of a parallelogram, with two sides protected by the Ganges on the short eastern and northern sides, and another river along the southern side, with more than five hundred towers and more than sixty gates. Also, and even worse, and again according to Satakarni, the King of the Gangaridae could summon at least two hundred thousand men, although most of them were poorly trained levies armed with only a spear and shield and no real armor. While this was daunting, if only because of the numbers, it still wasn't the worst of it; he also had twenty thousand cavalry, evenly split between lancers and archers, while still using two-man *quadrigae*, numbering two thousand, but what spelled the doom of Caesar and his army's plans was the fact that he used elephants, though it wasn't the animals themselves but how many he supposedly had at his command, which Satakarni estimated to be between three and four thousand.

    The problem confronting Caesar stemmed from the fact that they didn't have nearly enough naphtha left to douse that many animals; in its simplest terms, Caesar and his army had finally met a foe that, even if they could defeat these Gangaridae, there wouldn't be enough men left over to return back to Rome intact. Lord Senganan was still accompanying Caesar at this point, along with the two royal hostages, who remained with Caesar in a silent warning to Nedunj about the danger of ambition, and the Cholan nobleman had made the case that, while not lying, King Satakarni had been merely repeating what he had been told. This certainly seemed plausible, but in a subsequent conversation, the Andhran king convinced Caesar that he was speaking from experience, albeit secondhand, through his father Satakarni, the first of his name, who had launched an expedition against the city when he was crown prince. The defeat had been sound enough that Satakarni the First had never even hinted at making a second attempt, and on his deathbed, had sworn his son to refrain from making another try. They were, Satakarni had said in what would be their last conversation, simply too powerful to assault, even for the most formidable army in the known world. This didn't mean that Caesar completely abandoned the idea; even before he had left Muziris, he sent orders back to Parthia to replenish the naphtha supply, but even allowing for the amount of time it took for messages to make the arduous journey from Octavian in Susa, all that Caesar received was silence, nor did his army ever receive another shipment of the precious substance; while he would suspect it to be the case, Caesar was destined to never learn that this had been deliberate on the part of Marcus Agrippa, although on the express orders of Octavian.

Nevertheless, he led his fleet north as planned, while a reduced cavalry force remained ashore, paralleling the fleet, swapping out mounts and riders every fifth day, although in a reversal of his practice when they had sailed from Parthia, then from Bharuch to Muziris, Caesar hadn't landed the rest of the army every five days. Gradually, more than just the Centurions noticed that Caesar didn't seem to be in any hurry, not remaining under sail during the night but anchoring, even when the night was spent offshore. The tarrying was deliberate, and twofold; Caesar hadn't completely abandoned the idea of sailing as far up the Ganges as possible before disembarking to march on Palibothra, but to do that, he needed to ensure that his army didn't face the Gangaridae host at full strength. The second factor involved the naphtha, as he hoped that at any moment, the lookout who manned the small platform atop the mainmast would shout that there was a ship approaching from the south, and that instead of the normal array of merchant ships that they encountered in each direction on a regular basis, it would be a Liburnian, alerting him that his orders had been carried out. Although the naphtha was important, he had sent Quintus Salvidienus Rufus on an odyssey of his own, one that would fundamentally transform the political landscape in faraway Rome, potentially stopping what he had come to believe was another upheaval back in the city he still thought of as his home in the process. It wasn't to be; although Caesar remained in contact with the Pandya, the new supply base on Taprobane, and with Bharuch, receiving relatively regular reports, and even from Susa and its new Praetor Marcus Agrippa, though sporadically, neither the general nor most of the men currently in the army would ever have any contact with Italia ever again, and for the tiny portion of men who did reemerge from the far end of the world, it wouldn't be for the next several years.

To Caesar's surprise, once he finally stood before the army in the sprawling camp that had been constructed on an island in in the southernmost of the five mouths of the Ganges, where he essentially acknowledged his error about the location of Palibothra, a substantial number of the men, not quite a majority but close to it, clamored to continue on to the city, despite the distance. Even after he relayed what he had been told about the defenses, and the supposed numbers of defenders, emphasizing the number of elephants and pointing out how unlikely it was that their supply of the precious naphtha would be sufficient, while this persuaded some men, there was a stubborn contingent of men who persisted. These holdouts were men like Balbus, for whom the news of how heavily defended the city was absolute proof of the amount of wealth contained within.

It had led to several discussions during the evening meal in Pullus' tent that grew increasingly heated, with Balbus essentially repeating the same thing, "There's a reason that this Gangaridae king has an army that big! That place must be stuffed with gold, silver, and jewels. And," he would point out, not every time but with regularity, "if there are four hundred thousand people inside that city, we'll have a haul of slaves that will match the money we made from the sale of all those Gauls!"

Variations of these discussions that usually turned into arguments were taking place throughout the Legions, from the Centurions down to the lowest Gregarii, and it made for a tense several weeks, because Caesar refused to budge, both physically and in his decision to abandon Palibothra as an objective. His stated reasons for his refusal was that he was hoping that the Gangaridae king, whose name they had finally learned was named Agrammes, would dispatch a portion of his army, in numbers that the Romans could manage to defeat without a terrible cost, then sail the almost two hundred miles north, across the vast Ganges Delta to assault the city of Gange, which was situated on the northern bank of the northernmost mouth of the Ganges. Alternatively, he had hinted at the possibility that they wouldn't be forced to return from the Ganges emptyhanded, after arranging a heavy tribute payment from the Gangaridae, in exchange for what even the Gangaridae would have to acknowledge was the most veteran and formidable army in their world. This had the added benefit of being partially true, or at least appearing to be true, because within three days of their coming ashore to occupy the island camp, they were approached by a delegation composed of a dozen men, each of them on elephants. Although the Romans knew precious little about the Gangaridae, as Caesar and his officers were to learn from that first meeting, the Gangaridae, and their king Agrammes, who in fact did rule from Palibothra, was troublingly well-informed about the foreign invaders. So disturbed was Caesar that he summoned Senganan to his private quarters after the delegation left, and although their visit had presented a series of challenges, for Caesar, these other challenges were secondary to how the Gangaridae had learned so much in such a short span of time.

"Did King Karikala have any communication with the

Gangaridae?" Caesar asked the Cholan noble bluntly.

While Senganan still entertained hopes that Caesar would be good to his word and allow him to return to Chola, despite the probable danger he would put himself in at the hands of the Pandyan Lord Maran, who he had been informed by Caesar was now serving as the "temporary" administrator of Uraiyur, his larger concern was for Kumaran and Karthikeyan, the two surviving males of Karikala's line. By this point, he had had enough interaction with Caesar to somewhat trust the Roman general, at least to the point where he felt certain neither of the young Cholan princes had anything to fear from their captor; it was the Pandyan vipers now in Uraiyur who Senganan feared, particularly Lord Sundara.

Sitting across from Caesar at the table where the general took his meals, somewhat unusual in itself, Senganan answered honestly, "No, Caesar. I do not believe it even occurred to King Karikala to warn a kingdom so far to the north. Now," he allowed, "he *might* have thought to alert King Satakarni, if only because our relations with that kingdom were better than with Pandya, although not much." Nodding, he assured Caesar, "We were not the source of this information reaching King Agrammes' ear."

"Then it must have been Satakarni," Caesar muttered, then gave a hiss in frustration before he added, "It makes matters more complicated, and it puts me at a disadvantage with this delegation, not knowing as much about our enemy as they know about us."

This was a curious comment to Senganan, and he said as much.

"But has that not been the case ever since you arrived in India, Caesar?"

"Yes," Caesar and admitted, "and no." He stared down into his cup containing the fruit concoction that he drank even more than water, and Senganan had never seen Caesar drink *sura*, or even the *chai* that was also favored by his people. To Senganan, it seemed as if he was trying to decide something, and apparently he did, looking up at the Cholan. "Yes, once we left Bharuch in particular, we had much to learn about the southern kingdoms, and we didn't know very much, so in that sense, it's

24

similar. However, I had just won my Legions over after their...behavior in Bharuch by being true to my word and sharing the treasury of the Bharuch kingdom. The problem is," he leaned forward, "I was confident that my army could overwhelm the Pandya, thanks to what we learned in Bharuch about using naphtha as the best defense against elephants."

"But you still have that..." Senganan caught himself from using the epithet he normally employed when that subject came up "...substance, do you not?"

"No," Caesar replied quietly, forgetting and shaking his head as he said it, temporarily confusing Senganan. Seeing the Cholan's look of surprise, he elaborated, "At least, not in the amount we would need to subdue King Agrammes' elephants, at least not in one decisive battle. What I don't know is whether the Gangaridae divide their army into parts, or if they're allowed to return to their homes to be summoned if needed." Seeing that Senganan didn't grasp the importance, the Roman explained, "You see, Senganan, if Palibothra had been even a hundred miles upriver, as long as I knew the answer to that question, and," he allowed, "depending on what it was, we would be in the city by now." Although he wasn't sure why he did, just as Senganan did with him, Caesar trusted the Cholan nobleman, which was why he was willing to divulge what Caesar considered to be the true secret weapon that he and his army possessed. "What's made me so successful, going back to my time as Praetor in Hispania, is in my ability to move the men under my command more rapidly than my enemies. It's something I learned from reading about Alexander, with his Companion cavalry. But," Caesar smiled for the first time, and with a justifiable pride, "I did it with my infantry. When everyone else covers twenty miles in a day's march, my men can march thirty. And," he tapped the table for emphasis, "they can do that for days on end, because that is the standard that I expect. The same holds true with our fleet."

"Yes," Senganan agreed dryly, though with a tinge of bitterness. "We learned that when your Legate Pollio took Taprobane so easily."

"So," Caesar continued, "as long as I know enough basic information about our enemy, I can capitalize on the advantages we bring to the field in the form of the weapons that we've developed. But I don't know enough about the Gangaridae aside from their numbers to risk rolling the dice with my army. It is," he offered Senganan a twisted smile, "the only one that I have."

"What will you do?"

"If the Lord Chares is sincere in their offering ten thousand talents of gold in exchange for our departure, then I thought I knew what my men would want to do, and that includes many of my officers. Not all of them," he added, "but many of them. But now, there's a sizable portion of my Legions who want everything Palibothra has to offer."

"But ten thousand talents, if you shared that with your men, would make them wealthy!" Senganan gasped.

He would long remember the look Caesar gave him, one of a sardonic amusement at what the Cholan would realize later was based in his assumptions about what made these men of Rome march for their general.

"They already are wealthy, Lord Senganan." Caesar chuckled. "Granted, the women in the places we stay for any length of time end up with a great deal of it, along with all the other gamblers and hangers-on that follow us around. But not even Publius could have pissed away the money I gave them in Pandya."

"Then why do these men want you to order them to attack Palibothra if it's so strong?"

"Because we've reached a point in time where a good number of these men want the same thing that I want."

"And what is that?"

Caesar looked Senganan directly in the eye, and said simply, "Everything."

Caesar gained a certain amount of time by engaging in the negotiations between the Gangaridae in the form of Lord Chares and his councilors. Unlike most men with royal connections, Chares had proven to be incredibly close-mouthed about how he came to be the emissary that King Agremmes had chosen to initiate contact with the Romans, making only vague references to some form of familial connection. What Caesar *had* learned was that Chares was the chief administrator, similar to a Praetor, of the city of Gange that was located on the northern bank of the northernmost mouth of the Ganges, which put them almost two hundred miles away from the camp that, as Volusenus' chief deputy in his role of *Praefectus Fabrorum* Fuscus had predicted, was requiring a great deal of maintenance because of the constantly soaked ground of the island. In some ways, it was a blessing, because it gave his Centurions a way to keep their men occupied, but with every passing week, the discontent was growing, seemingly to be equally divided between pressing on to Palibothra, regardless of its location or danger, or turning about to return, at the very least, back to Muziris. However, in what more astute men would come to recognize, these two factions actually were unwittingly helping Caesar because of their squabbling with each other as they tried to come to a consensus that would satisfy the majority of the rankers in this massive army. The men wanting to return to Muziris were understandable, because they were either the relatively recent additions to the ranks in the form of Pandyans, or they were one of the hundreds of men who had taken up with a woman, either in Muziris or in Karoura, although Caesar also knew there was one exception to that, in the form of a huge Primus Pilus, who wanted to return to Bharuch instead of Pandya.

    Regardless of the wants and desires of his men, Caesar had already decided to, once more, risk all on a throw of the dice, and he spent a good part of every day standing at the northeast corner of the rampart of the camp, watching for the return of Volusenus. It wasn't until the end of the month of November, when a delegation composed of officers, although none of the Primi Pili and only a handful of Pili Priores from every Legion, including the stalwart 10th, approached the *praetorium* to inform Caesar they had finally hammered out an agreement among their own ranks. Rather than making demands, however, they made requests, invoking their rights as Roman citizens. They did this knowing that it placed Caesar in a more awkward position, given his status as Dictator for Life, and how he had predicated everything that led to the Civil War that made him First Man in Rome on a legal basis, according to both the laws engraved on bronze tablets and on customs that, in their own way, were at least as strong as the laws. The result was the delegation returning to their respective Legions to inform them that they had agreed to give Caesar until the return of Volusenus before he acquiesced, although he still didn't specify whether or not he would press on or turn back.

Volusenus didn't show up until early Januarius, but his arrival turned out to be an occasion that every man would remember for the rest of their days. It would have been memorable for the simple fact that, while he had departed on the *quinquereme Philotemia* and with two Liburnians, he returned with thirteen ships instead of the original three, but it was the size and construction of the newly added craft that betrayed their origin. Some of the more observant men had noticed these type of vessels sailing up the Pseudostoma River when they had been in Muziris, or in passing as they sailed their way up the eastern coast, although despite being more abundant on the eastern coast of India, they were still something of a curiosity. What was striking about them, besides the high prow and stern and their wide beam, were the two sails, a large one in the center of the ship and a smaller one at the bow, but it was the use of some sort of wooden slats that stiffened the sail so that, even when there was no discernible wind, the sails remained taut that made them so memorable. It was what was being carried on five of the ships, which the Romans learned were called *chuan*, that had the biggest impact on the wavering men. Yes, the rolls of brightly colored silk, the carved statues and figurines of jade, the pearls and jewels that Caesar put on display in front of the *praetorium,* under heavy guard of course, was impressive, and it definitely appealed to the men like Balbus. The fact that these men barely glanced at the mounds of shiny fabric, chests displaying the jade, and the glittering jewels was due to the presence of the other cargo, in the form of more than a thousand people, all of them female. Although Caesar's men had become accustomed to seeing women of different coloring, for the most part, their facial features largely resembled their own, but these women were exotic and completely new to the men, with almond-shaped eyes, smaller, flatter noses, and rounder faces, with a complexion that

Caesar Ascending – The Han

reminded some men of dried stalks of wheat, while others argued that the shade was closer to honey. And, in only the time it took to have the women paraded in the forum of the camp, men forgot all about returning to Rome, to India, or even to Parthia, many of whom had left families behind during their two-year occupation of what was now a Roman province.

Contrary to what most of the men thought, Caesar had always been aware that, aboard almost every ship of his massive fleet, there was at least one woman, usually more—Parthian, Bharuchian, and Pandyan—but this was on a completely different scale. The logistics of it alone was daunting, but Volusenus, who had sailed around what in later days would become known as the Malay Peninsula, then around the much wider peninsula to the east that would comprise the modern countries of Thailand, Cambodia, and Vietnam, to reach what was the southernmost part of the Han empire, had spent as much of his time on the long voyage in his capacity of *Praefectus Fabrorum*, the quartermaster of this massive army, as he had as an explorer, using the massive amount of gold that Caesar had provided him. Not all of his human cargo was female, either; accompanying him was the actual owner of the ten *chuan*; his name Long, one of the most powerful merchants who used the water route of the Silk Road from the port city of Ke Van (Vinh, Vietnam) on the eastern coast of the larger peninsula, along with more than two dozen guards and assistants, all male. It had certainly helped matters that the Han merchant had made the long voyage to the Andhra, Chola, and Pandyan kingdoms before, although he had only visited the latter once, but it would prove to be a seemingly unlikely person who would prove to be crucial to the effort of communicating with the Han merchant in the early days of their association with Long. It had actually been Diocles' idea, bringing it up while they were still in the Andhra kingdom, when the Greek had learned through Apollodorus that Caesar had tasked Volusenus with a monumental undertaking.

"Obviously, Achaemenes can't go," Diocles had argued to Pullus, only after giving the Roman time to absorb the most important news of Volusenus' pending departure. "But I think that Barhinder might prove to be extremely valuable to the

Legate, wherever he's going."

"How so?" Pullus asked, unconvinced at this point. "He's too young, for one thing. And," he pointed out, "it's likely that they're going to run into some sort of trouble."

"It's his youth that works to his advantage, Titus," Diocles had countered; neither master nor slave using their respective titles in private. "Surely you've seen how much the men like him, and he's very clever, with a quick mind. But," Diocles finished with what the Greek considered to be the clinching argument, "he picks up languages faster than anyone I've ever seen. I think he's at the very least Caesar's match in that, if not even better."

This elicited a chuckle from Pullus, who was only partially jesting when he warned Diocles, "Just make sure you never say something like that in front of anyone who might tell Caesar that." His grin faded, his weathered features assuming an expression that meant he was deep in thought, which made Diocles cautiously optimistic. "But you're right," he admitted finally, "I've noticed how quickly he picks things up. And," he sighed, "yes, I can see how it would be valuable to have someone within the Legion who knows about these Han bastards, given how sure we are that Caesar's trying to figure out a way to entice the men to give up on Palibothra." Finally, he shrugged his massive shoulders and said only, "If you can convince Caesar, and Barhinder agrees to go, I won't object to it."

Taking it as a victory, even if Pullus' enthusiasm was noticeably lacking, the Greek wasted no time, leaving the cabin to fetch Barhinder from where he was performing the strengthening exercises Pullus had given him, while Pullus announced that he was going up to take some air and pass the time with Balbus, fooling neither of them.

"Master Titus has a...task he'd like you to perform," Diocles had begun once they were back in the cabin, knowing that his wording had to be precise, aware that, for reasons he couldn't determine, young Gotra was in a state of almost constant fear that he would be dismissed by Pullus. "It's not dangerous," he assured Barhinder, hiding his smile at the Bharuch youth's crestfallen expression, "but it *is* very

30

important." Impulsively, he added, "Although, it *might* have some danger in it, all things considered." Rewarded by Barhinder's reaction, Diocles proceeded to explain the task, finishing by saying firmly, "And this has nothing to do with Master Titus being upset with you. In fact, it's the opposite. He sees the same thing I see in you, Barhinder. And right now, you'll serve Master Titus, the 10th, and the entire army best by doing this."

Diocles was certain that Barhinder would agree, but he was heartened to see that, rather than assenting immediately, the youth took a moment to think, then with a solemn expression, said, "So I am to be a spy for Master Titus and General Caesar, while translating for Legate Volusenus on his...task."

Sensing that, rather than being an impediment to Barhinder's agreement, the distinction was important to him, Diocles replied, "Essentially, yes. But it's to a good end, Barhinder. You're going to help Caesar and the army by learning more about what's east of us than we know now."

With Barhinder's agreement, and under the guise of submitting the daily report, Diocles was rowed to *Polynike*, where he found Apollodorus in the forward cabin that served as the army office, and was literally crammed with men, using flat pieces of wood they set on their knees to serve as desks.

"Barhinder agreed," Diocles said quietly as he handed the secretary the tablet.

He hadn't thought it necessary to inform either Pullus or Barhinder that everything else had already been decided, and that only Barhinder's agreement was keeping him from departing with Volusenus, who had initially resisted the idea based on Barhinder's youth, but he had been dissatisfied with the Pandyan who had claimed to speak Greek who Volusenus had hired soon after they settled in Muziris. Apollodorus' only visible reaction was a curt nod, then he followed Diocles out onto the deck, but when the Greek clambered down the rope ladder to his boat, Apollodorus continued towards the stern, entering Caesar's cabin without knocking. Barhinder was rowed to Caesar's flagship that evening, and the next morning when Volusenus, aboard the *Philotimia,* left the anchorage at Kantakosylla, Barhinder was with him.

"He's picked up the Han tongue quickly," Volusenus had informed Caesar the night of his return, forced to raise his voice even in the *praetorium* because of the uproar his arrival had caused, the men outside talking excitedly. "But it's more than that. He's so..." Volusenus finally came up with, "...likable that even Long, who's a suspicious, surly sort, took to him."

"I'd heard from Apollodorus that Pullus thinks highly of the boy," Caesar commented. "I'd like to bring him into the *praetorium* permanently, but," he offered a wry smile, "I don't need that kind of trouble from Pullus. He was unhappy about Gotra being with you, although it was temporary as it is. The gods know that the Equestrians and the 12th aren't causing the bulk of the problems, at least so far. But," he raised his cup in a toast to his Legate, "thanks to you, I think we might have quelled another...misunderstanding." Like every man who had been around Caesar for any length of time, they knew that he refused to characterize the uprisings against his authority, going back to Pharsalus, as a mutiny. In conversations that were always conducted in whispers, there had been much discussion about this reluctance, and there were many theories but no consensus. Turning his attention back to what was the more important matter, he asked Volusenus with genuine curiosity, "What made you think to bring women? And," he thought to add, "where did you find that many of them?"

"I thought about what I was missing most," Volusenus said with a grin, notable for its missing teeth. "And I realized that as nice as gold, silver, and jewels may be, none of those fill the hole a woman does."

"Or the other way around," Caesar murmured, pleased that it made Volusenus laugh. "But, are they slaves? Was there a war among the Han recently? Why so many?"

"That," Volusenus said, answering the last question first, "is something that I don't know. Barhinder says that he caught some talk among Long and some of his men about some sort of civil strife, but his Han isn't quite good enough yet to be certain. But," he continued, "no, that's not why these women were so easy to procure. The Han don't place any value on daughters, and they only keep the firstborn. These are all second, third, even fourth daughters. Long said it's very common, but yes, they're slaves."

"Sold by their fathers?" Caesar said, the contempt in his voice impossible to mistake. "That's barbaric!"

"Is it really that different than what we know our own Head Counters do, Caesar?" Volusenus asked quietly. "No, we don't sell them as slaves, but you know, especially out in the country, farmers will expose daughters because they can't afford to feed them."

This was true, but it wasn't something that Caesar wanted to dwell on, so he turned to more practical matters.

"You bought these women in my name?" Volusenus nodded, and Caesar began to pace, looking at the floor as he said, "My first thought was to essentially auction the women off, but I think that will cause more problems than it's worth."

"Why?" Volusenus asked. "The men have plenty of money. And," he pointed out with a laugh, "nowhere to spend it since we left Pandya."

"That's not what I worry about," Caesar replied. "I'm worried about the friction that's inevitable with an army that has a tail. Remember the trouble we had in Gaul? In Parthia, and in Bharuch, we had the advantage that we were leaving the women behind because the distances were so vast. But now, we have to concern ourselves with all manner of things, like food, and how to transport them."

"Was I wrong to do this, Caesar?" Volusenus was suddenly worried.

"No, you weren't, Gaius," Caesar assured him. "You saw how the men reacted. They're not banging on the wood outside the *praetorium* and asking about going home. You did the right thing. Now," he sighed, "I just have to think of how to make this work."

The solution Caesar came up with was accepted by the men, grudgingly, deeming that the women would remain the property of Caesar, who would allocate them equally among each Legion, but they would be housed and transported separately. Long also became semi-permanently attached to the army, serving as something of an assistant quartermaster, negotiating first with the native Mon, then the Khmer peoples through whose lands the Legions would be marching, although he was far less successful in his dealings with the Khmer. Finally departing the camp on the Ganges in Februarius with an army that was mostly united in their purpose again, with those who still wanted to return home overwhelmed by the number of men who wanted to find out exactly what these Han were all about, and to claim one of these women they considered the most exotic creatures they had ever seen for their own, Caesar honored his agreement by allowing Senganan and the young Chola princes to return to their kingdom. It wasn't all subtraction from the army, because along with Ventidius came the 14th, which was destined to be the last Legion sent from Rome, although they had been physically located in Africa, having undergone a new *dilectus* and with the sixteen-year enlistment just a few months before Caesar and his army had departed from Brundisium. Caesar had already sent the 22nd back to Muziris, while the 6th would be marching all the way back to Bharuch over the more arduous but shorter overland route from the Andhra kingdom, which was first used by the 14th and Ventidius, part of the agreement that Caesar had so feverishly hammered out with Satakarni during the week in Kantakosylla. With the arrival of Ventidius and the 14th, Caesar now commanded the Legions that would follow him for the rest of what was now more than a campaign. It would be a topic of debate for the next several years, around the fires of the rankers, and in the tents of the Centurions, about what motivated the men to continue to follow their general, but a consensus had never developed, other than the fact that the motivation was different for each man. For those like Publius Vellusius, one of the three surviving men of the original *dilectus* of the Equestrians who shared the same tent with Titus Pullus and Sextus Scribonius, and the only man of the three who never rose above the rank of *Gregarius* because he had no desire to, it was a simple proposition; the Legion was his home, and he couldn't fathom a life that wasn't under the standard. Not surprisingly, this attitude was most prevalent with the oldest veterans of their respective Legions. For other men, mostly in the Optionate and Centurionate, it was about the men under their command and their concern for their wellbeing, while for others, it was the allure of the kind of wealth that other men of the ranks had achieved, namely the veterans of Gaul. The fact that much of that wealth from the plunder, sale of slaves, and the bonuses paid by their general hadn't stayed in their respective coin purses long was something that didn't deter these men. Finally, there were men who followed Caesar because it was *Caesar* leading them, and they took as much collective pride in all that they had accomplished, even as they understood that it would be Caesar's name that would be remembered. Regardless of this reality, with every passing year, the number of men who felt this way would grow, commensurate with their budding belief that Caesar was more than a mortal.

For Pullus, it was a combination of these things, although the prospect of even greater wealth was the least of his concerns. Yes, he had always been fiercely ambitious, but money had always only been a means to an end for him, his goal being the man of the Pullus line who elevated his family from the Urban Tribes of the Head Count and into the Equestrian Order. The death of his family, including his son Vibius, two years before the beginning of this campaign had caused him to shift his ambition onto the shoulders of his nephew; if Pullus ever learned that, at that moment, he had a son who was now tottering about the palace at Bharuch, only the gods knew how differently things may have turned out, not just for Pullus himself, but for the 10th, and for Caesar. Now, all that mattered to him was that, with the arrival of the thousand Han women, along with the sight of the types of riches that the Han Empire had to offer, what the men would refer to among themselves as the second mutiny was averted. The third would occur in the territory of the Khmer people, after a particularly bad monsoon season where sickness was the biggest threat, as men contracted all manner of ailments, some of which they had become familiar with, and some that were new to them. After cutting their way through the dense *jangla* of the narrow Mon peninsula, where progress averaged barely a mile a day, once they crossed the thirty-five miles to the huge inland bay, the month they waited for Nero and the fleet to retrace the route Volusenus had taken ended up essentially serving as a rest period. It was during this month-long period that Volusenus' decision to buy the female slaves paid dividends, as the men spent their days lounging on the white sand beaches that lined the point of land that jutted out on the eastern side of the narrow peninsula, swimming and catching fish during the day, then carousing with "Caesar's Centuries" as they became known, albeit on a strictly controlled basis, enforced by Caesar on down to the Centurions. Every Legion had one hundred women assigned as theirs, and in typically Roman fashion, a system and schedule was developed that, over time, the men learned by heart, knowing when it was their Cohort's turn, with each Century having a day that was theirs and theirs alone.

The biggest concern for Caesar and the Primi Pili was the veritable inevitability that some of the men would develop attachments and start seeing a particular Han girl as something more than a temporary comfort and diversion, so very quickly, it was decided to rotate the "Centuries" between Legions to forestall this from happening, and while it wasn't a perfect system, it did keep the men from running rampant. The rules concerning the women's treatment was strictly enforced, not from any tender feelings, but from the standpoint of an investment; this, at least, was how Caesar characterized it to Tiberius Vetruvius and Bodroges, the two Tribunes he had selected for the task of managing what was in essence a moving brothel. It was more complicated than that; Caesar's proclivities with women, and his appreciation of them, were stuff of legend, but the one thing he had never developed was a taste for cruelty that seemed to infect so many other patricians and high-ranking plebeians. However, in this, there wasn't much distinction between the men of the different classes, and he understood almost from the moment Volusenus informed him of his human cargo that if he allowed those types of men to indulge themselves, he would quickly run out of women. Consequently, there was a weekly inspection by the Tribunes, aided by some of the *medici*, where they looked for bruises, cuts, or other injuries, and the only reason that Vetruvius and Bodroges hadn't rebelled at essentially acting as pimps was that Caesar had allowed each of them to select one of the women to be his constant companion and not shared by anyone else. Which Cohort had which "Century" as their own was always carefully recorded, so it didn't take all that long to narrow down the men who posed the greatest danger to the women. Rather than making an example of them, with a few whispers and liberal amounts of silver instead, those men were warned by their own comrades that their future would be very bleak, and short, if they continued to indulge their particular tastes. Although it was certainly unusual, Caesar actually drew on his experiences from Gaul, where the army almost always had a tail, and he believed he had developed a keen sense of when it was time to look the other way and when it was time to take action.

The Mon had posed no challenge for the time the army was cutting their thirty-five mile path and the subsequent rest month, and their contact with them was brief, but the Khmer had been another story altogether. They were ferocious fighters, as they learned fairly quickly once they began penetrating the inland from the river the natives called the Mae Nam, or Maenum, after a voyage of more than two hundred fifty miles from their camp on the eastern edge of the narrow Mon peninsula. That voyage should have taken perhaps five days, but it was double that because of incessant storms that, even in this relatively protected gulf, were savage and destructive. As skilled as his Rhodians were, and as much experience as they had accrued in the waters of this part of the world while performing a feat that would end up dwarfing all of Alexander's accomplishments, it was inevitable that mistakes were made and ships were lost. For Caesar, now that he had seen the *chuan*, all that mattered was maintaining the crews of the fleet of warships because they still relied on oar power, whereas the *chuan* and the other transports relied solely on the wind. Gradually replacing the original ships with the *chuan* had another benefit by allowing Nero as commander and Lysippos as chief *navarch* to shift crews and fill in missing oarsmen on the part of the fleet that still relied on this to power their vessels. As a result of this shift, Caesar had also resigned himself to a much slower pace once they began to replace other transports, but to his surprise, while they *were* slower, it wasn't by much, so that when the oar-driven part of the fleet would reach their nightly anchorage, depending on the wind, the *chuan* would arrive between a third of a watch to a full watch later. While it extended the time they were at sea, Caesar's Legions had become, if not accepting, then at least accustomed to life aboard ship, and they actually preferred it once they had gotten enough of a taste of hacking their way through a *jangla*, with all the sweat, toil, and dangers such as what had befallen Pollio on the large peninsula.

When Caesar and the army debarked at the mouth of the Mae Nam River, the expectation had been that the fleet would sail back to Long's home port of Ke Van located on the eastern side of the wider peninsula, where they would spend the time waiting for the army to march across the peninsula, a distance of almost six hundred miles, by refitting and repairing the ships they were going to keep, while either buying or paying to build more *chuan*, those repairs being effected for the first time since they departed Muziris. After their experience in cutting across the narrow peninsula, Caesar estimated that it would take between two to three months, the longest period of time he and his men had ever spent cut off from the fleet since their departure from Parthia. However, given the information he had learned from Long and the men who were the Han equivalent of his own *navarchae*, the merchant warning the Roman general of the treacherous passage around the bottom of the wide peninsula and the wildly unpredictable weather that was a hazard when navigating the strait, dotted with hundreds of islands, Caesar determined this was the best solution, reasoning that if he had to lose ships, he didn't want them loaded with his army. Instead of three months, or even four, which Caesar privately told his Legates he believed would be more likely, it would take almost nine months before they reached the village that was near the southern border of the Han Empire (Da Nang). The reason for the delay was from a combination of factors, of which the thick *jangla* was only a part. Caesar's attempt to create something resembling a Roman road that, much as the Via Appia did, connected an increasingly far flung swathe of territory in Italia proved to be excessively ambitious, although he quickly discarded the idea of using stones for the roadbed. Perhaps the most damaging factor was their discovery that the monsoon season in Khmer territory started earlier and ended later than it did in India, but even with this, Long and the few

Khmers who cooperated with these foreign invaders unanimously declared that it was the worst season in memory. Despite having switched to cotton tunics, very quickly, the Romans discovered that the climate was even more unforgiving on their leather footwear because it never dried out, and despite continuing the practice of beginning a campaign with every man issued two new pairs of *caligae*, before the first month was out, in which they had made barely a hundred miles inland from the mouth of the Mae Nam River, the majority of men were already on their second pair. The rain was incessant, and even now that they had three years of experience in the hotter and extremely humid climate, the men of the Legions spent at least as much time hauling the wagons and carts out of the mire as they did chopping down the dense vegetation and trees, the trunks of which were used as the foundation for the road. The horses of the cavalry, which, aside from one guard Legion every day, was the only part of the army that conducted military operations early on, suffered in a similar manner that they had during the nightmarish march from Pattala to Bharuch, their hooves never fully drying out. Fortunately, this time, their riders were more experienced in the care of their animals in this kind of climate, but it was inevitable that there would be losses, the pool of spares rapidly dwindling, while the draft animals were suffering in a similar manner.

The first clash with the Khmers occurred a week after their landing, when three *alae* of cavalry, scouting ahead of the Roman column, encountered a large village. The Decurion, the Galatian Arctosages, along with the Pandyan interpreter that every *ala* now paid to help translate, albeit with diminishing results now that India was behind them, rode into what appeared to be a deserted village, with Arctosages holding both hands out, while the Pandyan, Jai, called out in Tamil first, then switched to the Cholan dialect Telugu as they rode slowly into the village. Neither of them were certain what they did to trigger what came next, but from outside the village back where the rest of the men were located, a sudden explosion of noise in the form of male voices, followed an eyeblink later by the neighing of panicked horses, prompted the pair to spin their mounts about and gallop back along the slick mud of the path that served as the main street. What greeted Arctosages was the sight of lithe, bare-chested men surrounding his troopers as they hurled short javelins with an astonishing rapidity, their upper bodies glistening from the wet as the missiles struck both man and horse, with almost every rider struggling to keep their mount under control while the animal was trying to turn and flee. By this time, every *ala* of Caesar's cavalry was divided into roughly equal groups, with Parthian archers, the Galatians and some Pandyans providing a missile capability, while other Parthians, Galatians, Gauls, and Germans used their particular version of either the *spatha* or spears. The final contingent was the newest addition of Pandyans who were skilled in the use of the lance, but the sudden surprise of the attack had caused the troopers to become hopelessly muddled, so that the troopers who had the ability to rapidly close with the two or three hundred Khmer warriors were forced to negotiate a path between plunging, bucking horses, while the Parthian archers were completely useless because the constantly wet conditions rendered their compound bows useless. Only his fellow Galatians with their light javelins were able to retaliate, and it pleased Arctosages to see almost a dozen half-naked men lying in the mud, while he could see others limping off on their own or being helped by another man to leave the field. Then, so quickly that it might have been a figment of the imagination except for the bodies of men they left behind, the Khmer seemed to dissolve into the underbrush that surrounded the large, cleared area surrounding the village, leaving behind moaning men and horses whinnying in pain. Only for the span of a heartbeat or two did Arctosages consider pursuing the Khmer, but not only had they vanished in every direction, he had no intention of sending his men plunging through the kind of undergrowth that put cavalry at such a disadvantage. In terms of losses, they were actually light; he had three men and seven horses dead, or with the latter, so badly injured they had to be destroyed, with another dozen men wounded, and about as many horses with cuts or superficial wounds. What they had learned once they invaded Pandya was that, in this kind of climate, even seemingly minor wounds could corrupt with an almost astonishing rapidity, so he knew that his wounded troopers weren't completely out of danger. Despite not pursuing, Arctosages ordered his men into the village, which they ransacked but found very little of value, and because of the damp, it meant that firing the thatched houses in retaliation was next to impossible. It was his *Cornicen*, one of the dozen actual Romans in his *ala* who made a comment that he would have cause to remember.

"Maybe we should start bringing some jars of naphtha with us if it's going to stay wet like this."

The light was fading, and knowing their pace would be slowed because of the wounded, the Decurion ordered the search, which was now for hidden foodstuffs, cut short. It was as they were gathering back together that he was shown some of the missiles that had been thrown by the Khmer, noticing immediately that most of the points were simply fire-hardened wood, and what metal spearpoints there were, weren't iron but bronze. Their lack of armor didn't surprise him, at least that made of iron; as they learned almost immediately, keeping the links of a mail vest free of rust was literally a daily task, but none of the men he had seen even wore the stiff linen vests with rectangles of leather sewn onto them like the Pandya and Chola. As they made their way back to the main column, he thought about the attack, and while there were more questions than answers, he did arrive at a conclusion that was borne out, that the Khmer's use of bronze spearpoints was a matter of necessity, given how quickly iron could rust. He also wondered if this was an isolated attack because they had been surprised, or if this was going to be the way things were until they got across this cursed peninsula that, even just a week into the effort, he had come to despise.

Arctosages' question was answered the next day, when there were no fewer than five assaults on the column, all conducted in the same manner of men suddenly materializing from the edges of the quasi-roadway. Under ordinary circumstances, given the heavy armor of the Legions and their shields, it would have been a nuisance that inflicted more damage on the Khmer, who seemed to lose two or three men with every attack, although they always carried their wounded with them, depriving the Romans of prisoners. However, because of the almost constant rain—if a full watch passed without a downpour it was a cause for celebration—the men kept their *hamatae* rolled up in the greased cloth in their packs, along with their greaves, while the shield covers, which were now made of canvas instead of leather, stayed on. The only piece of protective equipment that the men continued to wear was their helmet, but only after, in another example of necessity being the mother of invention, semi-waterproof cloth covers were fashioned that provided some protection from the rain. It was far from ideal, and none of the men were happy about only having their tunics as protection, but every armor *immune* in every Legion had warned their Centurions that they simply didn't have enough of the materials needed to keep the millions of iron links that composed the *hamatae* for more than fifty thousand men constantly lubricated and protected. Their last supply of olive oil had been exhausted during their time in the camp on the Ganges, and the army had been using sesame oil on an ever-increasing basis since their time in Bharuch for cooking, but even as copious a supply of the sesame oil as they had on hand, of which Caesar had had the foresight to double what Volusenus had estimated would be needed, there simply wasn't enough. Those Khmer they encountered in the first two months of their progress were fierce, but they weren't particularly skilled on those few occasions where they were forced to stand and fight, nor did they seem very organized.

Things began to change as the army moved east, and once they reached the southern slopes of a line of low, heavily forested mountains that ran parallel to their direction of travel that Long, using what he said were his few trading contacts among the Khmer people, had insisted was the best route, several different but related events occurred. The first was an answer to a question that, to that point, not even someone as knowledgeable as Long seemed to know, whether or not the Khmer used elephants for the purposes of war, when another cavalry patrol came under attack by a Khmer force consisting of ten elephants, each one ridden by a *mahout,* but unlike their previous experience in India, they also served as a warrior, with a shield strapped to one arm and an extremely long spear that he used in much the same way as a lancer would, but with the height advantage that came with being on an elephant. There was a *howdah* of sorts, but with only two sides that were semicircular and made of bamboo that only offered a modicum of protection, while the platform was occupied by a single archer, and unlike the animals in India, although they were the same size, they weren't nearly as heavily armored as their Indian counterparts. These elephants were accompanied by infantry, and unlike the first Khmer they had encountered, wore an armor of sorts, also made of a combination of linen and pieces of bamboo that had been split to lay flat against the chest. They all had spears, with the shafts made of bamboo as well, and bronze points, while most of them carried bronze swords that were even shorter than the Romans' own *gladius*, but longer than their *pugio*. It wasn't a large force, and they were driven off by the arrows and javelins of the *ala*, but again not without inflicting casualties; the difference this time was that, either because they had thought he was dead, or for some other unknown reason, a Khmer was captured, and for the first time, Caesar had insight into these strange people who had resisted any attempts at contact.

Among the most important pieces of information, extracted by Long and one of his men who had picked up a smattering of their tongue, was that there was a city on the shores of a freshwater lake that was considered by the Khmer to be their capital, although whether they were organized along lines that Caesar would recognize, he couldn't tell. What was clearly apparent was that the Khmer viewed their arrival as a cause for hostilities, and as they drew nearer to this city, that they at least now knew was named Angkor, the attacks became more frequent. Meanwhile, as Caesar and his army struggled day by day, then week by week, the incessant rains from the worst monsoon season in memory made every foot, every pace, and every mile a struggle. Morale began to plummet, and while Caesar's Centuries helped, men began to become despondent, feeling as if not just the Khmer, but the land itself was fighting them every step of the way. By the time they had penetrated two hundred fifty miles into the interior, which was still less than halfway to go, it was already the Kalends of Sextilis, and it had taken Caesar's army more than two months. From the perspective of the rankers, what Caesar had done in effect was to strand them in the middle of a land that was even more hostile to them than India, where continuing forward to reach the eastern coast and at least the possibility of connecting with the fleet seemed an impossible task. Turning around, however, while the going would be much easier, and faster, also took them away from Nero, Lysippos, and the only available means by which they could return, if not all the way back to Rome, at least back to the more familiar world of Karoura and Muziris. This was when, on the Ides of Sextilis, the third mutiny by Caesar's army occurred, and it was by far the most serious of what would turn out to be the four mutinies before this campaign that would forever alter history ended.

Chapter Two

After it was over, none of the officers in Caesar's army could pinpoint the exact cause of what occurred, but there was general agreement that the series of events that escalated into the mutiny began because of what was, when all was said and done, a clerical error by one of the *praetorium* scribes. The error was simple enough, and had happened once before, weeks earlier, when two Cohorts were assigned the same Caesar's Centuries women, but the mood was quite different by the second time, resulting in a melee in the camp forum between the Third Cohort of the 8th and the Seventh Cohort of the 28th, as men pummeled each other, while the hundred women huddled in terror in front of the *Quaestorium* tent, where they were fed and examined when they weren't servicing a Cohort. Both Clustuminus and Cartufenus were summoned by their respective Pili Priores, but even their presence couldn't stop their men from releasing their pent-up frustration and anger as the battling rankers ignored the bellowed commands of their Centurions. If that had been all that occurred, it would have indicated a serious problem but one that could be addressed once tempers cooled, but then, a ranker from the 8th, who was being thrashed by one of the Centurions who had come wading in with their *viti*, reacted to the fact that it wasn't his particular Centurion by drawing his *pugio* and stabbing the Centurion in the eye. It wasn't a killing blow, although it permanently blinded the Centurion, but any chance of the brawl slowly winding down as men ran out of energy was ended as the rankers whose Centurion was wounded attacked the offending Gregarius, surrounding him and, even as he flailed wildly with his *pugio*, pummeled him senseless, the ranker falling face first into the mud of the forum. Even this would have been reparable, but rather than relent, the enraged men, who thought they were exacting justice for their Centurion, stomped the man to death, although there were some who believed he essentially suffocated in the mud before he succumbed to his injuries. Now, with blood being shed and a death, events quickly spiraled out of control, the uproar becoming loud enough to alert Pullus, who had been in his quarters reading as he waited for Diocles to prepare the evening meal. For the span of a couple of heartbeats, he cocked his head, trying to decipher the meaning of what, despite the huge size of the camp and being in his tent, he could clearly hear was a large group of men shouting. The instant he determined that these were voices raised in not just anger, but with the same kind of ferocity and urgency that he only heard during battle, Pullus leapt to his feet and strode to the hanging flap that served as his door, pushing it aside just as Diocles came rushing in, dripping wet and holding a steaming pot that contained the rice that was now the staple of the Legions' diet.

"Titus, there's a brawl in the forum, and Lysander said that it's the men of the 8th and 28th, and that someone's been killed!"

Turning to snatch up his *vitus*, Pullus was about to exit his quarters on his way out of the tent, but then, with a sense of real dread, decided to strap on his *balteus*.

"Run next door and get Valerius and Lutatius," Pullus ordered, then followed Diocles outside as the Greek rushed the short distance to the tent shared by the Optio, *Cornicen*, *Aquilifer* and *Tesserarius*, while Pullus turned in the opposite direction, facing the forum. As the senior Legion of the army, Pullus had been given the right to choose his Legion's location in the camp, but whereas it was normally a formality, with the Primus Pilus choosing the first streets nearest to the *praetorium* and forum, Pullus had bucked that tradition by choosing the spot on the opposite side of the camp from the latrines and stables, along one wall. This was one of the only times he cursed his choice, which he'd made for a variety of reasons, because it meant that he was almost a half-mile from the forum, making it impossible for him to see anything in the fading light. At least it's not raining right now, he thought, but despite the lack of visibility, he could tell by the sound that it was not only a serious matter, it sounded as if it was escalating, yet even as he stood there, he could see his men, those who were cooking the meal outside the tent joined by their comrades, all of them standing now and staring in the same direction. Before he could address them, Valerius came trotting up, lugging his large horn, with Lutatius beside him.

"Sound the call for all Centurions," Pullus snapped, then as Valerius hefted the horn and licked his lips in preparation, for the first time, Pullus addressed his men within earshot, bellowing, "*None of you cunni better take one fucking step towards the forum, because if you do, when I find out, I'll flay you!*"

Pullus was as aware of the men's mood as any officer, and he knew that he was running a risk of inflaming men whose tempers were already raw, but he was counting on the fact that he rarely issued these kinds of threats, and when he did, it was always in moments of emergency, so he was cautiously optimistic that his men would stay put. Valerius played the series of notes, but even then, Pullus could hear he wasn't alone, as from all parts of the camp came the same pattern of notes, with the slight variations that told every Centurion it was their Primus Pilus summoning them and not from another Legion. Naturally, Balbus was the first to arrive, and Pullus was relieved to see that he was armed as well, but by the time the other fifty-eight officers arrived, he saw that roughly half of them were only carrying their *viti*.

"Right, you can all hear something's going on," he had to raise his voice a bit, "but while we're going to head in that direction, we're not going to be in any rush, understood?" Accepting nods and murmured assents, Pullus turned to Lutatius, ordering, "You and the other Optios are responsible for keeping the boys from wandering in the direction of the forum. Let anyone who didn't hear what I said know what's going to happen if they disobey me."

Unlike the Centurions, Lutatius rendered his salute as he repeated the order, and only then did Pullus begin striding down the Cohort street that intersected with the *Via Principalis*, the road that bisected the camp from the side gates and terminated at the forum. Turning the corner, for the first time, Pullus had a glimpse of the forum, but his view was partially blocked by the backs of dozens of other men, all of them carrying their *viti* and all unified in where their attention was focused. With his brief hesitation, Scribonius caught up with him, but Pullus was already moving again, forcing Scribonius to scramble to keep up.

"That," the Pilus Prior said grimly, "doesn't sound good."

"No, it doesn't," Pullus agreed, though he kept his eyes on the crowd of men ahead of him.

Seeing that his fellow Centurions from the other Legions on this side of the camp seemed to be divided on how eager they were to investigate, Pullus quickly found himself first nudging, then more firmly pushing the other officers aside, some of whom whirled about to snarl a warning until they saw who it was, something that Pullus barely noticed. As he advanced through the other Centurions, he caught up with Balbinus, whose Legion was also on this side of the camp, and Flaminius, the Primus Pilus of the 30th, and only then did he slow down.

"What do you think?" Pullus asked the pair. "Do we wade in and try and break this up?"

"Do you have any idea what it's about?"

Pullus shook his head to Balbinus' question, although he allowed, "Lysander told Diocles that it's the 8th and the 28th involved, but I have no idea why."

It was natural that the Centurions with the trio gravitated to stand behind their respective Primus Pilus, but now that they had an unobstructed view, while it didn't stop their progress, they slowed a bit more.

"There! That's Clustuminus!" Flaminius pointed him out, but it took a moment to pick him out since the Primus Pilus, like all of the combatants, was clad only in his tunic, his only distinction being he was one of the few men with a *viti*, which he was even then slashing down onto the back of a ranker who was grappling with another man who was distinguishable only because his swarthy complexion marked him as one of the Parthians.

"It figures that it would be the fucking 8th," Balbinus muttered.

While Pullus silently agreed, he didn't say as much, aware

that the mutual loathing each Primus Pilus held for the other was no secret. However, in the aftermath, Pullus was forced to confront the possibility that the reason for his reluctance to get involved was because of his antipathy towards Clustuminus. While he didn't think so, given all that transpired, he would never truly be certain, because his hesitation meant that, when Pullus finally did decide to intervene, without consulting either Balbinus or Flaminius, and he began wading into the melee, bellowing and using both his physical strength and his reputation as he lashed out indiscriminately at any ranker who insisted on continuing their private battle, it placed him just two paces away to witness the murder of a Primus Pilus of Caesar's army. Perhaps if he had drawn his *gladius* and had it ready, he would have been in time, because in a manner similar to others he had experienced in the numerous battles over his career, the movements of the combatants around him seemed to slow down, so he had enough time to see a ranker, his face contorted with rage and hatred as he spun around in response to the slashing blow across his back, and in one continuous motion reach for his *pugio* in its scabbard, withdrawing it and pulling his arm back in what the detached part of Pullus' brain critiqued as a sloppy first position, before executing an upsweeping thrust that ended only when the handguard of the *pugio* struck Clustuminus' chest. The only solace Pullus could take was that he reached Clustuminus' side, with the man who had just murdered a Centurion standing dumbly, mouth open, before the Primus Pilus' body hit the ground. Catching his rival, Pullus experienced none of the negative feelings that were always stirred up whenever the pair had any contact, just an overwhelming sadness as he cradled Clustuminus and gently lowered him to the ground, completely oblivious to the fact that he himself was in a horribly exposed posture as he kept his eyes fixed on his fallen comrade, whose own eyes were wide with that shock and surprise he had seen so many times. Pullus could see that Clustuminus was conscious, but when he opened his mouth to say something, because his mouth was so full of blood, whatever he said was unintelligible, the effort spraying Pullus' face with his blood.

"Wait for me in Elysium across the river, brother," Pullus

whispered, offering a smile that felt foreign as he joked, "and we can argue about our boys again, eh?"

Watching until the dark part of Clustuminus' eyes suddenly went wide, only then did Pullus use one hand that was now covered in the Centurion's blood to gently close them before laying him on the ground. This was when Pullus become aware of two things: the noise level, while not gone altogether, had subsided dramatically, and that he was surrounded by his own Centurions, all of whom were armed now, holding their *gladius*, protecting their Primus Pilus from the fate suffered by the Centurion commanding the 8th Legion.

"We have four Centurions dead, eight wounded to one degree or another, the worst being Septimus Hastatus Prior Cinna of the 28th, who lost an eye and, from what we've been able to determine, was the first Centurion attacked. Of the dead Centurions," Caesar's voice had been flat and toneless, but for the first time, it cracked with some emotion, "Primus Pilus Clustuminus is the most grievous loss. However," Caesar's voice hardened, but for the first time, he looked over at Pullus, "thanks to Primus Pilus Posterior Balbus, we have at least taken Clustuminus' murderer into custody."

When he fell silent, there was a shifting among the assembled Centurions, which included Pili Priores, but it was Torquatus who finally broke the silence.

"What about the others, Caesar?"

Even in the torchlight, it was easy to see Caesar's anger, though it wasn't aimed at Torquatus, and he answered bitterly, "So far, nobody has stepped forward to identify anyone else who participated in the murders or wounding of the other Centurions."

More to forestall what he viewed as the inevitable recriminations, Pullus asked, "What about rankers, Caesar? What's the casualty total there?"

The general had to consult the tablet in his hand before he answered, in a clipped tone, "Fourteen dead, six from the 8th and eight from the 28th, along with almost thirty men with injuries severe enough to warrant being put in the hospital tent. One of the 8th's dead is the Gregarius who stabbed Cinna in the eye. He's a Parthian from the Second of the Ninth, and it appears as if he was actually the first man to die. But," he finished grimly, "he wasn't the last."

Neither Pullus nor any of the other Centurions noticed it, but it was Scribonius who did, and in what Pullus recognized was his friend's careful tone, asked Caesar, "When you say there are almost thirty men who are injured severely enough to be in the hospital, is that where they are now? Are they under guard?"

The look Caesar gave Scribonius, standing next to Pullus as he was, communicated that he understood what was behind the Pilus Prior's question, and that it wasn't whether the wounded were guarded, but he didn't hesitate to answer flatly, "No, Scribonius, they're not under guard because they're not in the hospital."

"May I ask why, Caesar?"

"Because, Papernus, it would mean that we'd have to shift men out who aren't criminals who have fallen to one of these agues and fevers to treat men who are going to be condemned anyway!" Caesar snapped.

Up to this moment, nothing that Caesar had said was a cause for concern, but now there was a definite reaction, as men glanced at whoever was standing next to them while muttering things that, while Caesar couldn't hear with any clarity, he understood was a negative reaction.

For Pullus, the expression on Caesar's face almost immediately brought him back to a moment from their shared past, and it prompted him to whisper to Scribonius, "I think Caesar is going to handle this like he did at Pharsalus."

He was half-hoping that his more insightful friend would disagree, but Scribonius' expression was grim as he gave a slight nod.

"It certainly looks that way."

For his part, Caesar clearly chose to ignore the mood in the room, and he broke eye contact to pretend to refer to the tablet again.

"As of this moment," he continued, "obviously both the 8th and 28th will be taken out of the rotation for the women." Even in this grim moment, there were some smiles at Caesar's steadfast refusal to use their nickname, but there was also another ripple of disagreement.

"The whole Legion?" Cartufenus, who had preferred to remain near the back of the crowd, couldn't contain himself. "But it was only the Seventh with my boys," he protested. "Depriving the other nine Cohorts isn't just!"

"Just?" Caesar echoed, and if he was feigning his incredulity, Pullus was certain his anger was genuine. "You want to speak to me about justice, Primus Pilus Cartufenus? One of *your* men," he pointed directly at Cartufenus, "murdered a Primus Pilus of another Legion! That is a stain on the honor of the entire Legion, and you need to drop to your knees and thank blessed Fortuna that I haven't ordered your entire Legion to be *decimated*! But," he finished by raising his voice to a level that few men had heard, "it's not too late for me to change my mind!"

The collective gasp was something that Pullus would remember for some time, and it was followed by at least two heartbeats of shocked silence before it was shattered by dozens of voices as Caesar's most senior Centurions expressed their refusal to accept this as even a possibility.

"Caesar, that's madness! None of my boys will stand for it!"

"Mine either, Caesar! Even if it's another Legion, they won't allow a decimation!"

"If you order this, Caesar, you'll lose this army. Just like Alexander did."

It was something that Pullus, the Centurions of the Second Cohort, and the men of the First of the Second had learned about Scribonius, that he had a way of being heard without sounding as if he was shouting; this time was no exception, and Pullus immediately saw that Caesar had heard this over all the other voices who were shouting their protests.

Turning his entire body to face where Pullus and Scribonius were standing, Caesar held up a hand for silence, but despite it taking several heartbeats, he waited, seemingly patient, for the Centurions to understand that something was taking place that they wanted to hear.

Once it subsided, Caesar asked evenly, "Would you care to

repeat that, Pilus Prior Scribonius?"

Ignoring his friend reaching out and clamping a huge hand around his elbow, squeezing it hard enough that Scribonius had to fight from wincing, he nevertheless repeated calmly, "I said that if you order the decimation of the 28th, and," he expanded, "I mean even if you order just the Seventh to be decimated, you...will...lose...this...army, Caesar."

The look Caesar offered Scribonius wasn't a glare, exactly, but it was close, yet the anger that had been present when he thundered at Cartufenus seemed to be missing when he commented, "That wasn't all that you said, Scribonius."

While Pullus had relented squeezing his friend's arm, he still held it, and he felt Scribonius tense, but the lanky Pilus Prior didn't hesitate to reply, "No, Caesar, it wasn't. I also said that if you go through with this, the result will be that you'll suffer the same fate as Alexander."

"Really?" Caesar replied sarcastically. "You mean that I'll be remembered as being the man who matched the feats of the greatest general in history?"

Don't say it, Sextus, Pullus pleaded silently. For the love of the gods, don't say it.

"I never had the impression that you wanted to *match* Alexander, Caesar," Scribonius countered quietly. "I've always thought that we were here to finish something that Alexander couldn't, and by doing so, you would surpass him."

And, there it was, at last, out in the open. The thing that had been an incessant topic of debate around the fires, and around the tables in winter quarters, with the men of every rank for at least the previous two years, when he had pressed on to Muziris from Bharuch, the belief among some that Caesar wanted so much more than just to reach the Ganges before turning back, while others insisted that once they reached the river and took Palibothra, it would be over and they could return back home. During the months they had spent in the camp at the Ganges, as the truth about what awaited them in Palibothra began to sink in, the men who believed the latter waited for their general's order to prepare to sail back south now that he had reached the spot that the Macedonian king had failed to reach. When it became obvious no such orders would be forthcoming, the mood discernibly shifted as the idea that Caesar wouldn't settle for the Ganges began to sink in with this faction. Then, Caesar had managed to turn the men around and agree to continue by what some muttered was a shabby trick, appealing to both the greed and the lust of the men who marched for him. Shabby or not, it had worked, and Pullus did believe that matters wouldn't have been this serious now if conditions had been the same as they had been in India, but none of them had been prepared for the brutally hard going that was much more difficult than what they had been forced to endure prior to this.

Somehow, the Centurions all realized the same thing, that it had to be Caesar who spoke next, and all eyes were on the general, but he was either oblivious to or was ignoring their gaze as he regarded Scribonius before he finally asked, "So, what if it's true, Scribonius? What if I do intend to lead this army to a level of fame and glory that the world has never seen before?" Now, he turned from Scribonius to sweep his arm to encompass all of the assembled officers in almost a challenging manner, as if he was daring anyone to argue. When no man said a word, he continued, "I could also point out that I am Dictator for Life, the supreme authority in Rome, and therefore I am in command of all the Legions of Rome. And," he pointed out, "there's not one man under the standard of this army who still doesn't have at least six more years of their enlistment to serve, and most have ten years or more, which means that you all are under my authority." Pullus saw some mouths opening, but Caesar held up a hand to assure them, "But I don't intend to rely on that. I want men who are willing to follow me, who will fight for me not because they have to, but because they want to share in all the fame and glory that still awaits all of us."

When nobody spoke up, Pullus took it upon himself to do so, certain that he understood the prevailing attitude, at least among his men.

"Right now, it's impossible for the men to see more than what's right in front of them, Caesar," Pullus began. Pointing in the general direction of the *Porta Praetoria*, beyond which the *jangla*, dripping, dank, and filled with all manner of dangers still waited, he continued, "All they see is more of the same. More chopping, slogging through the mud, more bugs, and more rain that never seems to stop. Most of them have been struck by sickness to one degree or another; we lose a man a week to one of those hooded *naja* or some other kind of viper, and at least a dozen of our slaves have been killed by tigers, and I don't even know how much of the livestock we've lost. And now," he held both huge hands up in a gesture that conveyed his helplessness, "they can't see this ending at all, let alone with the fame and glory, and all the money that comes with it."

"Then what do you suggest, Pullus?" Caesar cried out, finally unable to control his frustration and his concern. "If we turn around now, it's admitting that we've lost! It's saying that we weren't able to overcome any obstacle in our path, that we accepted defeat! Perhaps some of you can live with that, but I cannot! *Not after...the Ides*!" It was a show of raw emotion that none of them, not his Legates, not even Apollodorus, had ever seen before, but it was his mention of that day that shook his Centurions even more than Caesar's threats of punishment. Suddenly embarrassed, Caesar ended the meeting, saying, "I need to think about what to do about this. For now, all men are confined to their tents, and there will be no work until further notice."

He didn't wait for a response, nor did any of the Centurions try to ask him anything more. After a few moments, they all drifted away, returning to their men to wait, and try to keep a bad situation from getting worse.

That night was one of the tensest that any man could recall, even those who had been present at Pharsalus or during the dramatic encounter after Caesar and Pullus returned from Alexandria, when Caesar had confronted his most veteran Legions, including the Equestrians, in Campania, after their rampaging over the countryside outside Rome. In something of a blessing, the men didn't seem to have any desire to wander about the camp, choosing instead to huddle in their tents, talking in whispers about the day's events, while the Centurions did much the same thing, where they and their Optios gathered in the tent of their Pilus Prior, and while there was conversation, it was desultory, as every man strained to listen for some sort of sign that the violence had resumed. Inside Pullus' tent were some of the most veteran Centurions in the army, but they were all of a single mind, that this was a unique situation, one where none of them had any idea not only what Caesar would do, but what the correct solution even was.

"I don't think he has any choice," Gnaeus Asellio, Pullus' Hastatus Prior said. "I think we're going to have to turn around. I just don't think the boys have it in them to keep this up."

Pullus said nothing, but he was concerned to see that there were a couple heads nodding in agreement; that one of them was his own Optio was even worse. However, he had made up his mind to speak as little as possible, wanting his officers to express themselves freely without worrying about what he was thinking of them; at least, that was part of the reason. An equal part of it was that, for once, he had no real idea what to do either, because he was evenly torn between the two alternatives. That his reason for leaning towards the option of doing what Alexander had done and turning around was one that he would never utter aloud, the idea that, if they did so, it was likely they would retrace their steps that would lead them through Bharuch. Sometimes, in the privacy and darkness of his quarters in the night, he would think about how, if they did return to Bharuch, he might choose to remain there, even thinking that, because of his familiarity with some of the men of the 6th Legion from his time with the Seventh and Tenth Cohorts in Alexandria, he could persuade Caesar to appoint him Primus Pilus, thereby finally giving Balbus his chance to be Primus Pilus of the Equestrians. The fact that, if this came to pass, it would effectively put Felix out of a job was something he preferred not to think about, if only because, deep down, he knew that was all that it was, a dream. Still, he was as sick of this place the men had begun calling the "Green Hades" as they were, realizing now that he only thought he had been constantly wet and sticky when they had first arrived in India. Thanks to Hyppolita's advice, both with garb and diet, he had adjusted, even with their move further south, as had most of the men to one degree or another. This place, however, was different, and it wasn't just the climate; it was the seemingly never-ending *jangla*, where the clearings were usually manmade, and even those that occurred naturally weren't that large, rarely large enough for the daily camp. Through Apollodorus, Diocles had learned that this terrain remained the same as they moved east, until the final third, where it opened up...but there was a line of hills that had to be traversed to reach the coast. However, there was something he did share with Caesar, and that was the feelings unleashed by the unbearable prospect of what it would mean if they did turn around, because doing so couldn't be considered a setback, as at Gergovia, and Dyrrhachium, both of those turning out to be temporary defeats. If they turned around, Pullus knew as well as Caesar that they would never come back, that all of this would end. Perhaps, he thought as he sat there listening to the others debate, if I knew I had a future in Bharuch, I'd be willing to turn around, but the truth was that, with the death of his family in Brundisium, without Hyppolita involved, there was nothing that he missed about Rome. Oh, he did miss bread made from wheat, though not nearly as much as almost every man around him, especially Scribonius, and he had developed a taste for Falernian wine, but neither of these were such a Siren's call that the lure of them was irresistible. By the time Pullus was ready to send his officers back to their tents, the only thing he had decided was to wait to hear what Caesar had to say; whatever it was, he thought, it better be the best oration he's ever given, or the trouble has just started.

Caesar didn't disappoint Pullus, but even more than the words he spoke to what began as a surly mass of men who, while they were standing in their normal ranks, in their current mood were barely removed from the kind of mob that had stormed the Forum of Rome in past days, it was the tone their general adopted that was the beginning of turning the men's hearts and minds.

"My comrades," he had begun, standing on the rostrum that was constructed of crates, and even with ten Legions, thousands of cavalry troopers, and the thousands of faceless, nameless men who supported them, it was as quiet as Pullus had ever heard it. Pullus could also see in the faces of the men across from his spot to Caesar's right that Caesar addressing the men as his comrades, rather than his usual manner of calling them "my soldiers," had been noticed. "I begin this by offering you an apology. I," Caesar paused, and while it might have been due to his usual flair for the dramatic, Pullus didn't think so, if only because of the words, knowing how much they must have hurt their general to utter, "have failed you. That," he made an exaggerated show of shaking his head so that even the men more than a hundred paces away could see, "is to my shame, and for that, I humbly ask your apology." Fortunately, it wasn't raining, it having stopped about a third of a watch earlier, and while, like all Roman camps, they were standing in a large cleared area, the trees that towered over them beyond the perimeter of the camp were easy to see, and he pointed to them as he continued, "I know that you call this the Green Hades, that it has proven to be a miserable place, worse than our time in India, even for you," he indicated the Legions that were grouped together, "the men who marched with Legate Pollio south from Pattala. As much as I tried to prepare you for this, I have failed. There is no other way to put it." For the first time, his tone changed, becoming firmer. "But we now have a choice to make, my comrades, but before I give you those choices as I see it, I want to assure you of one thing." Another pause, but neither Pullus nor any of his officers, up to and including his Legates, were prepared to hear Caesar declare, "If it's your decision to abandon this campaign, to turn around and return, first to Pandya, then all the way back to Rome...I will honor that decision, and I will lead you home to collect the honors and accolades that you so richly deserve." In the shocked silence, he asked, as if he was inquiring about a minor matter, "Is this acceptable to all of you?"

It wasn't done with any unity, but there was no mistaking that the men of the ranks were shouting their acceptance, while Pullus stood there, nonplussed, wondering whether Caesar had actually gone mad from the events of the day before.

Caesar had to make a quieting gesture several times before he continued, "Very well, it's clear that you have accepted this. Now, I have one request, that you allow me to give you as accurate an assessment of our situation as it stands today as I see it that I can offer. Only after I do that will I feel that I have done my duty, not just to myself, but to you." It was more muted, but the response the men gave him was still clearly in the affirmative, and he began, "I believe that all of you are as aware as I am that our only hope of returning back to India, then Parthia, and finally to Rome, relies on our fleet." By this time, most of the men seemed content to let someone else voice their response, and in another ragged chorus, these unelected representatives signaled their acceptance of this premise, which Caesar acknowledged with a nod of his own. Pointing towards the *Porta Praetoria*, he went on, "Right now, our fleet lies in that direction. But," he didn't turn his body, instead pointing over his shoulder to indicate the *Porta Decumana* over his shoulder, "the way home lies in that direction, yes?" More agreement, but Pullus thought he saw the beginning of a dawning uncertainty on the faces of the men he'd been watching. Nevertheless, Caesar continued, "You all know what my purpose was in landing and building a road across what Legate Volusenus has assured me is this peninsula that is just as long from north to south as it is from east to west. And," he assured them, "if that was the only challenge, then I wouldn't hesitate to order the army to turn around, while sending our cavalry to the port city of Da Nang, where our fleet currently is by this time, waiting for us to arrive, with orders to come retrieve us. Remember," he reminded the men, "based on the information that I knew at the time, and after the struggle we had in clearing just thirty miles of the narrow peninsula, I thought I had calculated correctly the amount of time it would take us to negotiate this peninsula. And," he repeated, "as I said, I was wrong, not in the distance but in the degree of difficulty facing us. Right now, Legate Nero is expecting us within a matter of one or two weeks, when we are barely halfway there. I instructed him that, if a month passed beyond our anticipated arrival, he was to send a portion of the fleet, using our fastest ships, to retrace their voyage back down this peninsula south, then return to where we debarked at the Mae Nam River, my reasoning being that, thanks to your strong backs, he would at least have something approaching a road that he could send men to follow to find us." Now, Pullus was certain that what he was reading in the expressions on the faces across from him was a dawning recognition of the dilemma in which they found themselves. And, as they all learned, Caesar was far from through. "Even if the Legate made the decision to bring the entire fleet with him, not only would it take longer because of our heavier ships, but even if they found us back encamped in the spot we made by the river, we then will still have to sail south to get around the narrow peninsula, which we now know extends another five hundred miles farther south than the one upon which we find ourselves right now. Even under the best of circumstances, by my calculations, which," for the first time, he turned and indicated his Legates, pointing to one, "our *Praefectus Fabrorum*, and the best surveyor and navigator in the world has doublechecked and verified, it's likely that we won't return to our permanent camp in Muziris before Januarius." The men had begun to shift restlessly, murmuring to themselves, causing Pullus to turn his head slightly to try and overhear what the men of his own Century were saying.

"Januarius! That's months from now!"

"If he's telling the truth."

"Turbo, you know how fucking long we had to wait for the fleet to take us to the Mae Nam, and it took us three weeks longer to go thirty miles than we thought!" Pullus, recognized the voice as belonging to Aulus Clepsina who, like Turbo, was in his Second Section, and there was no missing the scorn as Clepsina asked sarcastically, "What, do you think Nero and the fleet stopped somewhere so they could get drunk and debauch before they came to get us?"

While he had no way of knowing, Pullus' hunch was that this was the tone of the conversations that had created the low buzzing noise that Caesar seemingly ignored, continuing now in a clear, logical, and relentless fashion, which, as Pullus had learned, was Caesar at his most formidable.

"Also remember this, my comrades. If we turn back around, we'll be covering ground that has already been picked clean of anything edible by our cavalry, and while we have enough of a reserve to enable us to return to the Mae Nam and stay for some time, we have no real way of knowing how long we'll have to wait before the fleet arrives." The buzzing had subsided as Caesar conveyed this last part, and to Pullus, the silence that followed was grim in its nature, as each man realized that their general was only speaking a simple, if unpalatable, truth. Every village encompassing an area that extended more than ten miles north and ten miles south from the crude road they were struggling to construct had been thoroughly ransacked and searched, which meant that it was extremely unlikely that foraging parties would return with anywhere near enough to keep the wagons and mules that transported their food supplies full, at least until after the coming harvest in October, still almost three months away. Caesar paused again, this time to survey his men, moving his head slowly across the sea of faces looking directly at him, and Pullus guessed that he was seeing the same thing that he saw in their expressions, which caused Caesar to point again, but this time back towards the east. "It's only ahead of us, across the land we haven't gone yet, where there's the prospect of food. But if it's your desire, then I, as your general, must find a way to keep you fed as we wait for the fleet to arrive." He fell silent, making Pullus wonder if he was done, and it was time for the army to decide, then Caesar said, "That said, I do have a suggestion to offer."

Like so many of Caesar's solutions, it was simple, yet also breathtaking in its scope. What Caesar deduced was that, if it wasn't for the intolerable climate conditions, the men would be, while not happy, still compliant and willing to follow his orders. Consequently, his proposal was that, until the monsoon season ended, the army pause where it was currently located to rest and recuperate while waiting for the dryer months to arrive. If that had been the only thing, Pullus suspected that it wouldn't have been enough, but Caesar had another idea, one that appealed to his Legionaries in a fundamental way, and that was through their greed. Slowly, in bits and pieces, thanks to several forays by Hirtius' cavalry, Caesar had learned more about the Khmer, and in particular, the city they called Angkor. Even accounting for the inevitable exaggeration, it became clear that Angkor was the most important city of the Khmer people, while Long had insisted that it was a wealthy city; not, of course, like the Han, but still stuffed with valuables. Using Angkor, Caesar also solved the dilemma of what to do about the two Legions who, while inadvertently, had triggered this crisis. Presenting the opportunity as a chance to redeem themselves, it was agreed that four Legions; the 8th under what at that moment was the provisional Primus Pilus, promoted from the Second of the First, the 28th under Cartufenus, along with the newly arrived 14th, commanded by Gnaeus Figulus and the 21st under Papernus, once they were sufficiently recovered, would march the sixty miles south under the command of Caesar himself to assault Angkor. Caesar announced that his decision to punish both Legions as a whole was suspended until after Angkor, where he would reassess his punishment decree. Nobody, not even the newest Gregarius from Pandya, was fooled; this was a way to preserve Caesar's *dignitas* as much as it was a chance for the two Legions who had ignited this entire mutiny to redeem themselves.

There was only one decision upon which Caesar wouldn't budge, and that was that the ranker who slew Clustuminus had to be executed, although he did relent by not requiring the traditional punishment of facing the comrades of his Century, armed with staves and ax handles. Truthfully, there was only token resistance to this, and the ranker was executed with only the officers of the 8th and the 28th present in the forum to witness it. As a whole, the men welcomed the respite, not from the physical exertion as much as from the ability to sit inside their tents and stay dry in a relative sense. The schedule for Caesar's Centuries was now double-checked by one of the Tribunes, who were still unhappy with their roles, and the only time the men were required to be in their armor was when they had the duty of guarding the camp. It wasn't complete idleness on the part of the rankers, especially in the beginning, as they went outside the camp to procure the raw materials to correct the one deficiency that plagued the men of the ranks. While most Centurions, particularly the Primi Pili and Pili Priores who had their own wagons, carried square panels of wood that served as the floor of their tents, the men didn't have that luxury, which meant that, even when they were only in the same spot for a day, the moist ground under their feet would become churned, sticky mud even under the cover of the canvas. No orders were given to correct this, and as far as Pullus could tell, it was both a spontaneous and almost unanimous decision made by the men of each Legion independently of each other. These makeshift solutions weren't elegant in any sense of the word; most tent sections were content to simply split logs of the same length, then lay them flat side up on the ground underneath their tent, although as days passed, some of the more ambitious men put time and effort into creating something that was a semblance of the smooth, and relatively even flooring that Pullus had long before taken for granted. Some of the Tribunes tried to organize a series of games to help pass the time in much the same manner that the Legions did in winter camp, but it didn't go very far; for the most part, what the men enjoyed the most was staying dry for an extended period of time. Another benefit was reported by the camp physicians, that the number of men with foot problems decreased dramatically, which had been another ailment that had plagued the army within a month of their sailing from India.

"When a man's feet are constantly wet and never dry out, the skin of their feet starts to shed itself," was how Stolos had explained it to Pullus. "That leaves the new layer of skin under the old exposed before it toughens up enough, and it can become corrupt itself. Of course," he had shrugged, "if this new layer stays wet like the first one, the same thing will happen until a man is walking on nothing but raw meat."

Of all the myriad ailments that had beset the army during this period of time, while it wasn't the most serious, it was the most prevalent, and as any soldier knew, an army marched and fought on its feet, and having men hobbled wasn't good for either. It was a gradual process, one where it was hard to tell from one day to the next, but tempers began to cool, while the complaining subsided back to a level of grumbling that was only slightly above normal. As hard as it was to see the incremental improvement from one day to the next, after three weeks had passed, Pullus and the other Primi Pili began to relax slightly. The change also had the added benefit of providing fodder for conversation around the charcoal fires and inside Centurions' tents.

"I don't know how he does it," Pullus broached the subject about a month into their halt. "I thought that this time he was going to throw Dogs, and that we'd be on our way back by now."

Neither of his friends, nor his nephew and his slave missed the wistful note in his voice, but it was a sign of their loyalty to Pullus that none of them ever mentioned any subject that could encourage Pullus to return back to Bharuch, even if only in his mind.

"I would have wagered the same thing," Scribonius agreed. "And," he gave a rueful laugh, "I would have been cleaned out of my Legion account, because I would have wagered everything I had on it."

"I *knew* I should have gotten you to take that bet!"

Scribonius' response was one of mild surprise, and he pointed out to Balbus, "But you and I agreed! You thought he was just as fucked as I did."

"I would have taken the risk just for the chance to make you go broke," Balbus retorted, but instead of addressing Balbus, Scribonius looked to Pullus, who only shook his head.

"Don't expect me to make any sense of that," he told Scribonius, "because if you can't, I certainly can't." Returning to the subject, Pullus mused, "I wonder if it was hearing Caesar admit that he made a mistake that did it."

"That may be, but he's also admitted making errors before," Diocles pointed out.

"Not like this." Scribonius just beat Pullus to saying the same thing. "Before, he always qualified it in some way. No, I agree with you, Titus. I think that did it."

"Now we just need to wait and see how long it lasts before the men act up again," Pullus commented.

"Maybe they won't," Porcinus spoke up. "Maybe they've finally accepted the idea that the only way to get home is to move forward, not backward."

Although it was still about two years in the future, Porcinus would learn this was a vain hope.

Six weeks into their idleness, for the first time, it didn't rain for a full day, and Long, who spoke enough Tamil for Achaemenes to understand to translate to Caesar, assured the general that the rainy season was coming to an end, although it was still another month away before it was fully over. This was what Caesar had been waiting for, and with so much time on his hands, his plan for the assault on Angkor was comprehensive and well-thought-out. While the men of the cavalry, and most importantly, their mounts took advantage of the rest, they did so on a rotating basis, Caesar unwilling to blind himself by recalling the *turmae* of troopers that were constantly roving over the area that their specific *alae* had been assigned as their responsibility to patrol. Only once was there any excitement and the prospect for the entire army to see battle, five weeks into their pause, when the Decurion that patrolled the area between their camp and Angkor sixty miles to the south sent a pair of riders galloping north to report a sizable force composed of more than two hundred elephants, several thousand infantry, and almost as many missile troops was marching north. For several days, the Legions had been put on alert, but the Khmer army only came within ten miles of their camp, whereupon they spent three days in place before retreating, a moral victory of sorts that played into Caesar's hands.

"They took one look at what they were facing and wanted no part of it. Now they're back in their city shaking in fear and praying to that god Buddha or whatever they call it that we don't show up," Balbus had declared on the night the scouts reported the Khmer withdrawal.

Knowing that his friend was far from alone in his consensus, neither Pullus nor Scribonius argued, and if the truth were known, Pullus in particular had limited interest in the activities of the Khmer. While he understood Caesar's rationale for selecting the four Legions he would be leading, it still rankled the Primus Pilus, but understanding that his men, and even some of his Centurions, didn't share that indignation at not being chosen, he kept his mouth shut, fooling no one who knew him. The day before Caesar departed with what the men had taken to calling the Angkor Legions, he called a meeting of all his Primi Pili and senior officers to inform them of his plans as it would affect them.

"I'm allocating a week to march to a point where I can examine the city with my own eyes and to prepare for the assault," he began. "Since we're traveling in relatively light order, we won't have to cut as wide a path, or make it as solid because most of the wagons and carts we're taking are going to be empty, and the others will only carry our artillery. And," he gave his officers a smile that could have been considered cruel, "enough naphtha to roast a thousand elephants."

This was no secret, but the Centurions responded with a guttural growl of approval, although Balbinus whispered to Pullus, "Any idea if these Han *cunni* use elephants?"

It was, Pullus realized, a good question, and a troubling one, because as much of an open secret as it was about Caesar taking their most potent weapon with him, it was also understood that, once they left India, and especially now, the supply of the volatile substance that they had on hand would, in all likelihood, have to suffice for the foreseeable future. Perhaps there was another source somewhere ahead of them to the east, but none of them, from Caesar on down the chain of command, were counting on it.

"Once I decide on the final plan, I will choose a day for the assault," Caesar continued. "According to every report I've received from Hirtius' men, the city is fairly large, and there are several stone buildings that appear to be temples or some other official structure. But," he offered another smile, "what they don't have is a wall made of stone or even wood. If possible, I want to entice their forces out from the city to engage us, then we can assault at our leisure once they're destroyed. All told," he concluded, "we'll be returning in one month from tomorrow to the day at the latest."

With that, the men were dismissed, and the next morning, they roused themselves to watch as the four Legions, whose men had been working through the night as usual, marched behind Caesar out of the camp. While tempers had certainly cooled, there was still what Pullus would describe as a wariness on the part of his Equestrians when it came to the 8th in particular, and he understood that there was still a vestige of bitterness between the two Legions that lingered because of the antagonism between the 8th's dead Primus Pilus and Pullus, and by extension, the Equestrians. It still wasn't anywhere near the tension between the 8th and 28th, and Pullus was certain that having the 8th as the vanguard and the 28th at the opposite end of the column was no accident; later, they would learn that the two Legions would always be separated for the entire time they were on their smaller campaign until the day of their return. Once they were out of sight, the men resumed their normal activities, returning to the never-ending dice games and the other games of skill and chance rankers indulged in to while away the time during their idle periods. One of the more popular activities was pitting some of the deadly vipers against each other, the men responsible for organizing the entertainment digging a pit in the ground deep enough that there was no danger of the combatants escaping, which would be surrounded by excited, shouting rankers who, of course, wagered on the outcomes. The more adventurous men, particularly among the Tribunes and Legates who had their own mounts, organized hunting parties, searching for the ultimate prize and returning with a dead tiger. Those that were successful then would display the pelt in some manner, including Pollio and Hirtius, who for a brief period of time wore the tail of the tigers they had slain, attaching it to their crest. For Pullus, however, what leisure time meant to him was to leave the camp where, just beyond the ditch that was still filled with water, there were ten large stakes that he had ordered be erected by his woodworking *immunes*, and stripped down to his *subligaculum* and armed with a *rudis*, he began his ritual, which had expanded to a full watch, thrusting, slashing, recovering, over and over. No man in the army who had been marching with Caesar thought of this as unusual, because it was a routine that Pullus adhered to with an almost religious fervor, although every now and then, men would come and stand on the rampart to watch, while others, usually the Centurions and Optios under his command, would come to join him, each of them having learned that, if they did so, it had better not be for the sake of appearance, because their giant Primus Pilus would notice, and none of them wanted the bruises and pain that would result.

Caesar and the four Legions didn't return a month and one day later as he had promised; instead arriving five days early, when the guard *Bucinator* sounded the initial call that a friendly force was approaching, which didn't create much stir since scouting and hunting parties were coming and going all the time. After the briefest pause, the second series of notes that alerted the men that their commander was approaching sounded, and the camp erupted into activity as men rushed from their tents, their dice games or wrestling matches immediately forgotten. Pullus just happened to be outside the camp at the makeshift stakes, but on this occasion, he had been joined by Porcinus, at Diocles' subtle but unmistakable message that his uncle was becoming peeved at his absence for these drills. It did serve to give the pair the first unobstructed view of Caesar's return, riding Toes in what, while none of them knew it, would be the last campaign for the horse who was almost as famous as his rider. Riding behind Caesar was his personal standard bearer, but when the approaching column drew closer, Pullus and Porcinus could see that, while it wasn't ivy, which was unknown in this part of the world, the shaft of the standard was wrapped in a similar kind of plant, as were the eagle standards of the four Legions. Porcinus prevailed on Pullus to curtail their training, and while Pullus grumbled it was more out of habit, the pair walking over to stand next to the *Porta Praetoria*, arriving immediately after Caesar, his staff and bodyguards entered the camp to the roaring cheers of men who came rushing from their tents to greet their general. The pair was in time to see that it was Cartufenus and the 28th in the vanguard, telling Pullus that his friend and his friend's Legion had been forgiven.

"Wait until you see what's following behind!" Cartufenus called out, but was gone before Pullus could learn more, consigning the pair to wait as the 28th marched past.

Seeing the second Legion in the column, Pullus remarked to Porcinus, "It looks like the 8th has forgiven the 28th."

One by one, the first three Legions marched past, but by the time the 21st had reached the cleared area around the camp, Pullus and his nephew could see at least part of what Cartufenus referred to, as a double column of gray beasts came lumbering past, causing the pair to gape at each other in astonishment, each animal being ridden by a man they had learned to identify as one of the Khmer because of their distinctive eye shape and coloring.

"We have elephants now?" Porcinus finally managed, but

all Pullus could offer was a shrug.

"It looks that way," he agreed, "but Caesar didn't mention that as part of his plan."

There was a total of fifty elephants, but as noteworthy as that was, it was the ragged column of men, six across, loops of rope around the neck of every man in each row, while their hands were bound, that gave Pullus his first indication of the scope of the Roman victory. It wouldn't be until later that night that Pullus, and the other officers who had remained behind, learned of something else, the first example of an event that would begin to germinate among the ranks of Caesar's army, until four years in the future, when it would be fully realized.

"The Khmer King recognized Caesar as a god," Cartufenus explained on the second night after their return from Angkor, accepting Pullus' invitation to the evening meal, making it sound as if it was the most natural thing in the world.

"What does that mean?" Scribonius beat Pullus to the question.

"It means that those Khmer prisoners aren't really prisoners, they're..." Cartufenus tried to think of the right word, coming up with, "...offerings, I suppose. The same with the elephants as well."

Like the other Primi Pili, Pullus had already heard the bare bones of the assault on Angkor, when, as Caesar hoped, the Khmer king and his army sallied from the city, arraying for battle a mile north of the outskirts. Proving that the Khmer were ignorant of the Romans' most potent weapon, the king sent his force of elephants, more than three hundred in number, at the waiting Romans, but in a tactic different from those used by the kingdoms of India, rather than try to use their mass in a headlong charge, they stopped about a hundred paces away so that the archers on each animal could launch a flurry of missiles at the invaders, presumably to soften the Romans up, who stood there absorbing the arrows, though not by going into *testudo*. Just as Pullus and the others knew the moment Caesar said it, the Khmer learned what a horrible mistake it was, Caesar having decided to refrain from using his *ballistae* early, even though it would have wreaked havoc when the Khmer were still more than three hundred paces away. Afterward, Caesar claimed that his reason for waiting was that he wanted to see whether this was a bluff on the part of the Khmer king before signaling for a truce. Ultimately, what mattered was that, even as the archers launched their first volley of missiles from their tiny platforms, both *ballistae* and scorpions began loosing, the bolts of the smaller pieces wrapped in a naphtha-soaked strip and ignited in the eyeblink before the *immune* who was assigned as the chief pulled the cord, the flaming bolts slashing into the unarmored animals, while the arcing pots of blazing naphtha descended to douse both animal and men. Just as had happened with Abhiraka's Harem, and the Beauties of Prince Divakar and the Chola, within an amount of time that none who witnessed could ever accurately convey aside from that it happened very rapidly, the Khmer host defending Angkor went from an army determined to defend their city to a screaming, panic-stricken mass of flesh, both animal and man who only had one collective goal, to escape the flames that seemed to chase them. Compounding the carnage, Caesar and the others present saw that the spear-wielding infantry was arrayed immediately behind the elephants, where they waited for what, up to that point for the Khmer, would be the inevitable collapse of their foe as their most potent weapons began their lumbering charge on the enemy lines, whereupon they would follow behind to slaughter the disoriented, reeling foes. Judging from the overall prosperity and wealth of Angkor, the Khmer method of fighting had clearly worked up until that day, but as every foe that used war elephants who faced Caesar's army had learned, there was essentially no defense from liquid fire that rained from the sky.

"We barely got our *gladii* wet." Cartufenus' words were slightly slurred, as Pullus had Diocles serve one of the last remaining jugs of *sura* as an incentive to get Cartufenus to accept his invitation over that of Balbinus and the other Primi Pili. "Those fucking beasts did most of the work." He grimaced at the memory. "It was like what happened with the Cholans at the pass, but worse, much worse." Taking another sip, he thought for a moment. "I don't think our *ballistae* loosed more than twice, at least with the *naphtha*." When Pullus looked at him with a raised eyebrow, he explained, "The survivors who

Caesar Ascending – The Han

didn't get stomped or burned alive ran into the city and took refuge in one of their temples, and they have a *lot* of temples. They're made of stone, and," the Centurion acknowledged grudgingly, "most of them are pretty big and well made. The largest ones had a wall around it, and about a thousand of the bastards holed up in each of the big ones, so Caesar had the *ballista*e breach the wall."

"How many people in the city?" Scribonius asked.

"I heard Caesar say that there were seventy thousand people, but a lot of them ran south out of the city. And," he finished with a shrug, "Caesar didn't send the cavalry after them. I think we rounded up about thirty thousand altogether as we moved through the city."

"Aside from the temples, was there much resistance?"

"Some," Cartufenus nodded, "but it was always small groups of men, ten, twenty of them together, and they always were in one of their other stone buildings, which is about half of the city, I'd judge. We had to go in and get them, so it took a couple watches to either kill them or round them up."

"And are those the prisoners?"

"Some of them, but only their spearmen. Their king had a royal bodyguard like all these barbarians do, and they were all swordsmen, but none of them surrendered. So," he said simply, "we cut them down."

"You said the king thinks Caesar is a god," Scribonius prompted, wanting to hear more about this.

"That's what Achaemenes said that Long told him," Cartufenus replied. "All I know is that the little bastard came out of his palace on his knees, blabbering and speaking their gibberish, and then kissed Caesar's feet. It was," he declared, "disgusting to watch. It's no way for a king to act." Seeing the expression of shared amusement, he said indignantly, "It's true! King Nedunj didn't behave that way. Neither did that Bharuch king, what was his name?"

"Abhiraka," Pullus supplied, ignoring Scribonius' sudden glance at his friend. More to get the topic out of dangerous waters, Pullus pointed out, "What about Phraates? He didn't die well, at all."

"No," Cartufenus admitted, but he wasn't willing to

concede the point, "but what about the Cholan? He killed himself rather than surrender to us!"

This caused Pullus, who was the only man in the room aware of the true circumstances to shift uncomfortably, but fortunately, Cartufenus was too drunk to notice.

"Where is this king now?" he asked quickly.

"Back in what's left of Angkor." Cartufenus laughed. "Praying to some god named Buddha and asking him to intercede with his fellow god Caesar and ask him to never come back."

The others burst into laughter, while Cartufenus beamed in drunken pleasure at his own wit.

Once the noise subsided, it was Balbus who asked, "So, has he changed his mind about using war elephants? I know he hated to abandon the idea once he found out that elephants aren't sailors any more than we are."

"Those aren't for war." Cartufenus shook his head, only after the laughter died down. Leaning forward, he tried to communicate his seriousness, but it was ruined when he belched before he said, "But Caesar swore me to secrecy about what they're going to be used for."

"He's going to use them to help us finish cutting our way to Da Nang," Scribonius said.

"How did you know that?" Cartufenus gasped, his eyes going wide as his befogged brain tried to work through the implications. "Be sure and tell Caesar I didn't say a word, Scribonius!" He stabbed a finger at his fellow Primus Pilus. "You too, Pullus! Swear on the black stone that you won't!"

"Cartufenus," Pullus' tone was gentle, and he was trying to keep from laughing, "Sextus just drew the obvious conclusion once you said they wouldn't be used for war. What else would they be?"

The Primus Pilus didn't answer, frowning instead, looking from one to the other, clearly trying to think things through, but he finally said in exasperation, "Just don't tell Caesar!"

Cartufenus only left after receiving assurances from each of the other men present, and Pullus escorted him to the flap of his tent, then stood to watch his counterpart stagger away.

From just behind him, Scribonius asked, "Are you sure he

Caesar Ascending – The Han

can find his way back to his area?"

"That," Pullus laughed, "is a good question."

The meal over, Scribonius stepped outside as well, and it was not much more than an idle thought as he mused, "I wonder what Caesar plans on doing with those men?"

"You mean, besides sell them?" Pullus shrugged. "I have no idea."

All answers to the various questions were answered the next day, when Caesar held a meeting of all Centurions, taking them outside the camp to do so while posting men on the ramparts to keep curious rankers away.

"The days of our men working like dogs to make it to Da Nang are over," he announced. "These men and the elephants given to me by King Kaundinya as tribute to leave the Khmer kingdom unmolested any further will be used for the hardest part of the manual labor that our men have been performing."

Despite the fact that no Centurion had turned a spade or swung an ax, although getting muddy to that point just supervising had been impossible to avoid, they cheered this news nonetheless, knowing that it at least meant a reduction in the complaining.

Once they subsided, Caesar continued, "I'm still working on the details of how this is going to work, but none of these animals was used for war, and they all have a handler who is essentially the same as a *mahout*. As always, our biggest challenge will be in language, but these men also know that their fate rests in my hands."

"Is it true that that Khmer king thought you were a god?"

To Pullus, and to some of the other more observant Centurions, Caesar's lack of surprise indicated that he had employed a common tactic and put Primus Pilus Flaminius of the 30th up to asking the question.

What Pullus found a bit more unsettling was Caesar's demeanor when he answered matter-of-factly, "Yes. And," he had to raise his voice slightly over the whispered comments, "what is important to understand is that so do these men who will be providing our labor force. So," he smiled widely, as if to assure his officers he was jesting, "if I begin acting like a

73

god, know that that's why."

The laughs this brought sounded more polite than from real humor, and Pullus saw several of his fellow Centurions look uneasy, making him wonder if their thoughts aligned with his; is Caesar really joking?

"What happens to these bastards once we reach this Da Nang place?" Batius asked.

Although he didn't hesitate, there was something in Caesar's demeanor that alerted Pullus that there was more going on than it might appear, but there was nothing objectionable in his answer, which was simply, "That will be decided later."

It was, Pullus thought, curious, and a glance at Scribonius informed him that his friend hadn't missed it either. For a moment, it looked like Batius would press the issue, but when he didn't, Pullus reminded himself that Batius' normal expression was that of a man who had an invisible *numen* waving a fresh turd under his nose.

When he saw Batius wasn't inclined to pursue the matter, Caesar said quickly, "We resume our march tomorrow, but we're going to return to this camp for another three days."

None of his officers reacted with surprise, in a sign that this had become normal during this phase of the campaign, when their daily progress was measured in miles in the low single digits, all of them learning very quickly that the men were more inclined to march a few extra miles to and from the camp when the alternative was to construct a camp that was usually less than three or four miles from the old one. Caesar dismissed the Centurions to return to their areas and spread the word, while leaving some of them to wonder about the details of how this new labor force was supposed to work. Like Pullus had, most of the curious Centurions decided to leave that to Caesar; they would find out soon enough.

Yuan, who had been born Liu Shi, but assumed the name Yuan when he ascended to the throne of what the outside world called the Han Empire, was worried, the sign of his agitation plain for his palace staff of courtiers and eunuchs to see by the manner in which he was pacing, seemingly staring at the inlaid wooden floor with a frown.

Finally, he stopped pacing to admit, "I fear that I should have taken this threat more seriously." He looked up to gaze directly in one man's eyes, saying simply, "I should have heeded your advance, Shi Xian."

The eunuch who, like most of his kind, had an ageless quality that made it impossible for even those who knew him to precisely determine his age, offered a deep enough bow that he was essentially addressing the floor. "You have many other issues to worry about, Bìxià," Xian assured him, using the term that loosely translated to the Western version of "Your Imperial Majesty." "And, I confess that I am as surprised as you are that these barbarians left India, not to return to the West, but to come in this direction."

"And now," Yuan said bitterly, more to himself, "they are nibbling at the edge of my empire."

As unpalatable as it was for Yuan, he now understood that when the word arrived that the pale-skinned army led by the Roman Caesar had been spotted on the eastern coast of India, he shouldn't have dismissed it out of hand as an Indian problem. The truth was that there hadn't been a disruption in the trade that was the lifeblood for his empire, one that even now was under threat, both from without, in the form of Zhizhi Chanyu of the Western part of the *Xiongnu* people, who had become increasingly aggressive in pushing for a military confrontation, and from within the Imperial court itself, as two factions competed for the ultimate prize in their world, access and influence with him. More than once, Yuan had wondered if both factions, divided between the one led by two of his former tutors, whose counsel he valued, and the other consisting of the palace staff, including Shi Xian, understood that he was aware of the infighting. He suspected that they did, although he also was fairly certain that they didn't know that not only was he attuned to this struggle that only took place behind his back, but that he was using both factions for his own purposes, as pieces on his *Go* board. Not, he thought ruefully, that this helps in the moment, because he realized that he was perilously close to being in a position where he would be reacting to the next move posed by this foreign invader instead of taking proactive steps. If only he hadn't been so dismissive when word had come to his court about the arrival of the Romans in India in the first place, but he had assumed that it had something to do with the Greek king Alexander in some way. Both of what were in effect the two remaining superpowers of their time were aware of each other, but as Caesar, and the other Romans in his army would learn, the Han knew far more about Rome than the Rome knew of the Han. However, in Yuan's mind, this made his lapse even more egregious, because he had been kept informed of the progress of Caesar and his army, beginning with the conquest of Parthia. It had been impressive, certainly, that the Romans could conquer an area so vast that it rivaled his own empire in size in a bit more than two years, but he had concluded that this was more of an internal matter in the settling of a grudge between the two Western powers because of the fate of the Roman Marcus Crassus. He had also heard about Pattala, which was interesting, but it was the capture of Bharuch that caught his attention because of its importance as a conduit for his most lucrative source of income in the silk trade, while the spices and cotton produced by India that returned through that city back to his empire was equally important. And, for a period of a few months, he had insisted on regular updates, but when there was no discernible disruption in the flow of goods, other matters became more pressing. Perhaps, he thought, *if I had done something then, possibly sending an emissary to this Caesar to establish contact, I would have a better idea of what their intentions are.* It was only a passing thought, however, and he returned his attention to the present, but when he asked another question, it wasn't aimed at Shi Xian.

"Master Zhou, what would you counsel me to do now?"

As Emperor, Yuan was neither required nor expected to address any of his subjects in a manner that might even hint at some form of equality, but Zhou had been one of his tutors, the man who had introduced the young prince to the teachings of Confucius, still the most influential philosopher in their history. His very presence in the imperial court was something Yuan knew created a great deal of consternation with the faction of which Shi Xian was a part, because of Zhou's relatively recent return from an exile that had been engineered by the scholar's rivals. As Yuan knew very well, addressing Zhou in this manner would undoubtedly irritate not only Shi Xian, but one of the non-eunuchs of Yuan's inner circle who opposed Zhou, his Imperial Secretary Hong Gong, who, as he always did, sat in a corner of the room silently recording this conversation.

Rather than answer immediately, Zhou, whose hair was now more white than black but was otherwise the only sign of his age, considered for a long moment, his fingers moving relentlessly over the string of black onyx beads that he was never seen without, finally saying, "I believe that you must send a delegation to these barbarians, Bìxià. But," he cautioned, "I also believe that you must be very careful in who you select to go, and if possible, someone who can communicate with them directly."

Yuan frowned; while he had suspected that his former tutor would advise him to make some form of contact, he hadn't expected this last condition, and, frankly, he thought it would be impossible.

"If there is anyone among my subjects who speak whatever tongue these Romans speak, I'm unaware of it," he replied. Then, thinking that it paid to be cautious, he asked the eunuch, "Are you aware of anyone, Xian?"

"No, Bìxià," Xian assured him, but even with the carefully blank expression that was a practical requirement for service in the Imperial court, Yuan was certain there was mockery there when the eunuch added lightly, "but perhaps Master Zhou has sources that we do not know about."

The older man didn't take the bait, but unlike Xian, he made no attempt to hide his amusement when he countered, "I was not thinking of the Roman tongue, Bìxià. These barbarians have been in India for, what is it, three years?" He addressed this not to Yuan but to the eunuch, who replied grudgingly, "From our information, yes."

"Then I think that it is not only possible, but likely that if the barbarian general has not learned either Tamil or Sanskrit, he certainly has someone who does. I can name a half-dozen men who are in the palace compound at this moment who speak one or both of those tongues, but there is one in particular who comes to mind."

Yuan did try to disguise his amusement at what only

someone who knew the eunuch well would recognize as a sign of his agitation, the stiffness of his bow towards Zhou, although his uniquely sexless voice that was commonplace among court eunuchs bore no trace of it as he conceded, "That is very true, Master Zhou, and it is something that I should have thought of myself." Xian turned to Yuan, and this time, there was no stiffness in his posture as he continued to bow. "And I offer my most humble pardon, Bìxià, and I beg your forgiveness for not thinking of this myself. I have served you poorly."

For a flicker of time, the Emperor thought of behaving in a manner that would suggest to the eunuch that, not only was he displeased, but he would remember, then decided that Xian had suffered enough for the moment. And, he reminded himself, he does have his uses.

Aloud, after assuring the eunuch there was nothing to forgive, he addressed the question to the others. "What should this message to the barbarians say?"

For the next *shi*, which the Han used in the same manner as the Romans used watches, and was roughly two-thirds of a Roman watch, Yuan allowed the factions to debate with each other until a consensus was reached. Only then did Yuan speak, having been content to sit and watch the proceedings to this point.

"I believe that this last version is suitable," he declared, using a tone that all of his courtiers knew marked a final decision. "Now, find the suitable man to carry it, and arrange a suitable escort for him." He rose, ready to retire, which meant everyone else in the room knelt, and as he swept out of the room, his floor-length silk robes making a barely audible hissing sound, he said, "Now we will see what these barbarians are about."

The progress by Caesar's army certainly increased, but it was aided as much by the fact that the incessant rains had stopped as it did from the additional labor force. Very quickly, a system developed, whereby the human prisoners performed the basic labor of chopping down the trees, bushes, and plants that had been the bane of Caesar's army, while the elephants were used to drag away the tree trunks, and most importantly, pull out the stumps as the first part of creating a relatively smooth surface that would serve as the foundation for the road. By this time, none of the original oxen who pulled the wagons that had departed from Zeugma remained, replaced by black beasts with a set of wide, curved horns that, on the males were oriented towards their back, but unlike the animals on the other side of Our Sea, the females of their type were horned as well, albeit smaller, and where it had taken two and sometimes four of them to rip out a stump, one elephant could do it with little effort, and with fifty animals at their disposal, the increase in progress was inevitable. This didn't mean the men of the Legions were idle, however. Even with their victory over the Khmer, and the belief of the Khmer king that Caesar was a pale god from beyond the edge of the world, there was always a Legion, armed and armored, five Cohorts on each side of the column. The *immunes* in every Legion were kept busy, particularly the leatherworkers, replacing *caligae*, while the woodworkers, under the direction of Volusenus, had begun experimenting more with the tree called bamboo, which, contrary to its appearance when they had first encountered it in India, had the combination of tensile strength and suppleness to be used in a variety of ways. Only after they had penetrated the large peninsula did they learn there were more varieties of the tree, including some that were quite large in circumference, which had quickly replaced other types of wood for use as the legs of their towers. The large bamboo logs were carried in wagons but were so much lighter that it made room for more cargo, and as it was the habit of Rome wherever they went, Caesar's army quickly adopted, and adapted, these new materials and new methods in an almost infinite number of ways. The Legions who weren't on guard duty were still expected to work, though they performed the less onerous tasks than those that had made them filthy and exhausted at the end of the day. They continued using logs cut to a uniform length as the surface of the road that the men had taken to jokingly calling the Via Hades, claiming that this was its ultimate destination. While morale was better, there was an air of resignation hovering above the men that meant that Pullus and the other Primi Pili didn't enforce the regulations as stringently as they normally did, the only exception being anything that smacked of disobedience, which was immediately punished, but in what the men called the "bathhouse justice" that never made it onto their Legion's diary, and by extension, to Caesar. None of the Primi Pili ever divulged to their rankers that this was actually by Caesar's order, recognizing that the idea the men were getting away with something from their otherwise omniscient general boosted their spirits in its own way.

"Men will never fuck their comrades over, or their Century, or their Cohort, or their Legion," was how Pullus' first Centurion and Primus Pilus Gaius Crastinus, who had fallen at Pharsalus as an Evocatus, had counseled him when he was a young Secundus Pilus Prior, "but fucking the army?" He would always accompany this with his bark of a laugh. "That's not only acceptable, it makes a man a hero among his comrades whenever he gets away with it."

It was something that Pullus had adopted as one of his own lessons on leadership, and this supposed ignorance by Caesar was an example of something that put a spring in a man's step, even if he was limping as he did from the thrashing he had just received, knowing that his transgression would never come to Caesar's attention. While this was one example, it was far from the only one of how Pullus and his fellow Primi Pili and Centurions across the army were using every single trick they had learned during their careers to keep the men moving forward, and most importantly, under control as they did it. Their route had paralleled the Dangrek Mountains until the low range curved to the north, and there was a brief span of time where the *jangla* thinned out, enabling them to make ten, and sometimes even fifteen miles a day. They were also reminded that, before they reached Da Nang, there was another range of mountains that were even higher than the Dangreks, but the only route that avoided crossing them was to swing far to the south and almost reaching the coast before turning back north to bypass them. Even Long couldn't provide more than a guess, made even more difficult because of the vastly different systems of measurement they used, but after many watches of discussion and calculations by Volusenus and his small staff of men who were experts in measuring distances for things like maps, the best guess was that it would add another three hundred miles if the general elected to avoid those mountains. Nevertheless, both in a sign that Caesar recognized his hold over his army wasn't as secure as it normally was, and because he was certain of the answer, Caesar had ordered another assembly of the entire army to present the alternatives to be put to a vote. It had been, Pullus and his friends agreed, one of the shortest such meetings that they could remember, the men roaring their decision that these mountains that stood in their way were no obstacle.

On their way back to their area, somewhat surprisingly, it had been Porcinus instead of Scribonius who wondered aloud, "If we didn't have those prisoners and the elephants, I wonder if the decision would have been different?"

As soon as he said it, his more experienced companions exchanged glances that communicated that this was a potentially good question, but Pullus indicated to Scribonius with a slight nod that his friend should communicate what Porcinus may have taken as a rebuke from his uncle.

"It's a good question, Gaius," Scribonius acknowledged. He smiled at the young Optio who had been promoted on the Ganges, as he added, "And it's also one of those 'what if' questions that it doesn't do any good to dwell on. What matters," he patted Porcinus on the shoulder, "is that we have those Khmer and their elephants, so it's something you shouldn't spend time worrying about. But," he spoke more firmly, "it's also the kinds of questions that a good leader needs to think about."

Pullus could tell by his nephew's expression that he had accepted this piece of advice from Scribonius in the manner it was intended, not in the form of censure or criticism, but as one more experienced leader imparting wisdom to a younger one. Reaching their area, Pullus immediately spotted two of the men from his Century behaving in a manner that immediately aroused a Centurion's suspicions, and he watched the pair as they cast a furtive glance behind them before rounding the end of the First Century's street. If only, Pullus thought irritably, all the problems were that easy to solve, as he stalked off in pursuit.

More times than he could readily count, Tiberius Claudius Nero almost talked himself into issuing the order for the fleet to make preparations to sail south, but not to stop at the small port of Da Nang that the barbarian merchant Long had given as the best spot for fleet and army to reunite. Instead, his intention was to sail further south, around the large peninsula that had clearly swallowed up Caesar and his entire army, followed by the longer, narrower peninsula that was the last obstacle between them and the eastern coast of India. However, instead of following the coast north to remain within sight of land, retracing their path as they had done to get there, he was determined to sail due west, across the open sea directly to Taprobane and the new depot at Palaesimundum, seeing it as the first step on the long journey from these barbarian wastelands and back to civilization. Fortunately, not least for Nero, what the patrician said he would do and what he actually did were very, very rarely anywhere near to each other, because if he had gone through with his plan in trying to cross the more than one thousand miles of open water, and if the *navarchae* had obeyed, it was highly likely that neither he nor any of the men of this massive fleet would have ever been heard from again. To his credit, Lysippos, after reaching a state close to panic the first time Nero had made this dramatic declaration, had quickly learned that Nero was a dog with no teeth, and that it was actually better to pretend to go along with the nominal admiral of Caesar's fleet by assuring him that preparations to depart were underway on every single vessel, then simply wait for the moment a day, perhaps two, later, when Nero's nerve would inevitably fail him. As much as he despised the man, however, they did share one thing: the Rhodian *navarch* was every bit as concerned about Caesar and his Legions as Nero, because in its simplest terms, it was as if they had simply vanished without a trace. Despite keeping a half-dozen ships at the port of Da Nang at any given time, of which at least two vessels were always the swift Liburnians, there had been no excited shout by the man in the high tower that had been constructed next to the dock here at Ke Van, which was manned through every watch, that one of those Liburnian was returning from Da Nang with a torch burning at its prow, the signal for

Caesar Ascending – The Han

which they were all waiting.

They had learned from the people of the town that was composed of mostly Han but had a small community of Khmer and other people native to this region before it had been conquered by the Han and whose features seemed to be a mixture of Han and Khmer, that this had been the worst rainy season in memory. There had been two storms, which the people called a *tai fun*, but while they had managed to avoid any damage to the anchored ships that filled the harbor at the mouth of the river they called the Song Lam the first time, the second storm had been much worse, the fleet suffering the loss of a *quinquereme*, a *quadrireme*, two *triremes*, and a half-dozen smaller craft, none of which had been salvageable. As far as Lysippos was concerned, it was this more than anything else that had ignited in Nero the urge to essentially abandon Caesar and his men to their fate, simply because he didn't want to face the Dictator for Life to explain the loss of his precious ships, particular the two larger ones. The fact that the loss had been a direct result of Nero's refusal to follow the Rhodian *navarch's* advice about sailing them farther up the Song Lam also meant that Lysippos had slept with one eye open in the time immediately after the disaster in the event that Nero panicked to the point he wanted the Rhodian silenced. Now, however, it was October, so that when Nero summoned Lysippos to inform him that he was considering sailing south, this time, the Rhodian didn't offer his normal assurances with the intention of doing nothing. This time, he listened to Nero, who at least could be counted on always stating his reasons, but while they were always the same, there were facts that Lysippos could no longer deny. It was at the end of the rainy season and given the length of the voyage Nero was proposing back to Palaesimundum at the minimum, a departure in the near future made sense. Nevertheless, the Rhodian still resisted, and he wasn't alone in that resistance. While there weren't many Romans who had been more or less permanently assigned to the fleet, there were originally three men of Tribune rank who acted as Nero's staff. The fact that they were there at all was only because Nero had insisted that a man of Legate rank should have at least a half-dozen Tribunes, but he had only been given three by Caesar, and only two of them were Roman. One of them, Rufus, Caesar had sent on a mission while they were in Kantakosylla that, while the general refused to share with Nero the details, he did inform Nero that Rufus wouldn't be returning. What was left was the Parthian Artaxerxes, and the son of one of Caesar's former Legates named Gaius Fabius Maximus, whose father Quintus had been left behind in Rome to aid Marcus Antonius, but for reasons Lysippos never learned, young Quintus was called Africanus. While his father Gaius had distinguished himself during the civil war, particularly at Munda, of his two sons, Africanus was the youngest, and from what the Rhodian observed, had to have been the dullard of the Fabii, but Nero found him useful, if only for his sycophancy. Consequently, it hadn't surprised Lysippos that Africanus had been parroting Nero's arguments for sailing from the first moment the Legate had broached the subject, but when Artaxerxes had added his voice, it had given Lysippos pause. The Parthian wasn't a natural sailor; if anything, the Parthians hated the sea more than the Romans, which, Lysippos thought, was understandable, but that was what made the young Tribune more impressive, because from his first day attached to the fleet, Artaxerxes had been diligent in learning all that he could about what was as much art as it was science in mastering the oceans. On what would turn out to be the night before Lysippos was forced to make a decision, the Tribune had appeared at the small house commandeered by the invaders that Lysippos was sharing with three of his fellow Rhodian *navarchae*.

"May I speak with you privately, *Navarch*?"

Lysippos normally teased the Parthian for his insistence on abiding by the strictest interpretation of protocol when addressing other men who held a post of some sort in Caesar's vast army, but his normal rejoinder never passed his lips when he saw the Parthian's face.

Stepping aside, he urged Artaxerxes inside, assuring the Parthian, "The others are either aboard their ship right now, or maybe at the brothel." Gesturing to the table that occupied the center of the room, Lysippos asked, "Would you like something to drink?"

"If it is *chai*," Artaxerxes grimaced, "or rice wine, then no, thank you." This made the Rhodian laugh, because he shared the other man's disdain for the new beverages that had become more prevalent with every mile east, and he dropped into the chair across from Artaxerxes.

The Parthian wasted no time. "I suppose you know that it is about time that Legate Nero is going to announce that we are sailing?"

This actually caught Lysippos by surprise, but after a moment's thought, he realized, "Ah, you are right. The last time was two weeks ago. And," he agreed, "that seems to be the pattern." He regarded the Tribune with a thoughtful expression. "But I suspect that you did not come to visit me just to remind me of that."

"No," the Parthian agreed. "I did not. I," he hesitated for a moment, then seemed to decide something, asking, "was wondering what your thoughts are on the matter?"

"The matter?" Lysippos echoed, but he was stalling for time as he tried to think why Artaxerxes had broached the subject. Deciding to trust his instincts, he posed a question of his own. "Is it safe to assume that you have begun to consider the possibility that the Legate might actually be right at last?"

He wasn't surprised at the flicker of irritation on the Parthian's face; *if you think I'm going to say it aloud first, you're mistaken, boy,* he thought, though his expression gave none of this away.

Like Lysippos, Artaxerxes was faced with a choice, and decided to trust his instincts as well, so there was only a bare lapse of time before he replied, "Yes, *Navarch*, you are correct in your assumption." When Lysippos didn't say anything in reply, he plunged on, "We are now into the Roman month of October, and we have not heard from Caesar and the army since late April. While we know that they were going to be forced to cut a path across this peninsula, and it is at least five hundred miles, we still should have heard something at Da Nang, if only from one of his cavalry scouts operating ahead of the army."

"That is true." Lysippos nodded. "And, it is troubling. Still," the Rhodian felt that he at least needed to make a show of confidence in Caesar, "forgive me for saying this, but I have been with Caesar since we departed Brundisium six years ago.

When we sailed to..." suddenly aware to whom he was speaking, he altered his words to avoid bringing up the reason, "...the other side of Our Sea, Caesar ordered me to navigate the shortest route possible, which meant sailing into the middle of Our Sea. Every one of his officers thought he was mad." Lysippos chuckled. "*I* thought he was mad, but we lost a total of ten ships, not the hundred that he expected and planned for." Taking a sip from his own cup, which he had filled with rice wine, despite sharing Artaxerxes' feelings for the beverage, he continued, "You *have* been with Caesar long enough to know that this is not the first time where Caesar has seemingly been defeated somehow. Whether it is by those Khmer savages we learned about earlier this year, or whether there was some illness that wiped them out, or," he shrugged, "the gods finally turning their face away from him this time, Caesar has always found a way before."

Knowing he couldn't argue this, Artaxerxes didn't try, instead using this statement of fact to his advantage.

"Which is all the more reason to believe that, finally, Caesar's Luck has run its course," he said quietly. "As extraordinary a man as he is, *Navarch*, he is a mortal man, and I am afraid that it is not only a possibility, but a likelihood that Caesar and the men with him have come to a bad end. After all," he reminded Lysippos with a smile, only because he wasn't speaking to a Roman, "this all began when Caesar decided to avenge the loss of Marcus Crassus and his Legions. If he had not been successful, the people in Rome would always wonder what happened to the *Crassoi*. As far as they were concerned, and would believe into the future, the truth would be that Parthia swallowed them all up. Is this any different, really?"

"No," Lysippos sighed, "it is not. And," he felt a twinge of guilt for admitting as much, "to be honest, I have been expecting some sort of catastrophe to befall Caesar and his army for some time. Although," he added with a laugh, "I gave offerings that that catastrophe happened on land and not when we were at sea, for obvious reasons."

The normally sober Parthian did give a soft laugh, though it was possible he was just being polite, and he returned to his purpose.

"I do not have to tell you that, in the past, we have ignored the Legate when he issues his orders," he said carefully. Knowing he had no choice, he told the Rhodian, "Tomorrow, if he behaves as expected and gives us the order, I intend to carry out my duties and put the things for which I am responsible into motion. I just wanted to warn you of that, *Navarch*."

No, you want me to tell you that I agree, and I'll give my *navarchae* the order to prepare to sail, Lysippos thought, though without any rancor. During their short conversation, Lysippos had come to realize that, finally, he actually agreed that it was time to leave.

"If Nero issues the order like he has before, then I will do the same," he assured Artaxerxes. "It is time for us to go home, with or without Caesar."

A very relieved Tribune departed shortly afterward, leaving Lysippos to stare moodily into his cup, wondering what it said about him that he was actually praying to Zeus and Poseidon that Nero wouldn't prove to be so predictable, thereby enabling him to postpone his own decision; it was to be a forlorn hope.

R.W. Peake

Chapter Three

    His name was Zhang Meng. He was the grandson of one of the Han's most famous explorers, Zhang Qian, and it had been his grandfather's influence and the example that he set that made Zhang the perfect emissary for this attempt to make contact with the Roman Caesar on behalf of his Emperor Yuan. Grandfather Qian was the first of their people to make the long, treacherous journey that comprised the overland route of the Silk Road, and in the process, gathered more information about the kingdoms that the Romans called the Indo-Greeks that had been founded two centuries earlier by the generals of the Macedonian king Alexander than the Han had ever known before. Grandfather Qian had died when Zhang was very young, but Zhang's father had carried on the family tradition, both of serving the Emperor, albeit in a post that was solidly in the ranks of middle management of Imperial affairs, and in learning more about the vast territory to the West; that they were also wealthy in their own right was what enabled Zhang's father to hire special tutors, men who had come from the land the Romans called India, to teach him the tongues spoken by the people who inhabited the kingdoms of the southern part of India. His father also was assiduous in gathering every scrap of information about the West, all of which he required his son to learn, but the one thing that Zhang's father lacked was the willingness to leave the comforts of home to actually view the sights Grandfather Qian had seen with his own eyes. More crucially for Zhang himself, his father had prevailed upon him to do the same and remain at home with his father by using his supposed health problems that, he would earnestly assure his son, his physicians said were extremely serious, and that he could perish at any moment. Unfortunately for Zhang, he was not only the oldest son, he was the only one who had survived to adulthood, and while he was currently unaware of the parallels, the oldest male of a family was the Han equivalent of the Roman *paterfamilias*, so Zhang had been forced to settle for what was certainly a less exciting and adventurous life, but one that had its own advantages. Because of his talent for languages, and an intellect that was far above even the high standards of his class, Zhang had been sent to study with Zhou, one of the two most eminent scholars and proponents of the Confucian philosophy. And, for a period of a few years, it had appeared as if Zhang's future was assured; it would be a period of time that Zhang would reflect on with bitter amusement at his own naivety about the reality of Imperial politics as practiced by the men who were part of the innermost circle of councilors, secretaries, and eunuchs who surrounded the Emperor. Zhang never learned exactly what had transpired, but that was only because Master Zhou, who had been the target of a concerted effort to remove him from a position of influence, refused to divulge a word about it.

"It is the way of this life, young Zhang," was all Zhou would say with a sigh.

Only later did Zhang learn how incredibly fortunate not only his Master had been, but he himself was, because the faction led by the Emperor's second cousin Shi had done their best to have Zhou executed, and over time, he learned that this punishment was usually extended to the condemned man's closest family, friends...and students. Fortunately, the Emperor Yuan had refused to sanction execution, choosing to exile Zhou instead, and Zhang seriously considered severing his ties with his teacher, thinking that it meant the end of any career he might have in Imperial service if he didn't. It had been the one piece of sage advice his father had given him, when to Zhang's utter shock, the elder Zhang had ordered him to remain with Master Zhou and follow him into exile, advice that now put him in the position he found himself in, summoned to meet the Emperor.

"Imperial court politics," he had counseled his son, "is like the ocean, my son. The tides come in, and they go out, in an endless cycle, and I tell you that this will pass."

"How can you say that?" Zhang had cried out, shocked

and, frankly, a bit scornful of his father. "The Emperor had him exiled, Father! His time at court is done, and he's in disfavor!"

Normally, his father didn't tolerate outbursts such as this, but this time, he remained calm and didn't even comment on his son's lack of discipline, saying instead, "That's exactly why you should stay with Master Zhou." Seeing that his son still didn't understand, the elder Zhang explained, "The fact that Yuan didn't have Zhou's head removed from his shoulders is a message to Shi and his faction, and it's one I'm certain they won't misinterpret." While he was unconvinced, Zhang was more amenable to listen, and he indicated for his father to continue. "When you remove a man's head, you remove the chance that he will ever offer counsel again. But," he had wagged a finger at his son, "a man who only has his presence removed and not his head, can be recalled. Trust me," he had finished placidly, "you will be better served to remain with Master Zhou."

It had been hard, certainly, being sent off to Hanzhong, mainly because of the lack of anything or anyone familiar, and being surrounded by rustic provincials had been a trial in itself. However, his father had been proven correct, and now here he was, at this moment being ushered into the presence of the Emperor himself! Master Zhou had been extremely cryptic in the purpose of the summons, only saying that he wouldn't be there, and Zhang was quite nervous, especially when the eunuch who introduced himself as Shi Xian had come to the entry hallway to escort him into the Emperor's presence because, in something of a rarity, the eunuch that Zhang knew was part of the faction that had been behind his Master's exile let his normally blank mask slip, perhaps intentionally, the cold hostility radiating from him as he went through the formalities impossible for Zhang to miss.

As Zhang followed, Shi Xian rattled off instructions in a manner that told Zhang he did this often. "When you enter the room, you will avert your eyes. When you are exactly four paces away, you will drop to your knees and abase yourself to the Bìxià. Which," he warned, "is a term that only a select few may use. And," for the first time, Zhang heard an emotion in the eunuch's voice that indicated this wasn't part of the normal instructions, because there was a note of satisfaction that was impossible to mistake, "you are *not* one of the select few." Since he didn't know if a response was required, Zhang said nothing, then before he could prepare himself, the large door was opened, but when he made to step through it, he was stopped by the eunuch, who hissed, "Wait here!"

The door was peremptorily shut in his face, though he didn't have to wait long before it was reopened, and Zhang stepped into the throne room and main council chamber of the Emperor of the Han. Somewhat to his chagrin, later, when he tried to explain to his father what had taken place, he could never recall anything of his entry, nor dropping to his knees.

His first memory came when a surprisingly deep and youthful voice said, "Rise, Zhang Meng." He did so, keeping his eyes averted, and he was certain he heard a sigh, then the voice said, "You may lift your eyes."

When he did so, he felt a little foolish as he realized that, while he hadn't known what to expect, the sight before him of what in every other way was an ordinary man, with a slight pot belly that the voluminous silken robes only partially hid, with a thin mustache and chin beard that only had a few strands of silver in it, hadn't been his mental image of what the supreme ruler of his people looked like. This was all he would allow himself, still terrified to look the Emperor in the eyes, which meant that he did an unconscious imitation of a Roman ranker when standing in front of an officer by staring at a point above Yuan's head, but the Emperor was accustomed to this.

"I have heard good things about you, Zhang Meng," Yuan said. "Like you, I was a student of Master Zhou. He is," for the first time, there was a note in the Emperor's voice that made him sound like a mortal man, of the kind of affection one had for a mentor, "a stern taskmaster, isn't he?"

What do I say? Zhang felt his first stab of panic, but he managed, "Yes, my Emperor." Then, horrified he had unintentionally insulted his teacher, he blurted out, "But it has been worth it, Emperor."

Now, Yuan made no attempt to hide his amusement.

"I see that Shi Xian has instructed you in not calling me Bìxià, eh?"

"Y-yes, Emperor."

"You may address me in that manner," Yuan said offhandedly.

Zhang felt the sudden surge of pride that he was now allowed to use this term, vowing to himself that he would serve Yuan faithfully, something that the Emperor knew quite well, and in fact, it was by his instruction to Shi Xian that he did so, having learned of this effect at seeming to bring a subject into the inner circle of his confidence.

"Thank you... Bìxià," Zhang tried to keep the emotion from his voice, but he could hear the throb of pride that he was experiencing.

"Master Zhou says that you excel in many barbarian tongues," Yuan said. "I met your grandfather once, did you know that? It was when I was crown prince."

"Yes, Bìxià, my father tells the story quite often," Zhang replied truthfully. With a bit less honesty, he said, "My father said that my grandfather spoke of the moment often and that he saw your greatness even then."

Again, this was nothing new to Yuan; almost from birth, he had been flattered, his supposed talents praised as being of a kind never seen before, his intelligence and learning being on a level with the great Confucius himself. And, he would remind himself with a combination of ruefulness and embarrassment, there was a time that he actually believed them.

More to forestall Zhang offering more praise that may or may not have been true, Yuan got to the point. "I'm sure that you're aware of the presence of the Romans?"

"Yes, Bìxià." Zhang nodded. "I first heard about them when we were..." with a sinking horror, he just barely stopped himself for using the world "exiled," and while he heard how it sounded, he settled on, "...away."

Yuan ignored this, mainly because he was still embarrassed that he had been persuaded by Shi and the others to banish Master Zhou, instead asking, "And what did you hear about them?"

Understanding that this wasn't an idle question, he thought for a moment, then began, "I have heard that they are very organized, very disciplined, and are formidable warriors. But," he stressed, "I believe that they are made more formidable because of their general."

"What makes you say that?" Yuan asked, and he truly wanted to know, having heard at least a half-dozen other alternatives.

"Because of the kind of man it would take to conquer all of Parthia (Anxi) and most of India (Shendu) in as short a time period as he has," Zhang replied matter-of-factly. "No amount of organization and training, no amount of discipline explains this. He is obviously very intelligent, but it's not his intelligence that makes him so formidable." He shook his head, realizing that, while he hadn't given it much conscious thought, he had clearly been ruminating on this Caesar for some time, and he was confident at least with this, but he said nothing more.

It was a man Zhang hadn't noticed, sitting in the corner at a desk with a small brush in his hand that served the same purpose as a Western quill, marking him as a secretary, who gave a quiet but unmistakable snort, but when Zhang waited for the Emperor to chastise the man, he was astonished when no such thing happened.

Instead, Yuan asked mildly, "What is it, Gong?"

Hearing the name, Zhang realized that this had to be the Imperial Secretary Hong Gong, one of the few members of the opposing faction that Master Zhou had been happy to express his feelings about, which from what Zhang could tell, was a combination of hatred, loathing, and if Zhang's instinct was correct, fear.

"Nothing, Bìxià," Gong said with a lack of sincerity that was impossible to mistake. Then, after a heartbeat where Yuan just looked at him, he tried to sound reluctant as he said, "Young Zhang is telling us something that we could learn in any brothel or *chai* house. Of *course* he is intelligent, and is obviously a fierce warrior. From what we know of Rome, they're bloodthirsty savages who live to make war and have barely any culture at all. This man Caesar leads them because he is obviously their greatest warrior! *That* is what makes him formidable!"

Yuan didn't reply to Gong, choosing instead to address Zhang.

"You said that it wasn't his intelligence," Yuan said, "while Gong says that it must be because of his prowess as a warrior." Spreading his hands, he asked, "So, what is this thing that you say is what makes him formidable?"

"His will," Zhang replied, without hesitation.

"His will?" Yuan glanced over at the secretary, who looked smug, then turned back and replied, "I don't even know that that means."

"It means that if this Caesar wills something to be so," Zhang explained, "his army bends to it and does his bidding." Seeing the glimmer of understanding on the Emperor's face, Zhang pressed his case. "How else do you explain how he has managed to maintain control of his army tens of thousands of *Li* from their homeland?" He asked, using the Han measurement of distance, which approximated a third of a Roman mile. "The Greek king Alexander was unable to do so. That is why he had to turn back from his quest to reach the river called the Ganges."

This prompted a reaction, this time from the eunuch, but while it wasn't a snort, there was no mistaking it was a dismissal, and while his tone was polite, there was no way for Zhang to misinterpret this, "As Gong points out, these Romans are bloodthirsty barbarians who live for war. As long as their general gives them opportunities to slake their bloodlust, they will follow him anywhere."

"Would you?" Zhang countered quietly. "Name something that you love more than anything in your life. Would you still be willing to leave your home behind to go to the other side of the world, to lands that you have never seen before?" Suddenly inspired, Zhang challenged Shi Xian, "Would you be willing to travel to Rome without knowing if you would ever return to your home here?"

This earned him a glare from the eunuch, but more importantly, it was Yuan whose words mattered.

"I believe we have found our emissary."

For the rest of their collective lives, however long they lasted, the men who marched for Caesar during this period of time, one that would shape the world in ways not even Caesar could imagine, the one thing that those who had contact lasting longer than a short duration with those men would have to endure would be hearing tales of Caesar's Luck, and how, by extension, it favored them as well. For men like Titus Pullus, who was one of the few men who served their general the longest, they would have more examples than they could easily think of, but there was one example of how much the gods loved Gaius Julius Caesar that only a handful of men would ever know the full story about. When Nero proved that, in this one area, his behavior could be relied on, the day after Artaxerxes' visit to Lysippos, when he announced his biweekly decision to sail home, as promised, Lysippos finally agreed, prompting preparations to begin immediately. Over the course of the next week, the *navarchae* drove their crews every bit as hard as Centurions drove their Legionaries, while both Africanus and Artaxerxes, with the help of Long's oldest son, who the merchant had sent with the fleet, scoured the countryside for every grain of rice that the villagers were willing to sell. The abundant rain had also made for a bountiful October harvest, and while they adhered to Caesar's orders to pay for goods instead of seizing them, it was only because they didn't have enough men to seize it that they did so. Caesar was aware of but largely ignored the fact that a large portion of the men who crewed the oared vessels had been pirates at one time or another, but their expertise lay in shipboard fighting, or with lightning-quick raids ashore where their rapid escape by ship was assured in order to avoid a prolonged fight. This adherence to Caesar's orders, however unwilling they may have been, proved to be particularly galling to Nero, who had spent his idle months trying to think of ways whereby he could use the manpower available to him to take what the fleet needed, while telling Caesar that he had paid for everything. Despite the significant amount of time he spent on the prospect, he never could come up with anything that wouldn't risk his execution, which meant that he was in a surly state of mind. While the Tribunes were busy, the crews were similarly occupied, although the one thing Lysippos had insisted on was maintaining the fleet to a point where, when the message from Da Nang arrived, the delay in sailing would be minimal, thereby speeding up the preparations.

At the end of a week, at Nero's insistence, a ritual was performed, where one of the native bulls was sacrificed, which Lysippos privately thought was a terrible idea for the simple reason that every one of the beasts in this part of the world was black, or at best a dark gray, and white bulls were considered most propitious by the Romans, and while they were plentiful in India they were almost unknown here. The lone augur with the fleet who, frankly, lived a miserable existence that made him think of committing suicide on a daily basis, also botched the job because, at least according to him, the various herbs that were needed to drug the animal into a docile state were unknown in this strange land. What that meant in a practical sense was that the portion of the crews who worshipped the gods shared between Roman and Greek watched in horror as the bull, spraying blood everywhere, went on a rampage, sending Nero, Africanus, and the other Romans with the fleet attending the sacrifice scattering like chickens. If there was a bright spot, it was that Aulus Varus Crispus, the augur, finally achieved the release of death that he had been too afraid to administer himself, even if it was an undignified end as, transfixed by one of the large horns, he spent his last moments attached to another being in its last moments as it tried to outrun its own mortality. It had been enough of a disaster that there was a sentiment on the part of the men that an omen such as this meant that the gods disapproved of their decision to essentially abandon Caesar and his army.

Nevertheless, on the early morning tide, the fleet, minus those ships that had sunk in the storm and those already in Da Nang, left the protected harbor of the river's mouth to begin sailing south. Aided by a northeasterly wind, the *chuan* had no problem keeping up so they made good progress the first day, but across the fleet, if the *navarchae* had been asked, they would have agreed that the mood was somber. Even the crewmen who held no love for Rome were aware that they were consigning men who had been passengers on their vessels to their deaths, it being inevitable that, given the amount of time at sea and the fact that Caesar ensured that the men were transported on the same ship, the men of the Legions had interacted with the crews of the ship transporting them, creating something of a bond between Legionary and crewman. There was also a feeling of shame, and regret, on the part of men like Lysippos; even Nero had qualms about what was being done at his order that weren't strictly aligned with his self-interest. Aside from the prospect of returning to Rome at some point in an undefined future to report that he had essentially abandoned the Dictator for Life, and the more than thirty thousand Roman citizens who still comprised the Legions under Caesar's command, it was the sense of bitter disappointment that surprised the Legate. He was aware of Caesar's opinion of him, just as he was that it was shared by his fellow patricians of Legate rank, but in a relatively recent development for him, he had come to realize that he was proud of being part of something that he was certain would go down in history, where Caesar, in the name of Rome, eclipsed the most famous man in history. Where Alexander had failed, Caesar had succeeded, and while he had been one of the most vocal among the Legates in arguing against going beyond the Ganges, now he felt a deep and abiding pride. Regardless of this feeling, the regret that he had initially felt quickly turned into something else, so that by the end of their second day at sea, he was already envisioning what was waiting for him in Rome; Tiberius Claudius Nero, the only Roman patrician to return from beyond the edge of the world. It didn't take more than a few watches, locked in what had been Caesar's cabin, to convince himself that he would be lauded as the Roman who had succeeded where Caesar had failed by returning. It was also true that every bit of cargo space would be crammed full of all manner of exotic and priceless goods from the lands that Rome had explored, so who would argue that, given his status as the Roman responsible for retrieving it, a portion of this massive wealth shouldn't be his? After all, it was the Roman way. Who knows? he thought as he lay in the hammock in what he now thought of as his cabin. Why can't *I* be First Man in Rome? So deep into this fantasy was he that it wasn't until the fourth blast of the horn that hung from a strap on the rear deck, blown by the man who had the tiller that he realized something was amiss.

"We're still fifty miles away from Da Nang," he grumbled

to his slave as he dropped out of the hammock, "so it's probably nothing. No pirate would be foolish enough to try us."

That was true, but as Nero quickly learned, there was a very good reason for the summons, which he learned from Lysippos, who had rushed up from the small cabin under the upper deck at the bow that he occupied when it wasn't used as the army office, reaching the rear deck before Nero. Since his back was turned from the bow as he scrambled up the ladder, Nero's eyes were on the Rhodian, who was pointing straight ahead, but it was what the *navarch* said that cut through his bowels like a cold knife.

"It's a Liburnian, dead ahead. And the torch is lit!"

The rush of emotions that flooded through Nero as he turned about and confirmed that what Lysippos was reporting was true would have been impossible for him to identify under the best of circumstances, but he did understand the most important thing; Caesar's Luck had held once again.

Caesar hadn't been fooled by Nero's explanation that he had made the decision to transfer the fleet to Da Nang to wait, but he chose not to press the matter because, in all truthfulness, he didn't blame the Legate for giving up hope. It had been the most trying period of this entire campaign, or series of campaigns, to that point, and another secret that he would never share was that he had been as demoralized, and as desperate, as the men he led, even more so than at Munda, when for a brief span of time he had been certain that that day would be his last on this side of the River Styx. The only thing that had saved not only him, but his entire army from falling apart and turning on each other to a greater degree than they already had was his certainty that any admission on his part of the depth of his discouragement would have triggered the very crisis he was trying to avert. Consequently, when Hirtius himself came galloping back to report that, at last, they could see the sea from the last of the series of hills that had been their final obstacle, he had almost shamed himself with a show of emotion so overwhelming that he was thankful that he was astride Toes to receive the news, or he would have collapsed on the spot. They were still a day away from actually reaching the small port of

Da Nang, but when he had followed Hirtius to the top of the hill, he saw what was nothing more than a small walled town whose buildings lined the curvature of the natural bay, with a scattering of small fishing vessels and a few *chuan* moored to the handful of docks. Then, almost literally overnight, by the time the cavalry was just a matter of a couple miles from the gate of the western wall, the bay had been transformed into a forest of seemingly limbless trees that they knew were masts, the tops just barely visible above the walls.

When the vanguard Legion, which, to the lack of surprise by the other Primi Pili was the 10th, drew closely enough for the men in the ranks to not only see but to understand what it meant, the uproar was such that it led Caesar to offer a wry comment to his Legates, "If there's never been a riot because men are so happy, then today might be the day."

It was said in jest, but he wasn't far from the truth; the Centurions, of every Legion including Pullus' Equestrians, had their hands full trying to keep the men in their marching formation and not breaking ranks to go rushing towards the gates, which were now open thanks to Long and his small band having been sent ahead to warn the townspeople of the approach of what the Han merchant was certain would be the strangest and most terrifying sight that these people ever witnessed. He had become somewhat accustomed to being in the company of these pale creatures who, even now, he still had trouble thinking of as men just like himself, but Long had the advantage over his fellow Han in that he had traveled to India, visiting the kingdoms of the eastern coast, and had even been to the island trading post run by the colony of Greeks. However, while these Romans did resemble Greeks, there were some startling differences; it hadn't been until he came into contact with Caesar, for example, that he realized there were men with blue eyes, which he always found unsettling when the Roman's gaze was fixed on him. He had learned from Achaemenes, the Parthian barbarian who was one of the only two through whom he could communicate with the Romans, that this feeling wasn't unique to him.

"I felt the same way," Achaemenes assured him, who Long thought wasn't a bad sort for a savage, but the Parthian went on to say, "and I have heard his own officers who are Roman like him talk about it. They say that it is as if Caesar can see into their soul, and he knows what they are thinking at any given moment."

This had unsettled Long, but he was cautiously optimistic that this wasn't the case, at least with him, because he had no doubt that, if Caesar had truly known what he was thinking, particularly in the beginning of their relationship, he would have been with his ancestors long before this. Now, he found himself astride one of the horses used by this foreign army that were much larger than the ponies of the Han, or any of the people in this part of the world, riding down the main street that led directly to the wharf, calling to the people who had come rushing out of their businesses and homes, telling them not to panic, that they weren't under attack, and they wouldn't be harmed, although he did stress that it was a good idea for them to return to their dwellings and stay out of the streets for at least the rest of this day. It was a third of a Roman watch later when the barbarian invaders, led by what was universally agreed by the townspeople to be a giant, walked through the gates, whereupon the men who seemed to be under his command did an odd thing from their perspective. As hundreds of terrified people watched through the slats of their shuttered windows, the barbarians broke off into smaller groups, each of them heading in seemingly opposite directions. The more astute of the townspeople quickly deciphered the meaning of this behavior, recognizing that these invaders were securing Da Nang, and presumably, searching for any sign of resistance. There would be none, every citizen of the town could have assured these pale creatures, if only because every single one of them was more terrified than they had ever been in their collective lives.

For Pullus, the first thing he noticed was how neatly arranged things seemed to be, with an air of tidiness that was lacking even among his fellow Romans. As orderly and settled as Romans liked things, outside of the Legions, a visitor to a Roman village, town, or city would be assured of seeing barrels haphazardly strewn next to a building, some of them overturned, along with broken crates, scraps of various items, and shards of shattered amphorae. None of that was visible here, but the other thing Pullus noticed, and put him on his guard, was that the streets of this town were completely empty. This was what prompted him to snap the orders that sent his even numbered Centuries to the northern side of the main street, and his odd numbered Centuries the opposite direction.

"Wait here, and when Scribonius gets here, tell him I want him to do the same thing," Pullus ordered Lutatius. "I want a Century covering every block of this town, all around the walls."

"You're not expecting trouble, are you, Primus Pilus?" Lutatius asked with some surprise. "This place looks deserted."

"It's not," Pullus snapped, but his eyes were still on the buildings aligned on either side of the main street. "I can feel it, we're being watched."

While he was right, it wouldn't be until a watch later that he was satisfied that the eyes that he had felt on him hadn't belonged to enemy soldiers lying in wait, but terrified civilians, something that neither Scribonius nor Balbus intended to let him forget. Caesar only entered after the last Cohort of the 10th was inside the walls, so that now when he rode down the street, it was no longer deserted but lined with his Equestrians, all of whom were roaring their happiness, and relief that, at last, they were reunited with the fleet that ultimately represented their only way to get home. Nero, Africanus, Artaxerxes, Lysippos, and the *navarchae* of the largest vessels were standing at the end of the street that led to the small port, where behind them was Caesar's flagship, the *Polynike*, along with the other *quinqueremes*, aligned in a row with their huge prows looming over the buildings that apparently served some function in the running of this port.

Nero waited until Caesar dismounted before rendering a salute, as he lied, "The gods favored us, Caesar! We had decided to relocate to Da Nang from Ke Van so that we could minimize any delay in embarking the Legions and our baggage, and it looks like we arrived just in time!"

"The gods," Caesar was smiling as he also lied, "truly did favor us, Nero! You couldn't have timed it any better!" More for the sake of appearance than anything else, after Caesar returned the salute, he stepped forward and offered Nero his arm, and when the Legate accepted it, his relief clear to see, Caesar pulled him into an embrace of the kind that only close friends exchanged, causing the rankers close enough to see it to erupt into cheers.

"I know why you're really here," Caesar had to raise his voice above a whisper, but since his mouth was next to the Legate's ear, he was confident the others couldn't hear, "you were taking the fleet home." He felt Nero stiffen, but when he tried to pull away, his mouth opening to protest, Caesar said quickly, "I don't blame you, Nero. In your *caligae*, I would have done the same. And," he assured the Legate as he relaxed his grip of what had been more than a casual embrace, "we'll never speak of it...to anyone. Agreed?"

Only then did he release Nero, looking down at the Legate with those icy blue eyes, but when all Nero could manage was a nod, Caesar decided this would suffice.

Turning away to face his other Legates, who had dismounted themselves and were standing there, Caesar beckoned instead to Pullus, the only Primus Pilus currently inside the town, and when he got close enough so that Pullus could hear as well, Caesar ordered, "We're not staying here any longer than we need to. I want to get the men aboard and settled so that we can sail as soon as possible."

As he expected, the other men saluted as they acknowledged the orders, but as Pollio and the other officers remounted, leaving Pullus standing there among his men, the Primus Pilus called to Caesar, who had turned back to Nero to issue his orders to the fleet.

Pullus had opened his mouth, but a quick glance at his men clustered around him made him think better of it, and he strode up to Caesar so that he could ask without being overheard, "And which direction are we sailing, Caesar? What shall I tell the boys?"

Pullus wasn't certain, but he suspected that the look of surprise on Caesar's face was feigned; *if it's not*, he thought, *he should have expected one of us to ask.*

"Why, we're sailing north back to Ke Van, of course, Pullus." Caesar smiled then, and the air of an almost boyish excitement that he was suddenly showing was completely genuine, Pullus was certain. "We've just barely reached the Han, Pullus. We can't turn around now; there's too much to see!"

Because of the prevailing winds, it took twice as long for the fleet to reach Ke Van as it had taken them to sail to Da Nang, but if the more observant men in Caesar's army noticed how the people of this town that was three times as large as Da Nang seemed to be surprised at their arrival, none of them commented on it. And, as had occurred at Da Nang, the amount of time that the men spent within its walls consisted of their march through it out to the area that Volusenus' *exploratores* had staked out for their camp. Unlike Da Nang, which was essentially surrounded by hills, there was flat land immediately outside the walls; that most of it was used for grazing and growing other staple crops besides rice, which required the fields to be flooded, meant that the farmers who owned the land were forced to watch their furrowed fields transformed into a town whose population was larger than Ke Van's. More importantly, because it was well inside the southern boundary of the Han Empire, it meant that the town administrator, who had already alerted his superiors of the departure of the fleet, along with his personal assurance that the barbarians were leaving for good, was now forced to send a courier north to Chang'An to inform His Imperial Majesty that, not only had the barbarian ships returned, they were carrying barbarian soldiers in numbers beyond counting. Unlike the inhabitants of Da Nang, the townspeople were witness to what, despite the fact that the men doing it had long before stopped thinking of it as noteworthy, was the astonishing sight of a massive military camp constructed, not in days, but in a matter of *shí*. What was not uncommon to Caesar's men was how the civilians in whatever place they were in openly gawked at the sight of thousands of men digging, with at least as many men cutting down trees, or clearing away any kind of underbrush or foliage in a swath hundreds of paces away from the outer edge of the ditch, all while at least one large group of men, subdivided into smaller units, stood like statues, their shields resting on the ground.

It was the turn of the 10th to dig, universally the most hated task in constructing a Roman marching camp, and it was Pullus who was gazing at the western wall of Ke Van, which was close enough that he could see that the wooden rampart was crammed with people, causing him to remark to Balbus, "At least they're not like those Gauls; where was it? Avaricum? Where they were calling us a race of midgets?"

This caused Balbus to give his version of a laugh.

"I had forgotten about that. And yes, it was at Avaricum. But," he shrugged, "those Gauls knew Latin." Indicating the watching crowd with his *vitus*, he said, "I'd wager all of my pay that none of those slanty-eyed people know a word of Latin."

"Just like we don't know a word of their tongue," Pullus reminded his friend, but Balbus' remark made him think, "I wonder if they think our eyes are as strange-looking as we think theirs are."

This caused Balbus to stare at Pullus, and with a shake of his head, he said, only partly in jest, "Sometimes I wonder if you've taken too many blows to the head. Who cares what they think? We," Balbus touched his chest with a thumb, "are the ones who look like the gods who made us, not them."

"How," Pullus asked with amusement, "could you possibly know what the gods look like?"

"Because they look like us!" Balbus retorted, then gave what he was certain was the clinching argument. "Look at all the statues of the gods if you don't believe me! Jupiter, Mars, Bellona, Juno," he used his fingers to enumerate them, "even Magna Mater. They all look like we do."

"Has it ever occurred to you that it's actually the opposite, that we make the gods look like us, rather than the other way around?"

Both of them spun about to see that Scribonius had reached them, but Balbus wasn't willing to concede.

"You don't know that either, just like he," he pointed to Pullus, "says I can't know that we are."

"What about that god the Pandya worship? Ganesha?" Scribonius asked, winking at Pullus as he did.

"Ganesha?" Balbus frowned, trying to recall. "Wait, is that the one that's a man with an elephant trunk?"

"Yes, that's the one."

"There's no way that Jupiter Optimus Maximus has a fucking elephant trunk for a nose! Or that Juno has eight arms!" Balbus snapped. "Besides," he grumbled, "they have too many fucking gods anyway."

"So do we," Pullus pointed out, then admitted, "although not that many."

"And," Balbus' tone could only be described as triumphant, "we look exactly like ours, because they made us just like them."

"I think you should give up," Scribonius suggested to Pullus. "You're never going to convince him."

Knowing Scribonius was right, rather than admit it, Pullus turned and pointed his *vitus* at one of his men who he knew wasn't doing anything worthy of being called out.

"*Oy!* Dolabella! Quit pulling your prick and dig, or I'll let the Pilus Posterior here use your ball sac as his coin purse, and you know he's been wanting to do that!"

"I only said that one time," Balbus protested. "And I wasn't serious."

He spent the rest of the time the 10th was laboring listening to his two friends assure him that he had, in fact, mentioned this predilection more than once, while the people of Ke Van watched this new reality in their world.

Even with a road system that rivaled Rome's, it took Zhang and his escort three weeks to reach the capital of the southernmost military district of the Han Empire's Jaozhi Commandery, Long Biên, arriving late in the month of *júyuè*, roughly coinciding with the Roman month of October, finding the city in a state of near panic. Since he was carrying an Imperial decree, the *Taishou* (Governor) of Jaozhi, Chang Zhi, offered a room in the provincial palace, mentioning to Zhang several times that, although he was under no obligation to do so, he was more than willing to accommodate any emissary sent by the Emperor, until Zhang assured him that he would mention his name to the Emperor upon his return to the capital. Aside from this, Chang wasn't a particularly useful source of information about the Romans, aside from knowing that they were currently in Ke Van, that they had arrived a matter of days earlier, brought there by the fleet that had been sitting in that city for a few months before it disappeared, then returned with the Roman army.

"Did you ever travel to Ke Van to see this fleet for yourself?" Zhang asked politely, though he suspected he knew the answer.

This was confirmed when Chang's face darkened slightly, admitting, "No, Excellency Zhang, I had too many of my regular duties to attend to, and as you know," he held both hands palms up in a gesture of helplessness, "Ke Van is located just north of the border between us and those Khmer savages and is not entirely safe. But, I assure you, that I have my best men there now, even as we speak, and they have been sending regular reports back." Suddenly thinking of something, Chang turned about and withdrew a scroll from the rack that lined the wall behind his desk, "In fact, Excellency, I made sure they performed an accurate count of every single ship that the *Gwai* possess, and of what kind it is. Which," he finished as he leaned across the desk to hand the document to Zhang, "was the most difficult part, apparently."

"*Gwai*?" Zhang frowned, and Chang laughed.

"It's what the commoners call them because they're so pale."

Zhang offered a smile to show his amusement at the fact the Romans were considered ghosts, but it vanished quickly as he read the scroll, and while he heard a gasp, he didn't realize it was his own.

"Is this accurate?" he demanded. "They have almost nine hundred ships?" Hearing the number aloud prompted him to shake his head. "Your men clearly miscounted. It's impossible to have a fleet that size."

"I thought so as well, Excellency," Zhi replied. "But I can assure you that this is accurate, because I sent three different men, over a span of several days, and they all returned with the same number." He paused, then added, "Within four or five of each other."

Zhang regarded Chang for a long moment; he was portly, in his late thirties, and he had an open expression that Zhang thought might be the face he wanted to present to the world and wasn't necessarily an indication of his true character. Being appointed a *Taishou* meant that Chang wasn't without connections to the Imperial court, but the question was, to which faction? Very quickly, he dismissed the idea that Chang could be deliberately exaggerating the size of the Roman fleet, simply because there was nothing to gain by doing so. He offered Chang a nod that signaled his acceptance, returning to read the scroll, and once again, his mouth pulled down into a frown.

"What does this mean?" He indicated the characters to Chang. "That they have ships that have only five oars on each side?"

"I was puzzled by that as well," Chang admitted, then pointed, "but if you unroll the scroll, I had one of the men draw what he saw. It's not," he laughed, "a good likeness. Hong has a terrible hand, but I think it will give you the idea."

Despite himself, Zhang gasped again at the crude but understandable rendition of a ship that, he quickly counted, had far more than five oars, but they were instead arranged in five rows, staggered so that, as he counted, he felt a sinking feeling in his stomach.

"These ships have *seventy-five* oars on each side?" Glancing at Zhi, he asked, "Did your men actually count the number of oars, or is this a guess?"

"No, Excellency," Zhi replied, "it's not a guess. They counted." Thinking to be helpful, he indicated the scroll as he explained, "The ships with four banks of oars have sixty, the ships with three ranks have forty-five."

"Which means that they're roughly the same length," Zhang mused; while it was an understandable assumption based on his lack of knowledge with maritime matters, he would learn fairly quickly he was mistaken. Deciding to turn his attention from the ships, he asked, "And what about their army? Did your men send any reports back of its size? How many horses?"

"No, Excellency," Chang answered readily enough, but now he was clearly nervous. "As I said, we only received word that the fleet had returned to Ke Van yesterday, and it was by one of my rice brokers who was there to purchase the surplus as the *Taiguan* ordered," he explained, naming the Imperial official in charge of purchasing various foodstuffs in the name of the Emperor. For the first time, Zhang noticed the beads of sweat on Chang's forehead, although it was a cool day; he understood why when Chang said, "He told me that the *Gwai* general had already sent his demons out and taken all the rice they could find."

Now I know why you're nervous, Zhang thought with a grim amusement, but while he was sympathetic, this also wasn't his problem.

Deciding that he had learned everything he could, he pointed to the scroll he had brought with him, and while he spoke politely enough, he also made certain there was no mistake that this wasn't a request, or that Chang could be as leisurely as he clearly had been about the presence of a barbarian fleet.

"As you can see, I've been given authority by the Emperor to requisition anything I need." Waiting for Chang to acknowledge this, which he did with a nod, he said, "I not only require fresh mounts for the last part of my journey to meet these...*Gwai,* now that I know that there are many thousands of warriors waiting, I require my bodyguard to be expanded."

"How many men do you have?" Chang asked cautiously.

"Fifty."

"And, how many are you requesting?"

"I'm not requesting anything, Prefect Chang," Zhang made his tone cold, "I'm ordering you to give me more men as part of my bodyguard." Realizing something, he asked, "How many garrison troops do you have?"

"Five hundred altogether," Zhi replied. "But three hundred of them are *Qiangmao*, (spearmen) while one hundred are *Qiangnu* (crossbowmen), and the rest are *liren* (swordsmen)."

"What about your *jingji?*" Zhang asked in some dismay, because he had intended to appropriate only the Han version of cavalry so that they could keep up with the pace he intended to set.

"We have none." Zhi held out his hands. "They were reassigned by Imperial authority to Xuwen." He hesitated, then ventured, "I assume you understand why."

"I do," Zhang replied, which was true, but it wasn't germane to the conversation; what was germane was that the only Imperial troops here at Long Biên was a force of spearmen, crossbowmen, and swordsmen, all infantry. Deciding that it made more sense to travel more slowly with men who could be sacrificed for his own escape in the event that the Romans were hostile and attacked him without provocation, Zhang said, "I will need those men to come with me."

Not understanding, Chang asked what he thought was a sensible question.

"How many?"

"All of them," Zhang replied, and for a moment, he thought the portly *Taishou* might faint.

"But that will leave us completely unprotected!" Chang gasped. "I can't do that!"

Zhang was about to snap at the administrator, then thought better of it, choosing instead to ask, "How many men do you think the fleet that your men described to you can carry?"

"More than can easily be counted," Chang replied. Chang's jaw set in a manner that Zhang concluded meant that the *Taishou* intended to be stubborn, but before he could do so, Zhang asked quietly, "And how much protection do you think five hundred men are going to give you and the people of Long Biên from numbers that can't easily be counted?"

It was the manner in which Chang suddenly closed his eyes that told Zhang he was successful. Not, he thought glumly, that it makes me feel better, because with my fifty bodyguards, even those from the Tigers Imperial Guard, it would only add a matter of heartbeats to my life. For the first time, Zhang began to understand the enormity of what he had been tasked to do, and the low likelihood that he would survive it. Any people, "*Gwai*" or not, who could design and sail ships of a type he had never even heard existed before, which could obviously carry so many men, presented a threat to his Emperor and his people that he had never imagined possible. And, he concluded as he strode out of the Imperial palace, a man who can command that kind of power must be a singular character.

The citizens of Ke Van finally came to the conclusion that,

for the moment, they weren't in any immediate danger from the *Gwai*; the fact that they had the distinction of giving these barbarians the name by which they would forever be known within the confines of the Han Empire would be lost to history, and they slowly began to venture outside the walls of their city. From the western wall, the barbarian camp was close enough that the townspeople could see down into at least part of the camp, although it stretched off to the west so far away that the six towers that lined the camp's western wall were barely visible. What they had no way of knowing was that they were seeing a unique configuration instead of the normal square, or sometimes rectangular shape with all sides being straight and equal. This camp, they noticed, had what seemed as if it was an appendage, in the form of a smaller square that was on the right side of the camp when looking west. None of them knew this was unusual, but what they did notice was that, while there were neatly arranged tents made the same way as the smallest tents in what was a small city, the occupants were exclusively female, and that there was a regular stream of male visitors into that part of the camp. While they found this interesting, not much was made of it, if only because some of their fellow townspeople who had spent time as men of the militia assured them that "comfort girls" were a common feature with the Han, so it made sense even for these *Gwai*. Until, that is, quite by accident, a farmer from out in the province, unaware of the titanic change in his world, came to Ke Van to sell some pigs. Giving the camp a wide berth, he entered the town, where he learned about the *Gwai,* that they had been there only a matter of several days by this point, and that, while terrifying to behold, they hadn't done anything provocative or aggressive to the town or its inhabitants.

"Is Long here, or is he still away doing his trading?" the farmer asked the woman he knew through her husband, the butcher with whom he did business.

Her initial response was to turn and spit on the ground, then she answered with obvious disgust, "Yes, he's here. And he came with the *Gwai*! He brought them here!"

Her husband, who had just finished inspecting the pigs, arrived in time to hear her, and he snapped, "No, he didn't, you silly woman! They were already making their way here, and when Long learned of it, since he speaks that dog language the brown people with the big noses speaks that he told us about, he offered his services so that he could spy on them!"

"So he says," his wife retorted, completely unmoved, but since this wasn't the first time they had this argument, she pointedly turned back to the farmer to ask, "Why did you want to know?"

"Oh, no reason," the farmer said vaguely, which was a lie, then excused himself and took a direct path to where Long's house and business were located.

The only reason he was going was because his shrew of a wife wouldn't let him forget what he had done by selling their second daughter to Long, but the farmer had refused to apologize, pointing out that it was a matter of simple economics; they couldn't feed an extra mouth, not with four sons and one daughter already. That hadn't made any difference to his wife, but the most he would agree to do was to speak to Long and try to determine whether the girl, Mèi, which simply meant second daughter, hadn't been sold into a worse situation than what she would have endured if he hadn't sold her, and this was his secondary purpose on this day. He didn't stay long, the merchant informing him that, not only had she been sold as intended, she was in fact not far away, and when the farmer asked the natural question why, Long told him that she was a member of Caesar's Centuries, although the merchant didn't use that common name, knowing that it would be meaningless. The farmer walked the streets of Ke Van for some time in a daze as he tried to decide what he would tell his wife, and the butcher's wife, seeing him pass by, called out to him.

"What troubles you? Did you see your first *Gwai*?" She laughingly said, "I don't blame you! I had much the same reaction the first time I laid eyes on them."

It was the manner in which the farmer stopped to turn very slowly to look at her that wiped the smile from her lips, but by the time the farmer was finished explaining why he was so distracted, he had unwittingly launched the first crisis between the Han of Ke Van and the *Gwai*.

"That Han merchant Long is at the gate, Caesar. He's requesting entry into the camp."

Caesar looked up from the tablet Apollodorus was holding open for him to read as he sat at his desk, simultaneously inscribing something in another tablet, responding to Tribune Bodroges irritably, "You know that the standing order is that he's allowed into the camp, Bodroges."

It was the manner in which the Parthian Tribune stood there, not moving, that hinted that something unusual was happening, and when Caesar returned his attention to the Tribune, Bodroges explained by saying hesitantly, "It is not just Long, sir. He has other people with him."

"Other people?" Caesar had been returning back to his reading, but now his attention was fully on the Tribune as he demanded, "What does that mean? What other people?"

"I am not sure," Bodroges admitted, "but I believe that it is Long's family."

This was enough to get Caesar to stand up and move out from behind the desk, striding out of his office saying only, "Come with me."

Because of the size of the camp, there were always horses available outside the *praetorium*, and Caesar leapt into the saddle of one of them, while the Tribune, who was the nominal commander of the guard Legion at that moment, did the same on his own mount, forced to kick his animal to catch up with Caesar, who was already moving at the canter towards the *Porta Praetoria*. When they arrived, rather than dismount to ascend the ramp, Caesar signaled to the rankers at the gate to swing them open. Standing there was, in fact, Long, a woman who, given her age, Caesar assumed was Long's wife, and what Caesar quickly counted were seven children ranging in age from a teenage girl, a slightly younger boy, and a baby that Long's wife had on her hip. What Caesar understood was potentially more important was the fact that behind the merchant's family, two men in rags were standing in front of a large and heavily laden two-wheeled cart pulled by one of the black horned creatures that resembled oxen. Suddenly realizing that in his haste he had forgotten to summon Achaemenes, Caesar sent Bodroges galloping back to the *praetorium* to fetch him, then beckoned to Long, indicating that they were all welcome to come into the camp. It was as the small procession entered the camp that, since he was still mounted, Caesar could look beyond them down what was now a crude road that led directly from the *Porta Praetoria* to the gate in the western wall of the town, and saw a large crowd hurrying out of the town through the open gate coming in their direction. While they were too far away to make out any details, he could see that they weren't soldiers, all of whom had fled long before when the fleet first arrived and who hadn't returned, but there was an energy in the manner in which they seemed to be hurrying this direction that deepened the mystery while also giving Caesar the first hint about why Long and his family were there.

"Optio, have your men close the gates," Caesar ordered. "And get your men off their walking posts to stand on the rampart with the gate section. I don't think we're going to have any trouble, but I'd rather be safe."

Once he saw his order was being obeyed, Caesar looked down, surprised to see that Long had dropped to his knees and was abasing himself, something that Caesar thought he had broken the merchant's habit of doing, but what was even more unusual was that every member of his family had followed suit, even Long's wife, who was clutching the baby, who was, Caesar was amused to see, the only member who didn't seem interested in behaving like the rest of his family, wriggling furiously in an attempt to get free of his mother's clutches, his face turning red as he began howling in protest.

Knowing it wouldn't do much good, Caesar still asked in Latin, "Long, what is it? Why are you here?"

The merchant straightened up, though he stayed on his knees, but he began babbling incoherently in a manner that Caesar was certain meant that even if he understood the Han tongue, Long would be talking much too quickly to be understood. Holding up his hand didn't stem the flow of nonsense, but now Long was at least pointing back in the direction of the town, giving Caesar his first hint that the merchant's appearance and the crowd that was coming this way were connected.

Finally, in frustration, Caesar snapped, "*Tacete*, Long!";

only when he put a finger to his lips did the merchant subside.

Thankfully, they didn't have to wait long, Caesar turning at the sound of the hoofbeats of the pair of Parthians cantering up.

After returning Achaemenes' salute, Caesar pointed down to the merchant. "It appears that we have some sort of emergency, Achaemenes, but I can't understand what he's saying because he's not even speaking in Tamil, but in his own tongue." Realizing that with the gates closed, his interpreter was ignorant of it, he added, "And there appears to be a mob of townspeople heading this way." Thinking of this, he called up to the Optio, "Is that crowd still coming this way, Optio?"

"Yes, sir." The Optio kept his eyes turned towards the town. "But now that they're getting closer, they're slowing down." After a few heartbeats of observation, he added, "It looks like they're having some sort of argument."

"Keep an eye on them, but unless they're armed and use them against us, you're not to do anything but watch, understood?" Not waiting for the Optio to acknowledge the order, he returned his attention to Achaemenes. "See if you can make any sense of this mess, Achaemenes." The interpreter did so, which actually took a fair amount of time, but finally, Caesar understood the situation, and before he could stop himself, he groaned aloud. "By the Furies, this is the last thing we need. But," he gave Long a cold stare, "ask Long why he assured me that the women he sold me weren't wanted? Because," he pointed in the direction of the gate, "we have a crowd of angry townspeople heading towards this camp!"

Achaemenes translated into Tamil, while Caesar divided his attention on the Han merchant and his interpreter in an attempt to get an idea of what to expect, but the Parthian's reaction once Long finished was to look puzzled.

"What is it?"

"I am not sure, Caesar," Achaemenes admitted, "because it does not make sense to me."

"Tell me what he said and let me decide."

"He used a word in Tamil that I am not familiar with," Achaemenes explained. "I have never heard it before. I only know that it seems to involve your Cent...I mean, the women."

114

Caesar Ascending – The Han

Hissing in frustration and ignoring the appellation, Caesar decided, "We can't turn them out of the camp, not without knowing why the Han out there are angry. If I abandon Long and his family now, we'll never be able to get any other Han to cooperate." He turned to Bodroges, "Tribune, I'm putting Long's family in your charge. Escort them to the forum and get the provosts to keep an eye on them, then go to Legate Volusenus to arrange for a tent for them to stay in. Put them on the Tribunes' street." Returning his attention to the merchant, he said, "Achaemenes, tell him that he's coming with us."

Waiting only long enough for the exchange, Caesar turned his horse, fighting the urge to go to the trot, but instead of heading to the *praetorium*, he led the other two men directly to the tent of the Primus Pilus of the 10th Legion.

"Tell Diocles that I need young Gotra," he instructed Achaemenes, who had deduced this would be the instructions and had already dismounted.

Knocking on the wood, the Parthian then thrust his head through the flap, and Caesar could hear the mumbled exchange before Achaemenes stepped aside as, blinking at the glare from the sun, Barhinder appeared, with Diocles behind him, who was quickly joined by Pullus, wearing only his tunic.

"Caesar!" Pullus exclaimed, actually forgetting to salute, his eyes going from his general to Long, causing him to frown and ask, "What's wrong?"

"That's what I'm hoping to determine," Caesar replied, but his attention was on Barhinder. "Gotra, we have a situation that I still don't understand. Long here has used a word in Tamil that Achaemenes is unfamiliar with, and it might be important."

"What is the word?" Barhinder asked his fellow interpreter and friend.

"Pēy," Achaemenes answered, then explained the circumstances, but Caesar's hope that Barhinder would immediately understand seemed dashed, because the Bharuch youth assumed an expression of confusion that had been identical to Achaemenes.

"I am sorry, sir. I do not have any idea why Long would use this word, because it does not make sense."

"What does the word mean?" Caesar asked impatiently.

115

"It means..." Barhinder thought for a moment, trying to remember the appropriate Latin word, but when he couldn't think of it, he switched to Greek, "...a spirit of some sort."

"Spirit?" Caesar frowned, then more to himself, he mused, "Is he thinking of a *numen*? A *pneumos*? Could that be it? That the Han thinks we're nothing but *numeni*?"

Suddenly, someone laughed, an incongruous reaction given the circumstances, and Caesar stared at Pullus, who had been the one who laughed.

"You find this funny, Pullus?" he snapped.

"Yes, sir," Pullus replied, then amended quickly, "but not in a humorous way. It's just that I think I know what he means." The Centurion walked over to stand in front of Long, but rather than address him, he simply pointed to his skin while raising an eyebrow in another of the facial expressions that seemed to be universal, prompting Long to nod emphatically. Turning to look up at Caesar, he explained, "It's our color, Caesar. They're using a word in their tongue that describes what they think we look like compared to them. And," he shrugged, "we're pale, like some people say that you can see a *numen* as an outline or...."

"Or almost white," Caesar finished, finally understanding. "The reason those Han outside the camp are after Long is because of the women he sold us. Apparently," he gave a sour smile, "the idea that he sold their unwanted daughters to us is a mortal insult, given they seem to believe we're otherworldly, and they drove Long from his business."

This was, in essence, the source of the rage by the Han of Ke Van aimed at Long, not that he had sold their children into slavery, but that he had sold them to the fiendish *Gwai*. So great was their anger that they actually came within fifty paces of the *Porta Praetoria*, but aside from the fear at seeing a solid line of *Gwai* warriors, all of them resting some sort of spear on their shoulders in an attitude they at least knew meant that the spears were to be thrown, they also realized in that moment that there was none among them who had any way of communicating with the *Gwai*. Nevertheless, they still remained there for a full Roman watch, staring up at the barbarians who were staring down at them before, finally, some of them turned away and walked back to the town. That night, Long's building was set on fire, and the merchant, who had been allowed the freedom of the camp for the previous months, stood on the rampart, tears streaming down his face. Yes, he had salvaged most of their valuables, most importantly the silver, gold, and jewels that he had hoarded away under a floorboard in his house, but as he watched the lurid, smoky light of the flames peeking above the town wall, he understood that he had now tied himself inextricably to these *Gwai*. There would be no returning to Ke Van in this lifetime.

The town was still in an uproar about this matter two days later when Zhang arrived with his mounted escort, having left the men on foot several miles behind once he determined that he wouldn't be intercepted by the barbarians. Once more, the Imperial decree gained him entry, and was met by the obsequiousness of the town administrator which, if anything, was even more pronounced than Chang's. Less than a *shi* after his arrival, he was escorted by the administrator to the western wall, but as much as he thought he had prepared himself, having had the time to take in the scale of the camp on his approach from the north, it took a massive effort of will not to show the dismay he felt when he looked down into the Roman camp. His first, visceral reaction was to think; how is it possible for mortal men to achieve this? While not specifically tutored in the art of warfare, Zhang was certainly familiar with the basic precepts, and like any man of his class and education, had been required to read and memorize the works of the masters like Sun Tzu, but what he was looking at went beyond tactics, and even beyond strategy. Without any experience, Zhang Meng instantly understood that these Romans possessed a level of organization and logistical capabilities that were, at the very least, equal to those of his own people, something that he had never thought possible. It was an article of faith among the Han, particularly of the upper classes, that one reason for their primacy was in their ability to organize and administer complex functions, whether it be in civil matters or in war. And, while he would never utter it aloud, he did wonder if the Han had within them whatever it took to travel to what was in effect the other side of their world, to the farthermost western edge of that world as these Romans had done in the opposite direction; it would be a question that he would answer, again only to himself, in the future. He also felt a certain satisfaction at what he viewed as the vindication of his characterization of the Roman leader that the eunuch had sneered at, and he had the thought, perhaps when I return to Chang'An, I can convince the Emperor to allow Shi Xian to come see for himself what I meant by talking about Caesar's will.

Since he had arrived early in the day, he remained on the rampart for the rest of it, although the administrator hurried off to find a chair that allowed Zhang to sit as he made notes, along with bringing *chai* and an umbrella to provide shade. Zhang watched what, to a Roman, would have been a dreadfully boring scene of a Legion camp where there were no duties being performed, but much later, even after he had been exposed to these barbarian invaders to a much greater degree, he would look back on this day as his most instructive, the day that opened his eyes to a reality that, just perhaps the Han had met their match. And, when he finally descended the stairs and was escorted to his rooms, he was not only exhausted, he was grimly determined not to fail his Emperor. Somehow, he didn't know how, these Romans had to be convinced not to wage war on the Han, because Zhang was acutely aware of just how perilous the situation was for Emperor Yuan; the Han simply couldn't afford another enemy right now, especially this one. He got little sleep that night, waking before dawn to a breakfast of cold rice and a few pieces of pork that he only picked at, then using one of the slaves belonging to the town administrator, he dressed carefully, wanting to ensure that he gave the *Gwai* general Caesar a proper impression of the Han. Waiting outside was the commander of the Tigers Imperial Guard detachment, Zhao Chongguo, who would accompany him on horseback to the gates of the *Gwai* camp, and he was dressed in his armor and wearing his helmet. Only a pair of men would accompany them, also members of the Tigers, and one of them carried a spear, not as a weapon but upon which was affixed a large square of white cloth.

As he was mounting, Zhao, who had made no attempt to

hide his contempt for Zhang, although Zhang had come to the conclusion that it wasn't personal and was simply how he viewed all men who weren't warriors, said, "You know, Excellency, there's not much chance that these barbarians are going to recognize that." He pointed to the cloth. "They're savages, and they clearly don't have any culture or honor. At least I have armor to protect me."

The smile he offered Zhang was a mocking one, but Zhang made no reply, climbing the set of portable steps that enabled a man to mount his horse in a dignified fashion, and he took care not to rumple the silk of his outer robes, which were floor length, black, and embroidered with the sign that every Han would recognize meant he was in the service of the Emperor. Only then did he speak, and it was just a curt command to begin moving, the four riders riding away from the Imperial palace, heading to the western gate. The townspeople who were out on the streets clearly knew what was happening because they dropped to their knees as Zhang and the others passed, and once they passed, some of them called out blessings and hope for their success in forcing the *Gwai* demons to leave their town, and their world. Zhang's mouth was incredibly dry, and despite the cool late October air, he could feel the sweat soiling his undergarments, which made him thankful for the black outer robes because the sweat wouldn't show. A pair of guards pulled the gate open, and there before him, about half of a Roman mile away, rose the dirt wall of the camp that, in its width, actually extended well beyond the walls of Ke Van in both directions. At first, he could only make out that there were men standing atop the wall, partially protected by a palisade made of what he recognized was bamboo logs, while the gates were made of bamboo as well; it wouldn't be until he actually entered the camp that he learned that they were split in half, but in the moment, he wondered if the *Gwai* had filled the hollow cores with dirt in order to offer more protection, which he knew his own military did sometimes. Once they were within a Roman furlong, he could make out more details, and as he surveyed the faces of the helmeted men lining the rampart, he understood the epithet they had been given, because they were indeed paler than any people he had ever seen.

"Those spears they're holding look odd," Zhao muttered. "I've never seen anything like them before."

"I suspect, *Sima* Zhao," Zhang was surprised how calm he sounded, "that we're going to be seeing many such sights with these barbarians."

To that point, the Romans standing there seemed to be content to just watch them approaching, then he saw one of them turn away to face inward, but very quickly, Zhang understood why when another *Gwai* appeared, and while he was wearing a helmet like the other men, all of them with what Zhang surmised were horsetail plumes, this man had what Zhang thought was a ridiculous-looking crest on his helmet that ran from side to side, apparently made of feathers given the manner in which they were moving with the stiff breeze. Immediately after his appearance, Zhang heard the sound of some sort of horn, but rather than stop, he kept his horse moving until, when they were perhaps fifty paces away, the *Gwai* wearing the strange helmet shouted something that, to Zhang, sounded very much like the barking of a dog.

"This is when they rain death down on our heads," Zhao muttered.

Ignoring him, Zhang took a breath, then called out in Tamil, "My name is Zhang Meng," making sure to indicate himself as he said his name, "and I come on behalf of..."

The Roman with the strange helmet cut him off with more gibberish, and he heard Zhao mutter to the other two Tigers, "Get ready to protect Excellency Zhang with your lives!"

And, at first, Zhang thought that Zhao's prediction would come to fruition, as the Roman gesticulated in his direction while shouting more nonsense, but when he saw the other men around him didn't raise their spears, or even make a move of any kind, it came to him.

"He's telling us to wait," Zhang said quietly.

"How could you know that?" Zhao asked, but even as he was saying the words, the *Gwai* who had been speaking turned and vanished.

What occurred next was even more nerve-wracking, because for a second time, Zhang heard a horn note, except this one was much, much deeper in tone, but when the Romans who remained on the wall didn't move in response, he relaxed, albeit only slightly. He could never recall how long they sat there waiting, but he could tell by the manner in which the *Gwai* who were watching him suddenly turned to look inwards, that the horn call must have been some sort of summons. Then, the Roman with the strange helmet reappeared, but this time, he wasn't alone, accompanied by two men.

Neither of them were wearing helmets, but Zhang immediately noticed the different complexions, and ages, of the two new arrivals, and it was the darker, younger one who called out, in Tamil, "Who are you? What is your purpose?"

Ironically enough, this settled Zhang's nerves a bit, because this was what he had hoped for, even if he hadn't truly expected it, and he replied, repeating his name. Then, in a Tamil that was strangely accented but understandable to Achaemenes, he delivered the message that had been decided a month earlier. He paused every few heartbeats to allow the dark-skinned Roman to speak to the other new arrival, who was tall, with features that, while foreign to Zhang, he admitted were pleasing to the eye because of the symmetry, although he noted with some amusement that this *Gwai* was balding but attempted to hide it by pulling the hair on one side over the top of his skull. In another quirk of fate, this also settled Zhang's nerves a bit, because he knew men of the Han, including his father, who were distressed at going bald and tried to hide it in the same fashion. However, it wasn't until about halfway through the exchange that it hit Zhang; could this be Caesar? he wondered, but the dark-skinned Roman had finished his part, and he had to continue delivering his message. Any doubt that he was gazing up at Caesar was removed when, once he had finished the prepared part of his message, that man turned and said something to the *Gwai* with the strange helmet, prompting the man to instantly disappear, then, within a matter of heartbeats, he heard the creaking sound of the wooden gates before they cracked open.

"You may enter, Zhang Meng," the dark-skinned Roman said. Zhang hesitated, but the man said quickly, "Gaius Julius Caesar, Dictator For Life of the Senate and People of Rome, guarantees your safety. You will not be harmed in any way."

"What did he say?" Zhao asked suspiciously; his hand had dropped to his sword when the gates began to open.

"Only that you don't have anything to fear," Zhang replied coolly, then before the other man could react, he kicked his horse and it began moving towards the gates, although he did think to say over his shoulder, "You can wait here, or you can go back into Ke Van. I'll return as soon as I've delivered the rest of my message."

"I thought you already did," Zhao muttered, but he signaled to his men to dismount to wait.

This was how the West of Rome established its first contact with the East of the Han Empire, in a moment that would change their worlds forever.

"Do you believe this Caesar can be trusted to fulfill his part of this agreement?"

It was now late in the Roman month of December, and this was Zhang's third trip back to Chang'An to report to the Emperor Yuan, who had asked the question. Despite having been in the Emperor's presence several times by this point, Zhang still got nervous whenever he was before him. And, Zhang understood, this was perhaps the most important question he would ever be asked in his life.

Nevertheless, the only reason he hesitated was because he didn't want to appear as if he hadn't given this much thought before he replied, "Yes, Bìxià, I do."

"How can you possibly know that?" Hong Gong asked. "You've met this Caesar how many times? Three?"

"I have been to Ke Van three times, *Shi Yushi* Hong," Zhang's tone was polite, and he had learned that Hong insisted on being addressed by his title of Imperial Secretary, "that is true. But I have spoken with Caesar several times. And," he addressed this to the man who mattered, "I have observed not just what he says, Bìxià, but the manner in which he says things, and what he does."

"Bìxià, it would solve more than one problem."

Yuan looked at Jin Chang, one of his Imperial Assistants, and while Zhang wasn't certain what his duties were, he had learned that the man was trusted by the Emperor.

"How so, Chang?"

"The whole reason behind your proposal to the Romans was because of the trouble we're having with Zhizhi and his...ambitions," Jin replied, and when Yuan nodded at him to continue, "But we cannot ignore the problem that has developed on Zhuya (Hainan) with General Xao either, would you agree?"

"You know I do," Yuan snapped irritably.

It was a sign of Jin's favor that he continued unperturbed, "Rather than shifting a substantial portion of our army to remove General Xao and his followers, what better way to accomplish two things, Bìxià? By agreeing to take his army to Zhuya and crushing the rebels and malcontents who have fled there and flocked to the General's banner for us, not only will he be removing a potential threat, as formidable warriors as these *Gwai* may be, they will still inevitably suffer losses, will they not? And," he spread his hands, the rustling of the silk sleeves of his robes sounding like whispers, "they cannot send to Rome for replacements for the men they lose."

Zhang was watching the Emperor intently, hoping that he wouldn't have to intervene, but when Yuan gave a thoughtful nod, he forced himself to interject, "Bìxià, while Excellency Jin is certainly correct about the impossibility of replacing men from Rome, I would be remiss if I didn't repeat what I have learned during my dealings with Caesar. They have been successful in filling their missing ranks with men from the lands they conquered. In fact," he realized that he hadn't mentioned this before, "the man who carries the rank of what they call a Tribune who is the only one among their officers who can speak Tamil, is actually a Parthian named Achaemenes, and I had the opportunity to talk with him about how he came to serve Caesar. Naturally," he acknowledged, "I assumed that, being the first kingdom that Caesar conquered, he must be a slave, and I found it curious that a slave from a conquered nation would be allowed to serve their commander in such close proximity." He hesitated, remembering his own shock at learning the truth. "But I was mistaken in my assumption. What I learned from this Achaemenes was that Caesar behaves in an extraordinary fashion when it comes to conquered peoples, because he doesn't make them slaves, and in fact treats them with great clemency. Every man of their army who isn't a Roman is there because they choose to follow Caesar, not because they have been forced to do so."

Indeed, of all the many things that Zhang had learned during this period of time when he was introduced to Rome, this fact had shaken him more than anything else. To a man of the Han, it had been inconceivable that any man would freely submit themselves to their conqueror; the idea that their service in the ranks of what Zhang now knew were called the Legions who marched for Caesar was voluntary was so foreign to him that he actually retired to the administrator's home in Ke Van, canceling a scheduled meeting with the Romans on the pretext of illness so that he could absorb this reality. At first, he had been certain that Achaemenes was lying to him, trying to present the Romans in such a way that it would convince Zhang that Caesar had, in essence, a practically infinite supply of men to serve in the ranks. It had been his contact with a young barbarian named Barhinder Gotra, who claimed to have once served the King of Bharuch, which, of course, Zhang knew of given its importance as part of the Silk Road, who had convinced Zhang that this wasn't a ruse of some sort. His warning, however, was immediately attacked by the eunuch, which he could have predicted.

"Master Zhang," Xian, as always, spoke with a veneer of amiability, but by now, Zhang had enough experience with the eunuch to hear the condescension, "while what you say is very interesting, surely you are not suggesting that our people would follow the path of these subjugated barbarians?"

Fighting his impulse to answer honestly, Zhang lied, "Not at all, Excellency Xian. I merely wished to point out that they still have a formidable army, and that they have been successful in integrating the men of Parthia, Bharuch, and Pandya into their ranks. And," he stressed, "training them in the manner in which they wage war."

"But the *Gwai* have never faced the Han," Hong pointed out, from his spot in the corner, and there was something in his manner that Zhang had begun to associate with a spider, which was how he thought of the Imperial Secretary, seemingly above the fray, spinning webs of his own making for reasons Zhang could only guess. "We have the mightiest army in the world, and once General Gan ends this problem with Zhizhi, he will demonstrate it by crushing these *Gwai*. However," as it always did, Hong's tone altered noticeably when addressing the Emperor, taking on the oily quality of the courtier as he inclined his head to Yuan, "I believe that Master Jin is correct in his assessment. We can accomplish two things at one time, and even though there is no question of our superiority, it can only help to further weaken the *Gwai* while crushing the insolent General Xao and his minions like a beetle under our shoe."

Despite the fact that Zhang wasn't a warrior, and had never participated in battle, he was still scornfully amused at the bellicose words coming from the sleek, well-fed Imperial Secretary, thinking as he did of Caesar, and the men who marched for him, one in particular, the giant they called Pullus, who was the most intimidating man Zhang had ever encountered. I don't know that it will be that easy, Hong. It's easy for you to say as much sitting behind a desk, knowing that you will never be standing there with a sword in your hand. Not, he admitted to himself, that he had any intention of facing the Romans on the battlefield himself.

There was a silence, as once again, the Emperor began pacing, head down and fingering his beads, face creased into a frown, and Zhang felt a stab of sympathy for Yuan, wondering what it must be like to bear the burden of upholding the honor of his house while caring for the people, and protecting his kingdom. Finally, Yuan came to a stop and turned to look at Zhang.

"Return to Ke Van and tell this Caesar that we agree to the proposal, and will abide by the terms of our agreement. We will provide them with enough rice and other foodstuffs to keep his army fed in exchange for his help in subduing Xao, and he and his army will be allowed to occupy Zhuya and use our permanent camps there for the next year, whereupon we will review matters and reassess."

Zhang dropped to his knees, performing his abasement as he assured the Emperor that he would fulfill his orders, but when he rose to leave the room, the Emperor had one more surprise.

"And Zhang," Yuan spoke in an almost offhand manner, "once you deliver the message and Caesar signs this agreement, you're to remain there with him. *Sima* Zhao will return with it."

Before he could stop himself, Zhang heard his own gasp of surprise, and dismay.

Struggling to recover, Zhang managed to sound calm as he asked, "And how long do I remain there, Bìxià?"

The change in the Emperor's expression was subtle, but now that Zhang had been in his presence several times, it was impossible to miss, and his words matched the coldness.

"For as long as I deem it to be so, Zhang Meng." He paused, and while he did offer Zhang a smile, Zhang wasn't fooled by it, nor by the mild way Yuan asked, "Will that be a problem for you? Do you have more pressing matters, perhaps?"

Assuring the Emperor that this wasn't the case at all, Zhang was just happy to be walking out of the palace, even if it was on wobbly legs. Only later did the scope of what he had been ordered to do hit him, which was why he made a point to visit his father, wondering if he would ever see him again.

Caesar Ascending – The Han

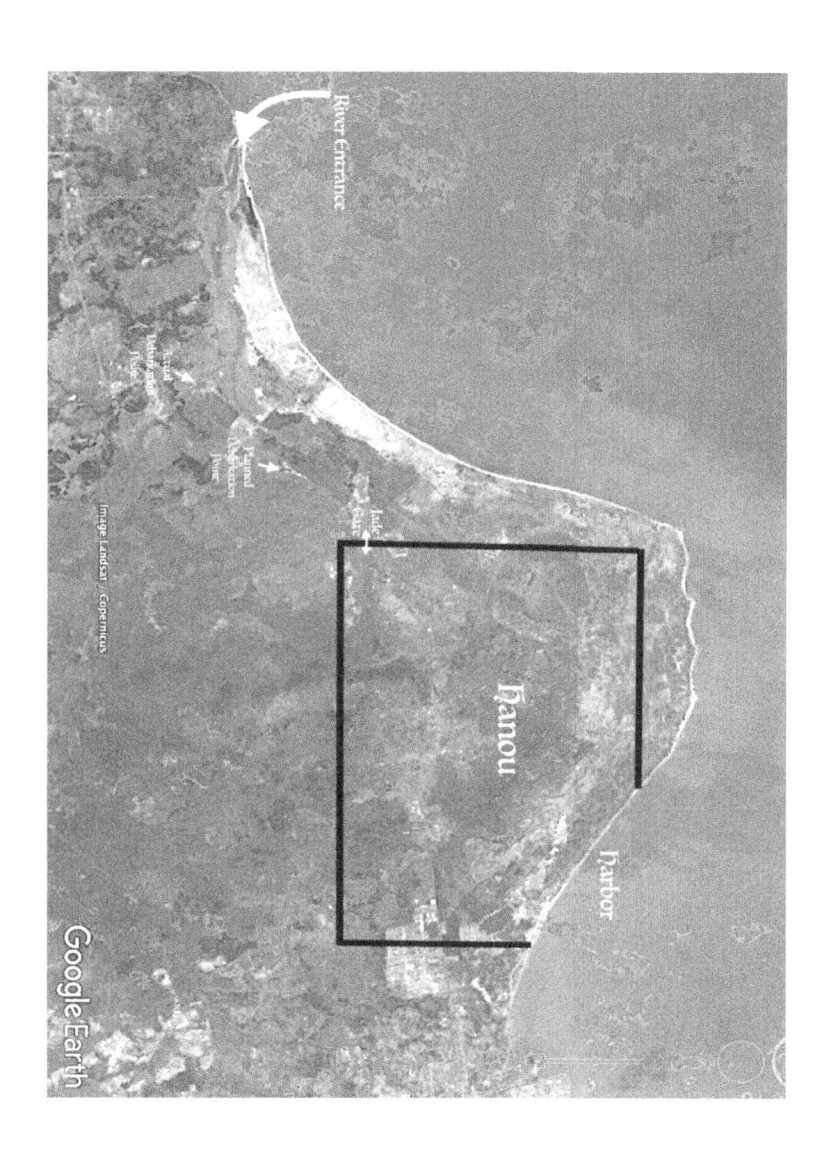

Yazhou
21st
Landing
Fort
Image Landsat / Copernicus
Image © 2021 Maxar Technologies
Google Earth

Chapter Four

One of the hallowed traditions of the Roman Legions was the sacred lustration ceremony that was held every Januarius, and for veterans like Pullus who couldn't easily count the number of these rituals he had attended, this one just two months short of six years since the Ides would remain as the most memorable because of what took place after the ceremony was over. Once the men were dismissed, Caesar led all of his senior officers back into the *praetorium* for a meeting, but the first thing that Pullus noticed was that on the long table where Caesar, his Legates, and the occasional Tribune dined, there were several amphorae of a style that told Pullus these were from their world, along with a cup for each man.

"This," Caesar announced as the *praetorium* slaves busily poured the contents into cups, "is the last of the Falernian that I've been saving for a special occasion."

"I don't like this," Balbinus muttered, as usual standing next to Pullus. "He's up to something."

"Oh?" Pullus chuckled. "What makes you say that? The fact that he's actually sharing his last stock of Roman wine?"

The truth was that Pullus agreed with Balbinus, but like his fellow Primi Pili, he didn't hesitate in picking up a cup before walking over to the stool that might have had his name engraved on it since it was his customary spot. Only the dead Clustuminus had ever attempted to usurp it, and that had only happened once and it had actually been Caesar who snapped at him for doing so.

Waiting for his officers, Legates seated on the front row and Centurions behind to get settled, the general raised his cup. "To Mars, Bellona, Jupiter Optimus Maximus, and to the shades of all of our comrades who are no longer with us."

There was a ragged chorus of acknowledgement, followed by the sounds of men either sipping or guzzling their cup and finished with the smacking of lips and low moans as men savored this taste of a home that, to one degree or another, they had resigned themselves to never seeing again. So absorbed were they in the moment that most of them, including Pullus, missed Caesar gesturing in the direction of the flap that served as a doorway, but all eyes were caught by the movement as Achaemenes entered, followed by the Han emissary Zhang, the pair coming to stand next to Caesar, facing the audience.

"What's that slant-eyed bastard here for?" Balbinus muttered, as always thinking that if any Centurion would know it would be Pullus, but all he received from the giant Roman next to him was a mystified shake of the head and a muttered "I have no idea."

Waiting for the whispered exchanges taking place among his officers that he had anticipated to die down, Caesar began, "As you know, I have been in contact with Emperor Yuan of the Han Empire," he indicated Zhang, "through Emissary Zhang Meng." Since this was common knowledge, he didn't belabor the point, going on to explain, "And we have been in...negotiations, I suppose is the best word, whereby we don't have to fight the forces of the Emperor...yet," he finished with a smile that seemed incongruous given the topic.

This was when Pullus noticed something and was about to whisper to Balbinus but decided against alerting his friend to the fact that Achaemenes wasn't relaying the translation of Caesar's words into Tamil for Zhang. Who, Pullus noted with amusement, was clearly upset about that, while Caesar continued in the same tone as Achaemenes remained silent.

"We've been given the opportunity to take an extended period of time to regroup and to replenish our stores, while spending the next few months under a roof made of wood and not canvas." To nobody's surprise, this was met with nodding heads and quiet exclamations of relief; as inured to life in a marching camp as they had become, it had been a subject of complaint, and not just from the rankers. Pullus wasn't the only officer who was waiting for the "but" he was certain was coming and, although there was no "but," he was still rewarded when Caesar continued, "There is one condition to this agreement, however. In order to ensure our food supply for at least the next year, we need to provide a...service to Emperor Yuan." For the first time, Pullus noticed that the map behind Caesar had been covered only when the general turned and yanked the cloth hanging over it away. This elicited another reaction from all but the Legates, since this was the first time the Centurions had seen this version of the map that was now filled with far more detail than the last time that they had seen it. Pointing to the outline of what was clearly an island, Caesar explained, "The Han call this island Zhuya, and as you can see, it's a good size. And," he offered them a smile, "as I'm sure your little birds told you, Legate Volusenus was gone for an extended period of time once again, which is why you're seeing what you're seeing." When Caesar picked up the stick that he used as a pointer, Pullus noticed him giving Achaemenes a subtle nod just before he indicated a spot on the northern side of the island as the Parthian began translating to the Han next to him. "This is the city of Hanou. Which," Caesar turned and bowed his head in Zhang's direction, "we have learned is rather a basic term that means 'sea port.' And, as you can see, is an apt name because of its position on this bay." The spot Caesar was pointing to was a semicircular indentation in the northeast part of the island closest to the mainland. "According to Zhang, Hanou has almost one hundred thousand inhabitants. But," he stressed the word to forestall the commentary on the size, "more importantly, until a few years ago, Hanou was the main headquarters for several garrisons maintained by the Han on the island, until Emperor Yuan gave the order to remove his troops."

It was just Caesar's ill luck that his throat had become dry and he was forced to pause to pick up his cup to take a sip, because the silence only lasted long enough for Pullus to ask, "Why did he do that, sir?"

Forced to swallow his mouthful in a hurry, which irritated Caesar further, he set the cup down hard enough to make an audible sound.

"If you had waited, Pullus, I would have told you," he snapped. Taking a breath, his tone returned to normal, "This island is inhabited, but not by people the Han consider to be their own. They're called," suddenly, Caesar looked embarrassed, turning to Achaemenes, who instantly understanding, spoke in Tamil to Zhang.

"*Li*," Zhang supplied.

"Yes, that's it. They're called the *Li*, and according to Zhang, they're essentially a people who have lived as bandits and pirates for generations, using this island as their base. They prey on the ships sailing east and west in between their island and the mainland in this strait." He ran his pointer on an east/west line in between the island and mainland. "That's why one of Emperor Yuan's predecessors invaded the island, to subdue the *Li* to stop their raids on the mainland and their piracy of Han ships. From what I can tell, this was seventy years ago. The problem is that the *Li* proved hard to subdue, because," he moved the pointer to a series of hatch marks that were roughly in the center of the island from north to south, but oriented more to the western side of the island, "of these mountains. They're apparently riddled with caves and hideouts, so what the Han did was to create a series of outposts that essentially ring these mountains." Pausing to take another sip, this time none of the officers broke the silence, although now Caesar was stalling for time, knowing what kind of reaction the rest of the information would cause. Recognizing he had no choice, he continued, "While the *Li* were effectively contained, Emperor Yuan decided that the effort to keep them in check was too costly, which was why he ordered the evacuation of the island. The problem is that a substantial number of his soldiers decided to remain on Zhuya with their families, including at least one of his high-ranking generals, named Xao. Xao has managed to attract other disaffected men in the Han armies, including other officers. And," he took a deep breath, "he has somehow managed to convince the *Li* to rally to him, apparently under the guise of offering them their independence from the Han Empire. Now, the Emperor has become concerned that Xao isn't content to have his own island kingdom because the raids on the mainland have resumed, and recently, there was an attempt on Xao's part to take the city of Xuwen," Caesar moved the pointer to a spot on the mainland, directly north of Hanou across the strait. "He wasn't successful, and he suffered heavy casualties, but he's still being joined by men from the mainland." Placing the pointer down on the table, Caesar finished, "In exchange for a permanent camp, and the delivery of enough rice and other food supplies for a year, I've agreed that we will land on Zhuya, find this General Xao and whatever he calls his army, and destroy them."

Afterward, every man attending the meeting agreed that this was the quietest it would be for the next watch.

Like the Emperor Yuan, the man who formerly held the rank of *Duwei*, the Supreme Commander of all military forces in the commandery of Jiaozhi Province, Xao Bang, was extremely interested in the arrival of the strange invaders called the Romans. Unlike Yuan, in that arrival, he had seen an opportunity, which was based on an assumption that, on its face, was both sound and logical, given the rapacity of the foreigners in gobbling up territory. It was when he was informed by one of the seaborne merchants who, like Long, served several purposes besides the transport of goods, of first the arrival of the largest fleet, composed of ships of a type never seen before in this part of the world, in Ke Van, that his idea first formed. With the arrival of the massive army, who, according to his limited information, had suddenly materialized seemingly out of nowhere in the port town of Da Nang, just south of Han territory, Xao began to become more ambitious.

"They clearly have heard that Yuan has most of the army thousands of *li* to the north because of Zhizhi," Xao had mused to his second in command Lei Zheng. "They must plan on taking advantage of that by invading Jiaozhi, starting with Long Biên."

While Lei understood his commander's reasoning and agreed that this was possible, he also cautioned, "Shouldn't we alert the Yazhou garrison? Perhaps send reinforcements since that is the closest safe landing spot to Ke Van?"

"I don't think that will be necessary," Xao replied, after a moment's thought. More to appease Lei, he said, "But I'll send orders to the garrison commander to send men to man the outpost on top of Shenjao, ready to light the beacon, as well as the others along the coast."

Sensing that this was as far as his commander was willing to go, Lei consoled himself that it was better than nothing.

What came next was more delicate, so he tried to sound disinterested and engaging in idle talk, commenting, "If the *Gwai* army does as expected, it will likely force Wu Qiang to respond with the Xuwen garrison, wouldn't it?"

Lei's suspicion was confirmed by the way that Xao nodded in approval, a broad smile on his face.

"I *knew* you would be clever enough to see it as I have! And yes, I believe that he will, because the garrisons at Qinzhou and Chongzou combined won't be enough to even slow the *Gwai* down when they move on Long Biên, even if their army is half the size it's supposed to be. And when that happens," he was still smiling, but it transformed into the kind Lei had seen before on his general's face and knew that it didn't bode well for their foes, "we'll make our return to the mainland, and then we will see whether the Emperor is as dismissive of my request as he was the last time."

"When do you think the *Gwai* will move?" Lei asked. "Should I make preparations to find shipping and summon our men from the south and the mountains?"

To Lei's pleased surprise, Xao actually nodded, saying thoughtfully, "That is a good idea, Lei. Yes, make it so. It will take some time, but I want to be ready to pounce when the *Gwai* force Wu to commit his forces in Xuwen to stop them from taking Long Biên. We," he smiled broadly, "will be ready to strike within days of that happy event."

With these words, Xao would become yet another man who underestimated Caesar and his army.

The reason that the plan had come together so quickly after Caesar's announcement was divined by Scribonius, who shared it with the others the evening after Caesar had summoned the Primi Pili.

"Either Caesar anticipated that the Han Emperor would make this part of the agreement and planned accordingly. Or," he smiled in a way that informed Pullus this was his belief, "he's the one who suggested it to the Emperor."

Pullus had learned not to argue with his friend once he had time to think through a problem, but there were still some lingering questions in his mind.

"How did he know that the Han were in such trouble with..." He stopped, unable to think of the name, which Diocles supplied, "...Zhizhi? And, how would he come up with this on his own?"

"I imagine that he learned from Long," Scribonius replied. "Supposedly, it's been going on for two or three years, and the situation on Zhuya has been going on for even longer. As far as how he came up with it on his own?" Scribonius thought for a heartbeat, then shrugged. "He's Caesar."

Even with this explanation, it was still a remarkable turnaround, even for Caesar, but while Scribonius was essentially correct in his guess, much of the credit went to the youngest member of the corps of translators that now dotted the ranks of the Legions. It was through Barhinder, who, as Pullus had hoped when he suggested him to Caesar, had developed a friendship with Long, the merchant agreeing to provide Caesar information about the Han, and when Caesar offered the merchant a sum that would have made Long one of the wealthiest members of his class, Barhinder had become a semi-permanent member of Caesar's staff, more or less indefinitely on loan from an unhappy Pullus. As determined as Long was to fulfill the terms dictated by the *Gwai* Caesar, it was still a difficult adjustment, and it wasn't surprising that the Han gravitated to anyone with whom he could communicate. Despite his trip to the island the Romans were calling Taprobane to do business at the Greek trading colony, he hadn't picked up more than a handful of words in their tongue, but he had become far more comfortable with Tamil, and in Barhinder, he found a friendly face and a good listener. More importantly, though Long only came to this realization later, Barhinder excelled at asking questions in a manner that was quite disarming, without arousing suspicion that he was gathering information. The consequence of this was that, by the time Nero arrived in Da Nang, Caesar already had an extraordinary amount of information about the Han and the political situation...and the formation of a plan. The next phase of

Caesar's strategy began when, once more, he sent Gaius Volusenus with the *Philotemia*, two *quadriremes*, two *triremes*, and four Liburnians, except now that Caesar was aware of the existence of the island Zhuya, Volusenus' mission was more specific.

In another change, Caesar sent one Century from the Tenth of the 25th Legion and half a *turma* of cavalry, along with extra ship crewmen in order to fulfill another task, with the small fleet departing a week after their arrival in Ke Van. They were gone until the Kalends of December, returning with not only a detailed map of Zhuya's coast, but with a good idea of what lay inland from the half-dozen possible landing sites that Volusenus had selected. And, once again, they returned with more ships than they had left with, with another half-dozen *chuan*, so impressed had Lysippos been with the vessels, and he had urged Caesar to acquire more. While Volusenus was away, Caesar was equally busy, albeit in a different manner, planting the seeds with the young Han emissary Zhang, a necessary but extremely frustrating process for the Roman who, more than any man, seemed to understand the value of time and recognizing it as the scarcest commodity in the world. As Pullus and every Centurion could attest, nothing was ever far enough, fast enough, or good enough for their general, but as relentlessly as he pushed his men, they saw that he pushed himself every bit as hard, and in many ways, much harder. He had long since perfected the art of functioning on only one standard Roman watch of sleep, which required Apollodorus to assign the small army of clerks in shifts, and it was the poor wretches who were consigned to the night watches for whom most of the men in the Legions felt sympathy. However, no matter how strong Caesar's will was, he couldn't change distance, and since Emperor Yuan showed not the slightest inclination to shift his presence and the administration of his vast kingdom south from Chang'An, the best he could hope for was to offer the Han emissary some suggestions that enabled him to cut his trips between the two leaders by almost a week. For Caesar, it was an excruciatingly slow process, but his normal impatience was curbed by his knowledge of the necessity for this work because, while he was using the Han emissary's youth against him, he was also acutely aware of the razor-sharp intellect Zhang possessed, and knew that one misstatement, one error in judgment, one lapse of any kind would expose the fact that he was manipulating not just Zhang, but the Han emperor into doing what he wanted. The reason was simple; Caesar understood that, more than anything, he owed his men stability, and when he had learned that, just two years before he and his army had departed from Brundisium, Yuan had ordered the abandonment of both the civil and military apparatus of the Han Empire on Zhuya, and by doing so, left behind complexes of sturdily built buildings scattered all about the island, he saw his opportunity. The reason Yuan had done so, from the recognition that his predecessors' attempts to subdue the native *Li* of Zhuya had proven far more difficult and costly than anticipated, meant that there would undoubtedly be a fight for these facilities and all that went with them. Caesar also possessed a shrewd insight into the men who marched for him; they *needed* a foe to defeat, an enemy who they could crush, and whose females and valuables they could take, especially now that his men had been introduced to Han women, who they considered the most exotic creatures in the world. In this, he was no different, except that it was a matter of scale, because Gaius Julius Caesar was driven by something that not even he completely understood, particularly because it was a relatively recent discovery about himself. When he had informed his men that reaching the Ganges would fulfill his ambitions, that by eclipsing Alexander, he would finally be sated, he had believed this to be the truth. It was when, sitting in the camp on the island in the middle of the southernmost mouth of the Ganges, he had come to the realization that he was dissatisfied, that there was still a completely irresistible urge driving him onward, recognizing this inner drive only after men like Scribonius had discerned it in him. After the nightmare with the Khmer it became even more crucial, and it was as they were struggling along the Via Hades, which he privately thought an apt name that, as he learned more about the Han Empire, the idea was born, albeit in a roundabout way that only later did he learn originated with young Gotra, then went through Pullus' slave Diocles, before going through his own Apollodorus. By the time they were reunited with the fleet, the basic plan was already formed in his mind; once Volusenus returned, it was only a matter of filling in the details of how it would be executed, performing the delicate dance with Zhang before gently nudging him in the direction he needed the emissary to go. And now, all was ready.

By the time Zhang realized that he had been manipulated by the *Gwai* general, it was out of the question that he would reveal this to the Emperor or anyone in the Imperial court; on what would be his last visit to Chang'An months later, he didn't even confide in his father when he visited him before his final departure that he had been outwitted by a barbarian. That it actually fulfilled the ambitions of his Emperor to remove the hovering threat represented by Xao and his army ameliorated some of the guilt he felt at being outmaneuvered by the *Gwai* Caesar, meaning that it was more of a personal humiliation than anything else. Despite his trepidation about being ordered to stay with the Romans for an indefinite amount of time, Zhang was nonetheless fascinated, and dismayed, watching the Romans essentially break down their huge camp, transfer the tons of supplies and equipment to their ships in a manner that reinforced his recognition that the Han weren't the only kingdom with superb organizational skills. What was most disturbing was that Zhang strongly suspected that these Romans surpassed the Han, and not just in this regard, but in the overall discipline and competence of the Legions, all of which was exemplified by the Legion commanded by the giant Roman he had learned was called Pullus. By this point in time, Zhang had recorded the identifying numbers associated with each Legion, having learned this was how the Romans did things, instead of naming them for an animal, or a characteristic that was important to the men as the Han did. Although the numbers in themselves were meaningless, it was from Achaemenes that he learned that, as large as Caesar's army was, the Legions represented by the missing numbers between one and thirty actually existed but were serving elsewhere. He had also learned of the destruction of two of those Legions, the 7th and the 11th, and that they hadn't been reconstituted for the simple reason that there weren't enough Roman citizens available. Not surprisingly, he had been extremely curious about the demise of these two Legions, but Achaemenes had been closemouthed on the subject; fortunately for Zhang, the other barbarian with whom he could converse, young Barhinder Gotra, had been more forthcoming. Once he learned that it was a combination of complacency on the part of the two Centurions commanding the Legions, and that war elephants had been involved, he realized that, while interesting, it didn't provide the Han any useful information. Although there had been attempts to employ war elephants by the Han over the previous centuries, they had been sporadic, and long before Yuan ascended the Han throne, those efforts had been abandoned.

 What he did learn that could be of use was also quite chilling, and he would recall the conversation with Gotra with great clarity for not as much what he said when describing the substance called naphtha, but the manner in which the young man shuddered and turned pale as he explained how the substance behaved. During the loading process, Zhang had happened to see the crates, all of which were marked with a large red circle on all four sides, transported down to one of the docks and loaded aboard one of the *chuan* that had been commandeered by the Romans, and he observed the manner in which the men doing the loading, all slaves, behaved. It reminded him of how one might handle a large crate of eggs, except for the naked fear displayed by the slaves as they gingerly walked up the gangplank, each carrying a single crate, but the most instructive moment came when one of the men tripped going up the plank, and for a span of a couple heartbeats as he struggled to regain his balance, how his fellow slaves scattered, most of them crying out in obvious terror. The process of preparing the fleet to embark had taken four days, and as daunting as it had been to watch, Zhang also noticed things that he thought could prove useful to his people. Achaemenes had obviously been warned, probably by Caesar, about divulging too much to Zhang, but he had managed to confirm something that he had noticed about the absence of a weapon the Han considered crucial, the crossbow. Deciding that he needed to give something to receive confirmation in turn, Zhang had told Achaemenes about the Han crossbow in a casual manner on the day before Caesar's part of the fleet had departed. Even as conversant in Tamil as the Parthian and Han were, Zhang had been forced to squat in the dirt, and using a stick, drew one, eliciting a sound from the Parthian that caused Zhang to look up at him.

"And you say this is carried by one man?" Achaemenes asked, and when Zhang nodded, he commented, "While the Romans have something that looks something like that, it is too large for one man to carry, and it is..." Realizing it would be easier, Achaemenes squatted and drew a crude representation of a scorpion. Standing back up, he held his hand at shoulder level. "It stands this high, and it takes three men to carry the pieces. There are now twenty per Legion, two to a Cohort."

Could this be our advantage? Zhang wondered as he nodded his understanding to the Parthian. The Han depended on crossbowmen heavily, meaning that their rough equivalent of a Legion, called a *Tu-wei-fu*, was composed of spearmen and crossbowmen in equal numbers, while swordsmen were about twenty percent of the total. Without knowing exactly what Caesar had planned aside from attacking Zhayou, he realized that the only way he would learn if this proved crucial to the Han when they inevitably clashed with Caesar was when he saw it happening. Not once did Zhang ever lose sight of what he considered to be a fact, that Emperor Yuan would never tolerate the presence of the *Gwai* for an extended period of time, and he considered everything he witnessed in that light, thankful that none of these barbarians could read civilized writing. He did find the wooden tablets coated with beeswax to be a useful convention, and he had begun making notes in them, but always transferred them to parchment at the end of every day in the small tent that had been allocated for his use, complete with a servant who spoke Tamil...and with a Legionary always standing outside the tent, day and night. He had never spent a single night in a tent before this, but he was resigned to this being his fate for the foreseeable future, and he was surprised that it was actually surprisingly comfortable, but he was also aware that the reason for that had been Caesar. He had been allowed to roam the camp, always with an escort, of course, usually Achaemenes but sometimes Gotra, and had been able to see inside the tents of the barbarians in the ranks and the packed dirt floor that, depending on the amount of rain could be mud, the low wooden cots, and the absence of anything remotely civilized, while he had a wooden floor made of square panels, a small desk, and a cot that was wider than those used by the soldiers. All of this was packed away and loaded aboard one of the ships, although he had no idea which one, but he had been allowed to keep his personal baggage, which was loaded aboard Caesar's flagship, including the large leather satchel that now contained several scrolls of the information he had gathered and hoped to send to Chang'An. He was invited by Caesar to stand on the raised deck at the rear of Caesar's flagship, which was named the *Polynike*, a ship the *Gwai* called a *quinquereme* that still filled Zhang with a combination of awe and dread, not only because of its size, but from the array of artillery fastened to the deck that ran down the center of the ship.

The air was filled with the shouts and curses of the Centurions, competing with the hollow thudding sound of hobnailed boots on the wooden docks as men filed up the gangplank of their assigned ship, each of them carrying their pack suspended from a long stick, another curiosity to Zhang, since the Han soldiers he had seen carried their loads on their backs. Since Caesar was occupied in his normal fashion, receiving clerks carrying tablets while sending Tribunes and other men of his staff on some errand, Zhang was essentially left to his own devices, so he walked to the railing to watch as the ship next to them was being loaded. Because it was still dark, every ship had a lantern lit at the bow and stern, and although the men were still little more than dark shapes, even in the gloom, Zhang could make out the giant Pullus, standing on the dock as his men filed by, and while he couldn't understand what was being said, he could tell by the tone that the Centurion was bantering with his men, something that Zhang couldn't imagine would happen with his people. Despite his lack of experience with the military, he knew that commanders of the status of Pullus were considered almost as gods by their men and were similarly unapproachable. He decided this was something to discuss with Achaemenes, thinking that his perspective as another foreigner to Rome would at least provide some insight into whether he found it as odd as Zhang. What Zhang also noticed was that Pullus was the last to board his ship, but even as he dropped down into it, the slaves on the dock removed the gangplank, while the man standing at the steering oar shouted something that prompted a pair of men with long wooden poles to shove them against the dock. More quickly than he would have thought possible, the ship carrying Pullus slipped away in the darkness and was replaced by another ship, and even as it was sliding into the vacated spot, Zhang saw men marching down the dock in a single file, the first man, carrying a pole with a piece of cloth attached to it reaching the gangplank within a heartbeat of it being dropped into place where, without hesitation, he strode up it and dropped down into his ship. This, Zhang thought, is both impressive and terrifying, feeling rooted to his spot and unable to look away from the smooth efficiency on display, while behind him, he could hear Caesar talking, using a tone that he had recognized as the one the general used when issuing orders. He noticed that it was becoming easier to see, but just as he was about to finally turn away to see if Achaemenes was disposed to talk, he saw something happen that would leave a lasting impression, one that he would think of often in the future.

It began with a shout of alarm, then a sudden lurching movement by one of the men ascending the gangplank that ended when he pitched headlong off the plank into the water with a large splash, the weight of his dropped pack making the stick strike the man behind him with considerable force, eliciting another shout, this one of pain. The men around him began yelling, which was understandable, but it was the manner in which the slaves on the dock behaved that caught his attention, as a pair of men each snatched up what looked like nothing more than a long pole, but whereas one of them shoved his pole out to strike the side of the ship, then was immediately braced by another man that kept the side of the ship from bumping against the dock, which he instantly understood because it could crush the fallen man as he tried to surface, Zhang saw that the pole in the other slave's hand was slightly different, with what looked like a loop of rope that he only later realized was actually made of iron, the loop end of which the slave thrust down into the water, right where the barbarian soldier had disappeared. No more than one or two heartbeats elapsed when the slave shouted, and Zhang saw the pole jerking violently in his hands, as some of the soldiers waiting to board rushed to him and, working together, pulled the pole up out of the water, at the end of which was a gasping, spluttering barbarian who had one arm through the iron loop. He was quickly hauled up onto the deck, dripping water and coughing, but extraordinarily to Zhang, while one of his comrades squatted down, the rest of the soldiers who had helped rescue him turned around, retrieved their own packs, and fell back in line as if nothing unusual had just taken place, that one of their comrades hadn't almost drowned.

"It *is* impressive, is it not?"

Zhang turned, recognizing Achaemenes' voice, and despite himself, he agreed soberly, "Yes, it is. I have never seen anything like it."

"Neither had I," the Parthian laughed, then admitted, "but I am a Parthian, and we hate the sea almost as much as the Romans do."

This surprised Zhang a great deal, and he wasn't sure that he believed Achaemenes, pointing out, "How can that be true, given all the time they have spent at sea? If they hate it so much, why are they willing to spend so much of their time on ships?"

Achaemenes simply pointed over his shoulder at Caesar, who appeared to be unaware of the small drama that occurred with the ship next to them as the Parthian said simply, "Because of him."

While the sun was fully up by the time Caesar's flagship *Polynike* slid away from the dock, it was only about a finger's width above the horizon, and it was as Zhang was trying to calculate how long it had taken that he noticed something.

Calling to Achaemenes, who had returned to stand with Caesar's secretary Apollodorus, Zhang pointed back at the docks.

"What about all those ships? Why are they not being loaded?"

"Because they are not coming with us," Achaemenes

replied. Seeing the Han's confusion, he hesitated, then realized there was nothing Zhang could do about it, being aboard ship as he was, so he explained, "Caesar is leading one part of the army to the city of Hanou, while Legate Pollio is sailing to the town on the western coast that is called..." he had to think about it, "...Yazhou, I believe it is called."

So, he's attacking Xao from two directions, Zhang thought, but his surge of excitement at the value of this information quickly evaporated as he realized, like Achaemenes already had, there was nothing he could do about it.

Because of the different distances, Caesar, leading the 5th, 10th, 14th, 25th, and 30th, along with half of the cavalry, which he placed under the command of Gundomir's brother Barvistus, with Decimus Silva second in command, departed three days before the other half, which was led by Pollio, his force composed of the 8th, 12th, 15th, 21st, and 28th, with Aulus Hirtius in command of the cavalry. While Caesar's part of the fleet observed the more traditional practice of following the coast, which arced in a northerly curve in the direction of Zhuya, and was a longer route but one that would require them to travel only twenty miles of open water between the mainland and the island, Pollio had to take the more direct, and potentially dangerous route across the open sea, a distance of one hundred eighty miles to reach the northwest corner of the island, then another fifty following the coast south to Yazhou, located at the southernmost part of the island. Although it was impossible to do so with absolute precision, Caesar's intention was to land both parts of his army as close to simultaneously as possible, at first light of the same day, which would be five days after leaving Ke Van. He also gave Pollio the discretion to postpone his landing at Yazhou by a day in the event they ran into foul weather while on the open water, knowing that, given the distance between what were the two largest cities on the island, there wouldn't be time for any kind of coordinated response. Between the two forces, Pollio's Legions had arguably the more difficult task, because they would be landing on the beach directly under the walls of Yazhou, similar to the landing at Muziris, but the walls of Yazhou were even closer to the low tide line than the Pandyan city had been. Caesar's force wouldn't face resistance immediately because they would be sailing up a river whose mouth was seven miles southwest of Hanou, but in another similarity to Muziris and the Pseudostoma, the river paralleled the coastline, and while the river eventually flowed past the walls of the city, it narrowed and was unnavigable by ships larger than a *bireme* a distance of four miles from the western wall. In both locations, Volusenus, guarded by a section from the Century accompanying him, had landed under the cover of darkness, moving into a position where he could examine the ground and the defenses of both cities while the *Philotemia* sailed back out to sea to a spot beyond the horizon with the other ships, with instructions to return every night. Taking care to stay under cover and moving slowly, Volusenus and the men with him spent two days outside Hanou, while Yazhou only required a day, but as thorough as he was, and with as much experience as he had in such matters, having scouted Pattala, Bharuch, and Muziris, he was equally aware of the likelihood he missed something, which he never failed to remind Caesar about. All he could do was hope that whatever it was didn't turn out to be catastrophic to their cause, making the voyage back to Hanou a trying time as he spent the time waiting racking his brain for anything he might have missed. In the case of Yazhou, while its proximity to the landing beach wasn't ideal, and they had learned that the Chinese used artillery, although not much was known about its range, the fact that the Romans would probably be within range of their artillery also meant the opposite was true, which was why Pollio had the bulk of the warships. Hanou's northern wall was more than five hundred paces from the shore, the city located in the elbow of the coastline where it curved from an east-west to a north-south orientation with a natural harbor formed by the coast continuing to curve to make an almost perfect semicircle, with the port that serviced the city on the eastern side of that semicircular small bay, with a sizable dock complex that was protected by the eastern wall of the city.

Unwilling to risk his men crossing the flat, level ground between the wall and beach on the north side, and unable to use his own shipborne artillery for support, nor willing to perform a repeat of their assault on Bharuch by running the ships of his Legions directly into the docks on the eastern side, Caesar's choices were limited. He had briefly considered swinging in a wide arc south after landing to essentially attack from the rear, but as thorough as Volusenus had been, he had deemed there was too much activity south of the city, where a sizable village had sprouted outside the walls that extended at least a mile south, leaving the western approach as the best option, but it had its own problems. In almost identical fashion to the Pseudostoma, the distance between the northern riverbank and the coastline was less than a mile wide, and the ground on either side of the riverbank was soggy, although Volusenus assured Caesar that it wasn't as bad as the ground north of Muziris, which was so bad that the 8th Legion had become so hopelessly mired that they couldn't even participate in the assault on the city. The question, which Volusenus couldn't answer to Caesar's satisfaction was whether or not the ground was firm enough for the heavy artillery to be transported, so it was left that only after they landed would Caesar make that determination. Another complicating factor was the river entrance, which was the narrowest part of the river at low tide, with only a hundred paces of it deep enough for the heavy ships to pass through, while at high tide it was almost three hundred. Like all experienced seamen, Lysippos had studied and made careful records of the tides in this part of the world, and Caesar trusted him enough to time their departure so that the tide would be high at daylight of the planned day of attack. Despite being confident in the overall plan, Caesar and his officers also knew that when the moment came, there would undoubtedly be something that went wrong, but they sailed with the confidence of the most veteran army, against the armies of more nations than any in history; whatever came up, they would adjust and prevail, of that they were all certain.

It had been a risk on the part of Lei to essentially go behind Xao's back, but he felt it worth the risk to send a secret order to the Qiongzhong, Lingshui, and the Qionghai garrisons, the three closest outposts on the southern side of the island, to shift all but one hundred men apiece to Yazhou, immediately. Of the three, he was most concerned with Qiongzhong, because it was inland, at the base of the Wuzhi Mountains, still the stronghold of those *Li* who had held aloof from Xao's offer of full rights in exchange for service to the general, but things had been quiet for the previous year, so he felt it worth the risk. He hadn't stopped there, sending similar orders to the garrison at Boon Siou, which was also on the southern side of the island, but at the eastern end, and the inland garrison at Tunchang, which was east of the Wuzhi. He also issued orders that placed the commander at Boon Siou, a grizzled veteran missing an ear named Yin Zhao, in overall command of what would be another two thousand men when the two forces met, directing them to march north to the village of Shishanzen, eight miles south from Hanou, knowing that having them arrive in the city beforehand would enrage Xao. He had taken another precaution as well, and that was to send his family to his estate inland, which he also did in secret, understanding that his general might view this as defeatist, but for all of Xao's bluster and insistence that there would be no attack on Zhuya from the *Gwai*, Lei could see that his commander was worried about that very thing. However, it suited both Lei and Xao's purposes that they carry out the pretense of preparing for another assault on Xuwen, which was why the harbor was now crowded with *chuan*. A good number of these *chuan* were now serving as floating barracks housing those *Li* who had chosen to follow Xao; Lei couldn't bring himself to call them soldiers, viewing them as not much better than a rabble of cutthroats, pirates, and thieves, though he had learned never to do so in front of the general. That Xao honestly believed that these men would prove to be reliable was yet another thing that had given Lei pause, but when he had decided to abandon his post in the Army of the Jiaozhi Commandery to follow the general, who had been enraged by Emperor Yuan's decision to give his rival Gan command of the Northern Army facing Zhizhi, he understood that their fates were now inextricably intertwined. All he could do was support Xao in every way he could; if that meant lying to him sometimes, then he honestly believed it was fated to be so, and now he had done all he could. There was nothing left to do but wait to see if Xao was right, or if Lei was, because he felt almost certain that they would be facing the *Gwai*.

Caesar's part of the fleet reached the finger of land that jutted out from the mainland that Volusenus measured as about twenty miles northeast of Hanou a watch before sunset on the day before the planned assault. This was the closest they had come to the island, and the tops of the mountains that dominated the central part of the island were just barely visible. While he insisted on his traditional meeting the night before a battle, it had been brief, and Pullus had returned to his ship sooner than Diocles had anticipated, meaning that he had to endure Pullus' grumbling that the evening meal wasn't ready, but Pullus occupied the time by holding a snap inspection of his Century. Which, of course, forced Balbus to do the same, despite the fact that he had already done as much while Pullus was gone. These prebattle inspections were only in name; this was when Pullus used the time to spend time with each of his men, which still was composed of Romans, being the First of the First, although there were now a handful of Parthians in the First Cohort, those who had served Rome since the first year of the Parthian part of the campaign, and one of them was in the Second Century. Normally, Pullus wouldn't have interfered with Balbus, but once he was through chatting with his men, when Balbus dismissed his own for a second time, he called to Mardonius before he could go below and he came immediately, standing at *intente* and, Pullus was pleased to see, looking very much as if he might jump overboard standing in front of his Primus Pilus, which was just how Pullus thought it should be.

"You know, Mardonius," Pullus spoke in a conversational tone, but the Parthian wasn't fooled into thinking this was a chat, "there's only one reason that you're in my Cohort. You know that, yes?"

"Yes, Primus Pilus," Mardonius answered immediately, not only because it was expected, but because he was aware that this was the truth, and he knew the reason.

"But if Pilus Prior Ausonius says you deserve to be in my Cohort, then that's good enough for me," Pullus said. Realizing something, he asked, "Did you know that he was the man who was the first to teach me how to fight?"

"I heard something about this, Primus Pilus," Mardonius replied cautiously, unsure how much to divulge, mainly because he had no idea how much was camp gossip and how much was fact.

"My best friend and I started pestering him when I was ten, and he was eleven," Pullus smiled at the memory. "But he kept refusing. Then," he laughed, "my sister told him one day, 'You may as well give in because Titus will never leave you alone.'" Realizing something, Pullus informed him, "He had married my sister not long before. But," he laughed again, "he held out for more than a year."

"When is the last time either of you heard from her, Primus Pilus?" Mardonius asked, then added with a laugh of his own, "She must not be very happy that her husband and her brother have been gone so long."

Pullus grimaced, not at the question but realizing he had inadvertently put the Parthian in an awkward position.

"She's dead now, Mardonius. She died a long time ago, when I was in Gaul."

"Oh, I am...sorry." Pullus waved it away, assuring him that no offense had been given, and Mardonius, hoping to move to a happier subject, unintentionally made things worse. "I did hear that you and your childhood friend joined together, and you were in the same section. And I know that Pilus Prior Scribonius was in your section; was that him?"

"No." Pullus shook his head, suddenly regretting having gone down this path. "His name was Vibius Domitius. He's back in Astigi. At least," he added, "he was when we left Brundisium. He left the Legion after our enlistment ended so that he could marry his childhood love."

This clearly startled Mardonius, who asked, "How long was your enlistment?"

"The same as yours," Pullus replied. "Sixteen years."

"And she waited for him all that time?" Mardonius gasped in surprise. "She must be quite a woman!"

This made Pullus laugh, and he shook his head as he assured the Parthian, "No, it didn't happen like that. She did wait almost seven years, but then she ended up marrying another man. But," he looked at Mardonius and grinned, "then he went and died, and made Vibius a happy man." He added quickly, "But yes, she was. She was quite a woman." Embarrassed now, Pullus returned to the original subject. "Anyway, I just wanted to let you know that tomorrow, you're going to have to show me that Pilus Prior Ausonius is right and prove that you're worthy of being in the First Cohort. Understand?"

Interpreting Pullus' tone perfectly, Mardonius stiffened back into a rigid *intente*, saluted, and said crisply, "I understand, and will obey, Primus Pilus." In a quieter voice, but in one that Pullus clearly heard the determination, he promised, "I will make Pilus Prior Ausonius proud, Primus Pilus, I swear it."

Rather than return the salute, Pullus grasped Mardonius by the shoulder, nodded, then said quietly, "Now, get below and try and get some sleep. A big day tomorrow."

He watched the Parthian hurry to the steep ladder that led down to the cramped space where hammocks were hung in tiers of four men, then turned and walked to the side of the ship facing the island. Why did I think about Vibius now? he wondered. Is it an omen? Will tomorrow finally be the day, the day when I'm a step too slow, or just unlucky? Shaking his head, he tried to banish the thoughts, knowing as always that giving in to them wasn't an option, and instead, as he always did, he began thinking of the practical things that he needed to remember for the next morning.

Hou-Chang Bao Xan, the commander of the guard for the night shift standing watch on the walls of Hanou was counting the *kè* (minutes) until they were relieved, wanting only to crawl onto his sleeping platform and get some rest. The one advantage of performing the night guard was that he and the seven *Sui* under his command, which in this period of time consisted of eleven men per *Sui*, wouldn't have duty until the sunrise after tomorrow, which meant that, after he rested, he would be able to go to the brothel and spend time with his favorite, Jiā, for whom he was saving up his money to buy from the brothel. Because his *Sui* were responsible for manning the ramparts of the northern and half of the western wall on this occasion, it meant that he spent most of his time walking back and forth since the northern side was almost ten *li*, while half the distance on the western wall was eight *li*. The boys of his seven *Sui*, which was how he thought of them because, for the most part, that was what they were, only needed a few swipes with his bamboo cane to remain alert and not for the first time did he think, For conscripts, they're not bad. They were all spearmen, part of the Leaping Dragon *Tu-wei-fu*, which was composed of spearmen and crossbowmen equally divided into eight *Hou*, four of each consisting of seven *Sui*, while there were two *Hou* of what Bao Xan longed to be a part of, the swordsmen who formed the backbone of the professional part of the Han army. He dreamed of distinguishing himself one day, and earning the attention of the *Hou-Kuan*, the rough equivalent of a Primus Pilus, because that was the one and only path to promotion, through the patronage of a superior officer. He himself hadn't seen much combat himself, participating in just two of what could only be called minor skirmishes back when General Xao was still loyal to the Emperor and was on Zhuya to bring the *Li* to heel and stamp out the last of their resistance to Imperial rule, and that had been more than eight years earlier, but that was still more than these conscripts had ever seen, and he liked to play the part of the grizzled veteran to them.

Like the other midlevel officers, he had heard rumors about the army of the *Gwai*, and because he consorted with the common people more than others of his class outside the military, he was certain that he had heard every tale of their savagery and their seemingly endless appetite for rape and slaughter. Being better educated than these people, Bao knew that these stories were undoubtedly exaggerated, but while he had been initially dismissive of these pale barbarians posing a threat to this island, it had been the behavior of General Xao's second in command, General Lei, that had made him take it more seriously. And, when several *chuan* owned by merchants that regularly sailed between the island and mainland had mysteriously vanished, it had increased the anxiety on the part of the populace that the *Gwai* were somewhere out there, lurking. Normally, this would have been easily explained as just another series of acts of piracy on the part of the *Li*, but there was now an at times uneasy cessation of hostilities between Xao and the part of his army who had chosen to follow him instead of vacating the island that had held for more than three years. The sudden increase in activity had been a surprise, as the Leaping Dragons, along with the other *Tu-wei-fu*, had been ordered to prepare for battle, but unlike the Romans, officers of the Han didn't feel the need to share anything with their subordinates when it came to reasons for whatever orders were given. However, much like the Romans, and the armies of every other nation, while there were secrets, there weren't nearly as many as the generals, and their Emperor, might have liked, and word quickly spread that the general was preparing not to defend the island, but to sail the ten miles across the Strait of Qiongzhou to try once again to take Xuwen. It had been the presence of the *chuan* gathering in the Hanou harbor that had convinced Bao this was the most likely, and he hoped that this time he would be allowed to participate instead of being left behind as part of the garrison, although he was thankful for it now, given the outcome of the assault. Such was his faith in General Xao that Bao was certain that being turned back from Xuwen twice wasn't possible, and given his own ambitions, it was vital that he be in one of the *chuan* on that day, whenever it came. This was what occupied his thoughts, even as he made what would be the last circuit of his part of the wall, the sky in the east turning pink, because once the sun was fully above the horizon that marked the end of the guard shift, and he wanted to time it so that he was at the end of his post on the western side, because the instant the horn sounded, his replacement and the men under his command would be waiting at the foot of the stairs.

By relieving his men from west to north, it meant that he would be closer to their barracks building when they finished, which in turn meant the sooner he could get some sleep. Since he arrived at the last post a bit early, with only half the sun showing, he occupied himself gazing at the sea, which was turning silver-gold from the light, lost in his thoughts and enjoying a moment of beauty as he thought of Jiā. He wasn't looking at anything in particular, yet something caught his eye, almost beyond the range of his vision, far out to sea to the west. Was something moving? he wondered, and it bothered him enough that he concentrated his attention, shading his eyes from the growing glare of the reflected light as the sun continued to rise. Bao was aware that there were giant sea creatures that roved in packs back and forth through the Strait; he had heard as much from the fishermen and the sailors who were happy to tell anyone who listened about their close call with one of these behemoths. He also knew that, while they lived in the sea, unlike smaller fish, they would come to the surface, and he had even heard that they used spouts of water that they somehow sent into the sky, but whether it was some sort of message to others of their kind, or an attempt to lure unwary sailors to investigate depended on which sailor was talking. Finally deciding that there *might* be something there, it wasn't enough to mention to the *Hou-Chang* who was relieving him; besides, the horn had just sounded, so he turned away to face the stairway, watching as his counterpart ascended the steps, whereupon they began the ritual of relieving Bao's men, and he quickly forgot all about it.

Like so many of Caesar's plans, his orders to begin moving south across the Strait while it was still dark so that they could reach the mouth of the river exactly when the sun rose to the point that it illuminated the narrow mouth of the river was timed so that they would be less than a mile away, ready to enter it at the first possible moment. While it was true that the mouth was seven miles from Hanou, and the walls were barely visible from where they were, several hundred ships filling the sea would look different enough to an observer even from that distance, so everything depended on the ability to sail through the narrow mouth three ships abreast, which was the most Lysippos would allow, as rapidly as possible, and Caesar had long before accepted the *navarch*'s expertise and deferred to his judgment. Even so, the men lining the rails of the outside ships of the first three vessels watched nervously as they slid past the sandbar on the eastern side, while the western side was a muddy, low bank. From Caesar's ship, in the middle of the first three, Lysippos shouted orders to the *navarchae* on either side because the narrowness of the channel wasn't the only challenge, the river then making a hard turn east towards the city immediately afterward, which remained the same width for about four hundred paces before it widened back out, meaning that the ship on the left had to make the hardest turn. Since they were first, they moved more slowly, but once the *navarchae* of the trailing ships, which were now arrayed three by three and sitting there rolling on the waves, watched Lysippos' maneuvers, they knew what to do, which did help speed up the process. Once the river opened out to its widest point of a half-mile, Lysippos maneuvered the *Polynike* closer to the southern side, which was heavily forested, allowing the ships carrying the Equestrians, followed by Batius' Alaudae, then Torquatus' 25th to row past. Aboard these vessels, men were making their final preparations, which for the Equestrians meant that only then were they required to don their armor, the sign that Pullus wasn't completely certain that Caesar's Luck would hold.

"If the boys have to swim," he had told his Pili Priores the night before when they came to receive their final orders from him, "I don't want them worrying about getting out of their *hamatae* in time."

Even as quickly as they were moving, the sun was more than a finger's width above the eastern horizon before the ships carrying the Legions and Caesar's part of the cavalry were past the entrance and at least rowing upriver, while the rest of Caesar's part of the fleet, the transports bearing supplies, remained off the coast where a small but still potent group of warships ringed the vessels that supported this massive effort. This portion of the fleet was commanded by Nero, and he had been given a potentially important task by Caesar; more importantly, at least to Nero, was how Caesar had characterized the task.

"I'm giving you an opportunity to exercise your judgment," Caesar had told him, then proceeded to explain what he wanted Nero to do.

Despite the manner in which he had put it, Caesar also knew that Nero would do exactly as he expected, in order to erase the stain on the patrician's conscience, not only for his decision to abandon the army, but because of the loss of the precious *quinquereme*, *quadriremes*, and the other craft that were now lying on the bottom of the bay at Ke Van. And, once the last of the ships carrying the men and horses who would be involved in the attack on the city negotiated the entrance, Nero wasted no time issuing orders of his own, leaving behind only three *triremes* to guard the transport ships, taking the rest of the armed vessels east, towards the city.

The first difficulty that Pullus encountered came when his *navarch* told him that he would have to debark a mile farther west than the plan called for, pointing ahead as he explained to Pullus, "See how much it narrows just up ahead? There is not going to be enough room to turn about safely once we unload you and your men so that the other ships can unload."

"But Legate Volusenus scouted this!" Pullus protested. "He said that it would be tight, but you should have enough room to head downstream back to the wide part of the river."

"He did," the *navarch* agreed grimly, "but he was wrong."

Pullus could just see the top of the mast of Caesar's flagship *Polynike* among the forest of smaller masts of the ships in between, but he could also tell that there was no practical way for him to communicate with Caesar, at least in a manner that wouldn't take too long.

Making his decision, Pullus told the *navarch* to choose a spot, then began bellowing, "All right, you lazy bastards! It looks like we're getting off early, so hurry up and get the ladders up on deck!"

It was, Pullus knew, a seemingly small thing, but now that the woodworking *immunes* had done enough testing to convince them that bamboo was actually superior in many ways to the solid wood ladders, it meant that each Century could carry more ladders, and more ladders meant the ability to get more men up on a wall more quickly. He had been one of the most skeptical, but once he had gotten, if not accustomed, then at least accepting of the fact that something could be as strong but at the same time be less rigid, and that just because it flexed it didn't mean that it would break under his weight, he had been convinced. There had been some experimentation with using bamboo as the shafts for javelins, but that hadn't been as successful. By the time the *navarch* nosed the ship up onto the muddy bank, Pullus' Century was ready to leap over the side,

155

and none of them were surprised when their Primus Pilus elbowed his *Aquilifer* Paterculus and the men of his First Section out of the way to hop up onto the side, then without any discernible hesitation, leap onto the bank...and promptly plunge calf-deep into the muck that had been disguised by the short, green grass. Later, it would provide for a great deal of amusement on the part of his men, but in the moment, none of them were foolish enough to laugh at the sight of their Primus Pilus struggling to extricate himself while bellowing with rage as he finally pulled first one leg, then the other free.

"Don't jump!" he shouted. "Lower yourselves over the side because by the time the First is unloaded, the other boys will be waist deep in this fucking mud!"

And, just that quickly, not only were the Romans farther away than the plan called for, but the actual unloading process would be much slower as, despite the warning, very quickly the ground on either side of the bow of the ship became a churned mass of black, sticky goo that was also extremely slippery, meaning that a significant number of men who struggled over to where their standard bearer had planted their standard on the northern bank were liberally coated with the stuff. Caesar's part of the attack was bogging down even before it got started.

Lei's extra precautions had paid dividends for the commander of the Yazhou garrison, Liu Zho, as the series of outposts atop the hills that were a feature of the southern shoreline lit the warning beacons as soon as the sentries manning one of them forty Roman miles from Yazhou first spotted the *Gwai* fleet materializing out of the hazy distance to the west. Within a Roman watch, Liu had been warned of the approach, giving him a critical full day to prepare for some form of action. General Lei had been maddeningly vague in the message that he sent alerting him to a possible threat and to expect reinforcements from the Qiongzhong, Lingshui, and Qionghai garrisons, the last of which had arrived the day before. It had made for cramped conditions in the two-story barracks located in the center of the small city of fifty thousand people, many of them refugees like himself from the mainland who were unhappy with the Emperor Yuan's policies, but the extra day gave him the time to think of a plan where he could use these extra men, though not within the city walls. The Han hadn't founded Yazhou; they had simply occupied what had been a sleepy fishing village that was fed by two rivers, the Sanya and the Linchun, which ran from north to south through the city, with the Sanya closest to the seashore, creating what was in effect an island that was almost two Roman miles long, upon which an earlier emperor of the Han had constructed the buildings that housed both the civil and military apparatus that was required to try and administer and control the southern half of the island. The southern end of the island terminated when the Linchun merged into the Sanya, which then made an almost ninety-degree turn to the west, where it emptied into the sea less than a half-mile away from the southwest corner of the city wall. Liu had briefly considered the possibility that the *Gwai* might try to sail up this channel but he quickly dismissed it; not only was it only two hundred fifty paces across, but on the other side of the channel there was the neck of a peninsula that jutted out in a southwest orientation that, when outlined on a map, reminded Zho of a half-eaten apple. At the top end of the apple closest to the walls, there was a hill, upon which a small stone fort had been placed, with the channel well within catapult and crossbow range. It was manned at all times, as it was now, but so convinced was he that the *Gwai* wouldn't attempt their landing there, he had stripped the pair of catapults to bring them into the city. If it hadn't been for the channel, which wasn't terribly deep but had a mud bottom, he would have concealed a force of men in the small fort, waiting to fall on the right flank of the *Gwai* who might be storming ashore. The road leading out of the western gate immediately turned north, following the rivers to where a small village was located a bit more than a mile from the northern wall, while the Sanya was half of a Roman mile from the shore. Although this might seem to be a perfect spot to land, the Han engineers who had constructed the defenses of the city had thought of this, because there was yet another small stone fort atop another one of the hills that broke up the area around Yazhou. It was too far from the beach for any kind of missile attack; while Zho was unaware of the *Gwai* capability with shipborne artillery, it would still prove too far for a *ballista* from one of the *quinqueremes*, which Volusenus had seen on his scouting trip.

Also helping his cause in protecting from an attack from a northern landing, just beyond the stone fort that would be in an enemy's rear when they moved towards the city was the presence of rice paddies in between the two rivers. The only other spot that was a possibility was the northwestern corner of the city wall on the opposite side from the southwestern wall, but again, this was where the hills provided aid to a defender. No, he was fairly certain that the *Gwai* commander would be landing on the beach below the western wall, but while completely ignorant of this parallel, like Nedunj of the Pandya, he wasn't willing to hide behind the walls for his defense. Unlike the Pandya, he had the advantage of the natural features in the wooded hills east of the city. This would be where the reinforcements from the garrisons would wait, and despite all that he had heard about the *Gwai* and their ferocity, he was coldly confident that there wasn't a force on earth that could defeat the Han, even without the help of the Emperor. There were two things that Liu Zho had no way of knowing, the first being that Yuan was hoping for a *Gwai* victory, but most importantly, he had never been alerted that several weeks before, the *Gwai* had already come to Yazhou, and had seen what Zho had seen...and had conceived a plan to defeat it.

The 12th with Pollio didn't face the same type of challenge as their comrades in the 10th, but it was equally as daunting, and more deadly, because Balbinus and his men were the first Romans to learn about the Han reliance on the crossbow. Things began well enough; because of the wide expanse of beach under the western wall of Yazhou, its proximity to the water, and the Han's ignorance of Roman artillery, as the plan called for, Pollio arrayed his warships broadside to the walls and began launching rocks and scorpion bolts. Meanwhile, what Balbinus guessed was at least eight or nine Han catapults carried out a counter barrage, loosing in the brief moment in between the incoming arcing rocks that were so devastating to these weapons, along with the scorpions with their flat trajectory that posed a threat to any Han who peeked his head between the high crenellations. Consequently, it became very clear to Liu that his artillery was inflicting minimal damage on the Romans as long as they remained offshore, ordering it to stop wasting ammunition. When Pollio ordered his *Cornicen* to sound the order for the ships carrying his men to head for the shore, Balbinus was standing in the prow of his *quadrireme*, watching the wall getting larger as the crew put their backs into their oars.

"Get ready to brace, boys!" he had shouted just before dropping to his knees onto the deck and grabbing the jutting prow just in time for the sudden shock as the ship slammed into the sand of the beach with enough force that it slid several feet out of the water in a spray of water and sand. Leaping up even as it was coming to a stop, like Pullus, Balbinus was the first over the side, calling over his shoulder as he did, "Who's going to beat me for the *Corona Murales*, eh, boys?"

While Balbinus' Legion had been part of the assault on Muziris, the 12th had been assigned the task that was essentially the one his friend and Pullus' rival Equestrians were carrying out now, although it was on a different city, and as soon as Pullus had learned their respective missions prior to their departure, Pullus had warned him about watching for some sort of surprise from the Han, similar to that pulled by Nedunj, back when he had been an untested Crown Prince. Consequently, he kept his attention on Yazhou, not on the ramparts, but on the ground between where he was standing and the wall, waiting for enemy warriors to suddenly materialize up out of the ground as the Pandya had when the 10th landed. Nothing of that nature happened, however, and once the First and Second Century had unloaded, their ship back oared while Balbinus ordered his last section to help by pushing against the prow to free it, and it slid away, leaving a huge gouge in the sand. Along the beach to his left, the other ships carrying the first four Cohorts of the 12th disgorged their passengers, led by their Centurions and *Signiferi*, who all rushed forward about thirty paces from the surf, with the rest of each Century using them as reference points to get into their formations.

Balbinus kept his eyes on the wall, particularly the large wooden gate, waiting for it to swing open as the Han defenders inside sallied forth, but when nothing happened, he began to relax, at least in a relative sense. Being the Legion on the right, and because the Romans knew a bit about the Han's capabilities with artillery, he had ordered his *Aquilifer* to align himself at a point that would put them out of range of any artillery that might have been in the small stone fort, perched atop the hill immediately to their right, the slope heavily forested save for around the top, which had been cleared to give the occupants of the fort a clear view. He had been informed of the presence of the fort thanks to the information Volusenus had gathered, and now that he had seen it, he concurred with the Legate's estimate that it could hold perhaps five hundred men but not many more. Nevertheless, Balbinus had already instructed his Primus Princeps Posterior in command of the Fourth Century, who would have normally aligned immediately behind Balbinus' Century, to instead array in a perpendicular manner facing the small hill, with orders to sound the alert if the Han somehow managed to hide more men out of sight, perhaps on the opposite side. What mattered to him in the moment was that the first four Cohorts of his 12th signaled their readiness to advance faster than the other two Legions in this first wave of the assault, Cartufenus' 28th, which was to their immediate left and in the center, aligning roughly with the western gate, with the 15th of Aquilinus on the opposite side, who had also been given the latitude to send part of his Legion around the corner of the northwestern wall to try and send men up the ladders on the northern side, while Balbinus didn't have that option for the simple reason that it would place the small fort to the rear of any men he sent to scale the southern wall. To his surprise and bitter anger, it was actually the *Cornicen* of the 15th who played the notes signaling they were ready to advance; that it was by a matter of heartbeats didn't do anything for his temper, or his coin purse. The 28th was ready a few heartbeats later, and as had been agreed earlier, the men of these three Legions immediately began their advance in unison at the last note.

"All right, boys," Balbinus bellowed, "we may not have been first to form up, but we fucking better be the first on the walls, or I'm going flay some of you!"

He was moving as he was shouting this, and over the

hissing sound of the waves crashing onto the beach behind them, he could hear his boys mumbling to each other, or offering up a prayer, while his eyes never wavered from the wall, his mind only on what was waiting for them. By this time, the Han had been introduced to not just the Romans' *ballistae*, but their scorpions, so he wasn't surprised that the gaps between the crenellations were empty of men. He also knew it couldn't last because Pollio would order the artillery to cease once he saw the Centuries leading the assault draw closer to the walls.

It was with this in mind, he called out, "All right, boys! We don't know much about these slanty-eyed *cunni*, but they're likely to have archers, so keep your eyes up, and be ready for the *testudo*!"

The ground sloped up gently from the beach, though only a couple dozen feet, so he could clearly see the ground between, and because of Pullus' warning, he was searching what seemed to be nothing but open earth, though dotted with a few stumps, trying to find any signs that the ground, which was covered with a short type of grass that was no more than ankle high, had been disturbed at all. He quickly determined that there wasn't a hidden trench where Han soldiers were waiting as had happened in Muziris, but he still alternated his scrutiny between the wall, which was now looming larger with every pace, standing almost fifteen feet tall and made of dressed stone, and searching the ground for the Han equivalent of Caesar's Lilies. They were close enough now that he could hear shouting drifting across the closing space between the wall and his men, though even if it had been distinct, he would have no idea what was being said, but to his ear, it had the same kind of urgency that indicated someone was giving orders. Then, as, his leading ranks reached an invisible line, the Han finally responded, as what was later counted to be fifteen catapults hidden from Roman eyes launched their deadly cargoes.

"*Ballistae!*"

Balbinus wasn't the one who shouted it, nor was he looking at the right part of the wall to spot the streaking rock just after it was launched, although dozens of his men did, including his *Aquilifer*, who cried out as he pointed to it, but the rock was moving too quickly for Balbinus to spot it. He heard the result, however, in a gut-wrenching combination of a sharp cracking noise accompanied by a scream of pain and cries of alarmed fear, so closely behind him that, despite knowing it could be fatal to himself, he looked over his shoulder, instantly wishing that he hadn't. The first rock had landed in the middle of the third rank of his Century, but it was the frantic motion of men scrambling to close the bloody gap in his formation that informed him that at least two men were either dead or at best, out for this action only. It was the sight of the blood splashed on the shield of his Third Section man, looking as if someone had thrown a large cup of red paint at it, that told him the former was a virtual certainty, and he tried to think of who had stood fourth from the right in his Third Section; was it Frontinus? While it was a distraction that only lasted a heartbeat, it also meant that he reacted late to the sudden appearance of Han soldiers who finally stepped out from behind the taller stone crenellations, although it wouldn't have mattered.

"*Arch...*"

That was all that the Sergeant of his First Section got out before, moving far more quickly than Balbinus had ever seen, a flurry of missiles shot out from the wall, but in a flatter trajectory that made Balbinus immediately think of their own scorpions. His Sergeant, Aulus Terentinus, had the unfortunate distinction of being the first Roman to encounter the Han crossbow, taking a bolt right through the mouth even as he was shouting his warning. In an eyeblink, the noise level dramatically increased, but it was the cracking sound of missiles striking shields that sounded to Balbinus more like a sling bullet that gave him his first indication they were encountering something new and, worst of all, unexpected. Even with the shouts of men voicing their alarm, competing with the shrieks of pain and the din of what, faster than he ever thought possible, became an almost constant patter of cracking noises as the shorter bolts of the Han crossbow savaged his men, Balbinus would later recall thinking, First it was naphtha that we didn't know about, then it was elephants we didn't know about, and now this?

"*Form testudo!*"

Hearing the shouted command of his Primus Pilus

Posterior Tiberius Macula, who had replaced Vibius Censorinus after he was decapitated during the river assault on Muziris, Balbinus bellowed more loudly than he ever had in his life, "*No! No testudo!*" knowing that it would give the Han catapults a huge target, but his command was drowned out by the *Cornicen* of the Second Century, playing the notes that relayed that order, although the *Cornicen*, in his excitement, forgot to play the two quick notes that told the rest of the Centuries the order was only for the Second Century.

Balbinus had drawn a shield from stores, and he did hold it a bit higher to provide protection as he twisted about and shouted at his own *Cornicen*, "Sound the cancel order!"

The words were barely out of his mouth when the *Cornicen*, Titus Barbatus, was struck in the upper chest by a bolt that had skimmed just over his own shield, the smaller round one strapped to his left arm that all *Signiferi* and *Corniceni* used to keep both hands free, knocking him flat.

"Keep going!" Balbinus snapped to Petronius, the 12th's *Aquilifer* even as he dropped to a crouch, but rather than checking on Barbatus, who was conscious and moaning, the bolt embedded half its length just below his right clavicle, the Primus Pilus snatched up the horn without a word to the fallen man. Remaining in his crouch, while holding the shield up and pointed towards the wall, Balbinus stood there, waiting for the ranker in the Eighth Section who served as the replacement *Cornicen*. Once he spotted him, Balbinus shouted, "Serpentius! Attend to me; you're the *Cornicen* now!"

Even as the Primus Pilus was doing what was necessary, the Second Century had already contracted into their *testudo*, and they had managed to move about five paces closer before whoever commanded the Han artillery had the three catapults within range adjust their aim to where the Second was moving, smoothly and currently intact, moving inexorably towards the wall. Just as Balbinus handed Serpentius the *cornu*, the first two, and a heartbeat later, the third rock came hurtling down to smash into the Second Century, and the noise it made was a sound that Balbinus would never forget. More crucially, one of his Centuries not only ceased their progress, turned into a stationary mass of human wreckage, but they blocked the Fifth

Century from moving up...and the assault had barely begun.

It took well more than a third of a watch before all of the 10th, and half of the 5th was unloaded and formed up, with a substantial number of the men coated in mud up to their knees, and in dozens of cases, their *hamatae* were caked with the foul-smelling muck; the mules carrying the pieces of the artillery, despite it being only scorpions and the lightest *ballistae* in their arsenal struggled the most, universally filthy up to their bellies. In order to expedite the process, Caesar had actually issued new orders for two of the other three Legions to debark wherever they happened to be along the river and onto the northern bank, but in a last-moment change, chose to keep the 14th aboard. Once the other Legions were all on shore and assembled, they immediately began the march towards the city, taking advantage of the firmer ground away from the river, but they still had farther to march than planned. Pullus, understandably, was in a foul mood, although he did offer a muttered thanks to the gods that only his lower legs below the knees were black from the muck, but the practical problems couldn't be ignored. The 10th had followed their orders, marching closer to the city to make room for the other Legions, stopping at the point where the 5th was supposed to align themselves to the 10th's left, while Torquatus and his 25th would be closest to the Strait, but the delay was chafing at Pullus, who knew that, if anything, his general was even more impatient. And, with every passing moment, the chance of any kind of surprise was rapidly vanishing, despite Caesar's order to debark the cavalry on the southern bank of the river, with orders to move rapidly towards Hanou to sweep up any of the peasants in the handful of ramshackle buildings interspersed between a combination of fallow fields and flooded paddies. There was a forest that began a mile from the western wall of the city that screened the Legions from being seen from the city walls, but the likelihood of a large body of armed men not being spotted by a farmer, or even a traveler heading into the city was high under the best of circumstances; the longer distance and the difficulty of the unloading process meant that Pullus felt fairly certain that their presence had already been detected. And, since Caesar was still aboard the *Polynike*, he made the decision on his own.

Turning to Valerius, he ordered, "Sound the alert to advance." The use of the *cornu* had been discouraged by the general but not expressly forbidden, and waiting to see the Cohort standards of his first line Cohorts dip in acknowledgement, once they did, he ordered, "Sound the advance."

Their original landing spot would have placed them a mile from the western edge of the forest, but with twice the distance to cover, Pullus decided that getting into the cover of the forest faster was more important than ensuring that the advance was coordinated with the other Legions. His Legion stepped off, the second line following the first, the third following the second, while Pullus alternated between scanning the ground ahead, and looking across the river, but to this point, the only movement he saw were mounted men that belonged to their own cavalry and who were now advancing on their own along the road that led to the city from the west. He briefly thought about the people whose lives would be ending; the farmers who, hearing approaching hoofbeats, stepped out of their hut to see men of a race they had never seen before just before they were cut down. It was only a passing one, however; this had happened more times than he could count by now, and it was something that every Roman under the standard knew about but rarely spoke of, how people whose only crime was to be in the way of the Legions as they brought death and destruction to their lands would inevitably die. He did appreciate that it was a bit cooler than he had expected, then reminded himself that it was still in early Februarius, and how the seasons in this world were only marked by the amount of rain and not the temperature. Every few paces, he checked on his men, but they were universally stone-faced, the files carrying the ladders no longer struggling as they did when they carried the heavier ladders made of solid wood. These had been constructed based on Volusenus' estimate of the height of the walls, and while he trusted the Legate, Pullus also knew that measuring things from a distance could be tricky, and he ran over in his mind what he would do if the ladders came up a few feet short, as they had during their assault on Seleucia. This was when he realized that he hadn't thought to assign men to carry any of their tools that might prove useful, specifically their axes or spades. He supposed that they could use their *gladii* to hack one ladder into enough pieces to allow them to lash the piece to another ladder to extend the distance, but he hoped that he wouldn't need to. It did serve to remind him of all the other times when, in the period just before the killing, and the dying, began, he would think of something that he had forgotten, and he did wonder if there would ever be a battle where he remembered everything, and if so, what it would mean.

"Primus Pilus?"

Looking over at Paterculus, he got the sense that the *Aquilifer* had called his name more than once, but he looked where Paterculus was pointing off to their right, and saw a mounted man galloping up to the opposite side of the river, recognizing Decimus Silva. Breaking into a trot, Pullus approached the riverbank, where Silva waited long enough to be sure he was heard.

"There was a group of horsemen," he called out through cupped hands. "We're sure that they were Han cavalry, but while we caught most of them, at least one got away!"

Despite suspecting this was going to happen, Pullus cursed bitterly.

"How long ago?"

"Not long," Silva replied grimly, "but long enough that he's already in the city."

Bao Xian had decided to eat before he went to sleep, so he hadn't been asleep long when his rest was shattered, and even before he was fully aware of what was going on, he was on his feet, blinking rapidly as he rushed to the door of his room that, as tiny as it was, was still a luxury in the Han army. Jerking open the door, the first thing he saw was one of his fellow officers, fumbling with his sword belt, and he called to him.

"What is it? What's happened?"

The other officer, who was concentrating on the buckle of the belt, barely glanced up as he said, "It's the *Gwai*. They're here."

"Their fleet?" Bao gasped, but his initial alarm was nothing compared to the feeling when his comrade, finally getting the belt buckled, looked up at him to say, "No, their army is here as well. And they're only five of six *li* from the city and marching this way."

Bao didn't have any memory of the next few moments; all that mattered was he somehow ran into the large room that served as the barracks for the spearmen of the Leaping Dragons wearing his armor and carrying his helmet, to find that his men were all moving and, even better, had donned their own armor and helmets so that he immediately began shouting orders to follow him outside. The large courtyard, surrounded on four sides by the two-story buildings that served as the barracks for the entire *Tu-wei-fu*, one of five such buildings in the city, was already filling up. The noise of all the shouted orders bounced off the walls in an echoing racket that made it hard to differentiate between officers, but gradually, order was restored to the point that *Hou-Kuan* Zhou Fang, standing on the second floor overlooking the courtyard, was able to address his Leaping Dragons.

"A cavalry scout arrived in the city to report that there is a large force marching towards us from the west, where they sailed several *li* up the Dongshui. They were spotted four *li* west of the forest on the north side of the Dongshui. General Xao believes that they don't intend to swing south to attack our southern wall but are going to assault the western wall. I asked General Xao for the honor of leading the Leaping Dragons as part of the force defending against these *Gwai* invaders." Zhou paused, then hardened his voice to shout, "The General agreed! We will be the men to crush the *Gwai* invaders when they try to scale our western wall!"

Frankly, Bao had never heard such a deafening noise as the one that erupted now, but his voice was one of them as the men of the Leaping Dragon *Tu-wei-fu* gave their commander their promise, but Zhou cut them off quickly with a clenched fist.

"We don't have time! All *Hou-Chang* attend to me for your orders! *Sui-Chang*, check your men and their equipment!"

Bao broke into a run, joining the other officers as they rushed for the stairs, jostling each other in their attempt to show Zhou that they were the most eager to reach him. Standing with

Zhou was Chun Guo, his second in command, the pair speaking in low tones as they waited for the others to join them to stand around Zhou, who had iron gray hair that was pulled back, while his mustache, which had more black in it, hung down below his clean-shaven chin; it was the milk-white eye and jagged scar that began above his eyebrow and traced what always reminded Bao of a lightning bolt diagonally down to the outer corner of his right eye, the scar ending on his cheekbone that made Zhou so intimidating to his officers and men alike.

"We will be on the wall, between the southwestern corner and the second stairway," Zhou began, then turned and, to Bao's surprise, addressed him. "*Hou-Chang* Bao, your spearmen will be the anchor on the left, and you will be supported by *Hou-Chang* Xun's crossbowmen. Go now to take your position."

Both officers offered the Han version of a salute, which to Romans appeared to be nothing but a quick bow, then Zhou dismissed them, and the pair turned and trotted back to the stairs, while Bao wondered; does Zhou know that we despise each other? In a sign that Xun's mind was moving along the same lines, he gave Bao a grin that had no friendship in it as he taunted, "You know that this means, Bao. Jiā is as good as mine now."

Bao, doing his best to sound disinterested, asked as they began to descend the stairs side by side, "How did you come to this conclusion?"

"Because," Xun replied cheerfully, "you will either be dead or *Hou-Kuan* Zhou will decorate me for bravery and mention me to General Xao, who will undoubtedly reward me!"

"Easy to say," Bao snarled, trying to hide how shaken he was. "But it will be the other way around!"

"We'll see," Xun sneered, but he was already heading towards his crossbowmen who, while they were wearing the same armor made of lamellar rectangles of stiffened leather sewn in overlapping rows, also had large leather bags slung over their shoulders that carried their supply of bolts.

Bao desperately wanted to offer a retort, but by the time he thought of something, Xun was already several paces away, where his men were surrounding him, so Bao did the same, calling his *Sui-Chang*, the rough equivalent of section leaders, to him.

"We've been given a great honor," Bao said, trying to sound as matter-of-fact as he could. "We will be anchoring the Leaping Dragons at the southwest corner of the wall, and the Leaping Dragons will be the first to face these *Gwai* demons!" He would have preferred a bit more of an enthusiastic response on the part of his *Sui-Chang*, but he couldn't really blame them, so instead, he said simply, "Gather the men; we have no time to lose."

The men obeyed readily enough, and Bao took a certain amount of pride in reaching the arched gateway that opened onto the street that they would have to follow to get to their spot before Xun's *Hou*, but it was short-lived, because he and his men stepped out into chaos. Only then did he realize that he had been hearing the panicked shouting of the people of the city, but he had been so occupied that he barely noticed. The street was packed with people, all of whom seemed to be heading somewhere, yet Bao didn't have the sense any of them knew where they were going, and he was quickly reduced to shoving anyone who wasn't quick enough to scramble out of the way before, finally, more out of frustration than any desire to cut down anyone, he drew his sword, eliciting shrieks of fright from both women and men. What mattered was that this did wonders to clear a path, and he quickened his pace until reaching the street that terminated at the western wall, then paused for a couple heartbeats, watching as his men caught up, trying to determine their state of mind. When the last *Sui-Chang* at the end of the procession thrust his spear into the air to let him know they were together, Bao resumed, but fortunately the traffic was considerably thinner. This initially puzzled Bao, until he decided that it was probable that the civilians had learned that it was from this side of the city the *Gwai* were approaching. Whatever the case, he appreciated the space, enabling him to quickly reach the stairs and lead his men up to the rampart, the surface made of thin layers of stone over a wooden deck and ten paces across, although more than half of its width jutted out from the wall, supported by stone columns upon which the wooden decking was lain. Puffing as he scrambled up the wooden stairs, he was pleased that he saw no sign of Xun, and when he looked in the opposite direction, his heart leapt at the sight; he was the first man to the wall!

Although, he thought guiltily, it was really he and his men, not just himself, but it still lifted his spirits, and he sounded almost merry as he shouted over his shoulder, "Follow me, men! We're not only the first on the wall, but we'll be the ones who spill the most *Gwai* blood!"

The ragged response, he told himself, is because they're out of breath, but he continued moving at a brisk trot, glancing to where the line of trees looked somewhat hazy in the humid morning, though this wasn't uncommon. Before he reached the corner, he saw another group of men moving at the same pace trotting west on the southern wall, heading for the same corner, and for a heartbeat, he felt a stab of dismay, thinking that it was Xun, but to his relief, while they were crossbowmen, they belonged to the Pacing Tigers *Tu-wei-fu,* whose barracks were closer to the southern wall. He only knew the *Hou-Chang* by sight, but whereas they were normally fierce rivals, today was a day for amity, and he gave his counterpart a genial wave.

"The *Gwai* don't know what's waiting for them, eh, *Hou-Chang?*" he called to the other man, who smiled and, with the same tone that meant his men could hear, just as Bao had done, he replied, "No they don't, but they're about to find out, and they're going to wish their ancestors had never been born!"

Bao made sure to laugh heartily, and he was encouraged to hear his own men just behind him do the same. Stopping so he was essentially wedged into the corner, he allowed his *Sui-Chang*, going by the number of their *Sui*, to array themselves so that a pair of men could defend each gap in the crenellation, although at first they would have to stand aside for Xun's crossbowmen until the moment the enemy reached the wall, when it would become his spearmen's fight. His mood was helped when he saw his rival, his face red and puffing from the effort, only coming into view once Bao's men had already arranged themselves.

"Good of you to join us, Xun," Bao called out, making sure he could be heard, not just by his own men, but by Xun's, and he was rewarded with a poisonous glare.

"We had to draw our bolts," Xun said stiffly, to which Bao made a show of yawning.

Before Xun could say anything else, he turned to look at the forest, saying, "We haven't seen any sign of them yet, but they will probably be here soon."

As he hoped, this quelled any urge by Xun to try and continue their bickering, which Bao knew was petty. More importantly, his stomach had started to clench as what they were about to face became more real, and Xun seemed to be of the same mind, the pair standing side by side, staring at the forest, the ribbon of water that could barely be called a river by the point it flowed along the southern wall a short distance away gleaming in the sunlight.

"I think it will be hot today," Xun said suddenly, but he kept his eyes on the trees, so Bao did the same, answering politely, "I agree. I'm already sweating, and," he glanced up at the sun, "it's not even close to midday yet."

"Maybe there will be a breeze soon," Xun commented. "It usually starts in the afternoon."

"That's true," Bao replied. "I've always liked..." He stopped, and without thinking, grabbed Xun's arm while pointing to the edge of the forest where the river ran just a few paces away to the south. "I saw something!"

"What?" Xun frowned. "I don't see..." Then, excitedly, "Yes! I see it too. It was a flash of something silver."

They weren't the only ones who had seen some sort of movement, and a sudden hush fell over all of the defenders arrayed near the southwestern corner, but they were forced to wait because nothing else happened that was worthy of attention.

After a span of a few dozen heartbeats where there were no other signs of any enemy presence, it was Xun who guessed correctly, "They must be waiting for something."

This was exactly what was happening, as the 10th Legion came to a halt more than a hundred paces from the eastern edge of the forest to wait for their comrades. Now that the element of surprise was gone, all that was left was an overwhelming display of power, and to that end, Pullus called for his runner.

"Head down past the Fourth Cohort and wait for Primus

Pilus Batius. Tell him that they're waiting for us, and I'm bringing my artillery *immunes* up front to assemble the small *ballistae*, and I suggest he do the same."

For the next third of a watch, the clash between Han and Roman would be nothing but a staring contest.

For Asinius Pollio, standing on the deck of the *quinquereme* that was his flagship, the feeling he was experiencing watching the 12th, 28th, and 15th being pounded by the Han defenders was eerily reminiscent of when he had been with Caesar at Muziris. No, there hadn't been any hidden bowmen outside the walls, but while the Pandyans had had artillery, it wasn't in the same numbers as the Han. However, there was something else going on that Pollio was too far away to see with any clarity other than the result, which was the leading Centuries of the three Legions slowing to a shuddering crawl that left fallen men in their wake, either sprawling in the sign all veterans knew signaled a mortal wound, or thankfully more commonly, rolling their bodies into a tight ball and dragging their shields over their bodies as they waited for aid. After the catastrophe when the Second Century had gone into *testudo* for reasons Pollio could only guess at, only to be immediately ripped apart by what he counted as three near-simultaneous strikes from rocks launched by the defenders, they had returned to an open formation like the other Centuries so that any strike by a rock wasn't as devastating. Yet, men were falling, despite Pollio straining to see the cause, searching the sky just above the wall for the arcing missiles that would tell him the Han had more archers than anticipated, but even after he called to the Rhodian first mate who served as the lookout because of his sharp vision, who assured him that there weren't any arrows being launched, it was still a mystery. It had to be something with a flat trajectory, like a scorpion, but they couldn't have that many scorpions, and the only other weapon like that was the sling, but Pollio had seen slingers from this distance, and their movement was distinctive and easy to spot, especially when it was dozens of men. More telling was that he could make out that there were a pair of Han soldiers stepping into the gaps between crenellations at the same time, something that would be impossible for slingers because of the room they needed to move their arms. Whatever it was, while it hadn't stopped the men completely, it had slowed them considerably. Finally, the First and Second Cohorts of the 12th reached the base of the wall first, reminding Pollio that there was undoubtedly some sort of wager involved among the Centurions that caused them to drive their men to be the first there. He heard a *cornu* call, but he didn't recognize it immediately, but instantly, the Centuries of the second line began moving to attach themselves to the rear of the Centuries ahead of them in the First Cohort of the 12th.

Realizing what Balbinus was doing, he turned to shout at the *Cornicen* who was standing a couple paces away, ordering, "Play the signal for relief in place, all Centuries, all..."

Before he was finished, however, there was an eruption of new sounds, in the form of *cornu* commands, as the other Centurions of the first four Cohorts of the 12th instantly understood what their Primus Pilus was attempting, which was quickly copied by the 28th, and the 15th. The second line Cohorts had already unloaded, marching up to the edge of where the ground was scarred and littered with the smooth round stones that marked the outer limit of the Han catapults, while the third line Cohorts were just beginning to leap over the sides of their transports. The casualties had been extremely heavy, but Pollio was too far away to see the shorter bolts that might have given him a hint of what type of weapon the Han possessed, although he was slightly heartened to see how many of the fallen had had the strength to pull their shields over them while curling up into a ball if they were small enough or weren't too badly wounded. It was something that Pollio had first learned in Gaul; not only did this help preserve Roman lives, it gave a commander an opportunity to see his losses, and on this day, they were already daunting. Pollio could only watch helplessly, unwilling to risk Roman lives with an errant scorpion bolt or rock in support of his assaulting men, and it was obvious the Han realized this, because now the gaps between crenellations were completely filled with men who, from that distance, appeared as if they were wearing black, although it could have been the distance. Finally, he saw the first ladder rising up above the upraised shields of Balbinus' Century, followed quickly by a second, then a third, reminding Pollio that they could now carry four ladders per Century because of the lighter weight of the bamboo. Tearing his eyes from Balbinus' Cohort, he scanned the line all the way down to the western gate, where the Second Cohort of the 28th was located, and he started to feel cautiously optimistic that they had absorbed the worst of the punishment. He turned to Africanus, who, over Pollio's objections, Caesar had assigned as his Tribune instead of Artaxerxes, preparing to order him to run the pennant up to the top of the mast that was the signal for the ships of the 8th and the 21st to begin rowing towards the shore, when he saw something out of the corner of his vision. Even then, it took him a moment to identify what had caught his eye, the figure of a man, a member of the crew of the *quadrireme* three ships down from his own to his right, waving frantically.

"Thrust your standard up in the air!" Pollio called down to his personal standard bearer, which was nothing more than a large rectangular piece of red wool with a large P stitched in golden thread on it, but of all Caesar's Legates, Pollio was the least vainglorious, taking the ribbing from his fellow Legates, and Caesar, with his usual good grace about such a simple symbol.

Keeping his eyes on the man, who was clinging to the top of the mast as he stood on what Pollio knew was a perilously small piece of wood fastened to the mast, the lookout waved an acknowledgement with his free hand, then after a pause, pointed in the direction of the shore. At first, Pollio thought that he was indicating the corner of the wall, and he spent a moment watching as a Centurion, wearing the white crest that identified him as Balbinus, had just begun his ascent on the ladder nearest to the corner, but as he stared, he didn't see anything that warranted this kind of reaction. He began to face back to the lookout to hold his hands out in a gesture that needed no translation, then he saw something, not anywhere along the wall but on the wooded slopes of the low hill. Something was moving through the trees, about halfway up the slope, yet he couldn't determine what it was, other than it was something large, and for a brief moment he experienced the flash of fear

Caesar Ascending – The Han

of the same type as the first time he had faced elephants on their march to Bharuch. Do the Han have elephants? he thought, with real dismay, although even as this came to him, he knew that down below were crates of naphtha, but then he realized what it was; it was a column of men, and they were using the cover of the trees on the slope below the stone fort, where nothing had stirred or shown any signs of life.

"They're trying to flank us."

Unaware that he was the one who said it, Pollio suddenly tore his gaze away and hopped down off the crates lashed together and secured to the deck that served as his platform, shouting at Africanus to bring the map as he did so.

To the Tribune's credit, he didn't hesitate, dashing into the cabin below the raised rear deck then returning with the map, which Pollio examined, though only for a brief moment. Turning back to his *Cornicen*, he snapped, "Alert the 21st that new orders are coming!"

As the horn player obeyed, Pollio jumped up back on the crates, but instead of facing towards the city, he faced out to sea, finding the *quadrireme* carrying Primus Pilus Papernus, identifying the ship by seeing the Centurion standing in the prow. Seeing Papernus looking at him, Pollio held both arms straight up, held them there long enough to ensure that Papernus was watching, which the Centurion signaled with a wave, then crossed them once, returned them to their original position, then did it again. Despite having gone over this more than once, Pollio was still relieved when Papernus thrust an arm up into the air, then turned and disappeared from view as he hopped down from the small, raised bow deck, but what mattered was that, suddenly, the oars that had been steadily hanging above the water suddenly dropped in with a splash, but thrust in the opposite direction than normal, and at the same time, Pollio heard the notes that he knew was Papernus' *Cornicen*. Waiting just long enough to hear the cacophony of discordant notes coming from the ships surrounding Papernus and see the ships beginning to slow, Pollio turned back to the beach, a smile on his lips that offered nothing but cruel satisfaction.

Feeling he should say something to Africanus, who hadn't been involved in the planning, he said jovially, "Well,

Africanus, it looks like the Han had a trick up their sleeve." He pointed over to the hill, where it was now impossible to miss the sight of what was clearly a large group of Han warriors making their ways through the trees, heading downslope, and when Africanus, following his finger, saw it, he let out a gasp, turning back to look at Pollio wide-eyed, who assured him, "Don't worry. We anticipated that this might happen, and we developed a plan in that event. Now," he turned back to the stern, seeing that the ships had begun reversing their course, "we have a trick of our own to play."

It was the wait that was hardest, not just for Bao, but for his men, and for Xun, who for once had nothing acerbic to say to his rival, nor did Bao feel like trading insults. After the first flash of silver, he had stared until his eyes watered, but it wasn't for several *kè* before there was another movement, though not in the same spot but in the direction of the shoreline. There was a shout from one of the other officers farther down the wall, unleashing another small uproar, but this time, it was Xun who spotted it first.

"There!" He pointed to a spot perhaps four hundred paces north from where Bao had made the first sighting. "It looks like a line of men!"

This time, Bao was able to spot them instantly, and his heart immediately began to gallop in his chest as he realized that he had been secretly hoping that this was all an elaborate ruse of some sort by General Xao to test their readiness. A few hundred heartbeats later, there was more movement, and this marked the moment where the coming assault became more distinct, as Bao saw what turned out to be a long line of armored men materialize out of the woods. Given the distance, it was impossible to make out any level of detail, but Bao could see that red seemed to be the predominant color at first, only gradually becoming recognizable as large shields. His next observation was more of a visceral feeling in seeing how neatly aligned the ranks were, and how precisely subdivided into what he determined was a series of larger units subdivided into smaller units.

"Have you ever seen anything like this?"

Bao glanced over at Xun in a little surprise; it was Xun who had more experience in combat than Bao, having participated in the failed assault on Xuwen, but he answered honestly, "No." Feeling obligated, he pointed out, "We're trained to keep our spacing like that as well."

"True," Xun granted, his eyes never leaving the approaching army, "but not to this degree."

It was true, Bao knew, but rather than dwell on it, he decided to do something practical; now that they were closer, it enabled him to do a count, which he announced, "They're marching in ranks ten men across, but you can see that there are files with men missing." Suddenly thinking of something, he said excitedly, "They're not organized all that differently than we are! We have eleven men per *Sui*, they have ten men in a rank."

He was surprised when Xun just nodded thoughtfully, then after a silence, he pointed out, "But it looks like they have ten *Sui* per *Hou*, while we only have seven. And," he moved his finger as he counted each Century, "they have six *Hou Kuan* per *Tu-wei-fu*."

Bao didn't respond immediately, not because he disagreed, but because a second line of *Gwai* had appeared from the forest, about a hundred paces behind the first line, and he noticed something.

"This first line has four *Tu-wei-fu*, but the second one only has three," he said, then added hopefully, "so that's not so bad, eh?" Glancing to his right, he could see a second group of men, differentiated not just by their spacing, but because he could now see another of whatever the silver thing was on top of a pole carried by a man, correctly intuiting this marked them as being a separate unit. "Adding them together, they have fourteen *Tu-wei-fu*, which is a lot, but we have our walls, and our catapults."

While Bao had been examining what he would never know was the 5th Legion, Xun had been watching the group of *Gwai* that appeared to be heading directly for them, and his voice was grim as he pointed, "There's a third line, Bao."

Turning in time to see that, in fact, there was a third line, this one also composed of three of the larger groups, it felt to

Bao as if his bowels suddenly turned to water. Then, from behind that line, there appeared a sight that he didn't immediately understand, and neither did Xun, but what he counted as six groups of four men, each of them carrying a large object, along with men leading what looked like ponies, all of them carrying some sort of load. Before he made any comment, he looked over at the second large group, seeing the same thing, but it was as he was looking in that direction he saw, on the far end of the western wall near the northwest corner about eight *li* away, movement that, while too far away to really distinguish, he quickly deduced was a third large group that he surmised would be essentially identical to these two.

"They look like...shields of some sort." Xun's comment tore his gaze back to the closer scene; a quick glance confirmed his counterpart's guess. "And now they're close enough for us to see the *Gwai* infantry, they're carrying something besides their shields. They look like spears of some sort, but they seem very puny. I can't even see the spearpoints."

Again, Bao immediately saw what Xun was talking about, but his mind was still fastened on the large pieces of what they could now see were made of bamboo.

"I think I know what those are!" he gasped, speaking rapidly as he pointed, "Those large things *are* shields of a sort, but they're for their catapults, which," he pointed to the animals, "are being carried by those ponies!" Xun's reaction was to curse under his breath, but Bao assured him, "We have our own artillery, Xun! Are you forgetting? I'm sure that General Xao is already ordering it to be brought to the western wall now that we know where the attack is coming from."

This prompted Xun to turn and stare at him for a moment, searching Bao's face for something.

"You don't know, do you?" Xun asked abruptly, their antipathy completely forgotten.

"Know what?"

Before he answered, Xun glanced around, but while he wasn't fooled that their men weren't avidly listening to their exchange, this was too important, and he whispered, "All of our artillery is gone."

"Gone?" Bao asked in bewilderment. "Gone where?"

"Every catapult has been loaded aboard the *chuan* that General Xao is taking to Xuwen!"

For a brief instant, Bao thought he might faint; somehow, he managed to maintain his composure, but he said nothing, instead turning to face the oncoming *Gwai*, and like his comrades, he was consigned to only watching as they began to methodically prepare for the assault.

Chapter Five

On his own, Pullus had ordered a pause of his Legion when they were about five hundred paces from the wall, thinking that by standing still, he might induce an overeager Han artillerist to betray the location of his piece and give him an idea of the range the Han artillery possessed. It also gave him an opportunity to more closely examine the ground, and he decided that what he was looking at were small garden plots that, since it was Februarius, were lying fallow, marked by low fences that would soon be crushed underfoot.

"I suppose these belong to people inside the city," he commented to Paterculus, then glancing over at his *Aquilifer*, shook his head as he added, "I still can't get used to that headdress."

"Why not?" Paterculus protested, but he was grinning. "Your nephew killed it, didn't he?"

"It's just...unnatural," Pullus groused. "It should be a lion's head, not a tiger."

"When was the last time you saw a lion, Primus Pilus?" Paterculus challenged.

"Parthia," Pullus admitted.

"And you were always complaining about how motheaten and ratty my headdress was," Paterculus pointed out, which Pullus knew was nothing but the truth.

"I know," he protested. "I just didn't think Caesar would say yes."

"Neither did I." Paterculus laughed again. In a teasing tone, he said something that few men could get away with. "But Caesar loves you, and he loves us, so..."

That was also true, but deciding that they had waited long enough, and seeing how Batius had drawn almost fifty paces closer without any kind of response, he cut his *Aquilifer* off to order Valerius sound the call to resume their march. When the 5th hit the four-hundred-pace mark and the only difficulty they encountered was their footing because of the fences that turned out to be made of bamboo, it convinced Pullus that the Han didn't have anything capable of reaching that far, reasoning that they would have begun loosing by now. By the time they pulled even with the 5th, Batius already had his men bringing his mules forward, along with the men carrying the mantlets that, like the ladders, were made with bamboo logs. There had been a vigorous debate between the more traditional *immunes* who didn't believe the mostly hollow logs, despite being from the larger trees, their trunks about as big around as a man's bicep, could withstand the pounding from artillery, but as with the ladders, this was quickly disproven by bombarding them with rocks from their own artillery. It also meant that the mantlets were lighter and easier to carry, and while it took four men, it was because of the size instead of the weight; perhaps most importantly, they had been designed in such a way that they could be quickly assembled, using wooden pegs to secure each log in place on the frame, which also came in pieces. When Pullus, followed by the other two Primi Pili, had recognized that the element of surprise was gone and they would have to use artillery in a more conventional assault, while there was an inevitable delay, it was minimized by the prefabricated nature of the mantlets, which could be assembled in the span of a few dozen heartbeats. Since the other Legion was slightly ahead of them, Pullus saw where Batius chose to halt, about three hundred fifty paces from the wall, and still, there was no kind of response, none of the Romans aware that none would be coming. The Han soldiers were now clearly visible, standing there in between the crenellations, watching but not doing anything else that he could see. This made his decision for him, so that when his front line drew even with the 5th, he didn't order the halt until they had gone another fifty meters beyond. He didn't have to wait long before he heard a shout, turning to see a man running towards him, crossing in front of his Fourth Cohort, then reaching the Third. Normally, Pullus would have allowed the runner from another Legion to get to him, but since this runner was wearing a white crest like he was, he broke into a trot himself, meeting his counterpart in front of his Third of the Second, the older Primus Pilus puffing from the effort.

"What are you doing, Pullus?" Batius demanded. "Trying to get a head start on my boys? Because," he said this more loudly than necessary so that Pullus' men could hear, "my boys will still be up on that wall before yours!"

Normally, Pullus wouldn't have ignored the taunt, but this time, he jerked his head towards the wall, then without waiting, walked a dozen paces in front of the men, turning his back to them, not only so they couldn't hear but in the event he was wrong about Han artillery and they would have some warning since they were now separate targets.

Reaching his side, Batius snapped, "Pluto's cock, what are you doing, Titus? We're already running behind as it is!"

Rather than answer directly, Pullus asked instead, "Do you think that matters now?" Pointing up at the wall, he went on, "Notice anything?"

Batius subsided a bit, hesitating before he replied, "Do you mean it doesn't look like they have any artillery?" When Pullus nodded, it was Batius' turn to point out, "Maybe it doesn't have the range ours does. Or," he said this, although he didn't really believe it, "maybe they have a commander who's just more disciplined than we're used to and is waiting for us to get closer."

"That," Pullus conceded, "is possible. Which is why I wanted to get closer, both to find out, and," now he paused, "because this is about the right range to use the naphtha."

Batius stared up at him, but rather than argue, he rubbed his chin as he gazed at the wall, yet while he wasn't overtly resistant, Pullus heard the skepticism in his voice.

"But we were told that most of their buildings are made of stone, for one thing, and if we're wrong, we could be climbing those walls into the fires of Hades."

"It's a risk," Pullus agreed. "But the element of surprise is gone now. They," he pointed up to the Han lining the walls, "are ready for us. We need something to take back the advantage."

"I see what you're saying," Batius admitted. "But I think Caesar will have our hides if we're not assaulting these walls by the time he gets here."

That, Pullus knew, was not just possible, it was likely, but then it was taken out of their hands when, from back in the direction of the forest, the sound of a *cornu* came rolling across the distance.

Turning, it took Pullus a moment to see why; realizing Batius couldn't see through the ranks of men standing there because of his height, he informed his fellow Primus Pilus, "It looks like we're going to find out, because that's Caesar coming."

For Bao and the Leaping Dragons, the continued delay was both excruciating and puzzling, but he did guess correctly when, emerging from the trees a group of horsemen came cantering forward, he was certain that this must be their leader, which partially explained why the *Gwai* seemed content to stand there. If he had known what the reason for the delay was, and what it would mean for him and his comrades, he might have abandoned his post to run to the brothel and taken Jiā and fled the city. However, in that moment, it was just a puzzle that at least helped pass the time.

"I wonder if this is their leader," Xun murmured, but Bao shook his head, certain that he knew differently.

"No, that's probably one of the leader's officers. *That*," he pointed down to the figure who had separated himself from the front line, "has to be their leader. Look at the size of him!"

The fact that Pullus was standing talking to Batius made his size obvious, but Xun wasn't certain.

"Then why is that man on the horse leading all the other horsemen?" he challenged. "See how they ride behind him?"

"Oh, he's certainly important," Bao agreed. "But he's probably the commander of their cavalry or something."

They were silent then, watching as the mounted man slowed his horse from the canter, then to the trot before walking the last few paces up to the giant and his companion. The two men on the ground made some strange gesture, which the mounted man returned, which Xun interpreted.

"The man on the horse *must* be the commander," he insisted. "The two *Gwai* returned what looks like their form of a salute."

Bao had seen the same thing and acknowledged, to himself, that Xun had been right; despite the apparent cessation in their private battle, he wasn't quite willing to completely forgive his fellow officer, so he merely nodded. As it happened, it wasn't either officer but one of their rankers, thankfully for Bao, one of his spearmen, who noticed something.

"*Hou-Chang* Bao! Look!" The spearman, who was standing a few paces away, was pointing, not down at the horseman and two standing *Gwai*, but farther back to the cluster of mounted men. "See that man on the gray pony? He's not dressed like the *Gwai*. I think he's Han!"

Both officers followed the spearman's pointing finger, and while it took a few heartbeats to pick him out among the thirty or so other horsemen, finally, Bao spotted a man, on a gray horse and wearing a long black robe that settled across the gray's hindquarters, but it was the distinctly different coloring of the man's face, which was the only flesh showing from that distance that convinced him.

"I think he's right!"

Xun's response to Bao's declaration was a nod, and when Bao, whose eyes were still on the man he was now certain was Han, noticed Xun wasn't saying anything, he glanced over at him.

It was the thoughtful expression on Xun's face that prompted him to ask, "What is it? Do you recognize him?"

"No." Xun shook his head. "He's too far away. But," once more, Xun glanced around them then returned to whispering, "I think I might know what it means."

"What?"

Xun took the extra precaution of cupping one hand as he leaned closer to whisper, "What if he's from the Imperial court? What if Yuan has made some sort of alliance with these *Gwai* to try to crush General Xao?"

Bao physically recoiled, leaning away to stare at Xun incredulously, his mind racing through the implications.

Finally, he whispered back, "What if you're right? What does it mean for us?"

Xun's response was a shrug, and in a normal tone of voice,

he replied flatly, "Nothing really. We," he indicated their men, "are still going to slaughter them," he pointed out to where the formations of foreign invaders were still standing, essentially motionless. Xun grinned, and added, "You and I alone will be enough since we're protecting Jiā, eh?"

Although he didn't want to, Bao had to laugh, realizing that Xun was right in both instances. Ultimately, even if the Han down there was representing Emperor Yuan, that was a matter far beyond the control of the Leaping Dragons, and his thoughts *were* about Jiā. All they could do was put up enough of a fight to make these pale foreign demons bleed and die at the base of their walls. In silent acknowledgement of his counterpart's words, Bao returned his attention to the scene below, and he had to admit that it was fascinating to watch the animals that looked a bit like ponies but were built differently, broader through the chest and hindquarters, and had much longer ears that, in his opinion, made them look a bit ridiculous, led to a spot in front of the leading ranks of the *Gwai* formation directly in front of them, where they were unloaded. Even with the lack of familiarity with these invaders, who were now close enough to see that not only were their shields and helmets identical to each other, they were all wearing what he assumed was armor, although he had never seen a mail shirt before, Bao did recognize the practiced ease with which the *Gwai* quickly assembled the pieces of what he was certain were several catapults, telling him they were veterans. All around him, the men of their *Sui*, both spearmen and crossbowmen were growing restless, but Bao wasn't inclined to order them to stop their murmured conversations and moving about, and it was clear that Xun was of a like mind. They're just as nervous as we are, he thought to himself, so I can't blame them. Finally, some of the men who had been helping with the preparations, which included placing the shields that were made of large bamboo logs attached to a frame a couple paces in front of each piece, trotted back to take their place at various spots in the formation, while what he counted were three men remained behind each catapult. Judging from the height of the *Gwai*, the shields stood a bit taller than a man, and were angled to a degree that he deduced was designed to deflect the missiles that would be loosed at them from enemy artillery. Which, he thought bitterly, we don't have because they're all on ships in the harbor.

"We don't have long to wait now," Xun said quietly, but while Bao agreed, they learned they were both wrong, because down below and outside the walls, the *Gwai* general was changing the plan.

Zhang had been surprised when the one-eyed Parthian he knew was named Teispes approached Achaemenes and said something to him that prompted the other Parthian to come to him.

"Caesar has decided that, if you desire it, you can accompany us to the city to watch."

Naturally, he had accepted, even as he tried to think of why the *Gwai* would want a potential adversary to witness what his army could do. It wasn't until, again with help in the form of a slave on all fours serving as a stool, he was swinging aboard a gray horse that he realized that it was precisely because of his serving as the representative of the Emperor that Caesar wanted him to watch. He wants me to see what they're capable of, he thought, even as he conducted a conversation with Achaemenes about something innocuous, both men part of a group of about thirty horsemen that followed Caesar, who had already begun moving at a canter. That means he's extremely confident that he can defeat Xao, because if he held any doubts about the outcome, he wouldn't want me to see a defeat. Somewhat to his surprise, this angered Zhang, thinking of it as the impudence of this barbarian to be so arrogant in his conviction that he would defeat men who, despite not being aligned with the Emperor, were still of the Han. Reaching the forest, he was forced to concentrate more on remaining aboard his mount as it weaved in and out between the trees and dense undergrowth, and not for the first time, he envied Achaemenes, who rode as if he was actually part of the beast between his knees, although he wasn't surprised. Even in the land of the Han, the Parthians were renowned for their skill on horseback, and a frequent topic of debate among Han noblemen was how the Parthians would compare to the nomadic tribes far to the northwest who had been such a bane to the Han for generations. I would at least like not to feel as if my spine was being jolted apart, he thought ruefully, noting that Achaemenes wasn't bouncing in the saddle like he was.

Finally, and thankfully, they emerged out of the forest, whereupon Caesar slowed, first to a trot, then a walk, and in that moment, when for the first time Zhang saw what three Roman Legions arrayed for battle looked like, did he truly understand why Caesar insisted on his presence. Just the sight of the ordered, neatly subdivided ranks of one Legion, which he had learned was more than four thousand men per Legion depending on their losses, and knowing that there were five Legions with Caesar, but was only half of the *Gwai* army, brought home in a visceral manner something that he had already understood intellectually, that however barbaric they may have been, these *Gwai* represented a threat that the Han had never faced before. Following Caesar, who rode through the gap in between two of the Legions, only when they arrived next to the first line of Caesar's men did Zhang see that the Legion to their right was the one they called the Equestrians, although he had no idea what that meant, but from horseback, it was easy to see the giant Pullus standing there with another Centurion wearing a white crest, recognizing the older man but not knowing his name.

"Caesar says to wait here," Achaemenes drew up at a spot just behind the second row of the first line of *Gwai* soldiers, and Zhang noticed how the hairy, smelly barbarians they called Germans had arrayed themselves around and behind him, although this amused him more than anything, understanding why. They sat watching as Caesar drew up and held what appeared to be an animated conversation between the general and the pair of Centurions, and he was surprised when Achaemenes began explaining.

"I think Caesar is upset because he expected the Legions to already be at the walls," he said, which made sense given the manner in which Caesar was behaving.

He did notice that, of the two Centurions, the short one, who Achaemenes identified as being named Batius, yet another strange name in an army filled with them, seemed more cowed by Caesar, while the giant Pullus stood there, holding the stick all the Centurions carried, behaving as if they were just holding an idle conversation, seemingly unaware that about four hundred paces away, the parapet of the fifteen-foot high wall was packed with men, their spears and the weapon called the *ji* just visible, waiting to kill them. It was, Zhang concluded, another sign that this wasn't the first time these Romans had been in this situation. Certainly, he had known that even before he had been sent by Emperor Yuan, but it was another example of the difference between knowing something in the mind, and experiencing it, sitting here in the hot sun, although he wasn't sweating nearly as much as the Germans around him, and he was certain that even if he had been, he wouldn't have emitted such an atrocious odor. As they sat watching, Caesar's gestures became less pronounced, Batius seemed less agitated, while Pullus hadn't altered his demeanor at all. Then, he saw Caesar give a curt nod before turning his horse and returning at the canter to where they were waiting. Drawing up, he said something in his own tongue that prompted a Tribune named Censorinus to salute, then spin about to canter back towards the forest, while Caesar turned and addressed Achaemenes, but he was completely unprepared for the Parthian, who was clearly surprised as well, to turn and address him.

"Caesar wants us to go with him," Achaemenes said, but then he hesitated and glanced over at the general before turning back to Zhang. "We are going to approach under a flag of truce to talk to General Xao to see if he is willing to surrender the city."

Zhang's first instinct was that, for whatever reason, the Roman general had decided to play a joke on him, but a glance at Caesar's face dispelled that idea; his first impulse was to refuse, although he quickly understood this wasn't an option.

"Caesar wants to know what the Han use for a sign of truce."

"Something white," Zhang explained, which seemed to surprise both Caesar and Achaemenes, and only then did the Han emissary understand that when he had approached them under a flag of truce, the Romans had assumed it was in recognition of their own convention, not realizing that it was shared, which made him wonder what the kingdoms of India used.

Caesar called to the German named Gundomir, then to Teispes, and the pair nudged their mounts forward, while Caesar trotted over to speak to one of his soldiers standing in the ranks of Pullus' Legion, wearing a white stripe on his shoulder, and Zhang noticed that there was something familiar about him, though he couldn't determine why.

It was Achaemenes who noticed the Han studying the Optio, who explained, "That is Optio Porcinus. He's Primus Pilus Pullus' nephew."

Zhang instantly saw the resemblance in the facial features, but whereas he was also taller than the men around him, unlike the brute Pullus, he wasn't heavily built. He understood what was happening when Porcinus produced a large square of white cloth that he had stuffed down the front of his tunic, then took one of the javelins from the man in the last rank standing next to him. Affixing the cloth to the point, he handed it to Caesar, who returned and passed it to the German, and only then did Caesar unstrap his helmet from his saddle and put it on, tying the leather cords. Before he began moving, the Roman turned and looked directly at Zhang, as if challenging him, and without thinking, Zhang kicked his horse and bounced up to draw even with the Roman. Then, with Gundomir leading the way, they rode slowly towards the city, angling slightly to align themselves directly across from one of the three large wooden gates, this one nearest to the southwest corner.

General Xao, accompanied by Lei, left the large building constructed with both stone and wood in the middle of what was now one of the larger cities in Jinzhou Province, of which Zhuya was a part despite being an island, riding horses that Westerners would have derided as ponies, in response to the request by *Hou-Kuan* Zhou, who Xao had named as the senior commander of the defenders on the western wall until he and Lei arrived. Thankfully, the streets were now deserted, mainly because Xao had issued citywide orders that gave his troops the authority to cut down any civilian who they judged was impeding them, and he ignored the faces peering out through windows or through a cracked door of those who heard the clattering sound of hoofbeats on paving stones. Reaching the wall, they were met by Zhou, who was standing at the bottom of the stairway immediately next to the Jade Gate, each gate of the western wall assigned the name of a precious object.

Bowing, Zhou waited for the pair to dismount before explaining, "The *Gwai* general is here, requesting to speak to you, sir." He hesitated, wondering whether it was wise to do so, then decided it would be worse not to, adding, "There's also a man who claims to be an emissary of Emperor Yuan with them."

Xao had already begun to ascend the stairs, but his foot hovered above the next step for an instant, and he stared down at Zhou with what appeared to be an equal mixture of disbelief and worry.

"What did you say?" Xao demanded; Zhou repeated himself, and the general looked at Lei, who was right behind him.

"I thought it might be a possibility, General," Lei said quietly, with even more trepidation than Zhou was experiencing, because unlike Zhou, Lei had witnessed what Xao did to those who displeased him, or who he felt were disloyal.

"And you didn't think to tell me?" Xao demanded angrily, but before Lei could respond, the general surprised him by grunting, "Not that it matters, I suppose."

Taking a deep breath, he turned back around, placed his foot on the next step, and ascended them, not seeing Lei and Zhou exchange a relieved glance. When they reached the rampart, the rankers of the Raging Tigers *Tu-wei-fu*, who had been placed next to the Leaping Tigers, scrambled out of the way, dropping their heads in a sign of respect, which Xao ignored, although he did return the bow of their *Hou-Kuan*, who was second in seniority to Zhou with the *Hou-Kuan*. Xao didn't approach the outer edge until Lei and Zhou joined him before walking slowly to the parapet, which was solid immediately above the gateway, without the crenellations, and looking down at where the five mounted men sat, seemingly patient, although he did notice the tails of their horses, which were larger than any animals he had ever seen before, were swishing back and forth, a giveaway of their riders' own tension. While Xao immediately saw that there was indeed a Han with these *Gwai*, he didn't recognize the man, who appeared to be in his late twenties, although he did recognize the embroidered symbols, stitched in a bright green with red accents, as belonging to the house from which Emperor Yuan came, and knew that anyone wearing a robe with those symbols represented him. Indeed, at one time in the past, his uniform had been adorned with the same design. He was the only man not wearing armor or a helmet, but Xao didn't need to be told who the general was, although not because of his armor, which was a gleaming silver single piece that looked much like the bare torso of a muscular man and was decorated with things he couldn't distinguish, and was different than those of the men immediately behind him, one of them a large, dark man with a hole where one eye should have been, and the other who had to be the hairiest creature on two legs that he had ever seen, while the hair was a pale yellow like the sun. It was the manner in which the *Gwai* sat his horse, completely without fear and gazing up at Xao as if this was a chance meeting of two strangers that identified him to Xao.

Making a point of ignoring the *Gwai*, Xao instead addressed the Han, demanding, "Who are you, and what is a civilized man doing in the company of filthy animals such as these?" Before Zhang could respond, he added, "And who do you speak for, dog? These *Gwai* savages?"

Since he didn't know the man, Xao couldn't tell if he had angered him, but it didn't sound like it when the man replied, "I am Zhang Meng, appointed as Official Imperial Emissary on behalf of the sacred and holy Emperor Yuan of the Han." Lifting a hand to indicate the *Gwai*, he continued, "This man is named Gaius Julius Caesar, and while his title is meaningless to us, I will tell you that he is the supreme ruler of Rome." Zhang paused, and there was no missing the scorn as he taunted, "Since I do not know how educated you are, do I need to explain who these Romans are? Or perhaps you might have heard of them?"

Xao heard Lei's hiss of anger, but he managed to retain control of his own temper, replying coldly, "I know of Rome. And I know that they have laid waste and pillaged their way, countless number of *li* and conquered other barbarian races from the other side of the world. But that does *not* answer my question, Zhang Meng; why are you with them?"

Before Zhang could reply, the *Gwai* general said something, not loudly, but Xao sensed that he was, if not angry, then at least perturbed. What happened next was even more curious, because instead of Zhang answering him, the fifth man of the party, who had barely rated a glance by Xao and was sitting his horse just behind but in between Zhang and the *Gwai* began speaking, clearly addressing Zhang.

"That must be their translator," Lei said quietly, and Xao realized this was undoubtedly the case, angry at himself for not seeing it first.

"So they have someone who speaks a civilized language," Xao observed, but Lei shook his head, frowning as he stood there, his head turned so that one ear was pointed in that direction.

After a couple of heartbeats, Lei replied, "I don't think they do, sir. While I don't understand the words, what the darker *Gwai* and Zhang are speaking has a different rhythm than our tongue."

This was the moment that the dark *Gwai* turned to Caesar and said something in what was now a third distinctly different tongue.

"Sir, I believe that the dark *Gwai* can speak the same tongue as the *Gwai* Caesar, and that Zhang can speak the tongue of the darker *Gwai*, but it's not ours. So," he concluded, "it's a three-way translation."

"Which means," Xao muttered, "this will take forever."

The Roman gave an abrupt nod that was clearly a signal, because Zhang turned back to address Xao. "My purpose here is my own business, General Xao. What I'm here for at this moment is only to relay a message."

"Oh?" Xao made sure to accentuate his scorn. "And what message is that, lackey?"

For the first time, and to Xao's satisfaction, Zhang exhibited signs of anger, but he didn't hesitate to reply, "Caesar is giving you an opportunity to surrender this city, for your men to lay down their weapons, in exchange for safe passage to the mainland."

Despite suspecting something of this nature, Xao was still taken aback, and the reaction of Lei, Zhou, and his counterpart *Hou Kuan* Lao, all of them gasping in shock, told him he wasn't alone. It wasn't just the arrogance of this *Gwai* making these demands, it was the realization of what it truly meant.

"Do you think the *Gwai* really knows what he's asking us to do?" Xao muttered to Lei. "We can't go to the mainland, not unless we take Xuwen. We must have the walls of Xuwen to protect us."

Whether Zhang possessed some magic that gave him the gift of hearing as keen as a dog's, or it was just a lucky guess they would never know, but he called up to them, "Yes, Caesar is aware that you're rebels and traitors who fled here to escape justice from our Emperor."

Now it was Xao's turn to be angry, and he snarled back, "The only traitor to our people is that weakling you call Emperor, *boy*! He's the one who abandoned Zhuya, not me! I've brought the natives here to heel..."

"You bribed them to fight for you!" Zhang cut him off. "Nothing more than that. You allow them free run of this island in exchange for loyalty so that you can pretend to be an Emperor yourself." Zhang indicated Caesar, and in a calmer tone, he said, "I suggest that you consider his offer carefully, General Xao, because I've seen what the *Gwai* can do."

The manner in which he stopped had an abrupt quality to it, which Xao understood when Zhang turned and spoke quickly to the darker *Gwai* translator, who shrugged then spoke to the *Gwai* general. Now that Xao was paying attention, he could also tell by the different cadences that Lei was correct that this was a three-way process, but whatever Zhang said elicited a curt nod from the *Gwai*.

Not needing it translated any further, Zhang turned and said, "General Xao, you should know something." Turning awkwardly in his saddle, Zhang indicated the Legions behind them, "These are just three of what the *Gwai* call Legions. And," he pointed behind him, "there are two more of these Legions hidden in that forest."

"Just all the more dogs to die against our walls!" Xao cut

him off, giving in to his growing fury. "You tell the *Gwai* scum that! Tell him that we'll feed the river with their blood, and that our livestock will become fat, and our crops will grow higher than ever before because their flesh and blood will nourish them!"

Zhang waited patiently for Xao to take a breath.

"That's not what you need to know." When Xao remained silent, Zhang continued, "Only half of the *Gwai* army is here. The other half is assaulting Yazhou today." Zhang chose this moment to look up at the sun, which was now almost directly above them before he commented, "Perhaps the city has already fallen." Returning his attention to Xao, his tone became flat and matter of fact. "You cannot defeat this *Gwai* and his army, General, not in the long run. Even if you succeeded in turning them away from your walls, they still have half of their army, and all of their fleet."

"Could this be true?" Xao asked Lei quietly, but his second in command actually smiled, certain now that any anger Xao might feel at his actions would be ameliorated by his relief.

"Even if it is true," he assured Xao, "it doesn't mean what they think it means."

When Xao looked at him in surprise, he quietly explained his orders to Liu and the reinforcements he had sent from the three garrisons.

"Why didn't you tell me about this?" Xao demanded, but before Lei could reply, he held up a hand, saying quickly, "Not that it matters, and I commend you for thinking ahead."

This news prompted Xao to address Zhang to tell him, "Don't be so certain that Yazhou will fall, minion. Indeed," his tone turned smug, "the *Gwai* are in for a...surprise at Yazhou. As far as your fleet?" He shrugged. "The river is too narrow, and our walls are too far from the seashore for them to do any damage."

For a brief instant, Zhang considered relaying what Xao said about a surprise waiting for Pollio's part of the army, but chose not to, although he couldn't have explained why, given the fact that his Emperor wanted the *Gwai* to completely crush Xao and end the rebel presence on the island. Instead, he related the essence of Xao's seeming indifference, and the part about the fleet. As he waited for Achaemenes to translate this to Caesar, he watched the general, who suddenly glanced up at the sky himself, as if he was measuring the time as Zhang had, and ignorant of what Caesar had set into motion with Nero as he was, wondered what it meant.

When Achaemenes nodded that he was finished explaining to Caesar, Zhang continued to Xao, "In order to persuade you that the wise course will be to accept Caesar's terms, he has arranged a demonstration for you."

"A demonstration?" Xao frowned. "What kind of demonstration?"

Rather than answer the general, Zhang again addressed Achaemenes, and once he was finished relating it to Caesar, the *Gwai* general responded, not verbally but thrusting an arm up into the air, which in turn spurred some activity at one of the pieces of artillery, causing the Han general to examine them for the first time.

"They use twisted rope like we do," Lei commented, "but I wonder why they have an iron basket?"

It was less the marking on the crate and more the exaggerated care one of the *Gwai* men took that caught their attention, but it was when the men donned leather sleeves that Lei assumed were dripping with what had to be water before taking out a clay jar that gave them the first presentiment.

"General Caesar says that he won't harm you or any of your men, but he is going to use your gate as a demonstration. He also swears by his gods that he will allow you to extinguish the flames without your men being attacked by his."

"Does the *Gwai* dog think we don't know how to use burning oil?" Xao sneered. "He must truly think we're savages. But," he feigned indifference, "if he feels the need, tell him that I also swear that we won't violate this truce. *We* are civilized men!"

Zhang dutifully translated, then a silence descended, all of the Han on the walls watching intently, especially those out of earshot of the exchange, which included Bao and Xun, who had to lean out between the crenellations to get a good view. From Xao's position, he and the officers around him could see how carefully the man wearing the sleeves carried the jar over and stood next to the metal basket; only then did Lei notice that the man holding the long cord was wearing the same sleeves as well. He also noticed how the *Gwai* Caesar and his party turned, and without haste, retreated from the Jade Gate, though not all the way back to where the *Gwai* army was waiting, but about fifty paces from the gate.

"Perhaps they've found some sort of oil that is even more volatile than the kinds we use," he suggested to Xao, but the general only grunted, his eyes never leaving Caesar, and he saw the Roman lift his arm again, then sweep it down in a clear command.

What happened next occurred very quickly; the jar was placed in the basket, resting there no more than a full heartbeat when the third man, also wearing sleeves, touched a smoking brand to the rag hanging out of the jar, and even less than that for the *Gwai* holding the cord to pull it, flinging the jar upward and away at a blinding speed. Despite it never arcing high enough to pose a danger to the Han standing above the gate, Xao's only consolation was that he wasn't the only man who instinctively dropped behind the solid stone parapet as the jar hurtled in their direction. They heard the impact, which sounded like it was, a jar shattering against a harder surface, but despite the flames not reaching up above the parapet where he could see them, Xao felt the intense blast of heat, along with a peculiar smell that he had never experienced before from the plume of black, oily smoke.

"You may extinguish the flames, General!"

Zhang had to shout this to be heard because of the extra distance and Xao hadn't stood erect yet, and he was still crouched as he snapped to Zhou to take care of it, the officer immediately rushing off, calling to a half-dozen men to follow him. They clattered down the stairs as Xao carefully rose, but the smoke was still thick enough that it was difficult to see the mounted party, forcing him to sidestep several paces to regain eye contact2. There were barrels of water, with buckets, at the base of the wall, a standard precaution against fire, so he wasn't concerned that the damage to the wooden gates, made with a double thickness of wood that was more than a foot thick, would be that severe.

"That was your demonstration?" Xao called down once the enemy party returned to its former spot, forcing a mocking laugh. "You make some smoke and fire?"

Zhang didn't have a chance to respond. Instead, from down on the street level, there were cries of alarm, but it was the shriek of pain that had Xao turning and snapping to Lei, "Go find out what's happening!"

Lei dashed to the stairway, racing down them as Xao tried to look calm and unperturbed as he waited, but it was difficult when he saw the *Gwai* general and the men with him sitting their horses impassively, although he did notice the animals were tossing their heads and beginning to move a bit, reminding him that animals instinctively recoiled from fire.

"General Xao!"

Turning away from the Romans, Xao hurried to the inner side of the parapet to look down to where Lei was standing in the street, just opposite the gateway, the expression on his deputy's face causing a stab of real concern; the continued screams of a man who was clearly in agony didn't help.

"General," Lei had to shout to be heard over the shrieking, "I don't know what kind of oil this is, but when the men doused it with buckets, it made the fire worse, and some of it splashed onto one of the men." Even as Lei was speaking, Xao heard another sharp cry, but with a gurgling quality to it, and only then did the screaming stop.

"Did you close the gate?" Xao snapped. "This might be a trick!"

"We did. But," Lei made a helpless gesture, "the outer part of the gate is still burning."

"General Xao! Please come back to the parapet!"

Recognizing Zhang's voice, Xao did so, where the mounted party still sat their horses, but before he could respond, he saw the *Gwai* who had placed the first jar in the basket place another one, quite a bit larger, but without a rag in it, nor was there any smoke. The man with the cord pulled it immediately, and because Xao was no longer directly over the gate, he forced himself not to flinch, watching as the jar made an arcing flight before briefly disappearing from Xao's sight as it smashed against the gate that was recessed from the outer edge by several feet. This time, however, there was no flame, nor was there any heat, and while he thought it was smoke at first, it was white and dissipated so quickly that he realized it was steam. So intent was he on this, he hadn't noticed the piece next to the first one being prepared, and it sent another jar to smash against the gate within a heartbeat of the first one.

"General Xao," Zhang called out. "It's now safe for your men to open the gate if they wish, so they can inspect it and make sure that it's no longer burning."

Xao shouted down the order, and he heard the huge hinges creaking, but he had already turned back to face Caesar as he demanded of Zhang, "What kind of sorcery is this, minion? What kind of oil is it, and why didn't water work, but whatever was in those jars did?"

He was forced to wait for the laborious process, hearing footsteps ascending the stairs, and he was joined by Lei, who said quietly, "Sir, I don't know what caused that fire, but whatever was in the jars they used to put it out isn't water. It has a stench I've never smelled before, so I don't believe it's water."

He was finished just in time for Zhang to relay what Caesar had said through Achaemenes.

"It's no sorcery, General. What's important for you to know is that this is something these *Gwai* used to conquer the elephants of the kingdoms of India, and defeat those savages the Khmer. He also says that only the *Gwai* know how to control it." He paused, because Achaemenes and Caesar had been conversing, and the Parthian relayed more, and Xao could see that whatever it was disturbed the Han emissary, but he didn't hesitate. "Caesar says that he will give you..." he had to stop for a moment to calculate, "...five kè to give us your decision, or he will rain this fire down on your heads, and there will be nothing left of the city or the people in it."

Xao opened his mouth to respond, but suddenly, Caesar turned his horse's head, going immediately to the canter, followed hastily by the others, including Zhang.

"What do we do, General?" Lei asked so that only Xao could hear.

"I don't know," Xao admitted, giving Lei a look of bitter

dismay.

Without another word, he beckoned Lei to follow him as he walked to the stairs and began to descend them, with the intention of removing himself so that he could have time to think and confer with the only man he trusted. Reaching the street level, Xao strode down Jade Street away from the gate, stopping far enough away not to be overheard, where he was immediately joined by Lei. Xao was just opening his mouth when, coming from deeper inside the city, they both heard the clattering sound of hoofbeats, in a rapid staccato rhythm that told them whoever was coming was moving at the gallop. Jade Street curved slightly, forcing them to wait a couple more heartbeats before the rider and horse causing the noise came into view.

It was Lei who recognized the rider, saying quickly, "That's General Shu's courier!"

"Shu?" Xao frowned. "He's down at the harbor."

Before they could speculate further, the rider reined in his horse, misjudging how quickly the animal could stop as it slid across the paving stones, forcing both Xao and Lei to leap out of its path. Normally, this would have earned the courier a punishment, but he was saved from this as, within a span of a couple heartbeats, his mistake was forgotten.

"General Xao! General Shu sent me to report that an enemy fleet sailed into the harbor, and before we could stop them, they set fire to our ships!"

Xao staggered back a step, his mouth open, temporarily unable to speak.

"Set fire to them?" Lei demanded. "What does that mean? Did they board them?"

"No, General." The courier shook his head. "They..." suddenly, he was unsure how to describe it, "...they hurled something from their ships, from a great distance away. And," whether the tears that came were from what he had seen, or his fear at being punished for bringing this message, neither general would ever know, "every one of our ships caught fire so quickly that there was nothing we could do."

"How many ships does General Shu think we lost?" Xao found his voice to ask, hearing it shaking but unable to stop it.

The courier now looked terrified, but he answered, "All of them, General Xao. General Shu said that they're all gone, burned to the waterline."

It was the last message the courier ever gave, because before Lei could stop him, Xao drew his sword and swung it in one single, fluid motion, sending the courier's head tumbling in the air, while Lei was struck by the spraying blood in the instant before the body crumpled to the ground, just barely beating its head, which struck the paving stones then went bouncing and rolling away. *He looks surprised*, Lei thought dully, *although I don't know why. He had to know how the general would react; perhaps that was why he began crying.*

Keeping these thoughts to himself, Lei turned to Xao and tried to keep his eyes off the dripping sword in his general's hand, hoping that he wasn't next as he asked, "What are your orders, General Xao?"

Xao smiled at Lei, but it was humorless, replying, "The *Gwai* either outsmarted himself or he was lying, Lei."

"How so?" Lei asked in real surprise.

"He told us we could sail to the mainland," Xao pointed out. "But then he destroys our fleet, the only way we could do that?" Shaking his head, he said flatly, "He never wanted us to surrender. He wanted to terrify our men with that fire that water can't put out. But now," Xao finished grimly, "we have no choice but to fight."

General Xao would be one of the relatively few opponents Caesar ever faced who divined the Roman's real intentions, not that he would survive to write about it.

As it would turn out, even with their assault on Yazhou beginning exactly on time, when Caesar judged that it was close to midday, Pollio's Legions still hadn't taken the city, despite being prepared for the surprise attack by the combined forces of the three garrisons that Lei had sent to Yazhou that Liu had deployed outside the walls, using the wooded hillside for cover. It hadn't been without a high cost; Balbinus' Fourth Century had sustained heavy casualties buying their comrades in the second line Cohorts enough time to change their alignment so that they were facing the small hill. The Fourth had done so, thereby enabling a counterattack by the three second line Cohorts, but as with Balbinus', Cartufenus' and Aquilinus' Cohorts, they were exposed to the Han crossbow, and it took their Centurions and Optios using every trick they knew to keep their men advancing into what was a murderous hail of bolts that were more powerful, and because of their flatter trajectory, were almost as difficult to dodge or block with a shield as sling bullets. It wasn't the weapon itself as much as that the Han infantry seemed to be equally divided between spearmen and crossbowmen, with the missile troops starting in the front ranks to pelt their advancing foes before moving quickly behind their spearmen once they came to grips. Even then, it didn't mean the bolts stopped coming, and as the Romans quickly learned, their Han enemies had clearly trained so that the spearmen in the front ranks were accustomed to bolts streaking past them in the gaps between the men currently doing the fighting along the front rank. It had forced the Romans to quickly adapt, compelling the second man in the file to keep a secure hold of the harness of his comrade with his right hand, while protecting him by lifting the shield and holding it just above the first man's head, similar to when being in *testudo*. Despite all of this, the Fifth, Sixth, and Seventh Cohort were able to stop the Han counterattack from quickly rolling up the assaulting Legions from the flank, and pin them in place long enough for Pollio's surprise, sending the 21st the less than two miles around the headland upon which the hill sat to land on the narrow strip of beach there, then climb the hill to slam into the Han force from the rear. What had been a close contest, with men standing toe to toe trying to slaughter each other with the outcome hanging in the balance was quickly turned into a slaughter, with the shattered remnants of the Han force reduced to small groups of men desperately using the cover of the trees to try and escape. To Liu's credit, when he saw this setback from his spot on Yazhou's western ramparts, he didn't hesitate to sound a general withdrawal, leaving a token force on the wall with orders to sacrifice themselves to delay the *Gwai* long enough for the second phase of his defense, which to Balbinus' dismay, was the cause for the current stalemate now, late in the afternoon.

"Why didn't we know that they had a fucking island like this in the middle of this city?"

To Pollio, who was now ashore and was standing with the Primi Pili of the three Legions performing the assault, the answer to Aquilinus' question was obvious.

"And how do you propose that Legate Volusenus would get inside these walls?" he asked the Primus Pilus in a reasonable tone. "He doesn't have wings, and we don't have anyone in our ranks who could pass for a Han, except for Long and that emissary. Would you trust either of them?"

Aquilinus didn't answer directly, settling for a muttered curse, but it was Balbinus who turned back to practical matters.

"I've sent my third line Cohorts towards the southern wall to see if there's another bridge that isn't defended, but I doubt they'll find anything, and they're also going to see if the river is shallow enough for us to wade across so we can at least surround these *cunni*."

"I did the same with my second line Cohorts," Aquilinus spoke up. "But they haven't sent a runner back, and I agree with Balbinus, I doubt they'll find any easy way to get around to the other side."

They were standing inside the western gate, but while they could clearly see the bridge several blocks away, which was blocked by what Pollio felt certain was a makeshift barricade, although it appeared to be made of blocks of stone, they were out of range of the crossbowmen, which they had just spent a few moments examining from one of the dead Han on the rampart.

"It works basically like a scorpion, but small enough for a man to carry," Cartufenus had observed, holding it awkwardly to his shoulder.

"And it hits like a fucking mule," Balbinus said bitterly. "Those bolts were punching through our shields once we got twenty paces away."

"So that's what was happening," Pollio nodded, his tone thoughtful. "I couldn't tell because I was too far away."

"And you can be sure that those *mentulae* over there," Cartufenus pointed at the barrier on the opposite side of the river, "are just waiting for us to try to cross that bridge."

It was, they all agreed, a difficult proposition. The part of the city west of the Sanya was now firmly in the control of the Legions, the evidence of that in the shrill, feminine screams from the Han women who had either been too paralyzed by fear to flee across the bridges, or for many of the unfortunates, had been turned away by the soldiers on Liu's command now that he was planning on an extended siege of his island redoubt. While the captured women were raped, they weren't put to the sword, nor were the noncombatant men, all of them being rounded up and led outside the walls to the beach, where they were guarded by the 8th, who rightly viewed their assignment as the reserve as punishment, but it was a sign of their current morale that most of the men were perfectly content with this development, if only because their Centurions chose to look the other way as the rankers indulged themselves with the captive Han women, who had already been defiled at least once by men from the assaulting Legions. At this moment, they were standing there, trying to decide how to assault the island, where the buildings were almost universally constructed of stone as part of the Han administration, with both the official buildings and the residences of the small army of bureaucrats that, as the Romans would learn, outdid even themselves when it came to organization, while the only flammable material was the wooden roofs. There was no wall lining the riverbank, but this part of the city had been constructed so that the rear of each building fronted the riverbank, with only a narrow strip of muddy ground between river and building. There was just enough room to place a ladder, but there were shuttered windows, all of them closed, that would expose anyone attempting this to a murderous crossfire, and that was only after finding enough small boats to row the one hundred-fifty paces across the river; surprising none of the Romans, the Han commander had taken the precaution of bringing every waterborne craft over to the island. They were alerted by a shout from outside the western gate, turning to see a panting Legionary who arrived in the gateway only to come to a stop so out of breath that he had to bend over and put his hands on his knees even before rendering a salute, his legs covered in mud to mid-calf.

Fortunately, Pollio wasn't the type of Legate to punish this kind of lapse, but he let his impatience show, snapping, "Who are you and what's your report?"

It still took a couple heartbeats for the ranker to reply, "Gregarius Sextus Longinus, First of the First of the 21st, sent by Primus Pilus Papernus, sir. The Primus Pilus sent me to tell you that we've driven what's left of the barbarian force that tried to surprise us up into those hills east of the city. He wants to know whether we should go up there after them, or if you want us to assault the city from the eastern side."

"Yes," Pollio answered immediately, then realized his error. "That is to say, yes I want him to assault the eastern wall immediately." Rather than acknowledge the orders then salute before turning back to make the journey back, the ranker stood there, prompting Pollio to snap, "What are you waiting for, Gregarius?"

"Er, it's just that I'm supposed to give you another message now, sir."

Pollio's mystification wasn't shared by the three Primi Pili, who exchanged knowing grins, although the Legate was focused on Longinus.

"What is it?" Pollio demanded, and Longinus, still uncomfortable, replied, "The Primus Pilus wants me to inform you that he thought you would order the assault on the city, so he's already started it."

For a moment, Pollio could only stare at the ranker, then he asked, "So if I'd told you the opposite, did Primus Pilus Papernus tell you to keep your mouth shut about it and just come tell him?"

There was no mistaking Longinus' distress, and he could only nod in reply, whereupon Pollio burst out in laughter, the ranker almost collapsing in relief.

"Tell your Primus Pilus that he's a wise man," Pollio said, and now a much-relieved Longinus did salute this time before dashing off, leaving the Primi Pili in a bemused state at the Legate's reaction. Seeing their faces, Pollio smiled. "I probably would have done the same thing if it had been me and I was reporting to Caesar." This elicited chuckles, but Pollio immediately turned back to the matter at hand. "I'm going to delay our assault from this side to give Papernus time to get over the wall. Although," he allowed, "I wonder if whoever's commanding the Han pulled those men back to the island on that side, which is what I'd do. So," he decided, "I want the artillery unloaded while we wait. In case," he finished grimly, "we have to burn those *cunni* out of their hole."

For Pullus and the rest of the men, who at that moment were unaware of their general's orders to Nero, the waiting was interminable, leading to widespread grumbling at being forced to hurry if Caesar was just going to ask for a truce and give these bastards more time to prepare their defenses. When the general ordered the demonstration by the artillery, it engendered a round of wagering among the men, and to Pullus' ears, his Century seemed evenly divided about whether the Han would be so terrified and demoralized by the sticky flames that the barbarian general would ask for terms, or whether they would fight despite seeing what they were facing. While Murena, the Equestrian's chief artillery *Immune* who had been selected by Caesar to carry out the demonstration, hit the target with the first smoking jar, his aim had been slightly off so that the jar shattered against the left-hand gate, which was about twelve feet wide and fifteen feet tall, and not squarely so that both gates were fully involved. However, this turned out to be better, at least as far as the watching Romans were concerned, because they saw the right-hand gate open and four men rush out, each of them carrying a bucket, the contents sloshing out in a silvery splatter that informed their foes that the Han were about to learn the lesson they had, but sadly for the men, there wasn't time to wager on who would be the unfortunate Han who got too close to the inevitable backsplash. As it turned out, the Han who had the misfortune of being splattered with the combination of water and the flaming globules of naphtha was the victim of one of his comrades, who hurled the contents of the bucket with particular force in an attempt to extinguish the flames. The water struck the clinging naphtha, splashing off the gate, the mixture of water and dissipated globules still aflame striking the victim fully in the face, and even from that distance, they could hear the screams as the stricken soldier clutched his face, so crazed with pain that he ran in circles, while his other two comrades at least had the sense not to throw their buckets at the gate. Finally, a soldier, helmeted and wearing a plume that suggested he was an officer strode out into view, waiting for the heartbeat it took for the pain-crazed Han to essentially run directly at him, whereupon the officer cut the man down while, Pullus noticed, taking care not to let the man touch him.

"They've figured out that that *cac* sticks to you at least," he commented to Paterculus, and proving they also recognized the futility of trying to extinguish the flames conventionally, they retreated back into the gateway and slammed the open gate shut.

Pullus guessed what the exchange that took place after this would be about, and they watched as Murena had to send two large jars of vinegar to smash against the gate before the flames were extinguished for the most part, although there were flickers as small remnants of the substance clung stubbornly to the wood. This was when the wagering became brisk, but only much later would all but a handful of Caesar's senior officers learn why the Han general still chose to fight, that he was essentially given no choice because Nero had sailed into the harbor and destroyed not only the Han artillery, but their only means to fulfill Caesar's demand to evacuate the island. What it meant in a practical sense was that it was well past midday when, once again, Caesar's *Cornicen* summoned the Primi Pili of the three Legions leading the assault, and Pullus was thankful that the general had chosen to place himself between the Equestrians and Batius' Alaudae, although Batius was actually closer given his position with the First Cohort. Pullus did notice that the Han Zhang had been allowed to stay with Caesar, although he was slightly separated and sitting with Achaemenes, and not for the first time, Pullus wondered if his general found it as difficult to read the facial expressions of the people in this part of the world as he did. Once Torquatus arrived, Caesar wasted no time.

"I offered terms to General Xao through Emissary Zhang, but the time limit has expired for his answer. So," he offered them a grim smile, "he's given us his decision." He hesitated, and Pullus understood why when Caesar said, "But there's going to be another delay, I'm afraid."

"Why?" Batius asked bluntly, and while his expression didn't betray it, Pullus was just happy that the oldest Primus Pilus fell prey to his natural impatience and beat Pullus to asking the obvious question.

"Because," Caesar snapped angrily, "I have ordered it, Primus Pilus Batius! That's reason enough." Uncharacteristically, Caesar took a breath then held up a hand, and in an almost conciliatory tone, said, "I apologize, Batius. I'm as anxious as you are to be done with this, but I'm also thinking of matters in the longer term. Which," he explained, "is why I sent Tribune Bodroges back to the ships to retrieve something that's going to be important to the men, given what I've decided."

For the next several moments, Caesar outlined what he intended to do, except that this time, the Centurion he could always count on to be his staunchest supporter was openly skeptical; more importantly, he expressed it openly.

"I think that's an awful risk, Caesar," Pullus said calmly, and while the general was looking at the large Primus Pilus, he saw Batius' and Torquatus' heads nodding at the edge of his vision. "We've never tried anything like that before, and this isn't the right time to try something new."

It was, Caesar conceded to himself, nothing more than the truth, but while he wasn't moved to change his mind, he did feel he owed it to Pullus to admit, "I understand your concerns, Pullus, and under different circumstances, you'd be right. This would be something that we would only do in battle once we tried it in training. But," he shook his head, "we're going to do it anyway."

"What are they waiting for?" Xun asked for what Bao was certain was the tenth time, but as he had done the previous nine, he said nothing.

Although, he knew, it was a good question, especially after *Hou-Kuan* Zhou made his way down to their end of the wall and informed them that General Xao had been completely unimpressed with the demonstration put on by the *Gwai* general, and that they would still have the opportunity to win glory by slaughtering these pale savages. Both officers and their men knew what was expected, and shouted their collective promise to uphold the honor of the Leaping Dragons, but Bao was certain that he detected something in his commander that was disquieting. He wasn't scared, certainly; Bao couldn't even fathom a warrior like Zhou feeling any fear, but there was a hesitance in the *Hou-Kuan*'s manner that troubled him, and as he quickly learned once Zhou returned to his own spot on the wall, Xun shared it.

"Something is worrying *Hou-Kuan* Zhou," Xun murmured. "I've never seen him like that, have you?"

Relieved that it wasn't his imagination and worried that it wasn't his imagination in equal measure, Bao shook his head.

"I wish we could have seen what it was that caused that fire," he said, earning him a look from Xun, although it was his counterpart's words that he would have cause to remember.

"I have a feeling, Bao, that we're going to find out."

Their conversation was interrupted by a shout from one of their men, who was pointing towards the forest again, the two officers seeing a two-wheeled cart emerge, drawn by one of those strange-looking ponies, followed by two more, but it wasn't until they got closer that they saw that the carts seemed to be loaded with the same cargo.

"I wonder if that's some sort of potion they give these *Gwai* before they go into battle," Xun commented. "That must be why they've been waiting."

It was certainly a reasonable assumption to make, and Bao agreed with his fellow officer, but instead of unloading the jars and passing them out to the men who, no matter what they were, had impressed Bao with their discipline, the lead cart stopped in front of the large group of *Gwai* directly in front of him, whereupon the men standing behind the first artillery piece trotted over and quickly unloaded several jars, carrying them and placing them next to the crates with the red spots on them. One by one, each of the artillery pieces were serviced in this manner until the cart was empty. While they were watching, Bao had looked off to his right, seeing in the distance the second and third carts performing the same tasks with the second and third large group. For the first time, the driver of the nearest cart used his whip, the pony going to a trot as the cart dashed away back towards the forest, using the space in between the two *Gwai* formations. By this time, Bao had deduced that the silver thing atop the pole on the right side of the line of men was some sort of bird, although it was still too far away to tell what kind, and for the first time, the *Gwai* carrying it, wearing a headdress that Bao deduced had to be a tiger's head just by the color, suddenly thrust the pole into the air. For the first time, Bao and his comrades heard the combined roar of their foes, unintelligible in whatever they were shouting but unmistakable in intent, and he was only vaguely aware that this demonstration was rippling down the entire length of the *Gwai* army. Gradually, the noise changed in character, as a handful of men began rapping the javelins they held in their right hands against their shields, which was gradually copied by their comrades, and while the sound of shouting didn't disappear immediately, the predominant noise became the rhythmic cracking sound made by thousands of men pounding their shields, until all other noise was drowned out. More than the shouting, which Bao had expected given that he would be exhorting his men to do the same very shortly, it was this absence of voices that unnerved him, the din echoing off the city wall in a steady, inexorable rhythm, the sound of thousands of professionals signaling their intent without saying a word.

 Suddenly, the giant *Gwai* wearing the white crest, who had walked out to a spot where he could be seen, and in a display of what Bao took as contempt for his foe, turned to face his men, as his soldiers continued with their rapping. It seemed as if the *Gwai* was content to let this go on, but then, without any signal that Bao could see, the giant sharply thrust his left hand up above his head, some sort of stick held in his fist horizontally...and the sound abruptly stopped, as if this was one giant beast instead of a group of men. Only then did the giant turn to stare up at Bao and his men, but despite being too far away to know with any certainty, Bao was sure that the giant *Gwai* was looking directly at him. So absorbed was he in staring down at the man that, when the note from a single horn sounded, back where the *Gwai* general was still sitting on his horse, he jumped slightly. The interval of time between that note and when the first artillery piece launched its cargo of smoking death was such that neither Bao nor Xun had any chance to say anything to their men, unable to offer words of encouragement or warning before their world erupted in flames.

As one would expect from the most experienced artillerist in the Equestrians, and one of the most experienced in the entire army, the jar of naphtha from Murena's *ballista* squarely struck one of the crenellations, creating a spectacular shower of fire, followed a bit more than an eyeblink later by the sight of the writhing body of the man whose misfortune was to be standing next to the stone upcropping, his entire upper body on fire, plummet the fifteen feet down to land at the base of the wall where, mercifully, he didn't move again. While Murena's was the first, all along the wall, at precise intervals, jars of naphtha were flung against the upper part of the western wall, although some hit a couple feet below the rampart, and one jar flew high enough to sail into the city. Almost as quickly, the air was rent by the screams of burning and terrified Han, drifting across the distance as thin cries which, Pullus noticed, were only audible because none of his men were talking, just watching in grim silence and reminding him that, even when it was a foe, watching men burn to death wasn't a sight many liked to watch. After the first volley, where every *ballista* launched at roughly the same instant, it was up to the crews to work at their own pace, which, as Pullus knew, was going to be slower than normal because of the care that the *immunes* were taking because of the dangers of the ammunition. Over the winter spent in Karoura, now two years before, there had been a debate among the Primi Pili about whether to pay the artillery *immunes* even more than the extra hundred *sesterces* a year they earned, in recognition for the greater danger using naphtha. Fortunately, at least as far as Pullus was concerned, the traditionalists like Ventidius, Hirtius, Batius, and handful of others were overruled by Caesar, but even with the increase, Pullus was aware that the *immunes* were secretly praying that the supply of this potent yet dangerously volatile substance would finally run out, especially now that they had learned from Zhang that they wouldn't be facing armored elephants any longer. Nevertheless, despite all the precautions; using the vinegar-soaked sleeves and keeping the naphtha far away from any flame until the last possible instant, it was inevitable that there would be accidents. Today was no exception, although Pullus was thankful that it had happened with one of the Alaudae crews and not his own. Slowly but methodically, the *ballistae* shifted their aim to deliver their deadly cargoes all along the parapet, until the entire length of the western wall was enveloped in the thick, choking smoke, through which the flames could be seen leaping and writhing, all while bodies of Han soldiers who were too slow to react added fuel to the fire.

"Sound the advance," Pullus ordered, just a heartbeat after the last stretch of the wall in front of his Equestrians was struck, and a heartbeat after that, the Centuries of the first four Cohorts began to march.

Pullus' concern that he had expressed to Caesar hadn't been based in this initial volley, knowing that they would be far away enough to avoid the risk of injury, but while naphtha did burn for an extensive period of time, unless there was some flammable material involved, it would eventually consume itself. Despite moving relatively quickly, Pullus could see the fires where the initial volleys had landed were beginning to flicker out, meaning that Murena and the other crew leaders would have to try and hit those spots one more time to give Pullus and his men the cover they needed without going into *testudo*, which moved more slowly out of necessity. As useful as the *testudo* was, it was universally hated by men, rankers and officers alike, because it was tiring, and for men who hated close, dark spaces, it was almost as hard on their nerves as the reason for the formation in the first place. Murena's choice for his first volley hadn't been random; it was close to the southwest corner of the wall, directly in front of the First Century, and would be the spot where one of the four ladders would go up against the wall. Most importantly to Pullus personally, it was the ladder he would be ascending, and while he trusted Murena implicitly, timing was crucial. Keeping his eyes fixed on the wall, he could see the tops of several helmeted heads, telling him that, while the Han had retreated from the parapet, they were still on the rampart, the width of which he had no idea but had assumed that it was several paces wide in order to accommodate the Han artillery, and that it had to be made of stone as well since the flames from the first jars were flickering out. Why they hadn't been bombarded by rocks from the enemy was a mystery, but it was a happy one as far as the Romans were concerned, and they were experienced enough not to question it, taking it as a sign of favor for their gods over those of the Han. Pullus and the front line had closed to within two hundred paces when a rapidly moving object trailing smoke caught his eye, the smoke enabling him to track the jar of naphtha on the last part of its arc until it smashed in another explosion of boiling flames just a matter of one or two feet from the original impact point, hitting just below the gap between the crenellation that had been struck the first time and the one next to it. This time, however, what Pullus noticed was that while he could hear shouts that communicated alarm, there were no shrieks of pain, telling him that the Han in that immediate area had removed themselves out of harm's way, which, he thought, could be a good thing, prompting him to make a snap decision.

"Sound the call to quick time, all Cohorts!" he ordered Valerius, lengthening his stride as he did so.

He was making an assumption, but it was one based on his years of experience. While it was possible that it was only the Han soldiers, or more likely an officer who commanded in this part of the wall who was behaving prudently, it was with a certain amount of confidence that he believed that, at this moment, none of the defenders were willing to risk being burned alive in the most horrible manner imaginable by coming to the parapet to defend it. The Han who had been immolated with Murena's initial volley had been the first enemy soldier who either fell or, in Pullus' view, more likely threw himself to his death rather than endure the agony, but he hadn't been the only one, and the base of the entire length of the western wall was littered with bodies, most of them still aflame. And, from experience, Pullus knew that as horrifying as the sight of another man burning to death was, even if he was an enemy, the smell of roasting human flesh provided the most visceral horror. It was the memory of other times, stretching back to the very first year of a campaign now in its sixth year when the 10th, and his friend Spurius' 3rd had been subjected to this weapon that had proven their salvation in the ensuing years that convinced Pullus to quicken the pace, gambling that even the staunchest Han wasn't willing to subject himself to becoming a flaming chunk of roasting meat, the odor of which was undoubtedly strong enough to smell from several paces away. His gamble paid off, at least in the sense that there was no flurry of missiles, either in the form of rocks, sling bullets, or arrows slashing down on any of the twelve leading Centuries of the Equestrians, but now that they were within fifty paces, Pullus had other concerns, which caused him to take his attention away from the rampart looming above them to look over his shoulder, trying to catch a glimpse of Murena.

There were too many men between them, eliciting a muttered curse from Pullus, then more loudly so that Paterculus, Valerius, and Vespillo, from his spot in the first rank of the first file could hear, "I don't know what Murena's waiting for, but he better douse that fucking naphtha or hope that I'm burned alive, because I'm going to beat him to death if I have to touch that *cac*."

Not only was it not an idle threat, it was a fear they all shared, but to their surprise, instead of sounding the halt to give the artillery the extra time, Pullus maintained his pace until they were at a point where they could feel the heat radiating from above them, and only then did he order the halt, where they stood just a few extra paces farther away than they would be when they raised the ladders.

"First Cohort! Ladder files!" Pullus bellowed the order, "Forward!" Immediately after this command, he warned, "Last five ranks, ready javelins! I don't think they're willing to be roasted, but if you see one of those slant-eyed *cunni* poke their face out, kill the bastard!"

In a sign of their trust in their Primus Pilus that, despite feeling the heat, and the random drops of flaming substance that was still dripping down from the outer edge of the rampart, there was no hesitation.

"It's now or never, Murena," Pullus muttered. More loudly, once he saw the ladder teams in position, he shouted, "Raise ladders!"

Again, the men reacted immediately, doing as he had ordered, but he saw on their faces the same apprehension that he was feeling, and it was all he could do to avoid grimacing from the blast of heat, as the man who would be bolstering the ladder he would be ascending by sitting with his back to the wall while holding the vertical supports had to be careful to avoid brushing against the smoldering corpse, who had one blackened arm extended outward, the charred hand pointing directly at Pullus as if accusing him of being responsible for his demise. Which, Pullus thought randomly, is nothing more than the truth. Nevertheless, when the ladder was raised and the top touched the wall just a few inches from the lip of the parapet that was still burning, Titus Pullus didn't hesitate to step onto the first rung, then begin climbing, trusting the gods and Murena.

If he hadn't seen it with his own eyes, Bao would have never believed, nor would he ever be able to describe it. The only thing he knew with any certainty was that *Hou-Chang* Xun had undoubtedly saved his life, shoving him, hard, towards the protection offered by the southwest corner, sending Bao sprawling in the instant before their world turned into a flaming horror. The screams were deafening, but because Bao landed face down on the stone rampart, he was actually saved from having his face and hands scorched. What he wasn't saved from was rolling over just in time to fully see what had to be Xun, his entire body from the waist up on fire, the flames wreathing his face, his open mouth emitting a shriek that didn't sound remotely human. There was a moment that couldn't have been longer than a heartbeat but Bao was certain lasted a *kè* where the two rivals locked eyes, even as the flesh around Xun's began to bubble and blacken, then, turning in what Bao was certain was a deliberate movement, Xun vanished as he threw himself over the rampart. There was too much noise for Bao to hear Xun's body hitting the ground, but now that his view of the rampart wasn't obscured, Bao heard a cry of horror that he only dimly realized came from his own throat at the sight of other writhing figures, arms flailing wildly, while some men now aflame retained their wits to drop to the stone rampart to roll over and over in an attempt to quell the flames, but as Bao watched in terror, he saw that it had no effect. More than one man followed Xun's example, throwing themselves off the rampart, some outward, but almost as many inward, landing on the paving stones of the street paralleling the wall. Between the chaos and the growing smoke as more jars of whatever vile magic potion was contained in them shattered in an explosion of flame, it was impossible for Bao to see any other officer, especially the *Hou-Kuan*, who had been standing at the opposite end of the Dragons by the second stairs, nor could he hear any shouting in the form of orders, the shrieks of burning men drowning out any officer who might be trying to impose order. Staggering to his feet, Bao instinctively began to stumble back along the western wall to the north, intent on gathering his men who weren't already casualties, but before he got a step, a rough hand grabbed him from behind. Turning in surprise, he saw the officer whose name he didn't know but recognized as belonging to the Pacing Tigers, who still grasped his arm in a firm grip.

"You can't go that way, *Hou-Chang*! Those men are doomed!"

"But they're my men!" Bao protested, jerking his arm out of the other man's grasp. "And not all of them are on fire!"

"No," the officer seemingly agreed, but then he pointed, "but look at what's happening to the ones who are trying to help."

Bao did so, just in time to watch one of his unharmed spearmen frantically kneeling next to a prone comrade trying to beat the flames out, only to have them transfer to first his hands, then quickly igniting the sleeves of his tunic, seemingly by magic. This proved too much for the spearman; he had retained his presence of mind to try and help one of his comrades, but now he panicked, and began sprinting north down the rampart, or at least tried to, almost immediately colliding with another man who was still standing, his upper body enveloped in flames, staggering and clearly close to collapse, the impact knocking the staggering man off his feet, while the first man caromed off and fell off the inner edge of the rampart and, as had happened with Xun, his scream abruptly stopped when his body hit the street. All along the rampart, as far north as Bao could see through the increasingly thick smoke, similar scenes were playing out as the *Gwai* rained what was clearly some sort of liquid fire down on the defenders, but as terrified as he was, Bao did have enough presence of mind to determine that, save for two or three jars that had sailed over the rampart to land down in the street or against the side of one of the buildings lining the opposite side, the enemy was trying to create a wall of fire along the outer edge of the parapet.

Bao had never been known for the power of his lungs, nor was he the kind of officer who used them to shout at his men, so he shocked himself by bellowing, *"Leaping Dragons! Off the rampart and down onto the street! Tell the others! Hurry!"*

He repeated this several times, until he saw that those men who were able to hear him begin to scramble to the second set of stairs; only then did he realize that his own path was cut off by the corpses of two of his men who had been standing next to Xun, both of them burning fiercely, effectively blocking that stairway. Spinning about, he had only gone a step when the *Hou-Chang* who had saved him by grabbing his arm now stepped into his path, hand on his sword.

"You can't abandon your post!" he shouted at Bao. "You'll be executed if you do!"

This shocked Bao, but he instantly understood why the other officer would see it this way.

"I'm not abandoning my post!" he protested, then pointed back over his shoulder to the flaming carnage of the rampart. "We've lost the rampart, at least on this part of the wall! I'm going to rally my men and *Hou-Chang* Xun's crossbowmen to meet them when they come down off the wall!"

The other officer didn't respond immediately, staring into Bao's eyes for a span that seemed impossibly long, before, suddenly, he gave a curt nod.

"That makes sense," he said. "We'll come with you."

"No!" Bao shook his head. "You need to stay here in case the *Gwai* try to use the southern rampart to get deeper into the city. Besides," he pointed to the officer's crossbowmen, "your crossbowmen will be in a perfect spot to slaughter the *Gwai* coming up the ladders since we won't be there to block your shot."

This time, it didn't take the other officer a full heartbeat to see and accept this, and he nodded again; more importantly, he stepped aside to let Bao run down the southern wall to the nearest stairway fifty paces from the corner, racing down to the street level then sprinting back to the junction of the southern and western wall. Rounding the corner, he was greeted by a sight that was similar to the base of the outer wall, though on a smaller scale, with burning corpses strewn down the street, but his immediate concern was how his surviving men, many of whom were still descending the stairs, while those down on the street were milling about, clearly close to panic. And, for the first time since he had been named a *Hou-Chang*, Bao Xian became a commander in more than name.

"Why are you looking like a bunch of scared women?" he roared at them as he strode in their direction. Drawing his sword, he pointed at the base of the first set of stairs nearest to the corner. "*Sui-Chang* Fang! You're responsible for defending these stairs! I'm giving you the *Sui* of Yong and Chun, but you're in overall command. If you let one *Gwai* set his filthy hoof on these stones, I'll kill you myself! Do you understand?"

"Yes, *Hou-Chang*!" Fang barked. "You can count on us!"

Bao was already moving down the street to a spot equidistant between the first two sets of stairs, where he shouted, "Crossbowmen of *Hou-Chang* Xun's *Hou*! Assemble on me!"

As he was organizing his men, Bao was also surreptitiously counting casualties, and he was disheartened to see that, of the seventy-seven men of his *Hou* and the seventy-seven crossbowmen belonging to Xun, fully a third of their numbers were missing, although it appeared that the losses were heavier among his own spearmen, which made sense given they had been standing closest to the parapet at the moment the barrage began. Bao was in the process of giving his orders to the crossbowmen, with the intention of sending them into the buildings across the street to loose from the windows of the second floor, which were shuttered at the moment, when he saw someone approaching from the direction of the Jade Gate. When he saw that it was General Lei striding towards him, hand on his sword with a look of fury on his face, it took a huge effort on Bao's part not to turn and run, and he did his best to appear as calm as the circumstances allowed.

"What are you doing, *Hou-Chang* Bao?" Lei snarled. "Why have you removed your *Hou* from the wall?"

Bao surprised himself once again, this time because he replied matter-of-factly, "Because the wall is lost, General Lei. The only thing that would come out of staying on the wall is seeing my men burn to death."

Lei's eyes narrowed, and Bao braced himself for an explosion of temper that, while not as volatile as General Xao, was still formidable, while he kept his eyes on the hand resting on Lei's sword, so he was completely unprepared when the general asked instead, "What is your plan, *Hou-Chang*?"

The shock delayed his response for a heartbeat, but he just beat Lei, who was opening his mouth to point to where *Sui-Chang* Fang and the survivors of his and the other two *Sui* were standing.

"I'm placing three of my *Sui* at the base of the stairs there, General," Bao explained. "The other four I'm placing at the base of the stairs next to the Jade Gate." Pointing to the second floor of the three buildings in between the sets of stairs covered by his *Hou*, he continued, "Putting the crossbowmen up on the second floor will put them in a position to slaughter many of the *Gwai* coming up their ladders, while my spearmen will be in position to stop them from descending to the street."

Before Lei could respond, there was a fresh set of screams from farther down the rampart, where another *Tu-wei-fu*, the Rising Cranes, was positioned, their *Hou-Kuan* choosing to remain on the rampart, and the general twisted about just in time to see a soldier, enveloped in flames, topple off the inner edge of the rampart onto the street below where, once again, the screams were cut short.

Whether this made Lei's mind up for him, Bao never knew, but the general turned back and gave a curt nod as he said, "Your strategy is sound. I'm going to talk to General Xao and recommend we do the same the entire length of the wall, before we all burn to death. Carry out your orders, *Hou-Kuan* Bao."

Certain that Lei was confused, Bao stammered, "B-but I'm only a *Hou-Chang*, General!"

"Not anymore," Lei snapped, then in a fractionally softer tone, said, "*Hou-Kuan* Zhou is dead, so you're now the Leaping Dragons *Hou-Kuan*. If you survive?" He shrugged. "It may be permanent."

Before Bao could say anything, Lei turned and moved at a quick trot back to the Jade Gate, leaving Bao with his mouth open.

"*Hou-Kuan* Bao? What are your orders?"

The reference to his new rank was what Bao needed, but he realized something, and asked the crossbowman, "What was your name again, *Sui-Chang*?"

"Jun, *Hou-Kuan*."

"Yes, that's right," Bao nodded, thinking for a moment, then pointed to the nearest building. "The entrance to this house is around the corner, so you need to hurry. Take your *Sui* and one other. Go," Bao ordered.

Jun called to another *Sui-Chang*, and they ran off while Bao hurried down the street in the direction of the Jade Gate, assigning two more *Sui* to the next building, then sending the final three to the building that was directly across from the second stairway, only then calling to the last four *Sui* of spearmen, giving them the identical orders he had given to Fang. By the time he was through, it was clear that Xao had agreed with Lei's suggestion, and he took a moment to savor the feeling of pride, though it wasn't destined to last long because, from that direction, the other surviving *Hou-Chang* of the Leaping Dragons came to get their orders from the new *Hou-Kuan*, which helped his nerves simply through the fact that he was too busy to be terrified anymore.

Pullus was certain that the feathers of his white crest were in danger of bursting into flames as he climbed his ladder, but just as he was raising a foot to ascend past the halfway point up the bamboo ladder, he had the barest flicker of warning of something hurtling above him before he was showered in liquid that he instantly identified as vinegar by the smell. More importantly, he heard the hissing sound that, while similar to that of water dousing normal flames, was subtly different, with a more sibilant quality. The liquid dripped down the rim of his helmet, fortunately not getting into his eyes, but when he glanced up, he saw that, while the flames weren't as fierce, they hadn't been completely extinguished, forcing him to make a decision. Temporarily stopping his ascent to let either Murena or one of the other crews send a second jar to fully extinguish the flames would be the prudent thing, and he actually intended to do that when he happened to glance to his left. There were now more than a dozen ladders leaning against the wall within his vision, although as expected, he was the highest of his men, but then he saw his Optio, looking directly at him on the third ladder over from his own, grinning as he scrambled up in a clear attempt to beat his Centurion. In that eyeblink of time, Pullus saw that the area just above Lutatius was fully extinguished, and the thought flashed through his mind that perhaps his Optio had rushed over to the nearest crew, not Murena but *Immunes* Sallustius, and offered him something in exchange for concentrating on the spot above Lutatius' ladder to give him an advantage over his Primus Pilus. Even as this was going through his mind, one leg was levering him up the ladder; what happened next occurred so close to simultaneously that it was impossible to determine what happened first.

Now that he had gotten closer to the gap in the crenellations where his ladder was aligned, he saw that, while there was still fire, the flames were only a few inches in height and flickering out. As was his habit, which had begun completely by accident during his first assault on an unnamed town in Hispania, Pullus intended on using the power of his massive thighs to vault up and over the parapet, not jumping or stepping through the gap between crenellations that most men favored. Because he was one of the few men, in any army, who had the strength to perform such a maneuver, he had perfected it over the years, using the mass of his huge body as his legs swung up and over to slam into any defender standing in that spot. With a crenellated wall such as this and when he had a shield, which he did now, he knew that he could use it by wedging it into the gap, gripping the handle to provide the necessary leverage to perform this move, while the final advantage was that it also kept his right hand free to grasp his *gladius*. The burning remnants of naphtha complicated this somewhat, but seeing Lutatius threatening to become the first man in the Equestrians, if not in the three Legions, to mount an enemy wall meant that this wasn't a consideration for a man whose desire to lead from the front bordered on an obsession. Consequently, he was beginning his move, reaching up to wedge the shield into the gap when, seemingly from nowhere, his shield was almost jerked from his hand, while he was showered with stinking vinegar as the jar shattered against the metaled edge of his protection. Along with the liquid were razor-sharp shards of pottery, and he experienced a now-familiar sensation as if someone had thrust a burning stick into his left cheek, although he was only barely aware of similar feelings at several points on his left arm. This was an annoyance; the shower of stinging vinegar in his eyes that temporarily blinded him was far more serious. Nevertheless, although he could have arrested the movement of his shield and paused to recover himself and, at the very least clear his vision, this was a moment where Titus Pullus was as much a victim of his growing legend as he was a beneficiary, the thought of pausing never occurring to him. After all, this was a move he had practiced so many times, albeit not exactly in this manner, he was certain he could have done it with his eyes closed. That was essentially what was happening, and he felt rather than saw the lower edge of his shield strike the stone of the bottom lip, whereupon he twisted his wrist to wedge the top of the shield against the opposite side at the top of the crenellation while thrusting up with his legs, both of which were now briefly on the same rung, twisting his torso to bring up then swing his legs like a door, with his left arm serving as the hinge and the shield serving as the doorjamb. He had prepared himself to feel the impact of his legs striking a defender, but there was nothing there, giving him less than an eyeblink to adjust to the change and prepare himself to land cleanly with both feet on the rampart, which he somehow managed to do. And, it was at this instant that another but even more important part of the legend of Titus Pullus asserted itself, the fact that, second only to Caesar, the gods truly loved him. The momentum of his movement meant that, when he felt he was on solid footing, he had to perform an unnatural motion in order to dislodge his shield from where it was wedged, which he managed to do so quickly and smoothly that, despite the fact that he was still unable to see clearly, to the Han *Hou-Chang* commanding the defenders of the Pacing Tigers on the southern wall nearest to the corner, it seemed as if the huge *Gwai* had seen the crossbowmen off of and slightly behind his right shoulder from their position farther down the southern wall and facing the western wall at an oblique angle. By appearance, it seemed to the *Hou-Chang* that, in the eyeblink, not before but after they loosed their bolts, the large *Gwai* swung his shield slightly across his body and into the perfect position to block them even as his head was only beginning to turn in that direction.

Whether they were shaken, or overeager by the sudden appearance of this pale giant, of the half-dozen crossbowmen who aimed at Pullus, four of them completely missed him, two bolts going wide to his left, one over his head, and one striking the stone of the parapet between his legs before caroming off into space through the gap in the crenellation. Two of them struck his shield, and if it had been anyone else, the shield would have been wrenched out of their hands; more importantly, if Pullus' shield had been made of its traditional poplar and ash and not the harder teakwood they had begun using during their time in the Pandya kingdom, the Han crossbow would have been powerful enough to completely penetrate it, although they protruded more than half their length as it was. It was only instinct and his own temperament that got Pullus moving, fast, in the direction of what he barely perceived as the nearest threat, and while he desperately wanted to wipe his eyes, he knew that he couldn't afford to, yet despite being unable to see with perfect clarity, his vision was good enough to perceive a Han charging at him from where the enemy soldier had been standing on the southern rampart a pace or two away from the southwest corner, cutting the distance between them by leaping across the space created by the corner to land on the western wall less than two paces from the Roman. He had a sword but no shield, and to his credit, the Han didn't hesitate, nor did he try to cleave Pullus in half with his longer sword like a Gaul might have, instead aiming a low, hard thrust that Pullus had to move his shield to block. The power behind the thrust was impressive, but it was the Han's speed that gave Pullus pause, thankful that, with the last couple blinks of his eyes, his vision cleared just in time to see his opponent's sword moving in a fluid arc so that, when the Han made another thrust, it was now from a completely different spot and angle, in what to Pullus would be a second position thrust, trying to drive the point of his blade into Pullus' face above the Roman's shield. Once more, Pullus blocked it, then he was done being on the defense, executing a thrust of his own while taking advantage of his higher shield position to execute a flawless first position thrust from underneath, violently twisting his hips at the last possible instant to add to the massive power he was capable of generating with just his arm. Later, when Pullus would reflect on this moment, he was convinced that this thrust had been one of the best he had ever performed, certainly in battle; to his intense frustration, his Han foe somehow managed to twist his body, not completely out of the path of the plunging point of Pullus' *gladius* but enough that Pullus could tell that the point hit nothing but open space, although he heard the Han yelp in pain as Pullus felt the edge of his blade slice into his foe's side. Just as he was recovering to try again, from behind him, he recognized Vespillo's voice.

"Primus Pilus! I'm here..."

Even before the last word was out of his Sergeant's mouth, Pullus heard the sharp crack that sounded much like a blocked sword thrust but was in fact a bolt from one of the Han crossbowmen, followed instantly by a sharp cry of surprise.

"They're using scorpions!" Vespillo shouted; more importantly, he was stepping into his spot to Pullus' left even as he did so.

Pullus didn't have the time to respond because his Han foe was already moving again, taking a slight hop to his left that put him into the southwestern corner so that he had the stone wall protecting him, a move which Pullus silently acknowledged. He knows what he's doing, Titus, so watch yourself. Even as the thought flashed through his mind, the Han renewed his attack, except this time, he feinted a high thrust then dropped into what was almost a crouch that allowed him to sweep his blade in a horizontal blow that Pullus recognized as an attempt to cripple his mobility and his base, aiming for the spot just above his greaves and below his knees. It was a desperately close thing, yet somehow he managed to block the Han's blade with his own, and this time, his own strength showed its advantage because, despite the momentum created by the sweeping move, it was the Han's blade that recoiled back in the opposite direction and not his own as it bounced back, which gave him the advantage he needed. Because his blade hadn't moved, and the Han was still in his crouch, his *gladius* was perfectly positioned for him to sweep it upward with a flick of his wrist, the edge already oriented so that it bit into the middle of the Han's lower jaw, and even with a backhanded attack, with enough power to cleave through bone, teeth, and tongue, sending the Han reeling backward. He would have shrieked from the pain of it, but his mouth instantly filled with blood, while, more importantly, he made no attempt to defend himself, though not from Pullus but from Vespillo's blade, which shot out between his and Pullus' shield to take their foe right under the breastbone. The Han collapsed to the rampart, blood pouring from his mouth, but instead of moving to step over the corpse and advance up the southern wall, Pullus grabbed Vespillo as the Centurion stepped backward, essentially swapping spots, although that wasn't his intent. All that transpired since his vault had taken perhaps four or five heartbeats of time, but it was enough for Tubero of the second file and Macula of the third to join them, both of whom Pullus shoved to stand next to Vespillo.

"Watch those *cunni*!" he snapped, pointing his *gladius* at the men of the deceased *Hou-Chang*, none of them looking particularly eager to step over their commander's body to engage the Romans, despite their longer spears. "And," he thought to add, "that bow they're using hits like a mule kick. It resembles a scorpion, but they can reload it faster, so don't drop your shields."

With this done, Pullus turned his attention to the larger situation, seeing that several of his men were already on the rampart from the other ladders, guessing that it was two men for each of the four ladders of the First Century. Lutatius signaled, waving his *gladius,* Pullus replying in kind with a wave of his own, and looking past his Optio, he saw that Balbus, his black crest identifying him despite his back being turned at the moment, was also on the rampart, which was no more than he expected. The smoke was still thick, but what flames he could see were clearly flickering out as the naphtha consumed itself, and the stone rampart was littered with corpses, though few if any of them felled by any of his men, Pullus noting that all of them were either still burning or smoldering. It was curious, Pullus thought, that none of the dead Han had been cut down by his men but had already been stricken by the naphtha, and he wondered what it might mean, though he didn't give it more than a passing thought. What mattered now was getting organized; this was the moment when not only would Pullus understand that the rampart had been abandoned, for the first time, Pullus and his Equestrians gained a fuller knowledge and appreciation of the Han crossbow.

Bao's first close look at a *Gwai* came when the giant wearing the white crest suddenly appeared as if summoned by the demons of the underworld, vaulting onto the rampart in almost the exact spot Bao had occupied not long before, but it was the manner in which the giant did it that convinced the Han that this being had otherworldly powers. Somehow, Bao wasn't sure how, the *Gwai* had used the large shield they carried as leverage to swing his body sideways, up and over the crenellations, and he was certain that the *Gwai's* massive legs would have at the very least knocked him off his feet if he had been standing there. When the *Gwai,* whose back was momentarily partially turned to the crossbowmen of the Pacing Tigers *Hou* on the southern rampart nearest the western wall, somehow sensed the threat and swung his shield around in what, to his eyes, was one fluid motion that appeared part of the same movement that brought him onto the parapet, any doubt that Bao had that this was a mere mortal man was erased. He had joined the first of his crossbowmen on the second floor of the building directly across the street from the southwest corner of the wall heartbeats before and his men had just pushed open the shutters, giving Bao and his men a perfect vantage point...and a perfect opportunity to kill this giant who had swung his shield to catch what Bao saw were two bolts, although he saw several miss. Yet, like the men standing with him, he was rooted in his spot, seemingly unable to move or to order his men to lift their crossbows to take aim at this *Gwai*. As long as it seemed, it couldn't have been more than a heartbeat or two of time, because from just behind the giant *Gwai*, another one appeared, although this man was of normal size and wasn't wearing that ridiculous white crest on the top of his helmet, but it was enough to jolt Bao from his trance.

"Loose on those *Gwai* demons!"

To their credit, the pair of men who could stand side by side in the window didn't hesitate, but they were too late, the shorter *Gwai* bringing his shield up just as his crossbowmen released their bolts, the sharp, cracking report of both bolts slamming into the wooden protection loud enough to be heard over the other noises. Bao had stepped away from the window to give his crossbowmen room, making it more difficult for him to see, but when he snapped the order for the first pair to step aside so the next pair could do so, both of them releasing even as they stepped close to the opening, he saw that the two *Gwai* had already been joined by another pair of men.

"I want three pairs at this window," Bao shouted, already moving to the door that led to another room where the second window in this building was located. "Don't let these *Gwai* off the rampart without filling them full of holes!"

He didn't wait to see if he was obeyed, even as the thought in the back of his mind was the reminder that these weren't *his* men, they were Xun's, but it didn't slow him down from rushing across the narrow hallway through the open door to the other room of the second story, arriving just in time to see that there were actually seven crossbowmen in this room, two of them kneeling down to reload as another pair stood over them, aimed for an instant, then loosed, the twanging sound of the bowstring snapping just audible, followed an eyeblink later by a sound that was music to Bao's ears, a scream of pain, followed by a shout that sounded as if it came from a different voice babbling some sort of nonsense. Hurrying over to the window, Bao saw that, next to a prone figure that was blackened and charred beyond recognition, a *Gwai* was lying on his side, although his upper body was obscured by his shield, having pulled the protection up and over his torso, perhaps in his last action on this side of the invisible barrier between this world and the next. For an instant, Bao considered ordering one of the men stepping forward to aim for the lower body, then decided against it, instead indicating the *Gwai* who was pointing his sword back in their direction, the tenor of his voice confirming that it had been the one who spoke what Bao assumed was a curse of some sort, or perhaps summoning more demons to aid their cause. The bolts from both crossbowmen struck squarely, the force sending the shield back into the *Gwai*'s body with enough force that he staggered backward, colliding with another *Gwai* who was just swinging one leg through the gap in the parapet. It was impossible to see exactly what happened with any clarity, but Bao heard a muffled shout of alarm, then the *Gwai* on the rampart, clearly forgetting his predicament, suddenly spun about, exposing his back, and as he did so, Bao saw that the gap was now empty, telling him that the ascending man had been knocked off the ladder he was using. While the *Gwai* immediately realized his error, judging by the manner in which he essentially made a full revolution in a desperate attempt to protect himself, two bolts buried themselves in his left side, although his momentum still brought him back around to face the open window. The shield slipped from his fingers, blood pouring from his mouth as he dropped to his knees before toppling face forward on top of his shield.

"They have the biggest noses I've ever seen."

Bao wasn't even aware of saying this, but it drew the attention of the men at the window, one of them turning around to grin at Bao, just as another *Gwai* appeared in the gap from which his comrade had disappeared, but this time, the man held a javelin. It seemed to happen slowly enough for Bao to shout a warning, but the man hurled the javelin just as he stepped up onto the rampart, putting his body into it so that it moved in a flat trajectory. From where Bao was standing, it appeared as if the crossbowmen who appreciated his comment sprouted what Bao could see was a narrow iron shaft, topped by a dripping triangular point that now protruded from just below his breastbone, so that it was now the turn of a Han to drop to his knees as blood sprayed from his mouth in a frothy foam when he tried to speak, and despite the difference in facial features, Bao was certain that his crossbowman shared essentially the same expression as the dead *Gwai* whose blood was still pooling on the rampart, beginning as puzzlement, then dawning into the realization of his mortality. Unlike the *Gwai*, when the crossbowman toppled forward, the point of the protruding shaft stuck in the wooden floor, leaving him propped up at a grotesque angle, his arms and head dangling for a brief moment before the shaft bent under his weight, and he finally hit the floor facedown. Bao's attention was torn away from this sight by another shout of pain, and he looked up just in time to see another of his crossbowmen who had just stepped into the window in order to loose another bolt suddenly reel backward, but this time, the shaft of the javelin didn't transfix him, instead hanging loosely from his abdomen.

However, when one of the remaining crossbowmen instinctively reached out to help his comrade, he placed himself directly in the window, and Bao snarled, "*Do not touch him!*" When the crossbowman looked at him in surprise and anger, Bao snapped, "You're making yourself a target! They have javelins!"

The crossbowman instantly dropped down below the window with a gratifying speed, but it gave Bao a better look at the rampart, dismayed to see that, as short as this moment had been, there were now several *Gwai* on the rampart, including another one with the strange crest, except this one was black, and Bao caught just a glimpse of the right side of the *Gwai's* face and head, which was brutally scarred and missing the right ear. It was what this *Gwai*, who Bao correctly assumed was an officer, was doing that was most troubling, arranging men in a line directly across from the window, whereupon the front row knelt behind their shields, while a second row stepped forward in between the kneeling men to place their shields on top of the shields of the front row, making something of a wall.

Bao shouted, "Drive those *Gwai* off the rampart! Hammer them and they'll fall back like that first demon, I swear it!"

The men obeyed; taking the time only to roughly shove the dead crossbowman aside, while another man dragged his moaning comrade, the javelin still protruding from his stomach, clear of the window as the surviving crossbowmen resumed working as a team, with two men loosing as the others reloaded. Bao stayed only long enough to see that, at least for the moment, they had at a minimum pinned the *Gwai* down, then went rushing out of the room, heading for the stairs. By doing so, he once again escaped death.

Chapter Six

Afterward, it was universally agreed that the gods had truly favored Caesar and his men when they reconstituted their shields with the harder teakwood, the extra weight that had initially been the cause of complaint proving to be well worth it. Even so, at a range of a bit more than a couple dozen paces, the bolts from the Han crossbows, which the men instantly nicknamed "little scorpions," penetrated to a disturbing degree, so that once a man's shield was hit enough times, there could be as many as a dozen sharp iron points protruding from the back of the shield that, unless they were removed, were still incredibly dangerous, and as they were about to learn, within ten paces, they penetrated all the way through, although they were robbed of just enough force not to penetrate very deeply into the part of a man's body protected by a *hamata*. Because the Equestrians were facing an otherwise inexperienced *Hou Chang* who nevertheless showed great initiative in recognizing the futility of holding the rampart and removed his men to the buildings across the street faster, they also suffered the most. Balbus' idea of making a form of *testudo* was quickly copied, including by Pullus with his First, but while they were protected, they were effectively pinned down, quickly learning that hurling javelins only worked when they had the element of surprise, the missiles not moving nearly as fast as the bolts that were slashing back at them in the opposite direction, and in several times the number. The other practical issue was the noise, sounding like hundreds of invisible carpenters whacking pieces of wood with mallets, which not only made it next to impossible to communicate, it made it almost as difficult to think. It was ultimately left to Scribonius to come up with the solution to the stalemate, although it was a grim one, and not something he decided lightly, but finally, after looking in both directions and seeing roughly the same sight, with three or sometimes four ranks of men on the rampart, with the men of the front rank kneeling less than a pace away from the inside edge of the rampart and the subsequent ranks resting their shields on the top of the men in front of them, he made his decision.

"Pusio," he shouted to the ranker of the third rank nearest to him. "I'm sending you back down the ladder to go to the Primus Pilus!" He had withdrawn a wax tablet from the satchel Centurions carried and was scribbling as he talked. Thrusting it out to the ranker, he finished by shouting, "Wait for my signal." Turning his attention to the rest of his Century on the rampart, less than half the total number with the remainder still at the base of their ladders, he spotted who he was looking for, and bellowed, "Caecina! Volusenus!" When the pair looked in his direction, he commanded, "You still have your javelins! When I give you the signal, I want you to fling them at the window across from you!" Seeing the look of alarm on their faces, he assured them, "I don't need you to take the time to aim. Just up and throw them, then get back down. We just need to make them duck!"

He saw the relief on their faces, for which he didn't blame them a bit, then turned to Pusio.

"Ready?" When the ranker nodded, Scribonius shouted, "*Release*!" then in the same breath, ordered Pusio, "Go!"

It worked, yet even so, while the Han crossbowmen did flinch, just as Pusio dropped out of sight below the parapet, a bolt skipped off the top of one of the men's shields to go streaking out through the gap where the ranker had been an eyeblink before.

"Now, we wait," Scribonius muttered to his *Signifer*.

Pusio scrambled down the ladder, although he had to curse at his comrades still waiting at the base of it to move out of the way, but when they demanded to know what was happening, he didn't take the time to explain, waving the tablet as he broke into a run along the western wall, heading south to the last ladder. Quickly finding it easier to move between the other ladders and wall, even with the handful of smoldering corpses, Pusio ignored the shouts of his comrades in the First Cohort, all demanding to know the same thing, reaching the ladder then scrambling up it as quickly as he could, before stopping just below the parapet. He hadn't seen the bolt that narrowly missed him, but he had heard it, and he wasn't willing to get a bolt in the face because he popped his head up like a curious rodent, so instead, he raised himself cautiously until the crest of his helmet was just above the stone of the gap.

"Primus Pilus Pullus!" he shouted, but there was no immediate answer.

Only after the third shout did he hear the growl that would normally send stabs of fear into his heart, especially now, because Pullus sounded more irritated than anything.

"Who is that? And what the fuck are you doing here?" Pusio quickly explained, and to his vast relief, Pullus said, "All right, reach up and hand the tablet to me." He did so, then realized Scribonius hadn't told him what to do after that, so when he began to lower himself, he suddenly stopped.

"*Oy*! Pusio? Is that you, you stupid bastard? What are you doing up there? What's going on?"

Recognizing the voice as belonging to an occasional carousing partner in the First of the First who was still waiting his turn to ascend, Pusio was about to tell him when Pullus called to him.

"Pusio! Go tell Pilus Prior Scribonius that I agree, that's the best plan." Pusio instantly began to descend; whether Pullus realized this was probable, or he had peeked over the side Pusio had no way of knowing. What mattered was Pullus barking, "Wait, I'm not through!" Naturally, Pusio froze as Pullus continued, "Before you do, you need to run back to tell Caesar that we need slaves or whoever is available to bring us the jars, as quickly as he can, do you understand? Otherwise, we're never getting off this fucking wall."

"Jars? What jars?" Pusio asked, more to himself, but it was loudly enough that Pullus snapped, "Of the naphtha, you idiot. What, did you think I wanted to give you greedy bastards the last of my *sura*?"

Pusio made no reply because he was already racing down

the ladder, but there was one benefit to being yelled at by the Primus Pilus; he didn't have to explain to the men at the bottom of the ladder, who had heard every word.

Lei had reacted quickly in accepting Bao's decision as the correct one and adopting it, and he knew he was running a risk in not conferring with Xao before he began issuing orders, but when the General was no longer standing across from the Jade Gate, Lei had taken it as a sign that Xao had rushed off to see whether or not the reports of the fleet being burned were exaggerated, leaving him fully in charge of the defense of the western wall. He was forced to use runners with the mounted courier dead, and, grabbing any man standing nearby, he sent several of them racing north along the wall, giving each of them a specific *Hou-Kuan* to find and pass along his orders to abandon the rampart, leave their non-missile infantry down on the street and congregated around each of the stairways and gates, and the crossbowmen to use the buildings across the street from the rampart. The smoke was thick and choking, and even if its acrid stench didn't make his eyes burn, it would have been difficult to see more than a handful of blocks in either direction, but he could somewhat track the progress by the movement he did see, and most importantly, that it was moving from his left to the right, away from the rampart, the sign that his orders were being obeyed. While he had no idea of the organization of a Roman Legion, he did think to move north beyond the Fourth Cohort of the 10th to determine the situation with his men facing what were the other two Legions. He had actually begun to move in that direction until one of the jars that was producing this ghastly fire and choking smoke sailed over the parapet, barely missing the rampart as it arced downward and smashed against the side of one of the buildings, just below the eaves of the roof. Despite being more than twenty paces away, he felt the intense heat almost immediately, while his vision was seared for a moment from the intense light, leaving only his ears to tell him that, while it hadn't struck the rampart, the contents had clearly spattered onto at least one of the warriors who had just descended down to the street, the man immediately shrieking in pain and terror. Lei could only catch glimpses, impressions more than substance as his vision cleared, of other men rushing to their stricken comrade, frantically trying to extinguish the flames by throwing the man to the street, yet the screams not only continued unabated, they seemed to grow in intensity.

Turning back because of the heat, Lei resigned himself to simply hoping that his orders had been obeyed the length of the western wall, deciding to remain at the Jade Gate for the moment. And, for a brief span of time, as he returned to Jade Street, it appeared as if it was working; all down the rampart to the southwestern corner, he could see the *Gwai* had been brought to a standstill, using their shields as a blizzard of bolts slashed across the street to slam into them, and he could see how they jerked from the impact. At least, he thought with some relief, they're not coming down off the rampart, but very quickly, he understood this was only a temporary measure at best. Yes, he could hear sudden shouts and screams of pain, and once he saw a *Gwai* who had been kneeling at the front suddenly topple forward, following his shield down to the paving stones, yet before he could blink, the *Gwai* behind the now-dead man stepped forward and knelt in the same motion, the gap in the shields lasting less than a full heartbeat, with the man behind him immediately resting his shield on the top of the first. Despite this encouraging sign, Lei knew that sooner rather than later, despite the fact that Xao had ordered twice the number of bolts for each crossbowman, they would soon run out. He briefly considered pulling the men from the three other ramparts who were waiting for the *Gwai* to attempt to scale the wall on their side, but since he didn't have any idea what the situation was, not having received any updates from the officers Xao had put in command of each one, he decided against it; he was only willing to go so far in exercising initiative. For the moment, he could see that many of the *Sui* consisting of the spearmen and *ji*, and the smallest group of men who used the sword, that weapon given only to the most experienced warriors, had chosen to shelter under the overhang of the rampart. He was about to order them to step out into the street so they were closer to the bottom of the stairway, but he took the time to examine some of the bodies, almost all Han, although he saw a couple of *Gwai* corpses, that littered the street. While most of them were clearly victims of the demonic fire weapon, he also saw a handful who been struck down by a javelin of some type, and that sight changed his mind. *We're going to need every man for the moment those savages leave the rampart*, he thought grimly; still, while the situation was serious, he felt confident in his infantry, knowing that the only way down was the stairs, the rampart too high to jump from safely under these circumstances. Lei also noticed that the smoke was dissipating in the direction of the southwest corner, telling him that at least the *Gwai* had stopped using the fire to drive the defenders off the rampart, and he was sure that the enemy would have to at least begin to try and leave the rampart very soon. He had positioned himself with his back up against the wall of the building on the south side of Jade Street; the *Gwai* just a few paces away and above him were still cowering behind their shields, but he was a veteran and no fool, presenting them with as small a target as possible as he waited for the moment he was certain was coming. Only then would he step away from the shelter provided by the stone wall of the building to take command of his men, for the moment contenting himself with switching his attention between the fighting south of the Jade Gate and to the north, and he just happened to be looking to the south when he saw Bao emerge from the building one block down, then race across the street to join the men under the rampart. Since he was looking in that direction, it was natural for his eye to be drawn to another movement, although this one was down at the southwest corner of the wall. It was too far away to make out any detail, but it was impossible to miss the sudden appearance of a *Gwai* wearing a helmet with a white crest of some sort as he stood erect. Lei could also see his arm draw back and, just barely, see the small object that he hurled across the street, but despite being too far away to hear the screams of burning men over the shouting, Lei somehow instantly understood what the object had been; if he had known this was just the first of many such scenes, he might have decided that his fate was sealed no matter what he did.

Pullus was unhappy to learn that, when the artillery *immunes*, their part done, rejoined their Centuries, they had left their leather sleeves with their pieces, but he had managed to scrounge up two skins of vinegar before he began in the event that there was an accident, while blocking out the thought that any accident would involve him being burned alive. Kneeling and protected by the shields of his Century, it was still hard to concentrate because of the noise as the Han bolts from the little scorpions kept hammering his men, and it took a supreme effort on his part to keep his hand from shaking as he prepared to strike the flint.

"I've only got one chance at this," while he was speaking loudly enough for the men around him to hear, to Paterculus, it sounded as if Pullus was talking to himself, "so I better not fuck it up." Only then did he glance up to remind them, "You have to move your shields the instant you see the rag catch, boys, you understand that? Or we're all going to be like those poor bastards down there."

The "poor bastards" he was referring to were in the small pile of corpses that, even under intense fire from the Han, his men had managed to shove off the rampart to make room, but he was assured by Turbo and the other men surrounding him that he didn't need to worry about them getting out of the way.

"Ready?" Knowing their Centurion expected more than a nod, they verbally signaled their readiness because his attention was solely on his task, prompting Pullus to strike the flint; the fact that it took three tries didn't soothe anyone's nerves, but then the rag burst into flame. "*Move!*"

The four Legionaries who surrounded Pullus obeyed instantly, yet even so, Pullus' shoulder struck the edge of Turbo's shield, staggering the ranker and causing him to collide with his comrade to his left, creating a momentary gap in the coverage. Given the concentration of fire from the Han, it could have easily been a fatal error, but Pullus had risen to his feet, drawn his arm back, and hurled the jar in one continuous motion and with unerring aim, right through the window directly across from them, doing it so quickly that none of the Han at the window, all of whom were in their last heartbeats of a life that would end in nothing but unimaginable pain, could react.

Everything happened quickly after that; knowing that the Han at the other window of the building across from them would at the very least be distracted by the explosion of fire, Pullus' orders had been explicit that the other men charged with breaking this deadlock by using this weapon that was so dangerous to friend and foe, wait for him to go first, and only then do the same. He also ordered that it be his officers performing the most dangerous part, which meant that Lutatius, on the opposite end of his Century was next, followed by Balbus, his ravaged features twisted into his version of a feral smile, although his throw was a bit low, the jar glancing off the bottom of the window, which, inevitably, he would declare he had meant to do. Certainly, the effect was even more dramatic, the contents of the shattered jar spraying outward and dousing the three Han crossbowmen who had the misfortune to be closest to the window, sending one of them hurtling out and down into the street, his agony ending when his neck mercifully broke from the impact. It was in this rippling manner that the Romans on the rampart retook the initiative, and in turn, it meant that it was Pullus who, even as his jar was still in the air, began moving for the nearest stairway first, located at the intersection of the western and southern walls.

With the death of their *Hou Chang*, the men defending the southern wall had retreated farther east down the rampart, content to allow their comrades with their crossbows pummel the *Gwai*, and when they saw the giant *Gwai* suddenly begin running towards the stairs, the spearmen were about fifty paces away. Without a leader, however, there was a moment's hesitation before one Han carrying the *ji* reacted and broke into a sprint down the rampart, although he was followed immediately by the rest of his comrades. Because of their position farther down the southern wall, they hadn't seen exactly what had happened when the giant had hurled a smoking pot into the window around the corner, but as these Han defenders raced to try and intercept the *Gwai*, understanding that these savages were attempting to get down into the city, they reached a spot where they could see black smoke billowing out of the building at the corner and hear the screams of men in horrible pain over the din. Whether or not this was what caused them to falter, Pullus neither knew nor cared; that they did so was all that mattered. He still carried his shield, though it was full of holes from the bolts he had yanked out of it, holding it in a position that protected him from the Han crossbowmen on the southern wall now that the immediate threat from the building was neutralized, and he felt it buck in his hand as a bolt slammed into it, the point protruding a couple inches just above the boss.

Seeing that he was going to reach the stairs first, Pullus had to make an instantaneous choice, and it was a sign of his faith in his men, and himself, that over the noise, he shouted over his shoulder, "Even sections on me down the stairs, odd sections with Lutatius to sort out these *cunni* on the southern wall!"

Knowing that it was the men of his First Section who were immediately behind him, while it superficially appeared as if Pullus was behaving with his usual hubris by disdaining the threat of the approaching Han, now three across the rampart with their spears leveled as they rushed towards the stairs, his reason for choosing to descend them and effectively place these closer Han to his rear was noticing their slight hesitation, and with a glance, he had seen that their attention had been drawn by the smoke pouring from the nearest window. It was a natural response, especially for these men who had already seen comrades incinerated, and he didn't hesitate to take advantage of it, judging that Vespillo and the rest of the First Section would still reach the stairs and be able to make the corner before the Han could, to protect his rear. Even so, it also meant that there was still a gap between Pullus and the men who would be supporting him in the fight to get off the stairs. That wasn't the reason he suddenly stopped halfway down the stairs, however; in the brief span of time that he had to observe the rude formation of helmeted and armored Han waiting at the base of the stairs, he noticed that, contrary to his first impression, they weren't all holding spears. In fact, they seemed evenly divided between spears of the type he had faced more times than he could count, starting two decades earlier in Hispania, and another type he had never seen before, with a spearpoint, but with an extra piece of iron attached just below that looked something like a crescent moon, with a sharpened edge and the end nearest to the spearpoint with a fine point, while the lower part actually curved a bit more and was slightly wider, not much but enough to be noticeable even with a quick glance. Behind him, he heard the shouts and the clashing sound that signaled that Vespillo and the rest of the First Section had closed with the Han defenders still on the rampart, but he didn't flinch nor did he bother to look, and barely a heartbeat later, he heard the clattering of hobnailed soles behind and above him, signaling the arrival of his Second Section on the stairs.

"Hold!" he barked, sensing that one of his men was only a step above him and about to get in front of his Centurion. Without taking his eyes away from the Han below them and seemingly oblivious to the struggle behind, Pullus warned, "See those spears with the extra iron piece on them? Be careful! I think they're going to use them to try and hook our shields!"

With this warning, he resumed his descent, dropping down one step when, without any warning and in a manner similar to how he scaled the rampart, Pullus, using his right hand as his fulcrum this time, although while still holding his *gladius*, vaulted over the wooden railing. It would be another moment that his men would be talking about, but with the element of surprise, the thrust by the nearest Han as he attempted to stab the Centurion in midair missed by less than a hand's breadth while, even as his hobnailed soles landed on the paving stones of the street, Pullus was punching out with his shield to bash that spearman before he could recover for another thrust. Striking the Han in the chest with the boss, the power behind his blow was enough that, even with the lamellar iron armor, he felt the snapping of the man's breastbone; more importantly, it sent the Han careening directly into another comrade armed with a *ji*, who was at that instant sweeping it downward at Pullus' shield, causing the blade to strike the paving stones instead, delaying Pullus' first moment defending against yet another new weapon. His right arm was moving simultaneously with his shield, though not in a thrust, instead making what seemed to be a wild, sweeping motion. This was done intentionally, however, both to force the two Han who were standing nearest to this part of the stairway and had been caught by surprise by Pullus' maneuver to hesitate for the instant he needed for the first of his Second Section men, led by their Sergeant, Tiberius Munacius, to reach the bottom of the stairs. It was still a risk, but Pullus felt confident that giving a warning about the probable use for this hooked spear would make his men sufficiently cautious, although even as he squared himself to face the pair of Han he had caught off guard, he saw Munacius engage with the man first jostled by the injured Han who had staggered backward and collapsed on the street, and he returned his attention to the two enemies just in time to learn firsthand how the Han employed this weapon by working in teams. The Han carrying the conventional spear, who in that instant Pullus judged was in his teens, his already narrow eyes barely visible as his face contorted into a mask of fear and anger that was universal no matter their differences, lunged with his spear in a two-hand grip, extending its reach by taking a step forward to coincide with his thrust, stomping his foot down hard on the paving stones as he did so.

To Pullus, it was crude and amateurish, but fortunately for him, he instantly discerned that it was at least partially done intentionally to distract him from the Han standing an arm's width from the spearman who, instead of thrusting with the spearpoint of his unusual weapon swung it down in an apparent attempt to cleave Pullus' helmet, and skull, with the long spear blade. Somehow—he had no idea how—Pullus understood that he wasn't the target, his shield was, so that instead of keeping it extended with his elbow locked into the hollow of his hipbone, he pulled it closer to his body while slightly leaning backward. There was a shout of obvious frustration from the second Han, who Pullus saw was older, and, he guessed, more experienced, when his weapon struck the metal ridge of Pullus' shield, but in between the blade of the spearpoint and the upper part of the curved piece of iron, which prevented the Han from simply thrusting the blade into Pullus' face. This also told Pullus that his foe had in fact been trying to bring the lower end of the curved piece of iron down on Pullus' side of his shield to yank it from his grasp, or at worst, pull the shield down. Even as this flashed through his mind, Pullus' right arm was sweeping upward, the edge perpendicular to the street, trying a maneuver he had used to great effect by slicing through the wooden shaft, but the Han was too quick, and Pullus' blade instead clashed against the point about halfway down its length in a shower of sparks as the Han snatched it back, the spearpoint rebounding upward from the power behind Pullus' parry, but while it wasn't successful, Pullus saw the purpose of the upper part of the curved piece of iron, not because of what the Han did but from what he tried to do, jerking his right elbow up while twisting his left wrist. He's trying to trap my blade with that thing and snap it! The lower part is to hook a shield and the upper part is to trap a blade! This recognition, while crucial to Roman success, both in this instant with Pullus and in the future to the rest of the army, didn't delay his left arm from moving as he saw the first spearman executing another thrust, exactly as he had before and aiming for the same spot. It was something no experienced warrior would do, and the only reason it momentarily saved the younger Han was because of his comrade who, thwarted in both attempts with his *ji*, now swung it at shoulder height in a sweeping blow designed to decapitate with the edge of the long spear blade. As experienced as he might have been, this Han had clearly never faced a man of Pullus' height, because his aim was off, requiring Pullus to barely raise his shield to block the swing. It was performed with a respectable amount of power, especially given the Han's size, but it barely moved Pullus' shield arm, which in turn meant that he was in a perfect posture to punch his shield, timing it so that just as the young spearman was recovering from his second thrust, he didn't have the chance to move the spear shaft across his body to either block, or more likely, at least reduce the impact of the blow from the raised metal boss that smashed directly into his face just below the nose, crushing his lower jaw. And, as Pullus had anticipated, no matter how skilled and disciplined a man was, seeing a comrade's lower face collapse tended to disrupt the concentration at the worst possible instant, so the giant Roman's right arm was moving simultaneously in what he supposed would be called a third position thrust, only because of where it was aimed as, even in this moment, he was critiquing his performance. When his decapitating blow was blocked, both ends of the curved piece of iron had buried themselves in the wood of the *Gwai's* shield, deeply enough that when Pullus punched with his shield, it yanked the Han off balance, and in less than an eyeblink of time, the point of Pullus' *gladius* punched into his side, just below his left armpit, almost half the blade burying itself in the man's body.

To an observer, it appeared as if both Han dropped simultaneously, but for the men of Pullus' Century who were higher on the stairs and, because they weren't currently engaged, were able to watch it happen, seeing their giant Primus Pilus dispatch two enemies in essentially the same movement was common enough that it would only warrant a mention around the fires that night. With this being the first moment Pullus had where he wasn't completely focused on staying alive, he paused for a heartbeat to make a quick assessment. Seeing that there were no Han to his immediate right, he pivoted to face north, giving him his first look at not just his immediate situation, but how the rest of his Cohorts were doing. It was difficult to make much out since the smoke streaming from the windows was trapped by the outer wall, and along with the bellowing and clashing of metal on metal, he could hear men coughing where the smoke was thicker. Most importantly, Pullus saw that his Century had descended the stairs first; he could see the black crest belonging to Balbus stuck about midway down the second stairway, causing a grin to form on his face. *It's just his bad luck that the Third Century was closer to the other stairs than he was, not that I'm going to tell him that.* Beyond his Cohort, it was difficult to tell anything with the smoke, and even if there hadn't been any, the mass of black-clad bodies of helmeted Han who had abandoned the rampart to put up their defense down on the street blocked any view. Having exhausted the heartbeat of time to the larger situation, he turned his attention to closer to home, and he was pleased to see that the men of his Second Section had made space beyond the bottom of the stairs. Although there were several Han bodies, thankfully, there were none of his boys, and the Second had been joined by the Fourth and Sixth Sections, giving him a bit less than thirty men now down on the street. *That's enough to get started,* he thought, but before he moved, he glanced over his shoulder up at the rampart, and saw that Lutatius and what he guessed were at least three of his odd-numbered sections had moved along the southern wall to a point where any view of them was obscured by the building on the corner. While it was too soon to tell about the overall situation, Pullus was certain that the deadlock at the rampart had been broken; now it was time to finish the job.

Bao was torn between elation that he had exited the last building before the *Gwai* started hurling their barbaric fire pots through the open windows of the second floor, while at the same time, he felt guilty for that sense of relief. When he dashed across the street to join his spear *Sui* gathered under the rampart, he had understood why they appeared to be behaving in a cowardly fashion, seeing several men, including some of his own, lying in the street next to the still-smoking corpses of their comrades who had perished in the first fire barrage, the wooden shafts protruding from the bodies of the unburned informing Bao why his men were reluctant to expose themselves. Once he joined them, he took a moment to examine one *Gwai* javelin that had missed its target and was lying in the street, and since he found it disconcerting to know that just above him were the men who in a very short period of time he and his men would be trying to kill as they did the same to him, he found focusing on the javelin helpful.

Nudging one of his *Sui Chang*, Kai Jun, he pointed at the spent missile, forced to raise his voice because of the clamor despite standing immediately next to the other man, "Do you notice anything, Kai? How the iron shaft is bent?"

"Yes, *Hou Chang*," Kai replied, unsure why his commander cared about such a thing at a moment like this; even under normal circumstances, he wouldn't have found it particularly noteworthy, but he guessed, "Their iron must be inferior to ours if it bends that easily."

"I don't think so." Bao frowned. "I think there's some purpose to this, but I don't know what it is."

Over the noise, Bao recognized the shout of the *Sui Chang* he had put in command of the men at the base of the southwestern stairs, turning in the instant after the smoking jar of naphtha shattered inside the upper story of the building nearest to the southwest corner and just in time to see a blazing figure either fall, or more likely, throw himself out of the window to land headfirst in the street, his shrill scream just one of many that were piercing the air with the higher pitch of men in mortal agony. It was the sight of the giant *Gwai*, who he assumed was taking advantage of one of his men throwing the pot into the building across from them to disrupt the hail of bolts, moving at not quite a run to head for the stairs even as the crossbowman was falling from the window that did it. If he had had an instant to think, Bao would have almost undoubtedly behaved differently than he did now, shouting at the nearby men to follow him as he ran to join their comrades at the base of the stairs, drawing his sword as he did. Despite the distance of about a hundred paces, even as Bao was running, he saw the giant descend the first few steps before suddenly vaulting over the railing, but this moment coincided with another *Gwai* above him on the rampart copying their comrade who threw the first pot. Just as he was crossing underneath that window, a *Gwai* wearing a black feathered crest whose arm was pulled back, instead of hurling it down on his head, the *Gwai* threw his pot at the window Bao happened to be racing past, causing him to flinch, but it was the sudden shouts of alarm from behind him that told him his men had followed without hesitation as they all felt as much as saw the effects of the exploding fire. Even under the circumstances, there was a part of Bao's mind that was gratified and surprised in equal measure that these men hadn't hesitated in following him. More times than he could count, he had been chastised for his timidity by *Hou Kuan* Zhou, yet here he was, racing down a street already littered with bodies, some of them belonging to his *Hou*, focused only on stopping these *Gwai,* led by a giant, from taking the part of the city for which he was responsible. Anything beyond that was out of his hands and a matter of fate, but this was something he could control, and within Bao was a resolve, and anger, that he had never experienced before, fueling him to immediately resume his pace as he reached the northern corner of the building closest to the southwest stairs.

    Whoever had thrown at the window just above him had partially missed, and the stone wall below the window appeared to be burning, something that just a day before Bao would have been certain was impossible, but in this moment and given what he had witnessed over the previous *kè*, seeing stone burn was now so common that he barely gave it a glance. Because his view was obscured by the backs of his men already in place ringing the stairs several deep, Bao couldn't see how the giant *Gwai* had done it, but he could see a pair of bodies lying at the giant's feet, and he had a clear view of the upper half of the *Gwai* towering over his own men, although everything below his neck was obscured by a shield. He was less than ten paces away when the giant stepped over the bodies, as one of Bao's spearman did exactly what he was supposed to do by thrusting his spear with a two-handed grip, striking the *Gwai*'s shield, but before Bao could rush to the aid of these men, the stairway was suddenly filled with the giant's soldiers, identically clad and equipped, the only difference to the giant being the plume of black horsehair affixed to their helmets that hung down their backs. It was the actions of the first pair of *Gwai* who, after blocking several thrusts from at least a half-dozen of Bao's men, and bolstered by their comrades behind and above them, used their shields to physically push the spearmen backward, clearly intent on making space at the bottom of the stairs.

"*Hold, Dragons, hold! Help is here!*"

Completely unaware that it was his voice shouting this, Bao arrived just as one of his spearmen staggered backward from the force being transferred through the man's spear shaft that had become embedded in one of the *Gwai*'s shields. Forced to choose between confronting the giant standing next to the staircase or trying to stop this incursion at the bottom of the stairs, Bao chose the latter by essentially lowering his shoulder to hit his faltering spearman in the back, and even with all the other noise, he heard the rush of the man's breath leaving his body. A fraction of a heartbeat later, the rest of Bao's group arrived, and he felt a hand grab his shoulder.

"I'll take your place, *Hou Chang!*" someone shouted in his ear, but while he recognized the voice, he couldn't match it to the spearman in the moment, not that it mattered.

Feeling as much as seeing the hand that suddenly appeared over his right shoulder and slightly above him to bolster the spearman who was still desperately clutching to his spear while pushing forward with all of his strength, Bao extricated himself before actually taking a couple steps backward to get a sense of the situation. The good news was that, with the arrival of his reinforcements, the giant *Gwai*, currently the only man standing on the street with his back to the stairs, was now completely surrounded; the bad news was that the sight of their comrades lying in pools of blood at the giant's feet, who he now recognized as belonging to his First *Sui*, meant that his men were wary of aggressively attacking this *Gwai*. While he didn't blame them all that much; this demon was the most intimidating creature he had ever seen, Bao understood that he was the key to successfully defending the southwestern stairs. He was also completely oblivious to the fact that there were small battles now taking place the entire length of the western wall as the attackers finally began pressing the defenders back from the rampart, not that it would have mattered. Bao was just moving into a position by moving quickly behind the ring of his men to get to the *Gwai*'s weak side, thinking to use his own sword to advantage, while his men with their longer weapons kept the giant at bay, when something happened on the stairs.

It began when Kai, who had just arrived a heartbeat earlier, panting from his run, lifted his *ji* almost vertically before bringing it down over the heads of his comrades, forced to extend his arms more than he had been trained because of the press of bodies between him and his target. That the lower edge of his *ji* landed exactly where he had aimed it surprised Kai as much as it did the *Gwai*, although he could only see the man's absurdly round eyes that suddenly went even wider just above his shield, but despite this, Kai didn't hesitate to yank with all of his might, feeling the lower blade catch the wood of the shield as he brought his arms back toward him with all of his strength, even adding to the force by leaning backward, normally a dangerous thing to do. There was a momentary resistance, accompanied by what he recognized as a cry of alarm from his target, then he experienced the sudden release of the tension, stumbling backward so violently that he ended up landing hard on his ass in the street. Consequently, he wasn't in position to see who among his spear wielding comrades performed the fatal thrust, but he clearly heard the result in the form of a combination of roars of savage joy and shouts of despairing anger, then through the tangle of legs he saw the *Gwai's* shield clattering down the last two steps. It couldn't have been more than a heartbeat before Kai was scrambling to his feet, snatching up his *ji*, but just as he was standing erect, there was a sound that, while he could tell it came from one individual, was unlike anything he had ever heard before, a combination of a towering rage and grief that was so overpowering that it stilled the other voices, both Han and *Gwai*, just for an eyeblink of time, but it was just long enough for Kai's eyes to move in the direction from which the sound came, meaning he was just in time to see the return of an old friend to the giant *Gwai* Titus Pullus.

As usually happened afterward, Pullus' memory of the event would be filled with gaps, nor could he ever articulate why it had been seeing Munacius take a spear thrust that sliced into his throat in the instant after his shield was yanked out of his hand that summoned this rage. He'd seen his men die before, and he always felt the loss keenly, nor could he say that he felt especially close to Munacius, who had been part of the second *dilectus* of the 10th after Munda, yet somehow, it triggered an event that, although it had only happened a handful of times in his life, was as much a part of the legend of Titus Pullus to men under the standard as any of his exploits over the previous two decades. It would be left to Diocles, Scribonius, Balbus, and Pullus' nephew, of whom only Scribonius had been present to witness it the first time, to try and convince Pullus that these volcanic eruptions of a rage buried so deeply within him weren't of this world. Even as skeptical as Scribonius was about the gods, not just about their power but their very existence, his normally incisive logic couldn't explain why these moments happened, just that when they did, it was always when not only Pullus, but the men who marched with him needed it most. What it meant in the moment, in a material sense, was that even as Pullus was bellowing an inarticulate but still clear message of his intent, he was moving, fast, aiming directly for the knot of Han spearmen at the base of the stairs. And, just as had happened the first time on an anonymous hill in Hispania, when a sixteen-year-old in his first campaign had rushed into a desperate fight to keep their makeshift defenses intact, the shield in Pullus' hand wasn't used once defensively, at least by intent, as he waded into the fight, using it to bludgeon and smash down anyone who tried to stop him. While he felt the shuddering impact, and heard the sharp cracking noise caused by his swinging the shield in a wide arc that, under normal circumstances, would have spelled his end because it exposed his entire left side, the blow was delivered with such force that, rather than knocking the three spears within the arc of his swing aside, the metal edge snapped the shafts of two of them, their iron points clattering to the street, while the third spearman's weapon was spared only because it was ripped so violently from his death grip on the shaft that it made the spearman stumble to his left, colliding with another comrade. It also meant that he was the first to die as Pullus' other weapon, his *gladius* that, like his shield, seemed to be an extension of his arm, wielding it as naturally and easily as a man would flex his fingers or point at an object, sliced across the spearman's throat. If that was all the havoc he wrought in the first of what would be a series of seemingly unconnected movements, most of his comrades would have been satisfied, but Pullus wasn't most men.

Taking advantage of the countless watches of practice, his slashing attack became a thrust in the fraction of time it took him to twist his wrist to orient the point of his Gallic blade so that it pierced the Han next to his comrade, who was still clutching his throat in a vain attempt to stop the spurting spray of bright red, the point striking the second Han in the jaw just a couple inches from the junction of upper and lower, slicing through the jawbone on both sides as if it wasn't there. If it had been anyone else who violated the unwritten but sacrosanct rule that a Legionary avoid cutting into bone, especially a thick one like a jawbone, because of the near inevitability of the blade being trapped there, a Centurion worth his salt would have exercised his *vitus* on the miscreant, provided the man survived, which wasn't likely. Pullus barely noticed, wrenching the blade free with such vicious strength that it created a yawning gap between the front of the Han's face and the rest of his skull, while his shield, which had naturally returned to its normal position from the momentum of Pullus' counter swing with his *gladius*, was shooting out again, this time in a straight punch that crushed the face of the last of the three Han spearman, who was still staring down at the splintered shaft in stupid surprise. It had happened so quickly that it was difficult for any of his men who witnessed it to describe, but Pullus was far from through, already pivoting on his left foot from its spot at the base of the outer edge of the stairs, while the Han who had been behind their three dead comrades reacted in different ways. Not surprisingly, one spearman backpedaled, trying to give his weapon enough room to be effective, but it was the Han who had fallen after yanking Munacius' shield who was clearly Pullus' target, the Roman knocking aside a thrust from another Han armed with the *ji* with his *gladius*, while his foe used his *ji* this time as a conventional spear. This was how it started, but as he had been trained, when Pullus' *gladius* struck the wooden shaft a few inches below the curved piece of iron, just as Kai had done with the shield, the Han yanked the shaft of his *ji* back towards him. Going just by the sensation, to the Han, it was as if his weapon had hooked a branch of a massive tree that didn't budge, but when Pullus reciprocated with a yank of his own, while the Han let go of his end, it wasn't quickly enough as he was jerked towards Pullus, stumbling forward two steps, effectively killing himself when the Roman's blade swung down from the vertical to cut deeply into the man's body at the junction of his neck and shoulder.

Pullus didn't even seem to notice, yanking his blade free even as he raised his shield to shoulder level as he twisted his wrist upwards so the shield was roughly horizontal, aiming the bottom edge at Kai in a punch similar to the standard method using the boss. The extra distance provided by the bottom half of the shield put the Han within range, but Kai managed to lift his *ji* just in time to catch the metaled edge of the bottom of the Roman's shield between the shaft and upper curved edge. Although he managed to soften the blow that struck him on the rim of his iron helmet and avoided being killed instantly, it wasn't enough to prevent an impact that simultaneously snapped his head back and creased his helmet. In something of a blessing, he was too dazed to recognize his death from a blade already coated with blood and still dripping with gore from the comrades of Kai who preceded him into the next world, and in fact, he was mercifully barely aware that he was now flat on his back in the street, the searing pain at the base of his throat lasting only an instant. The surviving men of Pullus' Second Section had already stepped over their dead comrade to take immediate advantage of the space that their Primus Pilus had secured, quickly kicking the corpses out of the way in order to form a line at the base of the stairs that curved around the side of the staircase. For his part, Pullus was already moving again, this time with the stairs at his back, heading directly across the street towards more of Bao's men, who had retreated a couple paces, needing the space for their spears and *ji*, something the giant Roman wasn't willing to give them. As often happened with Pullus, he didn't appear to be moving all that quickly, yet he was suddenly inside the points of a team of spearman and *ji* so rapidly that the spearman panicked, backpedaling with almost comical haste, isolating his comrade, who joined those Han already slain less than a heartbeat later.

Singlehandedly, and completely oblivious to the larger implications of his actions, Pullus was slaughtering any Han who stood in his path, with a ruthless efficiency that was completely at odds with the very fury of his attack, thereby giving his men the space they needed to begin filling the street around the stairs. In this moment, there was one and only one imperative in the mind of Titus Pullus, killing any man who stood before him, and in this sense, he was almost as much of a danger to his men as he was to the Han, some of whom had begun to take that first step backward, not to give their longer weapons the room they needed to be effective, but to preserve their lives. As any experienced warrior of enough battles knew, there was always a moment where matters hung in the balance, where one more act, of valor or of cowardice, could tip the balance. This was true in battles between massive armies or in smaller fights like this, and even if Pullus was unaware that this was the moment because of his frenzy, his men, hardened veterans in their own right, did. Consequently, they didn't hesitate, rushing to reach their Primus Pilus, now almost to the other side of the street, despite the fact that he hadn't issued such an order and still oblivious to anything but any Han who chose to stand their ground as he cut his way through them. Suddenly, and for the first time in this battle, Pullus was confronted by a foe who wielded a sword, the only Han who seemed willing to attack the giant Roman, in a desperate bid to prevent the total collapse of the effort to stem the tide of Legionaries now streaming down the stairs.

If Bao had been asked beforehand, before the appearance of the *Gwai*, and even up to the instant before he acted if he was likely to perform a deed of suicidal bravery, he would have assured the questioner that he had no desire to do anything more than his duty. Winning accolades for heroism was for men who were born to be warriors in Bao's view; he had come into his profession because he was a younger son of a minor functionary of the Han government, and this was the only slot currently available to him. However, while watching his men die from the evil fiery substance had horrified him, seeing this giant *Gwai* slaughtering them, and the contemptuous ease he was displaying while doing it, enraged him to the point that, without conscious thought, he found himself rushing at the giant, sword in hand, just as the *Gwai* giant was delivering a thrust to a spearman he recognized as belonging to his Third *Sui*, after deflecting the man's own attack by letting it slide off of his shield. In any other circumstance, Bao would have been revolted by the manner in which the *Gwai*, with only the strength of his arm, sliced through the lamellar armor to gut his spearman like one would a hog, but he barely noticed the gleaming offal falling out onto a street already shining with blood, so intent was he on ending this demon's killing of his men with this one. And, because of his angle of attack, coming from the giant's right side and slightly behind his shoulder, he felt certain that this gave him the advantage he would need to counter the *Gwai's* skill. Holding his blade out from his side and at waist level, Bao was unintentionally mimicking a Roman first position, albeit without a shield. How the *Gwai* knew he was coming, Bao would never know, yet just as he was drawing his arm back to deliver what he hoped was a fatal thrust, the giant pivoted to his right to face Bao. More crucially, his right arm was moving at the same time so that both opponents struck the other at the same instant, Bao's point striking the *Gwai* at the precise instant the edge of the *Gwai*'s blade sliced through the muscles, bones, and tendons of Bao's forearm, severing it so quickly that Bao didn't feel any pain for a blessed instant. Although he would never know it, Bao's thrust would have been fatal, striking Pullus just under his right ribcage as it did, and between his momentum and the force he had generated, it would have plunged deeply into the Roman's body and through vital organs, but it was fatally weakened with Pullus' slashing move. What it did accomplish was to snap Pullus out of the fit that had wrought such damage on his men, something Bao would never know, his last conscious memory hearing a bellow of pain as he stumbled past the Roman, his severed arm falling to the street along with his sword, collapsing facedown onto the paving stones, his left hand clutching his ruined arm underneath him, thereby saving his life.

In that moment, the pain Pullus suffered initially from the Han sword that penetrated his mail and plunged at least two inches into his right side rivaled his wounding at Munda, although it did serve to yank Pullus back to his senses, and there was a span of a couple heartbeats where he stood, panting and so completely defenseless that any of the surviving Han could have ended him right then, but seeing their *Hou Chang* fall had swept away the last vestiges of collective resolve, sending all of them fleeing. Most of them simply turned and ran down to the street paralleling the southern wall, turning the corner to vanish, but there were a handful so out of their minds with fear, they tried to rush past where Pullus was still standing, *gladius* and shield in hand, though both of them were hanging limply at his side. They barely spared him a glance, their attention instead on the men of the even-numbered sections of Pullus' Century who were the nearest to the corner they were heading for to escape, but only the first Han, who had dropped his *ji*, made it, sprinting down the street without a backward glance at his comrades. Those comrades were summarily cut down by Munacius' tentmates, despite two of the spearmen falling to their knees and holding out their empty hands in a clear plea for mercy, both of them dispatched with thrusts without a flicker of hesitation. With Munacius' death, it was left to Marcus Bestia to shout an order to stop two of his comrades who started out in pursuit of the lone survivor. Paterculus was the first to reach Pullus' side, and while the rent in Pullus' *hamata* was hidden by his dangling arm, his hand still gripping his *gladius*, the *Aquilifer* could see the blood streaming down his Centurion's side, falling in drops once it reached the hem of his mail to form a small puddle at Pullus' foot, which he gave no sign of noticing.

Alarmed and concerned, Paterculus, acutely aware of what he had just witnessed in the form of Pullus' rage, still spoke tentatively, "Primus Pilus?"

When Pullus didn't respond, he thought he hadn't spoken loudly enough to be heard because of the shouting going on around him, Lutatius having arrived to organize the Century as quickly as possible, and he repeated himself more loudly. He was about to shout a third time when Pullus, who was seemingly gazing up at the rampart along the southern wall that was visible from their vantage point, finally responded, not verbally but turning to regard his *Aquilifer* with an expression Paterculus had never seen him wear, stirring in him a great sense of unease, a vacant, empty look, as if Pullus had lost all interest in anything of this world.

"Primus Pilus, are you all right?" Paterculus pointed to Pullus' side, and was about to gently move Pullus' arm aside to examine the wound but thought better of it; he had been up on the rampart and seen everything, and while Pullus seemed out of his...fit, he wasn't willing to risk that he wasn't. Instead, he asked, "May I look at that wound, sir? It looks like it might be serious."

"Wound?" Pullus frowned, but when he moved his arm to look for himself, Paterculus heard first a gasp, then a muttered, "Pluto's cock, how did that happen?" Then, showing signs that he had returned to the moment for the first time, he looked around, muttering, "Where's Lutatius?"

"He's just around the corner, sir," Paterculus pointed to the street running along the southern wall. "I think he's rounding up the boys in the odds. They pushed those *cunni* down the southern wall a good distance, and I heard the Optio say that he was going to stop them before they went too far and got cut off."

"Good," Pullus grunted, then returned his attention to the situation around him. Spotting two close comrades of his Fifth Section bending over the bodies of the Han that Pullus had slain at the bottom of the stairs, he growled at them, "Flaccus! Gemellus! There'll be time for that later! Fall on the standard, now!"

While this wasn't unusual, Paterculus was nevertheless alarmed, asking quickly, "Shouldn't we look at your wound, sir? It looks like it might be deep."

"If it was, I'd be dead," Pullus replied shortly, but then he winced as if thinking about it made it hurt more, relenting, "but if it will make you feel better..."

He lifted his arm, trying not to grimace, while his *Aquilifer* grinned at this sign that the Primus Pilus he knew, respected, loved, and feared in equal measure had returned.

Paterculus' smile faded, and he glanced up at Pullus, not hiding his concern. "That's a nasty wound, Primus Pilus, but I can see that there are links missing."

"They probably dropped on the ground," Pullus remarked, which was certainly possible, but the *Aquilifer* immediately noticed that the Centurion didn't join him in examining the street around his feet.

Not that it was an easy task; the paving stones immediately around them were soaked with blood that was just beginning to congeal, there were bodies, and a body part in the form of a severed arm literally inches from where they were standing, but even after Paterculus squatted down to examine the closely fit paving stones that, even in the moment, he noticed and recognized as being of a quality that wouldn't be sneered at in Rome, thereby making it difficult for something as small as two or three links of iron dropping between the cracks, he couldn't see any.

Standing back up, he informed Pullus, who at that moment was watching Lutatius, the Optio having just returned with the men of the odd-numbered sections, "Primus Pilus, I can't find them lying about. I think they're inside you."

Next to being burned alive, it was widely considered the most painful death, when your own flesh and organs corrupted, becoming poisoned from the foreign matter that remained in the body after being wounded.

Pullus barely acknowledged Paterculus' words, saying only, "I'll have it looked at after we're done. Lutatius!" he shouted, and Paterculus saw Pullus wince, but he continued to use the same tone and volume, "Get me a butcher's bill while I go check on the rest of the Cohorts."

"Primus Pilus!" Paterculus pleaded as Pullus turned about to begin walking towards the gate he didn't know was named the Jade Gate. "At least let me bind your wound. You don't want it to reopen."

This did serve to stop Pullus, and Paterculus reached down between his *hamata* and tunic, withdrawing a clean but sweat-soaked bandage, one of which almost every man carried, usually in the same manner, and approached Pullus, who looked, if anything, amused.

"You think one bandage is going to work for me?"

The *Aquilifer* instantly recognized his mistake, looking up at Pullus with chagrin, but when Pullus made as if he was going to walk away, he said quickly, "Wait, Primus Pilus." He turned and beckoned to Valerius, who was standing a couple paces away, looking uncertain as he waited for orders. "Bring me your bandage, Lucius."

Valerius quickly trotted over, but unlike Paterculus, his rolled cloth bandage was in the small satchel that contained the items every *Cornicen* carried to keep their horn in good repair. Wasting neither time nor words, knowing that under the best of circumstances their Primus Pilus wasn't a patient man, Paterculus quickly knotted the two bandages together.

With a bit of trepidation, he asked, "Can you lift your arms for me, Primus Pilus?"

"Can I?" Pullus growled at him. "Are you asking if I can, or if I will?"

It was only by the glint in his eye that Paterculus realized Pullus was teasing him, but the Primus Pilus raised both hands, once again grunting a bit from the effort, although as always, the manner in which he was able to hold a heavy shield straight out from his body as if it was just his unburdened arm didn't go unnoticed by his men. None of them knew the effort it was costing Pullus at this moment; despite his seeming indifference, he was acutely aware that his men took vicarious pride in his exploits, part of which stemmed from making seemingly difficult things look easy, and impossible things look only slightly difficult.

If Paterculus noticed the set to Pullus' jaw as he endured the *Aquilifer* wrapping the combined bandages around his massive chest, he was wise enough not to comment, although when Pullus grunted as he pulled it tight, he asked worriedly, "Is that too tight, sir?"

"No, it's fine," Pullus lied, but he was also unwilling to waste any more time, and the instant Paterculus stepped away, he resumed his progress, muttering a thanks before saying more loudly so he could be heard by his men nearby, "Set the standard, Paterculus. I want the First ready for what comes next when I get back."

Then he strode away, seemingly unconcerned that just ahead of him, the fight for control of the street was still going on, where the Centuries of Balbus and Laetus had surrounded a remnant of Han infantry formed into something of an *orbis*, presenting a bristling circle of spears, while Balbus and Laetus stood together, conferring on how to go about the business of slaughtering these men.

Balbus' back was turned, but Laetus saw Pullus coming, and the Pilus Posterior looked over his shoulder, his eyes immediately going to the white bandage that stood out in stark incongruity to Pullus' grimy, blood-spattered mail, but he hid his concern, calling out, "What the fuck did you do to yourself this time?"

"You think I did this to myself?" Pullus retorted, then added, "And what do you think happened to the *cunnus* who did it?"

On its face, even under the circumstances, with men desperately fighting, this was their normal kind of banter, but Balbus saw something in Pullus' expression that warned him that all was not as it seemed. However, he understood now was not the time, and he tucked the thought away to find out later.

Aloud, he said, "I'd hope his guts are lying in the fucking street."

"His guts aren't," Pullus allowed, then gave the pair a ferocious grin, "but the fucking arm he stuck me with is." This was all the time he had for the topic, and he paused to briefly examine the immediate situation confronting his two Centurions, where about thirty Han spearmen were packed into a tight circle in the middle of the intersection of the wall street and one that ran eastward into the city. "What's your plan?"

"We're out of javelins," Balbus explained, "so we're going to have to go to the *gladius*. We're just trying to come up with the best way."

Pullus didn't answer, choosing to examine the Han, none of whom were shouting, and while he saw the fear, he couldn't determine to what degree they were gripped by it, thinking once again in a relatively short span of how difficult it was for him to read the expressions of the people in this part of the world. Aware that time was passing, he finally said, "I'll leave it up to you. I need to get to the other Cohorts."

He resumed walking without a backward glance, even when, once he had gone several paces, there was a sudden roar as Balbus and Laetus' men resumed their grim business of slaughtering their enemy, confident in his second in command to handle it with minimum loss. Spotting Scribonius, who was on the side of the street opposite the wall, calmly talking to his Pilus Posterior, Gnaeus Pacula, Pullus was still a few paces away when there was another shout, this one slightly echoing, his eyes moving in that direction in time to see his Quintus Pilus Prior leading his Century through the gate that had just been thrown open by men of Scribonius' Cohort, the most potent sign that the Equestrians had succeeded in their first mission of securing the rampart. He reached Scribonius and Pacula, and when both of them saluted, he only shook his head, pointing to his side, his eyes already looking farther down the street paralleling the wall, trying to make sense of what he was seeing, but it was difficult now that the Third and Fourth Cohort were at least partially down in the street. This was a moment that someone as experienced as Pullus knew presented the Han an opportunity, but only if they had a commander the caliber of Caesar, with the normally organized Romans temporarily in disarray as Centurions and Optios directed their men to assemble, making them vulnerable to a counterattack from a determined foe. He wasn't surprised when he saw some of his men emerging from one of the buildings that had an entrance that opened onto this street, or that they were carrying what appeared to be a statue and rolls of cloth that he could tell by the sheen was silk. Recognizing them as belonging to the Fourth Cohort, he reminded himself to talk to Nigidius about this lapse in discipline.

Ignoring Scribonius' pointed stare at his side, Pullus said, "It looks like the Alaudae are still up on the rampart. I guess they didn't do the same thing we did."

"What do you think Batius will do if you send us around to hit them from the rear, like we did in Pattala?"

Pullus briefly considered Scribonius' question, then nodded.

"Good idea." He turned to examine the men entering the gate, then spotted the red crest of Trebellius, but he surprised Scribonius, and concerned him when he muttered, "Call him over for me. It hurts too much to yell right now."

Scribonius did so, although he had to call his name three times before Trebellius heard, then came at a trot. As he approached, the Secundus Pilus Prior surreptitiously examined Pullus' side.

"It's fine," Pullus said shortly, without looking at his friend. "Stop looking at me like a mother hen." Before Scribonius could reply, Trebellius arrived, but once again, Pullus didn't return the salute under the guise of urgency, telling Trebellius, "You're going to take your Cohort," he pointed to the nearest perpendicular street, "and take the next street parallel to this one to head north and get behind those *cunni* who've got Batius and his boys still up on the rampart."

"Batius isn't going to like that very much," Trebellius commented, but with a broad grin on his face.

Normally, Pullus would have replied in kind, as happy about the chance to show another Primus Pilus that the Equestrians were the superior Legion, but he snapped, "I don't give a fart in a *testudo* whether Batius is unhappy about it or not. Stop wasting time."

"Yes, Primus Pilus," Trebellius stiffened to *intente*,

irritated and puzzled, but when he glanced over at Scribonius, the lean Centurion shook his head while he surreptitiously pointed at the bandage around Pullus' chest. Understanding, the other Pilus Prior assured Pullus, "I understand and will obey."

Once he had left, Pullus returned his attention to the larger situation, feeling but ignoring the ache in his side, or at least tried to do so. He had lost count of all the times he had been wounded, only considering the serious wounds, such as the one he suffered at Munda, the scar of which was still purple and knotted on his upper right chest even now more than six years later. Only a few days later would he think back to this moment, recognizing with hindsight that the reason this seemed to hurt more than it should was also the solution to the mystery of where the links of his mail had gone.

At the opposite end of the city, the Han defenders had been slower to recognize the futility of defending the rampart under the onslaught of fire falling from the sky; that two of the messengers sent by Lei suffered the misfortune of being the recipients of a jar of naphtha that missed the parapet to plunge down less than a pace in front of them as they were running side by side towards the northwestern corner meant that neither of the *Hou Kuan* who were the intended recipients of the message to withdraw received it. By the time Xao reappeared, it had become clear to Lei that the fight for the entire length of the western wall was lost; what also became obvious within a span of heartbeats after his commander's return was that Xao was no longer capable of commanding. In fact, given the exchange between the two when Xao returned to find Lei issuing orders, it appeared to the second in command that Xao wasn't all that interested in whether he lived or died on this day, nor did he appear to care about the fate of all of his soldiers who had answered his call to come to this island in his bid to become an emperor in everything but name.

"Perhaps it would serve our cause better that you return to the palace so that you can receive reports from the commanders responsible for the other parts of the city, General," Lei suggested carefully. "I haven't heard anything from them, so they may not be engaged, but I don't know with any certainty."

Xao had his eyes on the scene just a block away, where he could see through the smoke of the scattered fires that were still burning that the rampart was dominated by *Gwai* soldiers, only catching glimpses of the gray of their armor and helmets that contrasted to the red on the large shields they all seemed to carry. Neither a gate nor stairs were visible from their vantage point a block away from the western wall, which Lei had taken up when he saw that the fight for the rampart was essentially lost, removing himself out of the immediate fray, and at that moment, the only men they could see on the street were their black-clad soldiers, their backs all turned in this direction as they prepared for the coming onslaught from the *Gwai* who were descending the stairs at that moment.

When he finally tore his gaze away, there was a dullness in his eyes that alarmed Lei, but he did agree, "I believe that you're right, Lei. You can direct this effort to hold the western wall while I go to determine the situation elsewhere."

Lei bowed in their form of a salute, but when Xao mounted his pony, even as he knew it might not be a good idea, he asked, "Would it be correct to say that the report of our fleet being burned was accurate, General?"

"It is," Xao replied tersely, turning his pony's head as he spoke. For a heartbeat, Lei thought this was all he would say, but there was a crack in the general's normal stoic expression, although it was the sigh that preceded his words that Lei would remember. "All of our plans went up in flames, Lei. Without any artillery, not only does it make defending the city difficult, our assault on Xuwen will be impossible. I," he looked down at Lei for the first time, and in Xao's eyes, Lei saw the look of utter defeat, "made a grave error, General Lei, and for that, I humbly beg your pardon."

This was not just unusual, it was astonishing to Lei, who, up to this moment, had never seen Xao, who he had chosen to follow into self-imposed exile on this island, exhibit the slightest trace of doubt, or humility for that matter.

"O-of course, General," Lei stammered. "There is no pardon necessary." He felt a stab of desperation, and he tried to sound confident. "Once we drive the *Gwai* from the city, we can make new artillery. And," he thought to add, "I have a great deal of confidence in Liu Zho and his men defending Yazhou." Especially since I went behind your back and sent reinforcements, Lei thought, but understood this moment was not the time to remind Xao. "And remember, while they don't have as many artillery pieces as we do, they do have a good number of them, and we can send a ship for them while we recuperate from this effort. Which," he finished emphatically, "will be successful. The *Gwai* still haven't penetrated into the city, and we'll make them pay for every block in *Gwai* blood, I swear it!"

Lei bowed again when he finished, and although Xao acknowledged with an incline of his head, this was his only acknowledgement of Lei's attempt to revive Xao's spirits and Lei's promise, simply kicking his pony into a trot, heading to the city center and the administrative heart of Hanou. Not wasting another heartbeat of watching his commander depart, the only thing that Lei was certain of at this moment was that he was in command of defending against what appeared to be the main *Gwai* effort. He began striding towards the western wall a block away, but before he had gone more than a half-dozen steps, there was an echoing roar off to his left, in the direction of the southern wall, the noise such that he turned and raced back to the corner where he had just been standing, conferring with Xao. There was an echoing quality that betrayed the presence of a large group of men, the sound of their roaring voices bouncing off the walls of the dwellings in this part of the city, instilling a sense of caution in Lei so that didn't run around the corner, instead slowing down and sidling to the edge of the building before cautiously poking his head out. The sight that had arrested Xao, of men in gray armor and carrying red shields up on the ramparts now met his eyes but down on the street level as a large number of *Gwai* raced in his direction from the south, almost panicking the Han general, but just before he turned to flee, the *Gwai* leading them, wearing the same ridiculous crest, except this one was neither white nor black but red, suddenly turned to his left down the parallel street two blocks away. Matters deteriorated very quickly after that, to the point that Lei quickly recognized there was no point in trying to make his way to the western wall, and almost immediately, he was further consigned to the role of an observer, watching the sudden shifting of his men that he could see as they spun to their left to face south, accompanied by a dramatic increase in the noise. The clashing of metal on metal and the deeper sounds of iron striking wood once again added to the din, though not for long, the noise quickly drowned out by the din created by panicked men, hundreds of them, as the Romans repeated the tactic that had proven so effective, first in Pattala, then later in Bharuch.

He didn't do so, but Lei doubted that if he had counted he would have reached fifty before one of the men closest to him, in the rearmost ranks of spear and *ji* men turned about, and he was close enough to see the terror in the man's eyes as, without hesitation, he began running in Lei's direction. It didn't take much more than a full heartbeat before his comrades joined him, instantly threatening to either sweep Lei up with this human stampede or run over him and crush him underfoot if he tried to stand his ground, such was their panic. It was simple self-preservation that got Lei moving, although he also kept his wits about him as he turned to sprint east down the street away from the wall, hoping to get at least two blocks ahead of what was now a mob and was almost undoubtedly either occurring or was about to occur in both directions along the streets parallel to his. If he could get to a spot, then find a few *Hou Chang* or even a *Hou Kuan* from this rabble, he believed he could still rally these men, even if it was to fall back even further, perhaps to one of the three market centers in the city that was closest to the western wall. He regretted not choosing to keep his own mount nearby, though there was nothing to be done about it now, and in all likelihood the sight of a rushing tide of terrified humans would panic his steed despite being trained for the battlefield. His cause was instantly complicated when the terrified city dwellers, who had been issued stern orders to remain indoors with their shutters and doors secured, heard the uproar outside their homes as their protectors fled, panicking themselves to begin racing out into the street. One such civilian, an older woman, stepped out of her modest home directly into Lei's path, too frightened to even check to see if it was safe to do so, so he could neither slow himself nor change his direction enough to avoid her. Despite her small size, she was large enough that the collision sent both of them sprawling, although Lei was able to immediately scramble to his feet, his palms burning from the scrapes he suffered when he had tried to break his fall. Although he did spare the prone woman a glance, when he saw the spreading blood around her head, her eyes wide open and staring up at the smoky sky, he didn't attempt to help her, although he did draw his sword as a precaution and took care to run down the middle of the street as he resumed, brandishing the weapon as he shouted at the people just now flooding out into the street. He had to get to the Pearl Market, so named because it was on Pearl Street, viewing this as his only chance to stem the flood of retreat simply because it was large enough that several streets that ran east and west from the western wall emptied onto it, making it a natural collection point. He also knew he couldn't do it alone; indeed, this would have been the perfect moment for General Xao to be here to rally his men, and for the span of time it took him to burst out into the large area, empty of shoppers of course and with the wooden portable stalls all arranged neatly on the eastern side, he harbored a faint hope that perhaps he would find the General there, waiting. Those hopes were dashed the moment he emerged out into the market square, although it wasn't completely deserted, Lei spying what appeared to be an intact *Hou* standing on the eastern edge of the market in front of the stalls, and he headed for the *Hou Chang*, those officers actually wearing a crest that wasn't dissimilar to the horsetail plumes worn by the rankers of the *Gwai* army. His back was turned, but several of his men pointed, and he turned about, his mouth dropping at the sight of the second in command of the entire rebel Han forces on the island sprinting in his direction.

Lei saw that this *Hou* was composed of crossbowmen, and when he was still a couple dozen paces away, he demanded, "Where are the spearmen of your *Hou*, *Hou Chang*? And what *Tu-wei-fu* is this?"

The *Hou Chang* pointed behind him, farther east. "*Hou Chang* Qiang Mi took them two blocks east, General, and we are the Golden Lion *Tu-wei-fu* under *Hou Kuan* Shi!"

When he reached the young officer, Lei had to catch his breath, but he was still panting when he ordered, "Send one of your men to retrieve *Hou Chang* Qiang on my orders, and he is to..."

"*Hou Chang* Ning! There's movement on the other side of the market!"

Both men spun about to look in the direction the crossbowman who had alerted them was pointing, and to Lei, it appeared as if it was a surging black tide, with various bits of flotsam bouncing above it that he knew were the points of the spears and *ji* of the retreating men that they were holding vertically as they ran. Lei cursed the ancestors of these cowards, understanding that he wouldn't be given the time he needed, but he was determined that wouldn't stop him from trying.

Raising his sword, he started striding back across the market, snapping over his shoulder, "Send that runner, Ning! And then put your men to work using the tables and stalls to form a breastworks along the line where you're standing, from north to south across the entire market!"

He had no idea if the youngster had the mettle to carry out his orders, especially with his obviously panicked comrades rushing in their direction, but he had his own task at hand, which was to try and stem this flood.

Thrusting his sword into the air, he began bellowing, "Rally to your general! Rally to your general! Stop here!"

For a span of two or three heartbeats, he was certain that he was about to be run down by the men in whose path he was standing because they didn't even appear to slow, and he actually closed his eyes, determined that he wouldn't flinch, even if he was about to be crushed underfoot. Consequently, he only heard the scraping sounds as the fleeing men skidded to a stop; when he opened his eyes, to his immense relief, they had managed to halt a couple paces away, although he heard the alarmed shouts of protest as the laggards arrived and were unable, or unwilling, to stop their rush to escape, slamming into the backs of their comrades, jostling the men at the rear.

Knowing that he only had a handful of heartbeats to stem this tide and organize a defense, Lei first shouted, "All *Hou-Kuan* and *Hou Chang* come forward immediately!"

There was a stir in the crowd as a handful of men made their way out of the press, the larger group still growing in size as more retreating soldiers reached the market. Some of the officers refused to meet his gaze, but there were a sprinkling among what he quickly counted as twenty-two men who did, looking almost defiant, but Lei wasn't about to make an issue out of it now, needing these men to have any chance of success.

"We don't have much time, but I want a line, crossbowmen in front," he turned and pointed to where the men of the Golden Lions, having just been joined by their spearmen, were now overturning stalls and dragging them into a rough line bisecting the market about fifty paces from the eastern edge, "using those for protection. It won't be much, but we must stop these *Gwai*!" He took a breath, and more out of desperation, he shouted, "Your families are within these walls! Your parents! Your grandparents! Some of you have wives and children! Your ancestors rest just outside these walls! *We must stop these savages or we will shame them for eternity*!"

Whether it was the mention of their families or their ancestors, all that mattered to Lei was the response; while it wasn't as strong as he would have liked, knowing what they had just been through and what they were about to face, it would have to do.

"*Hou Kuan,* take command of your men!"

Lei was encouraged at the manner in which the officers didn't hesitate, but it quickly became apparent that their men were hopelessly jumbled, forcing Lei to grab each *Hou Kuan* and lead them to the spot he was making their responsibility, the *Hou Chang* then taking responsibility for rounding up their men and bringing them to their leader. It wasn't perfect, but the men worked quickly enough that they were at least on the eastern side of the market when the sounds of men approaching, not at a run, but with a rhythmic marching step that was in most ways even more intimidating, began echoing between the buildings to the west. Just as the Han had used the half-dozen streets that emptied out onto the market, the *Gwai* advanced in the same manner, pausing their advance only to widen their spacing once they emerged out into the square and weren't constrained by the width of the streets. Lei stood facing the

Gwai, using his ears to gauge the progress of his own men as they finished dragging anything that could be used to form a barricade which their enemy would have to clamber over while keeping his gaze on their enemy. Gradually, the noise level was reduced to just the sound of voices as the *Hou Kuan* and *Hou Chang* issued their last moment orders, although it didn't drown out the noise of the *Gwai* presumably doing the same thing, shuffling into spots as directed by the *Gwai* wearing the black and red crests, who appeared to be using sticks to point at their men. Smoke was now rising to his left, in the direction of the southern wall, but from deeper inside the city, and as it gradually grew quieter, he thought he heard the sounds of fighting on either side of him, although to this point he didn't see any smoke in the direction of the northern wall. While Lei was Xao's second in command, he wasn't the only officer above the rank of *Hou Kuan*, and Xao had given the next three men in their chain of command responsibility for defending the other walls, although when it became apparent that the *Gwai* were attacking the western wall, and back before Xao had seemingly lost interest in whether the city fell or not, he had ordered men shifted to Lei's command from the others. What remained of those men who had manned the western wall in the southern part of the city were present now, and because the Han didn't have the same level of organization as their enemies, Lei couldn't tell with any precision how heavy his casualties had been, and it was too late for him to demand the Han equivalent of the butcher's bill from the *Hou Kuan*, but he was certain that he had lost almost half of them, a good number of them in the worst way imaginable. It was this thought that brought his mind back to the fiery weapon, and even before he heard the rumbling sound of the carts arriving, he understood why the *Gwai* were waiting.

The area of the large bay serving as the harbor outside the eastern wall of the city was now effectively unusable because of the burned out hulks of the *chuan*, the unburned portion of most of them settling to the bottom so that many of their masts poked above the surface, looking like a strange forest of trees denuded of branches, while hundreds of bodies, some burned beyond recognition, were floating on the surface in that period before they sank into the depths. As a result, Caesar decided to send the ships carrying the 14th Legion to the far side of the bay, landing them four miles from the eastern wall, where Figulus and his men landed shortly past midday, but leaving their artillery aboard and with the first four Cohorts carrying ladders. Nor did they bring any of their consignment of naphtha with them, mainly because Caesar was becoming more concerned that they were being too profligate using this powerful weapon. It was certainly possible that a new supply would arrive from Parthia, but over the course of the year since they had left the Ganges, it had become increasingly obvious to Caesar that the lack of communication from Parthia Inferior was by design on the part of Marcus Agrippa, who was now the Praetor, aided by Gaius Maecenas, but he felt confident that this had been done at the behest of his nephew and not on Agrippa's own initiative. That, however, was a problem for later. He hadn't been happy being forced to use so much of the substance to secure the rampart, but once the element of surprise had been lost, his Legions needed every advantage they could get to negate the artillery that he knew the Han possessed, unaware of his fortune in that moment because of his counterpart's oversight.

It wasn't until the gates were opened, starting with the Jade Gate by the Equestrians, and Caesar entered the city through the center Gold Gate to find a scene that he would never forget, just one more of so many, the corpses of the freshly dead Han who had succumbed to the normal kind of battlefield injury trying to keep his men from advancing into the city mingled with charred remains of their unluckier comrades that in most cases were still smoldering fully bringing home to him that it was time to rein in the use of the naphtha. As he sat surveying the scene, the pall of the smoke that was still issuing from several upper windows, where the contents of whatever was contained in the rooms were now fully ablaze, hung just above his head like a low, dirty cloud, making his eyes water, although it was the stench that was the worst. He wasn't surprised to see that the Centurions and Optios were now more concerned with rounding up their men, and it appeared that his own casualties, while not insignificant, weren't as heavy as he had feared they would be because of their tardy assault, but he did notice the hundreds of used bolts lying scattered about on the street, making him curious enough to order Gundomir to retrieve one. Grumbling under his breath, the German dismounted, and in a form of petty revenge for being treated like a servant, he chose a bolt that was embedded in the chest of a dead Legionary just beneath the rampart. Returning, he handed the dripping bolt to Caesar, who pointedly ignored his bodyguard's obvious attempt to express his own displeasure, although he was sure to hold the bolt out from his body so that the blood didn't drip onto his thigh. Gundomir remounted, copying Caesar in his refusal to acknowledge the amused smile of Teispes, while Caesar examined the bolt.

"It almost looks like one of our scorpion bolts, but they're much shorter and not as thick," Caesar mused.

It so happened that he was overheard by a Centurion from the Alaudae who, despite appearances as he bawled orders to his men to assemble, had been listening to his general.

"That's because these slanty-eyed bastards use what the boys are calling scorpion bows, sir."

Caesar looked away from the bolt to address the Centurion. "Is that so, Canidius?"

Vibius Canidius, Tertius Hastatus Prior of the Alaudae, automatically stiffened to *intente*, but he refrained from saluting because Caesar was holding the bolt in his right hand.

"Yes, sir," Canidius replied, but then went further. "In fact, one of my boys picked one of them up from the rampart. It's a bit burned, but..." Suddenly realizing it would be easier to show rather than tell, Canidius spun about, scanning his Century still forming, then spying the ranker, shouted, "Columella! Come here, you dozy bastard, and bring that scorpion bow with you!"

The ranker immediately complied, except that he did salute Caesar, who nodded his recognition of the courtesy, reaching down with his left hand to take the crossbow that Columella extended to him. As Canidius had warned, the stock was badly charred, and part of the string had burnt away so that one end hung from an arm of the crossbow, but it was enough for Caesar to immediately see that it resembled a scorpion only superficially. Yes, it had two arms that were drawn backward, but unlike the larger Roman version, both arms were made of one piece of wood, and used a lever attached to the body of the crossbow to draw the string back, thereby pulling the arms backward, and in the body of the crossbow, aside from the iron lever, there was a simple iron trigger that released the bolt, which the crossbowman placed in the groove carved into the top of the wooden body. It was, Caesar decided, a simple design that would be easy to reproduce in mass quantities, the only somewhat scarce resource being the iron for lever and trigger.

Handing it back to Columella, Caesar observed, "I assume that it has a limited range, but at close distances like," he pointed up to the nearest window, ignoring the licking flames and black smoke boiling out of it, "from that building to the rampart, it's probably very powerful."

Canidius didn't answer directly, addressing Columella, saying, "Show Caesar your shield." The ranker, who had rested the shield on the ground in front of him hefted it, but while Caesar could see several holes in it, Canidius snapped, "Turn it around so he can see it, idiot." Columella fumbled with the shield but managed to turn it around as Canidius explained, "They punched through our shields, but they didn't penetrate all the way through, just about half the length. My boys swear on the black stone that it's because of the new wood we're using that kept it from skewering them. They say if we'd been carrying our old shields, we would have been slaughtered if we hadn't used the naphtha to burn those *cunni* to death."

Caesar didn't reply to Canidius, instead looking to the ranker, and despite the sudden rush of fear, Columella nodded vigorously, assuring the general, "Centurion Canidius has the rights of it, sir. There's no doubt in our mind that if we had been carrying our old shields, we'd all be across the river." Forgetting his discomfort at not only being in the presence of but speaking to a being that, like many of his comrades, he now secretly believed was at the very least a demigod, he displayed a grin notable for its missing teeth as he said, "I know we all liked to complain about these shields when we first started carrying them, sir, but you can be sure you won't hear another word about them, not from me or any of the other boys...at least in the Alaudae. I can't speak for those other bast...Legions."

Amused, Caesar looked to Canidius.

"Canidius, I believe Gregarius Columella has earned a reward." He smiled then, letting Canidius know that Caesar was aware of something as he said, "It's too bad that we've completely exhausted our stock of grape wine and *sura*. Otherwise, I'd double Columella's ration."

Understanding perfectly, Canidius offered Caesar a smile that was as much a grimace at this sign that Caesar was perfectly aware that most of the officers had their own private stocks of the highly intoxicating but sweet *sura,* over and above what had become a staple of the Roman supply train.

"I'll see if I can scrounge some up, Caesar," Canidius assured him as he saluted, which Caesar returned this time.

Turning away in a clear signal that he had devoted all of the time he had in the moment, Caesar spoke as if to himself, nudging his horse to move, reluctantly, farther away from the gate and closer to the flames flickering out of the second floor windows and some of the open doors on the street level, "We need to investigate whether or not these scorpion bows are worth making ourselves." Shaking his head, he said, "That will wait. Now," he addressed his bodyguards, "let's go see if we can find one of the Primi Pili to see what the situation is."

Neither Gundomir nor Teispes were surprised when Caesar turned his horse to the right and headed towards the southern wall and in the direction of the 10th, only exchanging knowing glances. Trailed by Apollodorus, looking as miserable on horseback as always, along with Achaemenes, Zhang, and a handful of other bodyguards, all of whom still rode in a casual but unmistakable cordon around the Han emissary, Caesar had to navigate around the bodies that had yet to be cleared out of the street. However, when Caesar looked over his shoulder to find Apollodorus, the secretary, having anticipated his master's order, assured him that he was already drafting the orders. Over the years, he had mastered the ability to write in a wax tablet while astride a horse, a skill that he heartily detested having to learn, but this was his lot serving Caesar. Only skilled horsemen could make their mounts obey their orders where death and fire were present, which meant that Apollodorus had long since resigned himself to having one of the Germans next to him with a hand on the scribe's horse's bridle whenever they were surrounded by such things. Even so, Caesar and the others had their hands full guiding their horses down the street, the animals even more reluctant whenever they were confronted by a charred corpse, and their progress was in fits and starts as each of them was forced to pause to calm their mount before they reached the part of the wall the 10th had been assigned. Spotting a red crest, Caesar steered his horse, not Toes, who had died shortly after they finished chopping their path on the Via Hades, but his offspring, although the malformation wasn't nearly as pronounced as it had been with his famous sire, heading for the Pilus Prior whose identity Caesar didn't know until the man turned around.

Seeing the general, Cyclops came to *intente* and saluted, and now that Caesar's hands were free, he returned it, asking as he did so, "Where's Pullus, Pilus Prior Ausonius?"

Grateful that Caesar was aware that, while he tolerated it from others, only close friends called him Cyclops, the Centurion turned slightly to point down the nearest street running from the western wall. "The last I saw him, he was heading down that street to check with Trebellius. We just entered the city, but one of the boys in the Fourth who took a bolt in the leg told me that Pullus sent the Fifth into the city a couple blocks north to hit these *cunni* holding up the Alaudae from the flank like we did in Pattala." Turning back to Caesar, Cyclops said, "That's all I know, sir, and I'm waiting for his orders."

"It clearly worked," Caesar remarked, looking past Cyclops to where at least two hundred Han were lying along the eastern side of the street just in front of the buildings, then on the far side, the bodies were not only thicker but were distributed across the street, his experienced eye telling him how the battle had developed and when the decisive moment had come during this small but vitally important fight for the wall. Returning his attention to Cyclops, Caesar said, "When I find him, I'll have him send orders to you based on what I decide we do next."

"Yes, Caesar," Cyclops acknowledged, exchanging another salute. "I understand and will obey." Caesar was already moving when Cyclops remembered something, calling the general's name. "Sir, I also heard that Pullus was wounded, but I don't know how badly."

"It couldn't be that bad if he's still performing his duty," Caesar answered, though he lifted a hand in acknowledgement as he resumed.

He was too far away from Cyclops to hear the Centurion mutter, "You'd think, but he'll kill himself because of you one day."

Chapter Seven

Pullus wasn't sure whether it was because of the wound or the bandage being bound too tightly that caused him such discomfort, but he didn't want to take the time to loosen it, especially since he would need help, which meant it was inevitable that whoever it was would want to examine the wound. Not surprisingly, the pain made him even more irritable, his Centurions bearing the brunt of his displeasure, which in turn meant that the rankers of those Centurions who felt Pullus' wrath subsequently felt the sting of the *vitus*. The problem was neither surprising nor unusual; once the Han fighting the Equestrians broke and fled, inevitably, men began to start kicking in the doors of the small but neatly ordered wooden buildings that were clearly dwellings, rushing in to grab whatever they could get in what they knew was the limited time they had before their officers appeared to stop the fun. It had been the same in Gaul, in Greece, in Parthia, and in every other town and city along the path of Caesar's army. And, as always happened, Centurions and Optios swatted, punched, and kicked their men in what was sometimes a half-hearted attempt to maintain order and discipline. Never far from the minds of any man wearing the Centurion's crest or the white shoulder stripe of the Optio was what had taken place in Bharuch, especially the officers in the Equestrians, not because of what they had done, but because of what their giant Primus Pilus had kept them from doing. It was something that was only discussed in low tones, in the privacy of a Centurion's quarters, and it was based more on a sense than anything tangible that any of them had heard, but even now, four years removed from that event, it was a topic of discussion, which in turn meant that it would be either Scribonius, Balbus, Diocles, or Porcinus that one or more officers would approach to whisper their concerns. And, it wasn't something that any of them refused to relay to Pullus; over those intervening four years, they had broached the subject on multiple occasions.

"The men still feel like they were cheated because of Bharuch," Scribonius had told Pullus on more than one occasion. "They had to sit there and watch while the other Legions were allowed to run wild for two weeks, and they haven't forgotten it."

This, and variations of it, had been related to Pullus innumerable times over the years, and Pullus' response had always been the same.

"I don't give a fart in a *testudo* whether they're unhappy or not," he snapped, or sometimes bellowed, "And any one of them that disobeys me the next time we're in a situation like that, I'll flay them myself! We're not fucking undisciplined rabble like those other bastards!"

Now, Pullus appeared dangerously close to carrying out his threat, but the delay in reorganizing wasn't nearly as long as he thought it was, so that by the time Caesar found him standing in the center of a street that ran north to south four blocks deep within the city, conferring with the six Pili Priores, there were seven Cohorts, each occupying one of the streets leading from the western wall, with the men in acceptable order, standing with their shields grounded as they talked in the excited manner of men who had just endured a period of intense combat.

"What's the situation with Batius and Torquatus?" Pullus asked first, beating Caesar, something that he would normally never have done, but Caesar had immediately seen the bandage, and how it was soaked red on Pullus' right side, shrewdly guessing that this was the cause for what would otherwise have been an intemperate thing to do.

More amused than irritated, though barely, Caesar assured him, "As far as I know, you're ahead of them into the city, Pullus. Now," he reasserted control, "what's *your* situation?"

"I've arranged each Cohort along one of these streets, in Century column order." Pullus, Caesar noticed, was careful to point with his left hand and not his right. "I've got Vistilia and his boys in my Sixth Century up on the rampart along the southern wall and down on the street to block any attempt to use that to get on our flank or rear, but my last report is that the Han don't seem all that eager to try." Caesar also noted the manner in which Pullus turned his entire body instead of twisting at the waist to point in the opposite direction. "On the Seventh's flank, his Hastatus Posterior is doing the same thing one street beyond them. And," he returned his attention to the east, deeper into the city, "there's a section from every Cohort I've sent ahead to get an idea of what's waiting for us on their street."

"What about the civilians?" Caesar asked, truly curious. "I saw a few bodies, and we can certainly hear them, but where are they?"

"They're inside," Pullus indicated the nearest dwellings, then knowing what was coming next, he assured Caesar, "and while we had some mischief early on, my Centurions have the men under control. They know better than to try and grab some loot before it's their time, and we don't want to cause a panic that sends these people out into the streets."

Caesar nodded his acceptance, but he was staring down the street leading east, which curved slightly, not much but enough that he couldn't see any Romans. He was about to ask when he heard a shout from the direction of the Seventh Cohort, turning his mount in time to see the section returning at a trot to be met by the Septimus Pilus Prior Titus Marcius, who had raised the alarm. After a brief exchange, Marcius turned and hurried towards them, prompting Caesar to kick his mount to meet him, which in turn ignited muttered curses by a Primus Pilus at having to run to catch up. *He always does this*, he thought sourly, trying to ignore the stab of sharper pain with every footfall. Pullus was gratified to see that, while Marcius rendered his salute, he waited for Pullus before he began.

"My boys have found a large group of Han, three blocks east of here. They say that it looks like it's a market or something, but the bastards have created some sort of breastworks along the eastern edge of the market, and that's where they're waiting."

"When you say large, how large, Marcius?" Pullus snapped, beating Caesar to it.

Reddening slightly, Marcius nevertheless answered immediately, "Sergeant Pulcher estimates that it's at least a couple thousand, but he said he also saw more of the bastards joining them from the northwest side of the city."

"Composition of the force?" Caesar asked, and when Marcius hesitated, he elaborated, "How many of them are those Han the men are calling the scorpion bowmen?"

"Ah, right. Pulcher estimates that almost half of them are bowmen, and the other half are spearmen, but they were too far away to tell whether or not they were just spears or those fucking hook spears."

"Hook spears?" Caesar frowned, but when he looked at Pullus, the Centurion said, "I'll explain later." Returning his attention to Marcius, he pointed at the street from which the section emerged. "Your boys advanced only on this street?" Marcius nodded. "How wide is this market? How many of these streets lead to it?"

"I didn't think to ask," Marcius admitted, then quickly added, "but they said they were at the southern end of the market."

"Which means that the Alaudae is the Legion that should handle it," Caesar mused. "Have you had any contact with Batius?"

"They were still at the rampart trying to break through," Pullus replied vaguely, but it was the manner in which he refused to meet Caesar's gaze that told the general the tale, reminding him of the fierce competition between Primi Pili. And, he was honest with himself, if Pullus did detach a Cohort to outflank the Han facing Batius like he had with his own Equestrians, Batius wouldn't be at all grateful. Regardless of this reality, Caesar didn't hesitate to make his decision.

"Here's what you're going to do, Pullus." Caesar made up his mind. "You're going to shift the Equestrians to align with this market, but at the same time, I want you to send one of your Cohorts back towards the western wall, and hit the Han facing Batius again from behind. We should be further along with taking this city as it is, and we still don't know what's ahead of us in a city this size."

As he expected, Pullus clearly relished the idea of being in a position to claim that he got Batius out of difficulty, and the Primus Pilus told Marcius, "You're closest to their area. Bring your Cohort out onto this street, then shake them out, a Century per block. That won't be enough to cover all of the Han, but the same thing will happen that happened with Trebellius. Once they see their left flank collapsing again, they'll turn and run." Instantly seeing the danger, before Caesar could point it out, Pullus added, "And I'll have the Sixth Century of each Cohort facing west and ready to cut them down when they head this way. It shouldn't be hard. They'll be in a panic to get away."

With the plan finalized, it was immediately put into motion, beginning with the Seventh spilling out onto the street, arranging themselves along each east/west street but facing west this time, then disappearing, while Gellius brought his Sixth Cohort out, leading them at a trot to the north, stopping six streets down, with each Cohort following suit. As the Equestrians made preparations, Caesar took the time to reverse his course back to the western wall before turning north, intent on determining the state of the 5th and 25th. As a rule, Caesar loathed assaulting a city because he had so little control once his men scaled the wall or breached a gate, and experience had taught him in a city this size, slightly larger than Bharuch, he and his officers had learned that in one spot a Primus Pilus could be winning the battle, managing the advance of his Legion beyond the crucial taking of the wall, and the report he gave Caesar reflected that, which was what happened with Pullus. However, that might not extend to the other Legions who were assaulting a wall that was well more than a mile long as this one was, especially with as much smoke as there now was, and his view was further blocked by a slight curve of the wall, whoever had built it originally following a natural contour. If he were to judge by his ears alone, it sounded as if the 5th was finally advancing into the city, which was confirmed by his eyes as he drew closer, seeing the standards of the third line Cohorts arrayed down the street, with the first and second line Cohorts no longer to be found, telling him that Marcius and his Seventh Cohort had succeeded in their attack.

As it had been with the Equestrians' part of the wall, there was a good deal of smoke, and he saw that the wooden roofs of several buildings had caught, the dancing flames visible in the afternoon sky, the smoke column now several hundred feet in the air. Normally, he would be concerned about the fire spreading; he didn't want another conflagration like what took place in Bharuch the night that King Abhiraka made his last, desperate attempt to retake his throne, but he had noticed something that he thought odd. Now that he had been several blocks into the city himself, his initial impression that every structure would be made of stone was incorrect; in fact, after the first block, the buildings were almost exclusively made of wood, using an architecture that, while similar to what they had encountered with the Khmer, was distinctly different yet still pleasing to the eye. Just as he spotted the Septimus Pilus Prior of the Alaudae, he drew up to examine the buildings in his range of vision to the north, noticing something; every building next to the western wall is constructed of stone, he thought, suddenly certain that this was no accident. One of Emperor Yuan's predecessors had taken steps to decrease the vulnerability of this city by ensuring that those structures nearest to the wall were constructed of stone, making them harder to burn. Of course, he would have to examine the buildings that lined each of the other walls to confirm his theory, but that could also wait. Pausing only long enough to find out if the Septimus Pilus Prior of the Alaudae had been in direct communication with Batius, the Centurion assuring the general that he had, then pointed behind Caesar at one of the streets leading deeper into the city.

"He's up there somewhere, sir. But," he grinned up at Caesar in what could have been called an impertinent manner to say, "I wouldn't disturb him right now. Primus Pilus Batius is...in a mood, sir."

As the Centurion hoped, Caesar wasn't offended, laughing instead, then rejoining, "Isn't he always in a mood, Salvius?"

Equally thrilled that his general knew his name and wasn't glowering down at him, he nodded his head. "That's true, Caesar. Primus Pilus Batius wakes up in a mood, but he's *very* unhappy right now, thanks to the Equestrians."

"I'll return shortly, but I need to check on Torquatus and the 25th first," Caesar said, ignoring the implied rebuke, then almost offhandedly, asked, "You know anything about their situation? It's hard to make out any details with the smoke."

"Only that Primus Pilus Batius is determined that Torquatus and his boys aren't going to move through the city faster than we are, sir. And," he finished with an almost defiant pride, "he's right. The Alaudae won't let anyone beat us, sir. Not even the Equestrians."

"Good," Caesar nodded in approval, but he was moving past Salvius as he did so, and he spoke over his shoulder, "I wouldn't expect anything less."

As Caesar discovered very quickly, Salvius' boast about his Legion was in serious jeopardy, finding that Torquatus and his 25th was several blocks deeper than Batius' men, but they were now meeting stiffer resistance.

"It's those fucking scorpion bows, Caesar," Torquatus informed his general, clearly disgusted and distressed in equal measure.

"I thought our new shields protected the men." Caesar frowned.

"They do," Torquatus seemingly agreed, "but only up to a point. Inside ten paces, Caesar, those fucking things pass right through. And," he said bitterly, "they clearly have an endless supply of them. I thought they would have run out by now, but they haven't."

Trying not to display how perturbed he was, Caesar asked, "What about flanking them? Pullus did that and..."

"Yes, sir," Torquatus cut him off, "we tried to do the same thing that worked for the Equestrians in Pattala, but the only way to do that was to move over into Batius' area. Besides, they've gotten organized here. They've dragged every single thing that can be used across the streets to block them, so we have to assault each and every one. And," he looked up at Caesar now, and the general saw the pain there, "I've already lost a lot of my boys trying to break through."

"So," Caesar said thoughtfully, "it's a matter of numbers when it comes to these scorpion bows?"

"Yes, sir," Torquatus affirmed. "I've never seen as many missile troops make up any of the armies we've faced. Not even the Numidians have as many," he finished, naming the kingdom whose king Juba had chosen to ally himself with the forces of

Scipio in what would turn out to be the second part of the civil war after Pompeius Magnus' death that had torn Rome apart.

Caesar considered for a moment, and while he didn't do so lightly, he told Torquatus, "Send someone back for your stores of naphtha."

The Primus Pilus didn't respond immediately, staring up at Caesar for a moment before nodding. Just as he was turning to issue the order, there was a shout from behind Caesar and his party, the general turning to see a ranker running in their direction, moving more swiftly than one would expect of a ranker, but as he drew closer, Caesar saw that his dark complexion wasn't because of exertion, and he vaguely recognized the face as one of the Parthians who were the first non-Romans to enlist in the ranks. More importantly, Caesar remembered that he served in the 10th, which also meant he was probably in the third line of Cohorts, but he didn't hesitate to kick his mount to meet the ranker, who slid to a stop. Despite the effort it must have taken to run almost a mile in armor, Caesar noticed that the young Parthian was only a bit winded, nor could he fault the precision of the salute.

In heavily accented but understandable Latin, the ranker addressed Caesar, "Sir, Gregarius Artaxades, First Century, Eighth Cohort. I've been sent by..."

"What does Cyclops want?" Caesar cut him off, sensing something important was happening.

The Parthian looked confused before understanding. "No, sir, a runner from the Primus Pilus came to find Pilus Prior Ausonius, then the Pilus Prior sent me to find you so the runner from the First wouldn't have to run as far." Understanding, Caesar indicated the ranker should continue, but Artaxades, suddenly realizing the import of this message, had to swallow before, clearly from memory, he relayed, "The Primus Pilus requests your presence immediately, sir. He says that there's a Han who is offering to surrender."

It was rash, even foolhardy, but Caesar *was* a superb horseman, and he put his mount to a canter that was as close to a gallop as the obstacles would allow, heading south with his party following behind.

It was the sight of the jars more than the number of *Gwai* facing them that had convinced Lei, but Xao's collapse had already shaken his resolve, triggered by the arrival of the minor clerk from Xao's headquarters to inform him that General Xao had gone into seclusion in his quarters, with orders not to disturb him. To Lei, it removed all doubt that General Xao had chosen to die rather than live through the humiliation of seeing his dreams destroyed, in the form of *chuan* now littering the bottom of the harbor. When he saw the *Gwai* unloading the carts with boxes marked with a large red circle on each side, and at a leisurely pace that was almost insulting, he only took a quick glance at the faces of the men behind him standing at the barricade before making his decision. The hastily built fortification was composed entirely of wood, as were the buildings on the eastern edge of the market; that they were also larger because they belonged to the merchants whose businesses were run paces away in the market only meant more fuel to burn. During the lull in the fighting, Lei had dispatched a party to the armory located in the city center with orders to bring the boxes of crossbow bolts that had been set aside as a strategic reserve. When they returned, he was informed that the reserve had already been partially depleted, and what they brought with them was all that remained. With five hundred bolts to a crate, Lei knew that the five crates seemed like more than enough, but just as the *Gwai* had been faced with new challenges facing the Han, the soldiers of the Han had never been confronted by an enemy force who used shields to the extent of the *Gwai*, and when they did, it was almost exclusively used by enemy cavalry, and the shields were smaller. More importantly, in Lei's experience, a shield provided minimal protection if the target was within fifty paces, yet he had seen with his own eyes when the battle for the rampart was taking place that the *Gwai* shields, while pierced, stopped the bolts from penetrating all the way through, and the range between the rampart and the buildings was a bit more than fifteen paces. Although he hadn't made a count, the fact was the shields protecting each *Gwai* provided coverage of the bearer from just above the iron greaves they wore to just below their chin, and that was if they didn't crouch down, from top to bottom, while only their right arm were exposed when measured edge to edge, and he had seen more shields than he could count studded with a dozen bolts or more that were still being used by their soldier. Whether that weakened them and made them vulnerable to the second volley his crossbowmen would lash them with as they closed the hundred paces between western and eastern edges of the market would only be discovered during the assault. Adding to that, the *Gwai* armor was unusual, the use of chainmail being unknown to the Han of this age, but it was clearly very strong. And, Lei thought, that's assuming that these demons plan on throwing those evil flaming pots by hand and don't use their artillery like they did on the rampart. Given their seeming lack of urgency, Lei suspected that they were waiting for that very thing, but he couldn't see beyond the ordered line of men with grounded shields to see anything that would indicate that they were bringing their artillery into place. It was when he turned to address the nearest *Hou Kuan* to his right, facing him north, that he saw there were now several columns of black smoke, and while they were faint, he could clearly hear shrill screams; whether it came from the throats of women being raped or both sexes being burned alive he couldn't tell, but this was the last piece of information that prompted Lei to act.

He had been about to order the *Hou Kuan* to make a last moment check of his crossbowmen's quivers, but instead, he ordered, "Find me something white."

The officer hesitated, but Lei saw his eyes look past him to something happening on the western side of the market, causing Lei to return his attention in that direction, and he saw that the huge *Gwai* wearing the white crest had appeared and was standing in front of his soldiers, but with his back to the Han. When Lei returned his attention to the *Hou Kuan*, he saw the officer already walking quickly over to a small group of men, unarmored and standing a short distance behind the rearmost ranks lining the barricade. These men were the equivalent of the Roman *medici*, and it was from one of them who, extracting a folded piece of white cloth from the bag slung over his shoulder handed it to the *Hou Kuan*, and on his return to Lei's side, snatched a spear from one of the men standing behind the first three ranks of crossbowmen. By the time he reached Lei, he had thrust the cloth down onto the point, handing the spear to Lei, then bowing.

"General, may I ask if this is a temporary truce? Or is this...?"

There was no need to finish, but Lei didn't know this officer well enough to determine by his demeanor where his thoughts lay, yet he also felt that he owed him at least a partial answer.

"Forgive me, *Hou Kuan*, but I've forgotten your name."

"Gao Zhong, General, of the Raging Tigers."

"What I'm about to tell you is meant for your ears, *Hou Kuan* Gao, and I need you to offer no reaction when I tell you what I have to say. Do you agree?"

If anything, Gao looked a bit offended, but he didn't hesitate to assure Lei, "Of course, General. Whatever you have to tell me will remain between us, and I swear on my ancestors that the men won't be able to tell anything."

Assured, Lei still made sure to turn his back fully on the men and to keep his voice low, "You have undoubtedly noticed that our commander General Xao is...absent." Gao nodded, and Lei continued, "The *Gwai* attacked our fleet, which as you know were already loaded with all of the artillery that the General intended to use in our new assault on Xuwen. Apparently, every *chuan* was destroyed, and while I don't know to a degree of certainty, from what the courier who informed General Xao and me of the attack told us, it appears that they used that same evil fire substance on the ships that they used to drive us off of the rampart. You saw for yourself how that substance behaves and how we can't seem to extinguish the flames from it." Just saying the words caused a rush of bitterness and hatred that Lei didn't attempt to hide, although he was encouraged that, aside from a slight widening of the eyes, Gao's expression remained impassive. Lei had to take a breath before he continued, "And I just received word from the headquarters that General Xao has gone into seclusion and ordered that he not be disturbed. It probably won't surprise you that when he returned after verifying that the courier was speaking truly, the General was...distraught."

He paused then, waiting for the true meaning to sink in, but

Gao proved good to his word, showing not a flicker of emotion.

"I see," he finally said. "The General has chosen death rather than being dishonored."

"That," Lei nodded, "is what I believe, although I haven't gotten confirmation."

"Forgive me, General Lei," Gao's tone was polite, but Lei heard the somber note, "what does the General's fate have to do with the rest of us? Especially," he indicated the waiting soldiers behind the barricade, "the men here?"

"Look over my shoulder to the north," Lei replied quietly. "See all that smoke? The city is burning. And," while he didn't point at them, he saw Gao clearly comprehended he was referring to those crates, "see all those crates? You saw what happened when the *Gwai* used them to drive us from the wall. Do you want to see this entire city go up in flames?"

"But what would the *Gwai* have to gain by destroying the city they're trying to take?"

It was a sensible question, but Lei realized in that moment that Gao hadn't been present to hear the exchange between Xao and the dog Zhang on the rampart above the Jade Gate that had taken place what seemed like a year ago.

"The *Gwai* are working for Emperor Yuan, *Hou Kuan*," Lei explained. "The Emperor is using these demons to crush us, the *Gwai* aren't doing this on their own. We've already seen what they were willing to do to secure the western wall, so why would they hesitate to completely destroy this city? And," Lei finished with what he felt certain would be the most powerful argument, "what do you think they will do to the people of the city? Yes, most of them are *Li* who have no love for us, but there are many thousands of Han who came here to escape Emperor Yuan's rule. Do you have a family?"

"Yes," Gao replied. "I have a wife and son. We live in the Imperial Quarter along with the other officers."

While it was no longer controlled by the Han Empire, the name for the part of the city, a neighborhood that not coincidentally was located just north of the administrative center of the city had stuck even now.

"Would you rather see your wife and son put to the sword, and only after your wife had been raped countless times, or see them burn to death, *Hou Kuan*?"

It was a grotesque question asked in a reasonable tone, but it also brought home to Gao the stakes, and the alternatives. His objection, however, was a practical one.

"How do we know these *Gwai* can be trusted? What if they do all the things we fear even if we surrender?"

"We don't," Lei answered simply, not seeing the point in trying to deny what was an obvious truth. "We know so little about these beasts with their pale skin and huge noses that that is an impossible question for me to answer. But what we *do* know about them now is what kind of destruction they're capable of. So," he held both hands out, palms up, "if they slaughter us because we refuse to surrender and fight to the last man, or if they accept the surrender, then kill us and enslave our families and every other person in this city, then that is what is fated to be, isn't it?"

"Yes, General."

To Lei's ear, the *Hou Kuan* sounded both reluctant but relieved at the same time, a sentiment with which he could identify quite well. Most importantly, Gao signaled his understanding and acceptance by shifting slightly but noticeably out of Lei's path, where he had been standing with his back to the *Gwai*, but when Lei began to walk towards the giant *Gwai* and Gao fell in step beside him, Lei was surprised.

"You don't have to come with me, *Hou Kuan*. Let the shame be mine and mine alone."

"You're doing what you can to save our families, General," Gao replied quietly. "Saving our wives, our children, and all of the Han in the city from being burned alive is not an act to be ashamed about. Although," he gave a small smile, "if we could save our people but roast these barbaric *Li*, it would make our lives easier."

Lei might have laughed, but his mouth was too dry now that he saw the giant *Gwai* had been alerted about their approach, and had begun slowly walking away from his men, some of whom had begun hefting their shields. The large *Gwai* apparently heard this, because he looked over his shoulder while gesturing with the stick in his hand, and his soldiers lowered them back to the ground. This was also when Lei

285

noticed the bandage wrapped around the savage's midsection, and he caught a glimpse of a red stain underneath his right arm, prompting a surge of a cruel satisfaction. So you *do* bleed, even if you are a giant from beyond the edge of the earth, he thought, and for a brief instant, he considered turning about and returning to his own men and resuming the fight. His sense quickly prevailed; even if they killed this *Gwai*, he had counted at least two thousand men arrayed behind him, but it was the signs of the fire that was still clearly growing in strength to the north of the market that dissuaded him from acting rashly. The pair of Han and the large Roman reached a spot roughly in the middle of the empty market, but both sides came to the same realization at the same moment.

"Where is the Han emissary Zhang?" Lei asked the question of the *Gwai* without thinking.

"I don't understand a fucking word of that gibberish except for Zhang," Pullus replied, equally unthinkingly, which created an awkward silence. Slightly inspired, Pullus spoke, but pantomimed as he did so, "I have sent word," he pointed back over his shoulder with the stick while rapidly moving the fingers of his right hand to meet his thumb repeatedly in what Lei understood was mimicking speaking, and Lei also noticed how awkwardly he was moving, "back to my general. He should be," he pointed in front of him to a spot between the two, "here soon." He touched his lips then moved his hand in their direction, "He will speak to you, and Zhang will be with him."

"Did you understand a word of that?" Gao whispered to Lei.

"Only one, and that was Zhang's name," Lei whispered back, "but I think that this *Gwai* giant might be simple in the head."

"Pluto's cock," Pullus growled, "how fucking thick do you have to be to not figure out what I mean?"

Then, a shout came from behind the *Gwai*, and Lei leaned over to see beyond Pullus, who carefully turned his body; they both saw movement several blocks to the west, determining that they were horsemen approaching, and Lei recognized the *Gwai* general called Caesar was leading the way.

"Where is General Xao? Why isn't he here?"

"General Xao," Lei replied coldly to Caesar's question, through Achaemenes then Zhang, "is no longer in command. I am."

Just as with the first time, both parties found the process frustrating and laborious, but it was still the best that they could do. Once Achaemenes finished, Caesar nodded his acceptance, then spoke some more to the Parthian interpreter, although his eyes never left those of Lei. He and his party had dismounted, leaving their horses back with the *Gwai* soldiers, and Pullus had remained, which Lei correctly guessed Caesar had ordered on purpose because, during the periods where his and Caesar's words were being translated into something recognizable, Lei found his eyes continually moving to the giant, and he was certain he could see the pain in the *Gwai's* expression. It didn't reduce his menace, and Lei acknowledged to himself that he was intimidated just being this close to the thing that may have resembled a man in some form but was clearly something other than a civilized human.

"Caesar asks what the purpose of this truce is," Zhang broke into Lei's thoughts. "He says that if you're trying to buy time, that you should know that there are two more Legions who are even now assailing your walls from the east, and from the south."

It took an effort on Lei's part not to react with dismay, but it also reinforced that he was doing not just the responsible thing, but the only one that made any sense.

Regardless of this recognition, he still had to control his temper as he replied, "What I am trying to do is stop this barbarian and his savages from burning Hanou to the ground with," he lifted his arm to point at the stack of crates behind and to Pullus' left, "whatever that is." While he hated to admit it, Lei went on, "This is a weapon that we cannot hope to defeat, and I've seen that he and his army are savages who would not hesitate to use that foul stuff to burn every man, woman, and child living inside these walls."

Zhang surprised Lei then, because he sounded genuinely sympathetic when he agreed, "Yes, it *is* a terrible weapon. When we entered the city, I saw what it could do, and it is truly horrifying." Lei saw Zhang glance over at Caesar then, sounding hesitant to do so, he continued, "But I will say this. I have been in his company for several months now, and I believe that, while he might be a barbarian, he is not without honor. His Legions are..." he tried to find the right word, settling on, "...formidable, and they fight like demons, but they are completely obedient to Caesar."

"So you are saying I can trust him?"

Zhang hesitated again, but before he could reply, Caesar interjected, addressing Achaemenes, while his eyes never left the Han emissary, followed by Achaemenes speaking in a tone that seemed meant to convey Caesar's ire.

"What did he say?" Lei asked, reminding Zhang, "and you didn't answer the question."

"Caesar does not like it when he does not know what is being said," Zhang explained dryly. "As to your other question?"

He didn't say anything, but he did give Lei a slight nod that was completely unsatisfactory to the Han; he also understood this was the best he could expect.

"What are the *Gwai*'s terms?"

This didn't take nearly as long to translate, and the reply was blunt.

"Unconditional surrender, and Caesar will decide your fate, but he also wants to know how he can be certain that you have the authority to speak for your entire garrison now that General Xao is no longer in command?"

It was a valid question, but Lei still didn't like it, and he had to control the anger it stirred in him, which he just managed to do.

"If he will give me time, I will send messages to my subordinates who are in command in the other quarters of Hanou and order them to lay down their arms."

It was a huge gamble Lei was taking, and he knew it; his authority as second in command was known to all, but of the three officers of comparative rank, one of them, Yu Wei, hadn't bothered hiding his disagreement with Xao's decision. He was currently commanding the Lotus *Tu-wei-fu* in the northern part of the city, which was also the part of Hanou that seemed to have the most buildings burning, which didn't surprise Lei at all, considering Yu a blustering fool who wasn't nearly as intelligent, nor as skilled in warfare as he thought, but came from an important family and clan that Xao needed to appease. In fact, Lei would have been shocked to learn that the Romans had essentially the same problem with some of their patricians, and he would never know that, once Caesar learned more about Yu and his actions that were taking place at that moment, it would make him think of Marcus Aemilius Lepidus, the disgraced and now-dead patrician who had been foolish enough to think he could usurp Caesar's authority in what was now the Roman Senatorial province of Parthia Superior.

"Caesar accepts this proposal," Zhang translated. Lei saw the flicker of...something in the Han emissary's expression, which he partially understood when Zhang went on, "with one condition, that you deliver the message yourself, and naturally, he and some of his soldiers will escort you wherever you need to be."

Caesar wasn't surprised by the vehement resistance to the announcement of his decision from Gundomir and Teispes, but he wouldn't be swayed.

"If we can end this without losing even more men, I'm willing to run the risk to me. Besides," Caesar smiled at the pair of bodyguards, knowing that between that and his calm demeanor, it would agitate both men even more, "you'll both be with me, and so will most of the First and Second Cohorts of the Equestrians. If you and Pullus can't protect me, then it's the will of the gods that today is the day my string runs out."

For this had been Caesar's final decision: he, Gundomir, Teispes, Achaemenes, and Zhang would ride on horseback, along with Lei, and three officers of his choosing, riding the mounts of the bodyguards who would remain behind at the market, preceded by the First Cohort and followed by the Second Cohort, minus both of their Sixth Centuries, which were still a block west of the market to stop any of the retreating Han who fled in their direction from the Alaudae's area. This naturally took some time to organize, and Scribonius took the opportunity to walk over to Pullus, who was giving instructions to the First Cohort Centurions, although he did wait until they moved away to inform their men to speak, with the exception of Balbus, who Scribonius called back.

"Are you sure that you're up to this?" Scribonius asked bluntly.

Pullus' reaction was alarming, because instead of snarling or blustering, he replied honestly, "I think so, Sextus. But," he allowed himself to grimace as he lifted his right arm a bit, "I won't lie. This hurts like Dis, but I don't really know why. I've been wounded worse than this, but this feels different for some reason."

"Because you're getting old," Balbus replied flatly, but Pullus' reaction was merely a lifted eyebrow and not his usual cursing rejoinder, causing Scribonius to give his scarred friend a worried glance, not encouraged by seeing the same concern on Balbus' face.

"Maybe you should let Balbus take over the First for this, Titus," Scribonius suggested, but while it wasn't with his usual fire, Pullus' mouth twisted in a scornful grimace.

"The day I can't lead my Cohort is the day you put me on the pyre," he snapped, but it was his expression that told the pair the matter was closed.

The delay was brought about because it took Lei time to select the three officers that would accompany them, the delay further aggravated when two of the men balked at mounting the horses provided for them, prompting a lengthy exchange that ended up with Achaemenes turning to Caesar, a bemused expression on his face.

"They say that our horses are larger than the horses the Han use, Caesar, and apparently not many of them ride to begin with."

Pullus was within earshot, and this was actually something he could sympathize with, having the infantryman's distrust of being on horseback, although he had come to enjoy riding quite a bit, something that he never divulged to his friends. As was the case with Achaemenes, a horseman like Caesar couldn't understand the issue, but he snapped an order to Pullus, who in turn called four of his men over, whereupon they each went to one of the horses, and while their expressions made their feelings clear about it, they obediently dropped to all fours. This broke the impasse, although Lei disdained the offer, leaping astride the horse from the opposite side, the rankers hurrying back to their spot in the ranks, muttering curses at their comrades who were clearly amused. Only then did the column begin moving, north across the market square, and the Centurions didn't have to admonish their men to remain quiet and stay alert. Only the first two Centuries of both Cohorts carried javelins, which had been taken from the third line Cohorts earlier. In order to maintain a fighting formation that fit in between the structures lining the streets, the number of files had to be halved, making the column longer and very quickly creating another problem when they reached the first intersection, Pullus calling a halt just before he and the first rank stepped into the intersection, ordering a pair of men to check in both directions before crossing through the intersection. Given the all clear, he gave the order to resume the march, but they had barely crossed to the other side of the street when there was a shout from behind that caused Pullus to turn, and he saw Caesar and his mounted party coming at a quick trot.

"The Han general says that you need to turn to the right here," Caesar called to Pullus, then added quickly, "but stop first. This isn't going to work."

After more back and forth, one of the Han officers, *Hou Kuan* Gao, nudged his horse ahead, carrying the spear with the white cloth on it, accompanied by Teispes, who offered Pullus a sour smile as they passed him to take the lead. They resumed, and before they had marched two blocks east, the sounds of fighting grew louder, not pleasing Pullus in the slightest.

"That has to be the 25th," he muttered to Paterculus. "That means that Torquatus got deeper into the city than we did, the bastard."

"How much did that cost you?" Paterculus asked, trying to hide his amusement; as much pride as he had in his Legion, and in his Primus Pilus, privately, he thought that it was good for Pullus to lose every so often.

"One of my last jugs of *sura*," Pullus replied, but before he could say anything else, the Han officer jerked the reins of his horse, causing it to rear up a few inches, forcing the Han to grab onto the saddle.

Pullus shouted the halt, then took a step to the side to see that two blocks ahead, a group of Han, all armored but wearing swords instead of carrying spears, had stepped out into the middle of the street. Teispes turned in the saddle, raising his hand so that he could be seen, bringing an immediate response as Caesar, with the Han general just behind him, and followed by the rest of the mounted party clattered up the street, forcing the rankers to move out of the way.

Caesar slowed, his eyes never leaving the scene ahead to order Pullus as he passed by, "Bring your First Section with you, Pullus. We may need your shields."

Since the men clearly heard, there was no need for him to issue the command, and he forced himself to break out into a trot of his own, the jarring impact sending stabs of pain so sharp that, while he managed not to cry out, he gasped loudly enough for Vespillo to ask in concern, "Primus Pilus, are you sure..."

"Shut your mouth, Vespillo," Pullus snarled. "I'm fine. Now keep your eyes open." Raising his voice so the rest of the section could hear, he warned, "These slanty-eyed *cunni* might have something planned."

Reaching where Teispes and the Han officer Gao were waiting and just behind Caesar and the others, Pullus divided the section into two parts, with one half up against the side of what he assumed was a family dwelling on one side of the street, while he led his half and did the same on the other, both halves ready and in position to rush out in front of their general and his party.

"Does General Lei know that man?"

Caesar didn't point, but he didn't need to, one of what Pullus counted were a dozen Han clearly standing out, not only for being slightly taller than his comrades, but because he was wearing the same device on his helmet as the Han general with them, the only real difference between Lei and this Han being that, whereas Lei had a mustache that Pullus had long surmised was the Han fashion, this man had a beard as well that was a bit fuller than what he'd seen before.

"Yes," Achaemenes finally answered after the translation, "General Lei says that this is General Yu Wei. He is third in command behind General Lei."

This prompted a slight shuffling, Caesar beckoning to Zhang, then pointed to where Teispes and Gao were still sitting on their horse, followed by gesturing to General Lei, who rode forward to place himself next to his officer. None of the men were talking, not even whispering, the tension being enough that their attention was completely fixed on the two parties who, on some signal that Pullus missed, began slowly approaching each other.

"Pullus, bring your men up to where we're starting from," Caesar ordered, though his gaze never left the other party. "It's out of javelin range, but you'll only have to go a couple of paces to get within range to provide us cover if there's any treachery."

He didn't wait to see if he was obeyed, which was delayed when Pullus suddenly had a thought, ordering the men of the second rank to hand over their lone javelin so that the First Section would have their normal complement of two. The delay was minimal enough that Caesar didn't notice, nor did the waiting Han observe that when Pullus arrayed his men across the street, he actually placed them four or five paces closer than where Teispes and the Han had originally stopped. It would put his men at the edge of their range, but it would save what could be a crucial heartbeat of time in the event things went to *cac*, something that Pullus fervently hoped wouldn't happen, his side hurting more by the moment.

"General Yu," Lei began, once they were within speaking distance, and having dismounted, although only his three officers including Gao followed suit. "Have you heard from General Xao?"

"What are you doing with these savages, Lei?"

There was no mistaking the hostility or the challenge in Yu's tone, but Lei was determined to not only maintain his composure, but control of this moment.

"That," Lei replied coldly, "does not answer my question, General. Do I need to remind you that General Xao was very clear in naming me as his second? And you," he deliberately pointed, something that was normally considered insulting, "are subordinate to me. So, as your commander, I ask again, have you heard from General Xao?"

Yu was clearly angered, but his manner became cautious, and he actually answered honestly, "A messenger arrived from General Xao, yes."

When it became clear that Yu had no intention of saying anything further, Lei snapped, "And? What was the message?"

Yu seemed to consider the idea of refusing to answer, but after a heartbeat, he said grudgingly, "That he has turned over command to you, General Lei. He has removed himself from command. And," Yu briefly closed his eyes, "removed himself from all matters of this world."

It took an effort for Lei to hide his surprise, since the message he had been given hadn't explicitly transferred command to him, but he assumed that Xao must have thought it was obvious.

Aloud, Lei lied, "Yes, I received the same message. Which means I am in command, and you will obey my orders."

Yu seemed to ignore this, pointing again at the *Gwai* general sitting his horse just behind Lei, repeating, "What are you doing with the *Gwai*...General Lei?"

Rather than answer directly, Lei turned his head slightly to look off to Yu's right, where the smoke was not only thicker, but he could now glimpse orange flames dancing just above the rooftops of the buildings between them.

Turning back to look at Yu, he asked, "How much of your part of the city is burning?"

"I have no idea," Yu replied indifferently, but Lei sensed that he was lying, not that Yu did not care, certain that he cared very much, if only because of the blow to his pride. "What I do know is that we've stopped the *Gwai* in their tracks!"

"Yes, so I see." Lei made no attempt to hide his scorn. "Judging from the noise and those fires, they're less than two blocks away from the northern edge of the Imperial quarter. We," he indicated Gao and the other officers, "came from Pearl Market, which is much less than halfway across the city."

"Perhaps you weren't facing the same resistance we are," Yu shot back.

Instead of answering directly, Lei actually turned and pointed to the large *Gwai*, who Zhang had whispered was named Pullus, Lei having seen Yu's gaze keep going back and forth between Lei and his party and Pullus.

"Does that *Gwai* look as if we didn't face resistance? It's true that he's a giant even among these *Gwai*, but anyone with eyes can see how formidable a warrior he is, and that white crest means that he commands one of the *Gwai Tu-wei-fu*. Now," Lei returned to the original subject, "as you have agreed, I am currently in command."

Yu refused to answer, glaring at Lei for a long moment, the tension growing to the point that the horses behind Lei began tossing their heads and lifting one hoof then another, which only in retrospect Lei realized should have warned him.

"Yes," Yu broke the silence, breaking eye contact at the same time. "You are in command, General Lei."

"And now, I'm commanding you to go back to the Lotus *Tu-wei-fu* and order them to lay down their arms and surrender to the *Gwai* forces that they are currently facing."

This seemed to catch Yu completely by surprise, affirming to Lei his thickness, his mouth dropping open to gasp, "I cannot do that!"

"You can," Lei snapped, "and you will." Pointing up at the nearest column of smoke, he spoke harshly, "Use your eyes, Yu! This city is in danger of burning to the ground!" Suddenly, he experienced a stab of doubt, realizing that he hadn't established one crucial fact, prompting him to ask, "How did those fires start? Did the *Gwai* use...something to start them?"

Yu shifted slightly, but it was his eyes darting over to the man Lei recognized as one of the *Hou Kuan* belonging to the Lotus that betrayed his answer before he gave it.

"Yes," he said grudgingly, "they threw smoking pots filled with something that is like honey in how it sticks to whatever it hits. Even," Yu's mouth twisted into a bitter grimace, "if it's flesh."

"So, you've seen it for yourself," Lei said, not unkindly. It was a horrible thing watching someone burn to death, and it was even worse when the normal things one did in that event didn't work at all. "I've seen it with my own eyes as well, and I've also seen the crates they carry this evil substance in, and they're too numerous to count."

While Yu didn't look as determined as a moment before, he was nothing if not stubborn. "The men of the Lotus are willing to sacrifice their lives for..."

"For what?" Lei cut him off, then realized something else. "Are you aware of what occurred in the harbor?"

"Only that there was some sort of attack," Yu said cautiously. "I assumed that it was the *Gwai* navy trying to cause us trouble."

Lei, thinking that Yu would work it out for himself, stared at his counterpart, but when it became clear that Yu hadn't made the connection, he said, "Not only did they attack, but they used the same fire weapon as they're using inside the city on our fleet. It was completely destroyed."

This succeeded in wrenching a shocked gasp from Yu.

"They were carrying all of the artillery and part of our force!" he exclaimed, and Lei felt a glimmer of hope that, at last, Yu realized the impossibility of their situation.

"So, General," Lei asked reasonably, "what exactly are we fighting for now? We have no way to execute General Xao's plan, who," Lei added forcefully, "is probably already dead by now. All that's left now are the people in this city, including our families."

"What about our honor?" Yu demanded. "How can you expect me to surrender to these...these...*savages*? They may look human, but they're clearly not!"

"Our honor is worth our lives," Lei seemingly agreed. "But is it worth the lives of our families? Of our wives? Our children? Our grandchildren? Will your line survive today if we continue to resist these *Gwai* with this horrible weapon?"

Yu seemed to seriously consider the question, rubbing his chin thoughtfully, but what finally alerted Lei was the manner in which some of the officers with him kept glancing to their right. While at first he thought that they were watching the nearest tower of smoke that had grown visibly larger since the parley had begun, he sensed that their attention was down on the street level, just around the corner from where Yu and his party were standing out of Lei's sight.

"Something's not right," Lei muttered, not loudly, but loudly enough for Zhang to overhear, and he heard the Han emissary speaking whatever tongue the darker *Gwai* spoke, who then babbled in an urgent tone to Caesar, prompting an equally sharp reply from the *Gwai* general.

Zhang was opening his mouth to address Lei, just after the dark *Gwai* relayed Caesar's words, when the reason for Yu's hesitation, and the distraction of his officers was revealed when, from the intersecting streets to their left, Han soldiers materialized from out of the smoke, rushing in their direction in a bellowing attack.

"*You fool!*" Lei roared at Yu. "*What have you done?*"

Yu had already turned to race down the street and out of range of the line of *Gwai,* but he obviously heard Lei's challenge over the sudden uproar, because he spun about to face Lei.

"I'm doing what you should have done, you cowardly dog!"

The last word was just leaving his mouth when a javelin came streaking down towards him, but while he tried to dodge it, his reaction was delayed just enough that the hardened point punched into his lamellar armor high on his right chest, knocking him backward. Two of his officers grabbed an arm to help him escape around the corner without wrenching the javelin, the point of which Lei could see just poking through the back of Yu's shoulder, and even with the other noise, he heard Yu shriek with pain as the butt end struck the street. That would be the last sight of Yu Wei alive that Lei would ever have, and he would quickly forget the man's presence in the span of the next few moments.

It was an attack destined to fail because of a lack of coordination on the part of Yu Wei, who had been alerted to the procession led by Lei under a flag of truce in enough time to devise what would have been a foolish strategy even if it hadn't been handled so ineptly. Even if he had alerted the *Hou Kuan* who had done a creditable job of stalling the advance of the 25th Legion to make a demonstration of some sort to tie Torquatus' men up, the only accomplishment would have been to inflict more casualties on the First and Second Cohorts of the Equestrians. Fortunately, thanks to the quick thinking of the

Quartus Pilus Posterior of the 25th, who just happened to spot movement through the smoke off to his right and thinking that the Han were trying to circle around their right flank, when he heard the sudden uproar, it was coming from an unexpected direction and nowhere near the Sixth Century of his Cohort, who he knew were four blocks south, whereupon he immediately sent a runner to his Pilus Prior informing him of this new development. Then, without waiting to receive permission, Publius Bassus dashed down the street running north/south, followed by his Century, to slam into the rear of the *Hou* of Han soldiers who were part of the force attacking the Second Cohort along a front of three streets. To the Quartus Pilus Prior's credit, he hadn't hesitated to order the rest of his Cohort to change their orientation from moving east to face south, spreading them across the three blocks, where they arrived within a span of perhaps two hundred heartbeats after his Second Century launched their counterattack.

The Han cause was further hampered by the nature of the attack itself, which relied on surprise and speed without using their crossbowmen first to soften up their enemy, and they were forced to go immediately to the spear, *ji,* or sword. They did achieve surprise, as the Romans were forced to suddenly shift their facing in time to meet the onslaught with their shields, several men falling as a result, and the Han attack did succeed in compressing the Roman lines so that the men in the rear rank had their backs literally pressed against the walls of the buildings on the opposite side of the street. The fighting was certainly furious, but it didn't last particularly long, nor was Caesar or any of the mounted men of his party ever in any danger. In the resulting collapse by the Lotus *Tu-wei-fu* that followed, when the Han still stubbornly resisting the 25th were suddenly confronted by their own comrades running towards them, shouting in panic that the *Gwai* were coming from a completely unexpected direction, it gave Lei the authority he needed to reassert control, so that by a third of a watch after Yu's failed attack, the fight for the city was essentially over, with the surrender of the Bear *Tu-wei-fu,* after the Han general who had been third in command had been slain by a Gregarius in the Fourth of the Third of the 14th when they finally reached and began their assault on the eastern wall. Once more, it fell to the very men who were responsible for creating the situation in the form of several fires that were in danger of getting out of control to stop it. That this task was given to Figulus and his 14th and Flaminius' 30th was appreciated by the men and Primi Pili of the other three Legions, although it was also expected. With a combination of a judicious use of the remaining vinegar and the razing of dwellings in key locations, the fires were finally brought under control shortly before sunset, whereupon the assaulting Legions were finally allowed to indulge themselves in the manner that, for many of the men, ranker and officer alike, made all the misery and suffering worthwhile. Of course, it was only allowed under a set of conditions, but unlike Bharuch, the passions of the men against the inhabitants of a city where they had suffered so much weren't as inflamed. Nevertheless, the rules developed by Caesar over the previous years had to be enforced by the Centurions and Optios, and while it was with varying degrees of enthusiasm, the officers patrolled the area assigned to their Centuries to ensure that the terrified civilians that were being dragged out into the streets weren't immediately put to the sword. In the case of the females, the only requirement was that they survived their treatment intact, in a relative sense, while the officers kept a sharp eye on those men of their Centuries whose taste for rape involved youngsters, of either sex. Of all the prohibitions, this was one where the enforcement between Cohorts and Legions was fairly uniform, which wasn't surprising given the fact that a majority of the men wearing the transverse crest or white stripe had by this time fathered children of their own, even if they were far away, and by now, scattered across the known world.

For the Primi Pili, most of them relied on their Optios to watch over their Centuries while they patrolled the entire part of the city they had been given, which meant that Pullus was moving from Cohort to Cohort, checking with his Pili Priores and their Centurions. Normally, this would have involved stopping long enough to banter with his men, listening to their stories of something that had happened during the fight, along with their complaints about the injustice that gave them a block of the fallen city that was clearly less prosperous than the next block over, which was being sacked by another Century. The fact that Pullus didn't do any of this wasn't lost on his men, and while they were all careful to wait until their Primus Pilus was out of earshot, the consensus among them was unanimous; they were worried about Pullus, who was inordinately pale and seemed to be weaving on his feet. Naturally, it didn't take long for the word to streak from street to street and Century to Century that, while he was with the Seventh Cohort, Titus Pullus had collapsed.

In Yazhou, Balbinus and his men, along with those of the other three Legions now inside the walls of the city, were unknowingly facing the same predicament in trying to counter both the power and ubiquity of the Han crossbow. As with any weapon, there were tradeoffs; while an archer using a conventional bow such as the Parthian compound bow could loose arrows more quickly, and the range was greater, in this situation, both of those advantages were negligible, while the crossbows wielded by the Han could be aimed with more precision, had a flatter trajectory that made it harder for a man to pick up with his eyes, and was more powerful at shorter ranges. When it became clear, based on what they had seen, that the Han forces were equally divided between spearmen and crossbowmen, it posed a daunting challenge, especially when combined with the fact that there were only three bridges across the two hundred paces of the river on the southern side, and only two crossing the slightly narrower northern river on the northern side.

"They'll be able to concentrate all of those fucking scorpion men to cover the bridges," Cartufenus complained. "We'll have to cross in *testudo*, all while these *cunni* pound us," he finished, then spat to reinforce his disgust.

In tacit recognition of this, Pollio had given the order to suspend any attempt to cross the bridges, directing the Legions inside the city to secure the quarter of the city in which they found themselves. Papernus' 21st had obeyed Pollio's command to assault the eastern wall, although there was no real need, because by the time they had driven off the survivors of the combined garrisons outside the city, General Lin had already deemed the walls lost and ordered the men who had drawn the duty of guarding the other three walls to withdraw to the island part of the city. In what would later be judged a rash decision, Papernus had lost men trying to rush across one of the bridges, hoping to surprise the Han defenders by moving more rapidly than they expected. Consequently, the First Cohort of the 21st had experienced an even stronger taste of the Han crossbow than the Legions belonging to Balbinus, Cartufenus, and Aquilinus, although afterward, just as Pullus and the Legions assaulting Hanou would acknowledge, the casualties would have been worse with their old shields. Recognizing the strong defensive position of their foe and resigned to this taking longer than he had hoped, Pollio ordered the artillery unloaded and transported into the city; more importantly, he had the Legion slaves unload every crate marked with a circle of red paint as well, although he kept half of them outside the walls on the beach, where the 8th was now laboring to build an enclosure for the several thousand Han prisoners, their numbers being added to as the Legions inside the city continued their search of every building.

Siting the artillery was the next challenge, Pollio sending a runner across the narrow neck of the river to inform the Primus Pilus that the 21st's role would be to support the three Legions, not wanting to take the time it would take for the 21st to retrieve its artillery from their ships, which would have to be hauled over the hills between the beach and the city. Each of the three Legions on the western side was assigned a bridge, with Papernus ordered to prevent any escape across the eastern bridges and if the opportunity presented itself, to cross the two eastern bridges to essentially attack the defenders from the rear. Compounding the challenge, the bridges were all constructed of wood, although the Han had, as Balbinus had guessed, stacked blocks of stone across the streets several feet high, not so high that it would require a ladder, but enough that an armored man couldn't hurdle it, even if there weren't defenders. Just as with the outer wall, there were blocks stacked on the top layer to form the same kind of protective barrier as a crenellation, offering defenders some added protection.

"We can't afford to drop naphtha onto the heads of the men defending the bridges," Balbinus' chief artillery *immune* explained to Pollio, "because if we're short even by a matter of a couple of feet, it will start a fire on the bridge."

Pollio didn't try to argue the point, having come to that conclusion on his own. Hissing in frustration, he began pacing back and forth, and Balbinus had the sense that the Legate was talking more to himself than soliciting advice. "Naturally, they pulled every single boat onto their side of the river, and there's no way for us to test the depth to see if we could wade across. And," he continued bitterly, "even if we could, we'd be like lambs to slaughter trying to cross the river with those scorpion bows they have." He stopped pacing and faced the Primi Pili. "Unless any of you have a suggestion, I think the only way is across the bridges, in *testudo*."

"What about using the naphtha behind them?" Aquilinus suggested. "That will at least give them something else to worry about."

"I can't tell what kind of buildings there are past this first block," Pollio countered, "and you can see they're made of stone. Judging from the difference between all of the other buildings inside the walls, my guess is that the island served essentially the same function as our Forum, with the Tabularium and the Curia, and stone doesn't burn. But," he added quickly to forestall what he was certain was Aquilinus' objection, "the roofs are made of wood, and it looks like they use timber as support beams and columns as well. That means," he concluded, "the question is how much damage we want to do if we're going to be occupying Yazhou for any length of time."

Since this was the first time the Legate had broached a topic that, to that point, he had steadfastly refused to discuss with his Primi Pili and Tribunes, it was to be expected that this piqued the interest of the three Centurions involved in the discussion, and Balbinus pounced on this unexpected opportunity.

"What *are* our plans for this *cac*hole? Although," Balbinus had actually been scanning their surroundings as he was talking, "we've seen worse places to stay for an extended period of time."

He didn't really expect an answer, yet rather than snap at him that this had nothing to do with the immediate problem, Pollio confessed, "I don't know, Balbinus. I honestly don't. In fact, at this moment, you know as much as I do, that we're doing this to ensure that your men are fed and don't have to worry about the Han Emperor sending his hordes after us for at least a few months." By returning his attention to the issue facing them now, Pollio actually took a breath before saying, "But I think that Aquilinus' idea is the right one. If we give these barbarians something just as dangerous to them as our assault to worry about behind them, it can only help us. And," he finished grimly, "if that means burning everything on that island down around them, that's what we'll do."

Liu wasn't happy about his command to cede the outer walls to fall back onto the island, but he knew it was the right decision to make. He hadn't stayed on the western wall long, just spending enough time to observe the manner in which the *Gwai* conducted their assault, and he had been sufficiently shaken to recognize that fighting for the outer walls would have cost him more than it was ultimately worth. This was especially true now that his plan of using the combined garrison troops in a surprise attack had been foiled, the aftermath of which he had forced himself to watch from the southern wall. Whoever was commanding this *Gwai* army was cunning, and despite himself, he felt a grudging respect for the pale savage, acknowledging to himself that he should have foreseen the possibility of using that narrow beach on the opposite side of the hill that towered over the southwestern corner of the city. That, however, was in the past, and now he was striding down the first street paralleling the river to reach the middle of the three bridges to conduct a final inspection. He didn't know why the *Gwai* had paused in their assault, although there was no way to miss the cries and shrieks of the civilian occupants of Yazhou who hadn't made it to the island. That he had ordered his men to turn the laggards away, forcing them at spearpoint to return to the outer part of the city, didn't trouble him overmuch, if only because his own family was safe and in the small house two blocks from the western river at the upper end of the island. He had issued a warning the day before that there was limited space available within what had once been the administrative center of not just the city of Yazhou, but the entire southern and a significant part of the eastern side of the island. Now, it was serving essentially the same function as it had under Imperial rule, except with General Xao as the titular head of what had become a haven for disaffected Han officers and soldiers, and while it was a topic that was never discussed openly, most of his subordinates knew that what Xao intended was nothing less than an island kingdom of his own, autonomous of Imperial Han authority. Liu had also known that there would be a reckoning at some point in the future, but he had understandably assumed that it would be with forces loyal to Yuan and not these *Gwai*, and certainly not this soon. Yet, here he was, inspecting the bridge defenses, and he didn't spend much time at the middle bridge, a quick examination telling him that they were as prepared as their comrades on the northernmost bridge.

It was when he was making his way to the final southernmost bridge that Liu paused, brought to a halt because he thought he had heard a cry of what sounded like some sort of distress behind him, but his view was blocked by the curvature of the street that mimicked the contours of the island. He was about to resume walking when he saw something, though not at street level, his eye catching the sight of a thin trail of smoke that had just begun to rise above the rooftops. While it was concerning, Liu wasn't particularly alarmed because he had ordered precautionary steps being taken to protect the flammable wooden roofs, placing barrels of water next to the structures he thought might be vulnerable to some attempt by the *Gwai* to set them on fire, while he had pairs of men whose primary task was to be alert and ready and positioned at strategic points throughout the city center. Resuming his progress, he reached the southernmost bridge, which was also the narrowest part of the island, being a bit less than four hundred paces across and because of that, it was lightly populated, at least by humans, instead serving as the stables for the livestock that provided various services, both military and commercial. Because of this, Liu was somewhat confident that this would be the focal point of any *Gwai* attempt to take the island, and he had shifted his manpower accordingly, reasoning that if he was wrong, it wasn't all that long of a distance to run to the north to bolster the men at the other two bridges.

There was one area of concern between the lack of cover for his crossbowmen and the fact that none of the stables and barns had an upper story to give them a height advantage. This was why the defenders of the southern bridge were commanded by *Hou-Chang* Bian Zhang, who was his nominal second in command, and his son-in-law, although Liu had assured the other officers that had nothing to do with his elevation when announcing his decision. Whether or not they accepted that assurance was another matter, but he didn't care; besides, there were more pressing matters to attend to, and when Liu emerged from between the line of stables and outbuildings, he immediately saw the array of *Gwai* artillery on the opposite bank, which the *Gwai* were hurrying to prepare. This got Liu moving at a quick trot to the stone barricade, behind which Bian was standing, giving orders to one of his *Sui-Chang*. The bridge was less than ten paces across, just wide enough for two carts or wagons to pass each other, but Liu had ordered the stone barricade to extend fifty paces on either side at this bridge because of the presence of a semi-permanent sandbar that bulged outward on the eastern bank that he was certain would be used by the *Gwai* either by leaping over the wooden railings of the bridge, or perhaps destroying them with a few well-placed rocks. He had intended to suggest to Bian that he deploy the relatively few crossbowmen he had been given out on the flanks to put the *Gwai* in a crossfire, but immediately saw that Bian had already done so, another example of why he had done well in elevating Bian. Despite this being the narrow part of the river, at a bit over two hundred paces, this was where the one weakness of the Han crossbow showed itself, putting the *Gwai* artillery at the very outer limit of the range of the weapon, and even if an exceptionally skillful crossbowman could arc his bolt to reach the distance, the force behind the shorter missile would be mostly spent, and now that Liu had seen the armor worn by these *Gwai,* while he was unfamiliar with chainmail, he could tell just by the color that it was made of iron, which prompted him to give explicit orders to every *Hou-Chang* commanding the crossbow *Sui* not to begin loosing until the *Gwai* were well within one hundred paces.

"The attack has already begun on the northern bridge," Liu informed Bian, but it wasn't until he turned around to face in that direction that he saw that what had been a thin trail of black smoke was now a column of grayish-black almost a hundred feet into the sky.

"It's been growing steadily, *Hou-Kuan*," Bian always made sure to address his father-in-law in the proper manner; Liu may have been unaware of the sentiment among his fellow officers because they held their tongue in his presence, but they hadn't been nearly as circumspect with Bian. "I suspect that we can expect the same thing?"

This turned their attention to the *Gwai*, who were close enough to see clearly, and they both noticed that a cart had arrived, pulled by a pony with absurdly long ears that neither of them had seen before, the contents of it quickly unloaded.

"I wonder what those red spots mean?" Bian mused.

"Nothing good for us," Liu muttered, then more loudly so the other men standing on the makeshift rampart could hear, "but it doesn't matter what these pale *Gwai* throw at us! They will rename this the Blood River after today!"

The resulting roar of agreement did serve to momentarily stop the *Gwai,* who turned to look across the river at the sound, but they quickly resumed their own activities. From the northern end of the barricade, some of the men shouted, tearing Liu and Bian's attention away from the *Gwai* across the river to see another plume of smoke joining the first one, yet with this one, the plume became thicker rapidly enough for them to see it expanding.

"I think that we need to be prepared for the same thing," Liu remarked.

"I did as you ordered *Hou Kuan*," Bian assured him. "I have barrels of water ready, but I only used one *Sui,* and they're spread out between the stables all the way to the Street of Cranes."

Although Liu would have preferred that Bian used a few

more men, in the event that multiple fires started at once, it didn't warrant a rebuke, nor was he inclined to countermand the order. As it turned out, they were just a matter of heartbeats away from learning the cause of these fires.

"*Hou-Chang*! Look!"

Turning to where the spearman was standing roughly in the middle of the part of the barricade blocking the bridge along with his comrades, the two officers were just hurrying to stand at the parapet when, above their heads, they spotted a smoking object flying overhead in their direction, tumbling over so rapidly that it made identifying what it was difficult. The results weren't, however, both men spinning about just in time to watch the object strike the side of one of the nearest stables and explode into a small but brilliant ball of fire that sent smaller globules of flaming substance splattering in a rough semicircle on the ground. Those would eventually burn out, the ground outside the stables nothing but hardpacked dirt, but more quickly than either Han officer had ever seen, the western wall of the stable began burning fiercely. Even as the frantic bawling of what were obviously oxen kept inside the stable began, four more buildings were struck in rapid succession. The change from what had been a normal scene of neatly arranged structures into what was now a series of small infernos of fire, the air filling with the sounds of terrified animals happening so quickly that not only Liu and Bian were temporarily frozen in place, their mouths agape in horror, although it was the *Hou-Chang* who recovered first.

"*Put those fires out*!" he bellowed, then made as if to drop off the rampart to rush the short distance to the first block of buildings, but Liu grabbed his arm with enough strength that it caused Bian to yelp in pain, stopping him in mid-stride.

When he spun about, his father-in-law was pointing across the bridge, his voice preternaturally calm.

"The *Gwai* infantry is already moving towards the bridge. Your men will take care of that."

Whether that was true or not, Bian knew, was less important than obeying a command, and he returned to the rampart, just in time to see what had been an evenly spaced formation of these strange creatures, an arm's length apart, suddenly begin to contract, the *Gwai* in the middle files lifting their shields above their heads as they moved, with the front rank raising their shields so the top edge almost touched the bottom of the shield held by the man behind him just above his head. Just as the Romans had experienced the Han crossbow for the first time, this marked the first moment that the Han of Yazhou faced the Roman *testudo*.

Balbinus' decision to begin early hadn't been made capriciously, although his fellow Primi Pili would never believe him. To the Primus Pilus, one of the most experienced in Caesar's army who had been part of the first *dilectus* of the 12th during the first year of the Gallic campaign, it was a straightforward proposition; if he delayed moving across the bridge, there would be a blazing inferno blocking their way. When he had examined the southernmost bridge and seen that the structures were more like those in the rest of the small city surrounding the island, made completely of wood and thatch, he understood that Legate Pollio had been thinking more about the other two bridges, especially the middle bridge, where almost everything they could see was constructed of stone.

"Form *testudo*, boys! We're not going to wait!" Balbinus shouted the order to his Century and Cohort, followed immediately by his *Cornicen* sounding the command to the other Cohorts.

Going more by his ears than his eyes, Balbinus heard the clattering sound of shields coming together, along with the scraping sound of hobnails on paving stones as they sidestepped into place, and the Primus Pilus wasted no time, bellowing the command to advance, hefting his drawn shield while Petronius stepped behind him, lifting his own round shield strapped to his arm. These Han may not have known the actual meaning of the eagle standard of a Roman Legion, but as with every foe they had faced, their enemies always recognized that the *Aquilifer* was second in importance only to the man standing in front of him, wearing the white crest of the Primus Pilus, the only Roman to do so. Knowing this and being able to do anything about it to ensure their safety were two different things, and the Primus Pilus moved as close to the *testudo* as he possibly could to improve his security, matching their shuffling pace, the hollow quality of the sound informing him that they were on the wooden bridge since his eyes never stopped scanning the barricade ahead of them.

"Remember, boys, there's a reason why that barricade is so much longer than the ones blocking the other bridges, so we can expect those fucking scorpion men to be out there on the flanks, waiting for us, so keep it tight, especially you outer files!"

Satisfying himself with the hollow-sounding ragged chorus that signaled he had been heard, Balbinus tried to calculate when the first volley would be heading their way. Having experienced a taste of the power of the weapon that he and his comrades still thought of as smaller versions of their own scorpion, what he didn't know was their range, but his instinct told him that it would suffer from the same restriction on range as the larger Roman version did. Ahead of them, while it was difficult to see, Balbinus felt confident that there were now defenders being pulled from the wall to attend to what was an astonishingly fast-moving fire, the air now thick with smoke, some of which was beginning to drift in their direction because of a lack of breeze pushing it in any direction. Reaching the spot he had marked in his mind as the most likely point to come within an acceptable range, Balbinus' caution was rewarded when, after remaining either crouched down or behind the blocks acting as crenellations, helmeted figures appeared off to his right, but it was more their manner than actually spotting their crossbows that prompted Balbinus to sound the warning.

"Get ready..."

Before the words were fully out of his mouth, what Balbinus guessed was twenty missiles came streaking from his side, flat, black, and fast, forcing him to turn his body to more fully present his shield, feeling it jerk in his hand twice, though the impacts were so close together that they could have been simultaneous. All around him, there were cracking sounds that he had first equated to sounding like sling bullets, but there were no shouts of pain, and he offered a prayer to Bellona that it stayed that way, though he knew it would probably be in vain. He had judged that they were now just within a hundred paces of the Han crossbowmen, and the impact of the bolts wasn't powerful enough to loosen his grip on the handle of his shield, but it was still considerable, with half the point protruding on his side of the shield. Intending to warn his men in the front rank to prepare for this, his voice was drowned out by another volley, bringing Balbinus to the realization that the Han were working in pairs, with one man loosing while the other reloaded, and while he had no idea how these small scorpions worked, what he had already learned during their assault on the wall was that they were able to reload much more quickly than a scorpion crew. What it meant in the moment was Balbinus and his Century taking a pummeling, the shields of every man in the outermost files and the front rank studded with bolts by the time they were within the last ten paces to the barricade. Somehow, and in something of a miracle, Balbinus hadn't heard, or been informed by any of his men that one of them had been struck by a bolt, but he also knew that this was about to end. He had debated with himself about the need for javelins, which they had been given the opportunity to replenish after the assault on the wall, compromising by telling his Cohort to only carry one, and now was the moment to use it. With this incessant hail of bolts, of which the Han seemed to have an endless supply, Balbinus also steeled himself for the inevitable, but he still clamped the bone whistle between his teeth, choosing to use it instead of the *Cornu* because it would put *Cornicen* Barbatus into too much danger. Blowing the three sharp blasts that warned his men a command was coming, Balbinus paused, then, realizing that there was no point in trying to time the movement to a more open formation when there was a lull in the barrage, he blew a long blast, at the end of which he opened his mouth to let the whistle drop from his lips. Events occurred rapidly after that, beginning with the men essentially performing the move that put them into *testudo* into reverse, as the men of the inner files dropped their shields back into position, but within less than a heartbeat, Balbinus heard the first shout of pain, from the far side of the formation in the middle ranks, followed instantly by the thudding vibration of first a shield then a body dropping to the wooden deck of the bridge.

Ignoring this and deciding to give the order even as the men were still taking their shuffling sidestep outward, he bellowed, "Ready javelins!", followed a fraction of a heartbeat later, with, "Release!" Ignoring the screams and cries of alarm from the Han who had been an instant slow in ducking or moving behind one of the taller blocks, he drew his *gladius* as he went rushing forward, shouting, "*Kill these cunni!*"

Even in that moment, it always gratified Balbinus when he was instantly drowned out by the voices of his men answering his challenge, and just as Caesar expected from his Primi Pili, Balbinus led the way.

Bian quickly forgot the presence of his commander, but Liu didn't intervene when his son-in-law gave the command to their crossbowmen to wait until the *Gwai* reached the fourth pillar supporting the bridge that marked the halfway point, although he would have preferred to wait a bit longer. In fact, he barely noticed, becoming increasingly distracted by the heat and smoke radiating from behind them, caused by what he had counted as four structures now fully involved and enveloped in flames, although it was the shrieks of the animals trapped inside and out of their mind with fear that was almost as disorienting. He was fortunate in one sense; he didn't witness the fate of most of the unfortunate men of the *Sui* that Bian had designated to fight the fires, but just as the *Gwai* reached the spot that unleashed the torrent of bolts at them, he heard a man shouting from behind them, turning to see a spearman running down the street leading from the bridge, or more accurately, staggering towards the barricade. Even if he had known the identity of the spearman, there was no way Liu could have recognized him, but what he first assumed was black soot covering his face and hands turned out to be quite different, taking an extra heartbeat to understand that every inch of exposed flesh was charred black, only because he had never seen anything like it, but as he instinctively moved towards the spearman, the man collapsed a half-dozen paces away, Liu then rushing to kneel by his side. He wasn't particularly concerned about the fate of a lowly spearman, but if the man had endured what was unimaginable pain to reach his commander, Liu felt certain that it was important.

He had to drop to both knees and lean down to hear the man, his voice almost unrecognizable as belonging to a human, whisper, "Water...water..."

Assuming that the dying spearman was requesting a last drink of water, Liu looked about, trying to find a bucket and dipper to slake the man's thirst, but even in what was his last, pain-wracked moments, this lowly spearman, a man who Liu would barely deign to recognize, retained enough of his wits to understand what his commander was doing.

Reaching out and grabbing Liu's forearm with a surprising strength, he managed to whisper, "No, General! I do not need...water...water does not work on the fire. It...makes...it...worse."

It would be the last words the spearman ever uttered, and in some ways, it left Liu more mystified than enlightened, and he spent a moment watching the fires, trying to understand what the now-dead man meant. Just as he was about to turn away, he saw another pair of men, each with a bucket, throw them against the wall of a stable at the same time in a coordinated effort to douse the flames, leaving Liu only able to watch in horror as the inevitable backsplash created by hurling liquid at a solid surface seemed to take tiny bits of flames back towards the men. It's almost as if this fire is using the water to carry it! This was Liu's thought even as he saw that, of the pair, one of them was fortunate enough that the tiny globules of flaming substance splashed mostly on the ground, although some got on his lower legs, prompting the man to drop the bucket to begin frantically beating at the flames that clung and continued to burn the man's trousers with a stubbornness Liu had never witnessed before. As unusual as it may have been, it was still better than the second man, who, being closer and in something of a crouch, had gotten a face full of the splashing fire water, the spearman immediately erupting into screams, and to Liu it looked as if the man was vigorously slapping himself in the face as he began staggering in a rough circle. The scream was unnerving in itself, but it was the sight of a man who had tiny spots of fire dotting his face that would be seared into Liu's memory, yet he still instinctively took a step in the afflicted spearman's direction, thinking to knock him down then use his hands to beat the flames out in an unconscious reaction to the horror his eyes were seeing. He took one step but not another, his progress abruptly stopped when another smoking jar came tumbling down from behind him to land in between him and the spearman. The fact that the jar shattered on the ground closer to the spearman alternately saved his life, as he recoiled from the sudden explosion of fire to land heavily on his ass, even as he felt the skin of his face begin to blister, and doomed the staggering spearman, now completely engulfed in flames, while his comrade went from just a few flames on his lower legs to having his entire right side covered in sticky fire. For a horrifying instant, Liu was certain that the man who had been struck in the face would run directly into him, his arms out in front of him as he blindly groped for something, shrieking with a pain that Liu couldn't even imagine, but thankfully, he only made it two staggering steps before collapsing, while the other spearman had dropped onto his right side, screaming in the same kind of agony as he tried to smother the flames. Despite the roaring clamor behind him as the *Gwai* infantry on the bridge closed the final few paces to close with Bian and his men, Liu couldn't tear his eyes away, which was when he saw that, for reasons he would never understand, when the writhing spearman who still lived finally succumbed, rolling over onto his back, his screams turning into a low moan as he slipped into the next world, the flames that should have been smothered were still burning fiercely. It could have been his imagination, but Liu didn't think it was, certain that the flames seemed to have gained in strength as it consumed the dead man's flesh, and even with the noise behind him, he both saw the sudden spark and heard a distinct pop, making a sound that he recognized often occurred when roasting a pig and the fire touched some fat. This was enough to make him turn away, shuddering in revulsion, and the blisters on his face were quickly forgotten as he returned his attention to the bridge just in time to see a *Gwai* with the largest nose Liu had ever seen before, his mouth twisted into a rictus of savage fury that was impossible to misunderstand and wearing a helmet with an equally ridiculous-looking white crest, make a thrust with a short but broad sword in between the highest blocks, the point punching into and through the mouth of the man standing next to Bian to come bursting out at the base of the spearman's skull in a shower of blood, brain, and bone. Not surprisingly, the spearman collapsed, but there was an instant of delay as another spearman, this one armed with the *ji*, tried to kick his dead comrade out of the way to take his spot hard up against the parapet, just a bare moment when Liu and the *Gwai* locked eyes. Even if he could have understood the words, it would have been impossible for Liu to hear the *Gwai* as he shouted something, but it was the sword, still dripping blood and matter that the *Gwai* pointed directly at him that needed no translation. He was being challenged, not as a commander but as a warrior, and before he knew it, Liu was on his feet and striding towards the rampart, his sword already in his hand.

For Balbinus and his men, the spears of the Han defenders didn't prove much of a challenge, if only because by this moment, the Romans had had so much experience facing enemies for whom this was the primary weapon. The same didn't hold true for what appeared to be the weapon every other Han seemed to carry, which, having no previous experience with what would become known as the halberd, although the Han called it the *ji*, posed yet another new challenge they had never faced before. This weapon, he was convinced, had been conceived by Dis himself, and he had been forced to watch how it was used on Quintus Papillo, the Gregarius of the first file of the First Section who stood next to Balbinus, serving the same function as Vespillo of the Equestrians, the best Gregarius with a *gladius* in his Century. After blocking a Han spearman's attack using a conventional spear, another Han who Balbinus couldn't see because of the angle, pushed his weapon out beyond the makeshift wall, but rather than a straightforward thrust, he lifted the iron point above Papillo's head before bringing it down. At first, Balbinus thought it was an attack more commonly used by Gallic tribes, an overhand blow that swept down to strike the opponent on the top of the head, but he instantly saw that whoever was wielding this weapon hadn't extended it out far enough, so that all Papillo would have to do was move his head back while the strip of iron that lined the edge of the Roman shield would protect it from the iron spear blade if the Han actually managed to strike his target. You stupid bastard, he thought smugly, who do you think we are? Some *Tirones* who have never fought before? That sense of satisfaction died in the amount of time it took for Balbinus to understand that the Han hadn't missed his target, because with a dexterity that bespoke of watches of training, the instant the shaft of the Han weapon struck the top of Papillo's shield, instead of thrusting forward, it was jerked backward, the curved iron blade hooking the top of his man's shield and yanking it.

To his credit, Papillo didn't lose the grip on his shield, but the force of being tugged away from the strict vertical posture that was one of the first things *Tiros* were taught dropped the top of the shield down several inches, which was when, with a blinding speed, the weapon then changed direction, the slender spearpoint that topped the weapon plunging into Papillo's eye. Dropping his shield, Papillo's scream was only matched by the competing sounds of the despair of his comrades, Balbinus' voice among them, and the triumphant roar of Han spearmen on the opposite side of the double thickness of stone blocks. This would be Balbinus and his men's first experience with the *ji*, but it was far from their last, becoming another weapon that they would have to develop tactics to combat; what it did in that moment was unleash Balbinus' rage, and when the ranker in the second rank started to step over Papillo's body, as the Gregarius of the third rank crouched and grabbed his dead comrade's harness to drag him backward, Balbinus savagely shoved his man aside to take his spot. Between the space created by the makeshift crenellations, Balbinus saw a pair of faces that, to his eyes, were identical, their eyes barely visible, their mouths open as they shouted their gibberish, one of them reacting a bit more quickly than his comrade to jab his spear out, aiming at Balbinus' head and neck area, the only part of his body even partially visible between the height difference and his shield. Balbinus caught the thrust on his shield, noticing the point that barely poked through despite the power behind the blow, but when the Han recovered it for another attack, Balbinus threw himself up against the wall of stacked stone blocks. Now, he was at an almost impossible angle for the Han, the only way to attack him being by leaning out through the gap, and he wasn't surprised when no such thing happened. However, what applied to the Han equally applied to him; there was no way for him to execute a thrust of his own without exposing himself by standing back up, so instead, he took this moment to gauge how his men were faring. Aside from Papillo, he saw that one of his tentmates in the First Section, in the seventh file, a veteran named Sido, was scooting himself backward between the files, the mangled links of mail high on his right shoulder revealing a puckering wound from which blood was flowing freely, though not in a spray, telling him that the wound wasn't immediately mortal.

Clamping the bone whistle between his teeth, be blew three short blasts again, then the long sound that signaled a shift relief, which was made more difficult by not only the range of the Han spears, but the hooked spear that, now that he understood how it worked, posed a more potent threat. Although he was intending to remove himself from the immediate fighting, just as he began to backpedal, a Han, either having forgotten that Balbinus was directly underneath the opening or unaware of his presence leaned out through the gap as he jabbed his spearpoint at Papillo's replacement from the second rank as he was sidestepping to allow the third man to step into his place. Balbinus didn't hesitate at this opportunity, standing up straight so quickly that the Han was still recovering the spear for another attempt, and the Primus Pilus' blade shot through the gap, the detached part of his mind noticing that he didn't even have to shatter the man's teeth because his foe's mouth was hanging open in surprise, the point only meeting resistance as it bit into the back of the spearman's throat, followed less than an eyeblink later by the grating vibration any experienced veteran knew meant he was cutting through bone, followed by the greater resistance as the point punched through the iron of the Han's helmet. He was prepared for the manner in which the Han so quickly collapsed that his blade was still partially in the man's mouth, but he was no Titus Pullus, so he didn't even try to hold his arm rigid as he withdrew the blade, instead allowing it to be pulled down and using the dead weight of the Han's collapse to free it without twisting it. It wasn't long, perhaps a half of a normal heartbeat, but for an instant, Balbinus spotted another Han, this one with an iron-gray mustache and wispy beard, locking eyes with the man.

Since his sword was still extended, it was natural for him to point it directly at the Han as he bellowed, "*I'm going to gut you myself, you slant-eyed yellow cocksucker!*"

The brief moment ended when another Han appeared in the gap, but unlike the man Balbinus had just slain, this one was armed with the hooked spear, and while it seemed to move ridiculously slowly to Balbinus, it must have happened more quickly than he could react as he seemingly just watched as the shaft of the hooked spear slammed onto the top of his shield just below the curved piece of iron, whereupon it was immediately yanked backward. Knowing the Han was attempting to kill him in the same manner as Papillo, he was at least prepared, tightening his grip on the shield, but his refusal to let go meant that he felt himself drawn back towards the base of the makeshift wall. Feeling his feet sliding across the wooden deck of the bridge, more out of desperation than with any thought to make a counterattack, Balbinus not only stopped resisting, but he threw himself forward, and by doing so, his shield slammed into the blocks of the wall...and he felt them move. No more than two full heartbeats elapsed as Balbinus thought through how to exploit what none of them had noticed, that the large blocks of stone weren't mortared.

Having returned to his spot at the base of the wall, Balbinus shouted at the top of his voice, "Do you boys remember what the Equestrians did to the *Crassoi* at Susa when they attacked that wall?"

When the response was a ragged but rousing shout that Balbinus took as affirmation, the Primus Pilus felt his lips turn up into a smile, one that held no warmth, one that was his promise to make these savages pay for Papillo and all the men he would lose this day.

It had been the one disagreement between Liu and Bian, but the overall commander of the Yazhou defense had prevailed in his decision not to use mortar to attach the blocks of stone, although he did admit, only to his son-in-law, that it was less than ideal.

"If we had time, I would, Bian," he assured the younger man. "But the *Gwai* will be here in a day, and you know that it takes time for mortar to dry enough to keep the blocks together. Besides," he offered his real reason, "we used the foundation stones that had been left over by the previous garrison, and they're too heavy for even two men to move."

This was certainly true, but it was left to Bian to witness the sudden shift among the *Gwai*, who he had observed bolstered each other in a manner that he thought could be useful in the future, with one arm extended to grasp on to a leather strap that ran vertically down their back, which was attached to the belt from which their sword and dagger were attached. Even if he had been able to understand the words, he couldn't have heard Balbinus' challenge over the noise made by his own men at the parapet who were working in teams of two men with spear and *ji*, but he saw how, instead of extending their arms, the entire formation of what he guessed was roughly the size of a *Hou* began shoving the man in front of them, shortening the depth of the *Gwai* formation. It was what he sensed more than what he saw that warned him of the danger, because he felt the large blocks used to create the parapet shift under his feet, not much at first, but it quickly became clear what the *Gwai* were attempting to do.

"The demons are trying to shove the barricade over!" Bian shouted this, but he was drowned out by the cries of alarm from the men around him who had felt the same movement under their feet, forcing him to repeat this several times.

Even as he was shouting this, he saw that the *Gwai Hou* directly behind the one now trying to topple the barricade had moved rapidly across the bridge to close the distance, even as they were savaged by the hail of crossbow bolts as his crossbowmen shifted their aim to this second group. Bian had become aware that the fire from his crossbowmen was slackening and had intended to send a man to demand to know why, but then this happened, and he correctly deemed this to be the more dangerous development. The front rank of the second group reached the back of the first, and when they threw themselves against the backs of their comrades, there was a lurching movement under his feet that was strong enough to stagger Bian and several other men. It was at this instant that Bian became aware of another presence, and he turned in surprise to see that it was Liu, sword in hand and immediately behind him, an expression on the older man's face he had never seen before, one that made him hesitate to give the order without consulting his father-in-law first.

"General, we're about to be knocked off this barricade." He had placed his mouth next to Liu's ear, not wanting to be overheard by the men, acutely aware of the continual glances in his direction. "If it topples over, we're going to lose men!"

Even as the words came out of his mouth, there was another noticeable shift under their feet, strong enough to make Liu sway, but this seemed to make no difference to the general.

"We will not abandon this barricade!" He shouted this for all to hear. "I will cut down the first man to step off this rampart!" Then he turned his attention back to Bian, but he dropped his voice so that only Bian could hear. "Including you, *Hou Kuan*."

Events happened quickly after this, what would turn out to be the last exchange between the pair, because within a span of perhaps three or four heartbeats, the stone blocks of the section of the parapet on the right side of the bridge were pushed far enough backward to reach the tipping point, and while neither Bian nor Liu saw the beginning, they were alerted by the sharper cry of alarm as one of his spearmen, who turned out to be the fortunate one, fell backward as the block he was standing on toppled off of the row of blocks serving as the platform. Turning just in time to see that part of the parapet collapse, with the topmost blocks suddenly toppling forward in the direction of the bridge, Bian did hear a sudden scream of pain from the other side, though he had no time to savor the moment, because even as the dust was rising in the air, this new gap in the parapet was filled by a pair of *Gwai* warriors, leading with their shields as they clambered over what was now a jumble of stone blocks, one of them stumbling slightly as he lifted one leg.

"They're inside the wall!"

Bian recognized Liu's voice, but he was already moving

towards the enemy; at least, this was his intention. Before he had taken two steps, just as had happened with the first spearman, the ground collapsed from under his feet. What followed was more sensations and scraps of visuals, although the intense pain he felt as he fell and landed on his side, striking the upturned edge of one of the rampart blocks and, even protected by his armor, he heard as much as felt the snapping sound of at least two of his ribs. His momentum was such that he was more like a passenger in his own body as he felt himself rebounding off to hit the ground on his back, his vision impaired by the dust while unable to spit the dirt that filled his mouth because he couldn't draw the breath he needed. He was vaguely aware of movement next to him, as one of his men was trying to climb to his feet, shaking his head in a manner of a man trying to gather his wits, and he was just standing erect when another figure appeared in Bian's vision, holding a large shield that, despite his dazed state, the Han recognized, but it was the manner in which this *Gwai* used it that Bian had never seen done before, the savage thrusting it directly into the face of the spearman who, while on his feet, was still bent over at the waist. The large round iron boss struck the spearman in the face, and Bian saw his man collapse, dropping immediately back down onto the jumbled blocks, his body quivering and twitching in a manner Bian had never witnessed before. Aware that he was completely helpless at this instant, Bian accepted his coming death the moment the *Gwai* looked down at him lying there, but instead, the savage stepped over the spearman's still-quivering body without a glance, his back to Bian. Within the span of a heartbeat, it became clear to Bian that the *Gwai*, whose helmet bore a white feather crest, was intent on closing with one man in particular, but it was through the slightly spread legs of the *Gwai* he saw his father-in-law, standing there with sword in hand, clearly waiting for the *Gwai*.

It was a serious error, and one that usually proved costly to the man who made it, but Balbinus forgot about being a Centurion, or a Primus Pilus, his focus completely on the gray-haired Han who was now standing a couple paces beyond the ruined barricade, his own sword out and held point down slightly from his body, clearly waiting for the Centurion.

"Your mother must have been a pig and your father a goat," Liu snarled, which of course, Balbinus didn't understand, but there was no mistaking the contempt the Han showed as he pointed to the Centurion's shield then shifted the point towards the ground, "Only a woman would cower behind a shield, not a warrior!"

Balbinus certainly couldn't understand the words, but he understood the intent, although all this earned the Han was a smile that was more of a snarl.

"This isn't the gladiatorial games, you slanty-eyed, yellow *cunnus*. I don't fucking care about fair. If you think I'm going to drop my shield..."

He was moving before he finished, but Balbinus wasn't surprised to see that hadn't caught the Han off guard, the older warrior managing to twist at the waist backward and to the side enough that the boss missed striking him altogether, only being grazed by the curved wooden part of the Roman's shield. More quickly than Balbinus anticipated, the Han shifted his balance, and his momentum, pivoting slightly on the ball of his left foot as his sword, about the length of a Roman *spatha* snaked inside Balbinus' shield to gash the Roman's arm. It wasn't a particularly damaging blow, but in that moment, the Primus Pilus felt a stab of fear that, perhaps, he had met his match. He moves as fast as Pullus does, he thought, vividly remembering the day he had brazenly challenged his fellow Primus Pilus to a sparring bout, which turned out to be a foolish decision from which he carried the bruises for more than a week, but the memory that flashed through his mind served him well as he performed the rough equivalent of the Han's attack with his own blade, executing a third position thrust, despite the Han's lack of a shield. While the Han managed to dodge yet again, Balbinus hadn't expected it to land, needing only to keep the Han from resetting himself, and in this he was successful. In what Balbinus sensed was a desperate move, the Han made a slashing sweep of his blade that the Roman blocked with his shield. He's fast, but he's not nearly as strong as Pullus, Gnaeus, and you might be a bit stronger, so use that. Again, even as the thought was going through his mind, he was moving, still using his shield, not to punch with it, but by putting his weight directly behind it as he rushed at the Han, who backpedaled, his blade flashing over and over, and while he came close again with a slash across the eyes of his foe, Balbinus managed to dip his head in time to catch the blade on the iron strip of his helmet. To this moment, no more than two or three heartbeats from the instant Balbinus launched his first attack, Balbinus had only executed one thrust, but just as the Han's blade bounced off of his helmet, the Centurion performed a blind one, this time from the second position over the shield. Normally, an experienced Centurion wouldn't tutor a *Tirone* on executing an attack when he didn't have a clear view of his target, but Balbinus' vision was impaired from the Han's blow to his head, the impact causing an explosion of tiny stars in front of his eyes. However, he had begun his thrust in the fraction of an eyeblink before the Han struck, and he felt rather than saw that his aim was true from the jarring impact that traveled up his arm, while his reward was a bellow of pain from the Han. This time, when the Han backpedaled, Balbinus didn't press, needing the time for his vision to clear, while the Han's left arm now dangled uselessly by his side, blood pouring from the wound just below his clavicle, his face twisted with pain. It was Balbinus who recovered first, rushing to close the gap again as one of his men stepped into the spot he had just vacated, just in time to block the spear thrust that one of the *ji* men launched at the Primus Pilus' unprotected back. Balbinus heard the sharp crack that signaled iron striking wood, but he was far too experienced to let it distract him from his quarry, anticipating the counterattack from the wounded Han.

Despite knowing it was coming, even with his left arm dangling by his side, the older man's speed was blinding, and Balbinus found himself unable to block the thrust at his face with his shield, forced to rely once again on his helmet by dropping his chin. The difference this time was that it wasn't a slashing blow but a thrust, which he felt the full force of in a tremendous impact, but it was the brilliant stab of pain as the iron point pierced his helmet and sliced into his scalp that forced him to be the one to recoil backward. This time it wasn't from inside his skull but from the blood that streamed down his forehead less than a heartbeat later, dripping into his left eye that obscured his vision. More dangerously, it was the side from which the Han's blade was coming, and he would never know how his left arm moved his shield over in time to block the second thrust from the Han, which was even more powerful than the one an instant earlier. It also sealed the Han's fate as, despite the tougher teakwood of the shield, the point of his sword penetrated several inches, and Balbinus, veteran of countless similar moments, immediately twisted his left wrist with as much force as he could. In a manner similar to when a man's blade was trapped by bone, the torque created by this simple move meant that when the Han yanked on his sword to free it, it didn't budge. Not for long; if he had had the time for a second attempt, he would have yanked it free, but without a shield, and with a useless left arm, it took the eyeblink of time for Balbinus' *gladius* to slice into his neck, just in front of his spinal column before the Roman pulled the horizontally oriented blade straight back towards him, severing both large vessels and windpipe. For a second time, Balbinus' face was drenched in blood, some of which sprayed into his open mouth just as he bellowed his victory, but he didn't care, reveling in the sight of the gray-haired Han collapsing at his feet. I bet this is the widest your eyes ever got, you *cunnus*, he thought as he spat the mixture of his own saliva and the Han's blood into his dead foe's face.

"Primus Pilus! What are your orders?"

When Balbinus spun around at the sound of his Optio's voice, he realized that it wasn't just the vision in his left eye that was obscured, so he could only hear the gasp of Domitillo at the sight of his blood-covered face, but when he lifted his right hand to use the back of it to wipe his eyes, it was also covered with blood and did nothing to clear his vision.

"Cerberus' balls!" Domitillo exclaimed, his Optio hurrying to him while yanking his own neckerchief off to hand to his Centurion. "You've got a fucking hole in your helmet, Primus Pilus! How are you even alive?"

It was a good question, but Balbinus didn't reply immediately, taking the time to wipe his eyes first so that he could see properly. His Century was now almost completely across the ruined barrier, while what he estimated to be at least fifty Han in the immediate area were down around the jumble of stone blocks. His ears were ringing, giving the shouting an echoing quality and he supposed it was from the blow to his head. Only when he saw that the immediate area was secure did he bother to answer Domitillo.

"That," he admitted, "is a good question."

Bian had been consigned to watch as the *Gwai* with the white crest slew his father-in-law, then, to his disappointment, when another *Gwai* soldier stood over him and, seeing he was alive, drew his sword back, the point hovering for an instant before plunging down, Bian was resolved to look the savage in the eye to show him how a man died. Just before the soldier thrust his arm down to plunge the point into Bian's throat, there was a guttural shout that, while it meant nothing to Bian, clearly meant something to the soldier, because he stopped to look over his shoulder. Bian's helmet was wedged between two of the fallen blocks and he couldn't turn his head, so he was forced to see out of the corner of his eye that another *Gwai,* identically dressed as the soldier, with the exception of a white stripe of cloth sewn onto the shoulder of the strange armor, was pointing down at him while barking like a dog. Unaware that what Domitillo was pointing at was his ponytail crest that denoted his status as an officer, Bian experienced a mixture of relief and disgust with himself for that relief when the soldier dropped his sword arm but lifted a foot instead, and he braced himself for a kick. While the soldier did kick something, it was only Bian's sword that was lying next to his hand, sending it skittering over the blocks; only then did he bend over, then with his left hand, grabbed Bian's belt, clearly intending to unbuckle it. Bian would have used that as an opportunity to lash out, with his right fist, his left being pinned under his body, but the pain from the belt being jerked from around his waist was so intense that he lost consciousness. By the time he came to, he found himself lying next to a half-dozen other of his men, all wounded, although a couple of them were sitting up. When he instinctively tried to move his arms, he discovered they were bound, undoubtedly with his own belt, but when he attempted to roll over onto his back, the agony was so intense, he almost passed out again.

"*Hou-Kuan* Bian," while he couldn't see, he recognized the voice of *Sui-Chang* Kong, "can you hear me, sir?"

"Yes," he managed to get out, even this causing a stabbing pain in his side.

"General Liu is dead, and the *Gwai* are moving into the city," Kong informed him, then added what Bian knew was Kong's larger concern, as it was his. "What will happen to our families, *Hou Kuan*?"

Now that Bian was fully alert, if in tremendous pain, he knew he could roll over from his left side so that he could at least look at Kong, as he also knew that it was the duty of a good *Hou Kuan* to attend to his men, but it would also mean he would be able to look north, able to watch the results of his failure to stop these *Gwai*, so he remained as he was, although he felt guilty for not answering Kong.

"I don't know, Kong," he finally managed. "I do not know."

While he was destined to live, for the next Roman watch, as Bian was consigned to listen to the final assault by the *Gwai* that resulted in the fall of Yazhou, it was the most painful memory of his life, and if he had been asked in the moment about ever seeing the *Gwai* as anything other than his mortal enemy, he would have thought that person mad to suggest otherwise. Nevertheless, a year later would find Bian Zhang marching again as a soldier; more accurately, as he would learn, he would be called a Legionary.

Chapter Eight

By this point in time, Caesar and his army were accustomed to the idea that, once an assault on a town or city was successful in crushing the last bit of resistance, the Romans would find themselves spending almost as much time quelling the fires that had been created by naphtha. Yazhou was no exception, but unlike Bharuch, which was a much larger city, the fires started around the area of the three bridges were quickly contained, although as the sun set, the entire island part of the city was still almost obscured by the pall of smoke trapped in between the buildings.

"It's a good thing that we were able to get these fires under control," Pollio observed to the five Primi Pili who were now assembled in the square in the rough center of the island. "We're completely out of vinegar, so we would have had to start tearing down buildings to stop it from spreading. And," he indicated the two-story structures surrounding them, "these things are built very well."

Balbinus was the only one among them not wearing his helmet, a thick white bandage wrapped around his head, with a large red spot on it, and once the Legate and his fellow Primi Pili determined that, while his wound was certainly painful and required more than a dozen stitches, he wasn't in any danger, they wasted no time in jesting with him that he had been inspired by their time with the Pandya and Chola to wear what they called a turban. If he hadn't had a pounding headache, he might have enjoyed being the object of their lighthearted mockery, which in reality wasn't any different from what the rankers took such delight in inflicting on their comrades in a similar situation. The large square in the center of the island was now the initial collection point for the Roman wounded, a sight that wasn't humorous to any of the senior officers, even if many of these men didn't belong to their Legion. It had been a bloody fight, but they also knew that it would have been much worse if they hadn't employed their fiery weapon that forced the Han to devote warriors to try to quell the flames, even though they were unsuccessful. Like their supreme commander Xao in Hanou, these men were ignorant about the properties of naphtha, but unlike what occurred in Hanou, the soldiers were aided in their efforts by hundreds of noncombatant civilians, both men and women, of the few thousand that had either lived on or fled to the island the day before the assault began.

As competitive as Primi Pili were, it was Cartufenus who addressed Balbinus. "Thanks for sending a runner to let me know those barricades weren't mortared together. That saved me a lot of my boys."

Before Balbinus could reply, Aquilinus echoed Cartufenus' sentiments, but this was aimed at Cartufenus. "And thanks for doing the same, Cartufenus. And," he turned to Balbinus, "to you as well."

"I didn't," Balbinus confessed. "It was Macula who was thinking on his feet." He offered a rueful smile as he pointed to his bandaged head. "I was too busy trying to copy Pullus in picking a fight."

"But the bastard who did it is dead, neh?" Papernus asked, though he was still out of sorts because his Legion hadn't played a decisive role in the final phase of the fight for the city.

"He is," Balbinus confirmed. After a slight hesitation, he confessed, "But for an old man, he was fucking quicker than Pan. He almost did for me."

"An old man?" Pollio frowned. "One of their rankers was an old man?"

"No, sir," Balbinus shook his head. "He was wearing a different helmet, not with a ponytail that their officers seem to be wearing. It," he used his hand to indicate, "ran front to back like your crest does, but it was made of iron, and it had gold leaf, like those Parthians of the royal bodyguard did." Finishing with a shrug, "If he was their general or whatever they call it, he died at our bridge."

This, Pollio realized, made sense; unlike what was taking

place at roughly same moment in Hanou, with the death of Liu and the incapacitation of Bian, none of the other *Hou Kuan* felt they had the authority to speak for the surviving members of the garrison, which was what had forced the Romans to continue inflicting and absorbing punishment as they hacked down smaller groups of Han soldiers until defenders in that group began throwing down their weapons. None of these veterans were surprised that most of the survivors had been wielding either a spear or what their Legionaries had begun calling the crescent spears, while the Han whose weapon was a sword that was similar to a *spatha* but was slightly curved fought to almost the last man. This had been the way of it since they set foot in Parthia; the lowest classes of Parthians had been armed with only spears and a wicker shield. Pattala, and Bharuch, had been different, but as they knew, this was due to the Macedonian influence over those two kingdoms. Pandya, Chola, the Khmer, and now the Han, armed and equipped their standard infantry with pole weapons, and it was their elite warriors and upper classes who relied on their version of the sword. And, as they had all learned, nobility or high ranking men were more inclined to die rather than accept a life where, for the first time in their collective experience, they might end up being treated in a manner not all that different than the one in which they treated those of their comrades carrying spears.

"What are we going to do with their warriors?" Aquilinus asked Pollio. "Did Caesar give you orders about what to do with them?"

"He did," Pollio nodded, but there was a reluctant note that Balbinus in particular noticed, and he braced himself to hear something that the Legate suspected wouldn't be popular. At first, Pollio didn't seem disposed to continue, but acutely aware of the stares from the five Primi Pili, he sighed before he went on, "They're to be kept separate from the civilians, of course, but they're not going to be sold."

He wasn't surprised that this was met with a chorus of dismay, and some anger, although of the five Primi Pili, the new Primus Pilus of the 8th, Quintus Junius Felix, voiced his protest more as a matter of form. Not only was he acutely aware that the Legion once commanded by Clustuminus was still under a cloud for what had occurred on the Via Hades, he was equally cognizant that the fact that he was the twin brother of Marcus Junius Felix, Primus Pilus of the 6th, was viewed as being the real reason for his promotion from Secundus Pilus Prior to Primus Pilus in the aftermath. The fact that the Primus Pilus Posterior, who by custom would have been promoted, had the same attitude as Quintus Balbus of the Equestrians, having absolutely no desire to don the white crest, wasn't something known outside the 8th, and Felix had heard the whispers among the other Primi Pili about his elevation.

"What's he going to use them for?" Balbinus asked, then answered his own question, "As crewmen for the fleet, I suppose."

"That's one possibility," Pollio agreed vaguely, then changed the subject by addressing Felix. "So you've built an enclosure outside the city walls?"

"It's almost finished," Felix replied. "I ordered that it be made as a holding pen and not a camp."

Understanding what this meant, that rather than the dirt wall being inside the ditch, it was the other way around, Pollio asked, "How large?"

"Enough to accommodate two Legions' worth of people. We've got more of their civilians in it right now, so it's a bit cramped. They have just enough room to sit down but that's all."

"I doubt we're going to have that many of their soldiers to hold," Pollio mused.

"They put up a hard fight," Aquilinus acknowledged. "And, they're actually fairly skilled, especially with those crescent spears."

There was a murmur of agreement, but it was left to Balbinus to inadvertently touch on the reason for what was coming, "They worked in pairs, like a team the way we do, just on a smaller scale. That's something we haven't seen that often."

"No," Pollio, who knew why Caesar had ordered that the captive Han soldiers be saved from slavery, at least immediately, agreed, "We haven't."

329

"I believe," Stolos informed Caesar, "that the Primus Pilus' liver might have been nicked by that sword thrust. But," he added quickly, "I also am certain that there are still links of his mail inside his body."

Nobody, not his Legates, and certainly not the other Centurions of the 10th who were gathered around their general would know what it took for Caesar to retain his composure and his *dignitas,* as, at this moment, he realized something. Like the Centurions standing there, and the men under their command, he had begun to believe that there was nothing that could kill Titus Pullus.

Even now, as he glanced over at Pullus, lying supine, eyes closed, face gleaming with sweat as his massive chest rose and fell in a disturbingly ragged rhythm, he found it hard to fathom what it might be like not seeing this giant Roman standing in front of the 10th Legion.

"What's the most immediate danger now?" he asked Stolos. "The damage to his liver? Or those mail links?"

The physician, who had been the man who sewed up and treated most of Pullus' wounds for the previous six years, stroked his beard as he thought about it.

Finally, he began, "As soon as we got his *hamata* and tunic off, I had him rolled onto his right side. And," his tone turned grim, "there was a *lot* of blood that came out of that wound, but I also smelled it, and it had a bilious odor to it, which is why I believe that his liver was at least slightly cut by the tip of the Han's sword." He sighed, then admitted, "I had hoped that flushing the blood out of the wound would help expel all or most of however many links are still inside his body, but none of them came out."

"When can you get them out of him without killing him?"

Stolos grimaced at Scribonius' question, and he didn't meet the gaze of the lean Roman, although he knew that the Secundus Pilus Prior wasn't the type to take his anger out on him just for being the bearer of bad news. Fortunately, neither was Caesar, but he was still reluctant as he admitted, "I do not know that I can, Pilus Prior. I have no idea where those links are, and if he moves at all when I fumble around in there, I am likely to hit the major blood vessel in his liver. And if that happens," he finished unhappily, "he's crossing the river."

Understandably, it was a grim group who left the building that had been appropriated by the Romans to serve as the hospital, in the administrative center of the city, but Caesar didn't linger to commiserate with Scribonius, Balbus, Cyclops, and the other Pili Priores of the 10th, only these Centurions allowed to be at Pullus' bedside, although both Porcinus and Diocles were allowed to be present as well.

"I need to check on the other Legions," Caesar informed Balbus, who was now the acting Primus Pilus, and while he seemed to be his normal detached, businesslike self, neither Balbus nor the others were fooled. Just before he left them, Caesar said quietly, "I'm going to be making sacrifices to every god I can think of, and I suggest you do the same."

He didn't return the collective salute, striding away in a manner that made his *paludamentum* swirl behind him, which they all knew was one of his favorite affectations, but as Scribonius watched their general crossing the large square to the opposite side, where he knew the highest-ranking Han prisoners were being held and followed by what was now Caesar's party of five other men, even in the torchlight, he could see Caesar's head was bowed. Whether it was from the heavy weight of his burden, or because he was praying, Scribonius didn't know. As for himself, he was at a loss, which he expressed to Balbus.

"Right about now, we'd be in Titus' quarters going over the fight. I'm not sure what to do right now."

Normally, Balbus could have been counted on to at least try to take advantage of such a moment; instead, all he said was, "Neither am I, Sextus."

Zhang was exhausted, and he was aware that not only was he young, he hadn't done anything nearly as strenuous as Caesar, and yet, here in the darkness of the night after Lei's surrender, the *Gwai* showed no signs of slowing down. And, since he had been required to accompany the general, along with Achaemenes, the secretary Apollodorus, and the two bodyguards, of course, he was determined not to show his fatigue. He was at least thankful that he had been kept outside of the three-story building that the *Gwai* had appropriated to serve as a hospital; enemy of the Han they may have been, but he had seen more than enough gruesome sights this day, nor did he particularly like to watch others suffer. As Caesar strode past, he was nudged, none too gently, from behind by the German Gundomir, causing him to stumble a bit, earning him a sympathetic glance from Achaemenes, who said in Tamil, "Gundomir doesn't like your people very much, but don't take it personally. He doesn't like the Romans much more."

This seemed odd, and it prompted Zhang to ask, in a whisper so that Caesar wouldn't overhear, not certain that he believed that the *Gwai* was unable to understand any Tamil, "So why does he serve them?"

Achaemenes' answer was to simply point at Caesar's back, just as they reached the opposite side, where an identically sized building was located. Unlike the hospital, which only had two men standing guard at the entrance, this one had what Zhang quickly counted was eight men, all of them still armored, while their shields were leaning against their legs. The section stiffened in what Zhang knew was the same sign of respect and obedience as the Han bow, but only one of them saluted, and he saw the white stripe, which he had learned meant the man was an Optio. Caesar returned the salute, which Zhang found a bit ridiculous and a waste of time, but their conversation was brief, then Caesar walked to the double wooden doors. It was when he looked over his shoulder directly at Zhang that the Han knew he was expected to enter this building, and he gave Achaemenes an inquiring glance.

"This is where your officers are being held," Achaemenes explained in a whisper, and before he could say anything, Zhang was pushed once again, towards the door.

On his entrance, he was shocked to see that what he estimated to be at least three dozen of his fellow Han weren't bound, and in fact, some of them were stretched out on mats on the floor, while others sat against a wall, talking quietly. They were guarded, of course, and the room, which Zhang assumed had served some sort of Imperial function before the Emperor's order to abandon the island, was now devoid of any furniture, but it wasn't overtly oppressive; if the situation had been reversed, there would have been almost as many guards, they would have all been armed with clubs, and they would have bashed any of the prisoners who tried to speak, either to them, or to their fellow prisoners. It was just another unusual custom of a people who Zhang was beginning to suspect weren't quite the barbaric, bloodthirsty, and uneducated savages that he knew his Emperor and his court assumed them to be. Competent at warfare, yes; by this moment, Zhang felt certain that Yuan now understood not to underestimate the *Gwai* when it came to martial matters, but the assumption was that this was all these Romans knew to do. Caesar paused to speak to another of the guards, and while this one wasn't wearing his helmet, he was armored and wearing his sword, although it was the stick he held in his left hand that informed Zhang that it was one of their Centurions who was responsible for the eight other *Gwai,* stationed in pairs around the room, their backs to the wall. When the Centurion pointed, Zhang naturally looked, seeing that it was Lei who Caesar was asking about, the general actually standing with his arms folded as he spoke to a younger officer. While they had been allowed to congregate and speak, it wasn't lost on Zhang that none of the men were wearing their armor, nor did they have any weapons, or belts for that matter, dressed only in their cotton trousers and long shirt that was dyed black. There was no doubt that they were prisoners, nor was there any doubt that the *Gwai* weren't watching them carefully, even if they did allow them to freely discuss what Zhang guessed would either be a discussion about their possible fates, their families, or about the possibilities of escape. Caesar beckoned to his party, but this time, Zhang moved without being pushed, and he noticed the Parthian's grin at the muttering from the German, guessing that Gundomir was disappointed he didn't have another chance to shove him.

  Caesar crossed to Lei, who stood there without moving towards the Roman, arms still folded, his face betraying nothing, not even to a fellow Han like Zhang, and it was the *Gwai* general who started the process, Zhang asking after Achaemenes' translation, "Caesar would like to know if you are being treated well? Is there anything you need?"

  This time, Zhang was certain that he saw a flicker of

surprise on the defeated general's face, but he answered immediately, "Tell Caesar that we have been treated well enough considering our status as prisoners." Zhang saw him take a breath, and he wasn't surprised when Lei said, "We would all like to know the fate of our families, Emissary Zhang. If Caesar wants to do something for us, that would be something that I know the officers would appreciate."

"I will ask," Zhang replied, but he was about as certain as he could be that it would be rejected out of hand.

To his utter shock, once Achaemenes was finished, Caesar turned to his secretary, who reached into his leather satchel and withdrew two of the wooden tablets that Zhang had found quite useful.

"Caesar asks that you help with this task," Achaemenes explained to Zhang. "He wants the names of the family members General Lei and his officers are asking about, and a possible location."

For a moment, Zhang felt like refusing, offended that he would be viewed as nothing but a clerk, but he quickly realized, and with some chagrin, that he was currently the only person in Hanou, and probably in the entire Han empire who could perform this task.

"I will help you, General, as soon as Caesar is finished," Zhang replied to Lei, and this time, the relief was easy to see on the man's face, but it was brief.

"And what does he want in return for this...generosity?" Lei asked coldly. "Because you can tell him if he expects me to do more than I have already done, I will not cooperate." Seeing the flash of uncertainty on the emissary's face, Lei pointed out, "Yes, he has taken Hanou, and if he is not lying about Yazhou, if they have the same...weapon that the *Gwai* here did, then it has probably fallen as well. But we have several more garrisons around the island, and if he expects me to travel with him to those garrisons and dishonor myself further, he may as well kill me now."

Internally, Zhang was torn; his Emperor wanted the entire rebel army conquered and subjugated, yet he couldn't fight the instinctive feeling of pride at this sign of Han honor, but he managed to hide this as he related Lei's words to Achaemenes.

He watched Caesar carefully, yet there was no sign of the anger that Zhang was expecting, and instead, he saw the *Gwai's* upper lip curl up in what he took to be a sign of amusement.

Listening to Achaemenes, once the Parthian was finished, Zhang told Lei, "Caesar says he would never expect you to do such a thing. Your actions today were necessary, but he understands why you refuse."

Lei's eyes narrowed, Zhang feeling as if the older man was staring at him for a sign that this was some sort of jest, but after a heartbeat, he gave an abrupt nod. Zhang, however, was completely unprepared for Lei's question.

"What happened to the giant *Gwai* who was at the Pearl Market? The one with the white crest on his helmet?" Seeing Zhang's surprise, Lei shrugged. "I noticed that he was wounded." He hesitated, then added, "Even so, he was quite formidable."

"He is," Zhang agreed unthinkingly. "His name is Pullus, and I have been quite close to him on several occasions. He is...fearsome, and he was considered the greatest warrior in the *Gwai* army."

"Was?" Lei asked, eyes going slightly wider, but before Zhang could explain, Caesar snapped something to Achaemenes.

"Why are you speaking about Primus Pilus Pullus?" the Parthian demanded, adopting Caesar's tone as his own.

"General Lei asked about him," Zhang replied stiffly. "Remember, the Centurion was the first man from the ranks of your army to speak to the general. And," he did offer what could have been considered close to a smile, "Pullus is hard to forget."

Achaemenes' tone softened. "He is," he agreed, then explained to Caesar.

"Why did you refer to the *Gwai* in the past tense?" Lei asked, ignoring the exchange between Achaemenes and Caesar. "Is he dead?"

"No," Zhang replied. "Not yet."

"Why is he in danger?"

Since Zhang didn't know, he waited for Achaemenes and Caesar to finish, then asked the Parthian about Pullus' condition. For a long moment, Caesar didn't seem inclined to explain, but then he spoke to Achaemenes, who in turn related what Stolos had said, which Zhang related to Lei.

Once he was finished, Lei didn't respond for a long moment, and instead seemed to be considering something.

Zhang found out what it was when Lei said quietly, "Tell Caesar that I might be able to help."

When Titus Pullus regained consciousness, the first thing that greeted his eyes almost undid all the work that had been performed trying to save his life, as he tried to sit up, alarmed at the sight of three Han, standing side by side and looking down at him, the fact that they were uniformly old, with iron gray hair and straggly beards not registering with him. As it was, the pain was so intense, and ruptured several stitches in the process that his first period of consciousness only lasted a matter of two or three heartbeats. When he came to a second time, he immediately realized that his wrists were now tied to the frame of a cot, while he could tell that he was further restricted across his legs and upper chest. Thankfully, the first face he saw this time was Diocles, who, as he would learn, had been summoned to sit next to his master's side after the mishap that Pullus would be informed had taken place two full watches earlier.

"Don't struggle, Master." The Greek stood and leaned over so that Pullus could see him clearly. "You're in the hospital, and the Han you saw when you woke up are physicians."

It took two tries before Pullus managed to croak, "Why are you letting those slanty-eyed *cunni* touch me?"

Despite knowing that the Han couldn't understand, Diocles still glanced over at them apologetically, but the three men, sitting next to each other on a bench on the opposite side of Pullus' bed just stared at him blankly.

To Pullus, he began hesitantly, "That's...hard to explain, Master. But," he hurried on, "Stolos says that they saved your life."

Bits and pieces began coming back to Pullus, but they were only after he had been wounded, remembering the agony that was only marginally less now than it had been. More importantly, he also remembered why it had been so excruciating, but Diocles, seeing Pullus' expression change, anticipated what his master's alarm was about.

"They retrieved four links from your wound, Master," he assured Pullus, and there was no mistaking the relief on Pullus' face as he relaxed, "and we matched it to your *hamata*. There are no links missing, so that's all of them." Now, Diocles thought, for the bad news, which he delivered carefully. "But as dangerous as they were, your liver was damaged."

"Damaged? Damaged how?"

"Probably from the stab wound," Diocles explained. "But thank the gods it didn't penetrate deeply. Stolos says there's a huge blood vessel that's located in the middle of our liver and if that had been severed, or even punctured, you'd be across the river."

Pullus was listening, but he was also finding it hard to concentrate, and he was also exhausted already.

Before he fell asleep, he asked, "What did those Han do that Stolos couldn't do?"

"I'm not sure," the Greek admitted. "I think some of it has to do with the kind of herbs they use here that we either don't use or we're not familiar with. But," he said firmly, "Stolos doesn't doubt that they saved your life, Master, so try not to kill them when you wake up again."

While he was too weak to laugh, Pullus did fall asleep with a smile on his lips, and while he would be the first Roman saved by Han physicians, over the course of the next several years, he would be far from the last; more crucially, he would be saved one more time.

In a manner similar to what had happened in Bharuch and Muziris, Hanou and Yazhou were taken over by the Legions of Rome, but the Romans would quickly learn that, while they were able to maintain control and order in the two largest cities on the island, the interior was an entirely different story. Part of it was what turned out to be the intransigence of the *Li*, those people the Han considered to be not only native to the island, but to be inferior to themselves, while to the Romans, Han and *Li* were completely indistinguishable from each other. It was a common subject of conversation among the men, how the Han could even tell whether a stranger was Han or *Li*. For the men of the 10th, it was what began as a comment by Scribonius, made as he sat by Pullus' bedside during his hospitalization, which lasted two weeks.

"I've tried to explain it to Quintus," he told Pullus, smiling at the memory, "but it's like talking to a rock. But we can tell a Greek from a Roman at a glance most of the time."

Pullus was sufficiently recuperated by this point to engage in conversations, although he found his mind was still a bit foggy, and he pointed out, "That's not always the case, though, is it? If you put a Greek in a toga, or in a soldier's tunic, you might not be able to tell the difference."

"That's true," Scribonius seemingly granted, "until they open their mouths. But no matter how well they may speak Latin, you can tell they're Greek. And," he added, "the other way around."

"That's true," Pullus grunted.

Going on, Scribonius said, "Just because we can't tell the difference between that gibberish the Han and *Li* speak, that doesn't mean they can't."

While this was mildly interesting to Pullus, which he took as a sign that he was on the way to recovering, there were larger issues on his mind.

"Now that we've solved that mystery, how about you tell me what the fuck is going on?"

"I knew this would happen," Scribonius sighed. Somewhat grumpily, he complained, "Why can't you just worry about recovering and not concern yourself with things that you can't do anything about right now?"

"Why do you always answer a question with a question?" Pullus countered, earning a laugh from Scribonius.

"Fair enough. Let's see, where to begin?" He thought for a moment, then continued, "As of this moment, we're the only Legion still in Hanou. The others are out in the countryside right now, taking control of the rebel garrisons east and south of the city."

"They're going to have a fight on their hands," Pullus said grimly, "if they have as many of those scorpion bows as the bastards here did."

Caesar Ascending – The Han

"That's what Caesar believed as well," Scribonius agreed. "But it's not turning out that way, at least so far. I've only heard about the 5th and the 14th, but they sent couriers back to inform Caesar that with the suicide by General Xao, and having his second in command as a prisoner, I seems to have taken away their will to keep fighting."

This was good news, but Pullus frowned as he thought about it.

"But how would they know that? That this Xao is dead and that other *cunnus* is a prisoner?"

"Because Caesar came up with a plan for that," Scribonius explained. "Of all the Han soldiers we captured, we bagged a fair number of officers. The first night, General Lei asked Caesar to find out about the families of his officers, and naturally, Caesar agreed. They were found and they were unharmed." Scribonius' expression altered slightly, and he amended, "I mean, for the most part. They were alive. The wives?" He shrugged, though not elaborating.

"All right, but what does that have to do with what we're talking about?"

His impatience is another sign he's on the mend, Scribonius thought ruefully.

Aloud, he explained, "Because every Legion has at least one or more of those officers with them to inform the garrison commanders of their situation. And, the prisoners have been very persuasive, at least so far."

"So Caesar must have found other Han besides Zhang who can speak one of the tongues we use in the army," Pullus mused. "Otherwise, there would be no way to tell if these prisoners are being straight with their comrades. For all we know, they could be telling those commanders to fight to the last man."

It was true, Scribonius knew, but he was also aware of another fact that Pullus wasn't, which he explained, at least partially.

"Yes, that was a concern, but Caesar thought of that." He fell silent, waiting for Pullus to work it out on his own, but for a long moment, his friend's expression communicated only confusion.

He was about to open his mouth when Pullus gasped, "He's

holding those families hostage!"

"Not all of them," Scribonius replied, somewhat defensively. "But yes, he found officers with families, but who only had one son, since the Han only value their male children."

It was something that every Roman found distasteful, although Scribonius was honest enough with himself to acknowledge that it was less the idea that Han females were devalued, but to the degree they did, since Romans placed more value on their male children as well.

Pullus signaled his concession of the point by moving on. "So, how long will that take? Does Caesar have any idea?"

"Balbus just got back from a meeting as your representative," Scribonius replied. "And he said that Caesar estimates that, provided the rest of the garrison commanders behave as the first two or three did, it will take a month to cover the entire island. Pollio and his Legions are taking care of the garrisons on the southern side of the island, but he's actually almost done because it turned out that General Xao ordered the entire complement of three garrisons to march to Yazhou."

"Fortunate bastards," Pullus grumbled. He revealed his true cause for concern. "You know that Balbinus and Cartufenus will never let me forget that their part of the army took care of their business first."

It was heartening for Scribonius to hear Pullus carping about the never-ending competition between Primi Pili, but he would have cause to remember this exchange for a different reason, as it would turn out that Pollio's Legions were far from through.

Zhang had been dreading the coming confrontation between himself and Caesar, but he knew it couldn't be put off any longer, now three months after the fall of Hanou and Yazhou. It had been an admittedly confused and confusing period of time, exacerbated by the fact that, unlike the Indian kingdoms, the number of Han who knew even a smattering of other tongues— Tamil, Sanskrit, Telugu chief among them— who had been on the island could be numbered on two hands, with fingers left over, and Zhang was one of them. At first, Zhang assumed that Caesar's continued delaying of the discussion about the other part of the agreement that, without undue pride, Zhang had been instrumental in creating on behalf of his Emperor was because of the difficulties arising from the *Gwai's* inability to communicate with a civilized people. As the weeks went by, Zhang grew increasingly suspicious that Caesar was using the problem as a pretext for delaying what, to the Emperor, was the most crucial aspect of the agreement. Finally, on a rainy day in the Roman month of October, a year removed from the Roman resumption on the Via Hades, Zhang approached one of the men with whom he could communicate. That it wasn't Achaemenes but Barhinder was a calculated gamble on the part of the Han emissary, understanding that, given the Bharuch youth's utter devotion to the huge *Gwai* Pullus, who was back on his feet and seemingly back to normal, Barhinder might go directly to Pullus. It was a mark of Zhang's desperation that he did it, lingering around the Prefect's Palace in Hanou that the Romans now called the *praetorium*, watching for what he had determined was Barhinder's daily trip to drop off a report of some sort. When Barhinder arrived, Zhang was worried because the young clerk was chatting with another *Gwai* that Zhang recognized as being attached to the 10th Legion, but he did his best to make it seem like an accident when he walked directly across the pair's path.

"Zhang!" Barhinder's surprise seemed genuine, making Zhang believe that his ploy had worked, and as usual, the younger man was smiling. "I have not seen you for several days."

"I have been out in the countryside with Legate Hirtius," Zhang explained. Glancing at the other clerk, who seemed more curious than wary, Zhang asked, "Once you are finished with your business, may I speak with you for a moment?"

Barhinder's smile faded a bit, and Zhang thought he saw a flash of suspicion in his eyes, but Barhinder didn't hesitate, much.

"Of course. When I come back outside?"

Naturally, the Han agreed, and he was relieved that Barhinder didn't tarry, returning outside very quickly.

"I will walk with you," Zhang began. "I know that you are busy." When Barhinder nodded, Zhang began, "I have a problem and I need your advice."

While they were unaware of it, the first four Cohorts of the 10th were now housed in the same barracks that had once been the home of the Leaping Dragons, and the quarters belonging to Bao were now occupied by Optio Lutatius. The barracks had been thoroughly looted, of course, none of which mattered as Zhang, being as honest as he was willing to be, explained his dilemma. Barhinder listened, his normally cheery demeanor becoming thoughtful.

When Zhang finished, he said carefully, "So you are concerned that you are disappointing your Emperor by not confronting Caesar, but he has refused to be in a situation where you are able to bring the subject up."

"That is exactly the case," Zhang agreed. "But I do not know what to do about it."

"All I can tell you is what Diocles told me about what Master Titus does in similar situations," Barhinder replied.

For the next few moments, Barhinder talked, Zhang listened, and once the young clerk was through, while he didn't know it, he triggered what would be the first crisis of what would become a longer relationship than either Han or Roman knew.

"Caesar said he does not have the time at the moment."

Zhang wasn't surprised at Achaemenes' statement, standing in the outer room of the large building, and the Han could see that the door to Caesar's private office was shut, which the staff understood was a signal that he didn't want to be disturbed. Nor did he fault the Parthian, who he had come to both respect and like, but this time, instead of Zhang acquiescing, without saying a word in reply, he gently pushed Achaemenes aside and began walking towards the door.

"You cannot do that!" Achaemenes gasped, but when he turned to call for the clerk who normally sat at a small desk near the door who served as an unofficial gatekeeper, the cursed Greek wasn't there.

Probably off gossiping, Achaemenes thought bitterly, but when he hurried to intercept Zhang, reaching out to grab one brocaded sleeve, the Han turned and regarded him with cold eyes.

"Touching an emissary of Emperor Yuan could be considered an act of war, Parthian." He didn't say it loudly, but there was a tone in Zhang's voice that Achaemenes hadn't ever heard from the Han.

Nevertheless, while he was flustered, he was also angry himself, and he snapped, "And disturbing Caesar could get your head parted from your shoulders...Han!"

"If that is to be my fate," Zhang said quietly, with a calmness he didn't really feel, "then I am willing to die for my Emperor."

He would never know whether it was his words or his tone that got Achaemenes to relent, but while the Parthian stepped aside, Achaemenes muttered, "Let it be on your head."

And, with a pounding heart, Zhang reached for the latch, and without knocking, walked into Caesar's office, the next step in what would become a period of time all involved would remember.

"He *what*?"

Zhang responded to Emperor Yuan's gasped question as calmly as he could.

"He says that he has decided that it would be unjust to turn General Lei and the other officers on your list to you, Bìxià," Zhang repeated. However, he couldn't keep the scorn from his voice when he added, "He said he believes that General Lei is an honorable man, and that his aligning with the traitorous General Xao was done out of a sense of duty." He did think to explain, "Apparently, he and General Lei have become friendly, and Lei has dined with the *Gwai* on more than one occasion. I believe that is how Caesar knows that Lei served General Xao for almost fifteen years."

"Did you warn the *Gwai* of the consequences of this action?" Shi asked, igniting in Zhang a flare of anger at the idea that he wouldn't.

"Of course, I did," Zhang just barely kept his tone under control, never forgetting that he was treading in dangerous territory, where one never knew who was an enemy and who was a friend. "I was very explicit in what the *Gwai* could expect."

"And what did he say to that?" Yuan asked, somewhat unusually seated on a chair that would have rivaled that belonging to the dead Chola king Karikala in the quality and ornateness of its carvings.

He looks pale, Zhang thought, experiencing a pang of worry that wasn't focused on himself. Before he answered Yuan, he had to take a breath to explain what was, in essence, a bitter truth.

"Caesar has determined that the island is capable of producing enough food to sustain his soldiers, without any further aid from us." He had to swallow before he delivered the part of the message he had been withholding and had been dreading delivering for the weeks he had been traveling to Chang´An. "He also said, 'If the Han emperor wishes to take General Lei and the other officers on the list presented to me, he is invited to come and take them.'"

He wasn't surprised at the shocked silence, and Yuan grew even paler; for the first time, even the Imperial Secretary Hong wore a stunned expression, the brush in his hand poised above the parchment, and Zhang noticed a drop of ink falling onto it, everyone seemingly frozen in place. He's going to have to rewrite his notes, Zhang thought idly as he waited for a response, from anyone present.

"That...that...*worm*," Yuan finally muttered. "Who does he think he is?"

"Clearly, he is what we thought he was, Bìxià," Shi said, and Zhang heard a smug note in the Emperor's cousin's tone. "An utter barbarian savage, with no understanding of how civilized nations conduct business."

"We can't let this go unanswered," Xian insisted, reminding Zhang that the eunuch was an ally of Shi's. "We must send an army to Xuwen, and sail across the Strait to crush these insects!"

Zhang wasn't a warrior, and he never considered himself to be even partially inclined to martial matters, but the scorn he felt for the palace eunuch was almost overpowering as he thought, So you say standing in a palace far away from these *Gwai*!

It was this thought that prompted him to speak, without thinking, "Bìxià, I have seen the *Gwai* in battle. I know what they're capable of." Thinking of something, he asked of nobody in particular, "Did anyone get my report from Hanou?"

He didn't add "this time," given his certainty that at least one such dispatch he had sent never made it to the Emperor, so he was relieved when Yuan nodded.

"Yes, I did. And I read it," he added, which seemed to have some hidden meaning to both Xian and Shi, the latter visibly stiffening. "It was," Yuan said soberly, "a very thorough report, and very disturbing." Thinking for a moment, Yuan asked suddenly, "Your description of this substance naphtha was quite enlightening, and I directed all of my *Taishou* to send any knowledge they have of a similar substance in their provinces, but to this moment, while there are certain flammable substances that come from the ground, none of it has the consistency that you describe. So," he leaned forward, "how much more of this substance do they have?"

Zhang had anticipated and dreaded this question, because he could only say, "I was unable to determine that, Bìxià, although I tried, but as you can imagine, the *Gwai* were very careful about what they allowed me to see, and while I have learned their word for naphtha, I don't know enough of their tongue yet to know anything other than it was a topic of discussion." He thought for a moment, then said, "I will say that there is a building that is under heavy guard, but more importantly, it's the only building on its block in the Imperial center of Hanou, and I once saw some of their slaves carrying crates out that are marked with a red circle. That is what they carry the jars of naphtha in, but while I know where it's located, I don't know how much they have on hand. But," he felt it important to emphasize, "I also know that none of the ships that have sailed into Hanou since I've been there have been of Roman design. Only *chuan* as far as cargo vessels."

"What does that matter?" Shi scoffed.

"Because it indicates that none of the ships have sailed all the way from Parthia, Excellency," Zhang replied. "That is the only source for the substance, and it stands to reason that the ships carrying such a cargo would be part of their merchant fleet of Greek or Roman ships from Taprobane."

"It *is* a vast distance between here and Parthia, especially by sea," Jin Chang, who Zhang knew was aligned with his own Master Zhou, who was absent because of an illness, spoke up for the first time. "So it's likely that if they do not have more on hand, their supply is running low."

"You said you know where this naphtha is stored?" Shi asked Zhang, and the emissary nodded, but rather than address Zhang, Shi turned to Yuan. "Bìxià, I'm certain that Emissary Zhang would be willing to return to Hanou and sabotage that supply. Then, we can sail from Xuwen in sufficient numbers to overwhelm the *Gwai*, who would be without the one weapon that makes them so formidable."

Zhang felt as if his blood had frozen in his veins, and it was a struggle to remain calm as he replied coolly, "While it's true that their supply of naphtha is a distinct advantage, it would be foolish for anyone to think that this is the only thing that makes them so, as you say, formidable." He noticed out of the corner of his eye that the Emperor's lips curled up in a small smile, making Zhang think that he appreciated what Zhang had said; encouraged, he went on, "Again, with all humility, Excellency Shi, I have seen Caesar's army and what they're capable of, with and without naphtha. You have not."

Zhang's reward was a poisonous stare from the Emperor's cousin who, if rumor was to be believed, had long felt that the wrong member of his clan was sitting on this ornate Imperial throne.

"While I agree that the *Gwai* have insulted *me*," Zhang wasn't alone in hearing Yuan's emphasis, "I also recognize that young Zhang is vastly more qualified to assess their capabilities than anyone in this room, including me. So," the Emperor looked at Zhang directly, "what is your counsel, Emissary Zhang?"

It was thrilling and terrifying in equal measure, but Zhang had also had much more time to contemplate their predicament, and had reached his conclusion many days earlier.

Nevertheless, he didn't reply immediately, not wanting to betray his mind was already made up, and he tried to sound as if he was thinking it through as he said, honestly, "I don't believe there is anything we can do, not at this moment, Bìxià. Yes, it's an insult, one that at some point in the future must be answered, but the *Gwai have* fulfilled your larger goal of ending the threat posed by General Xao and his rebels. And," he pointed out, "the reason you adopted that wise policy was because it would have required you to divert forces from General Gan in his fight against the *Xiongnu* and Zhizhi. Which, as I learned on my return to Chang'An, has become more of a threat, is that true?"

It was left to Xian to answer reluctantly, "We have suffered some...setbacks, that's true. But," he insisted, "it's nothing that General Gan can't handle."

"Can he handle it with less troops?" Zhang asked, and while he suspected he knew the answer, he also wanted to be certain, but this time, it wasn't the eunuch who replied.

Instead, Xian gave Shi a glance that Zhang caught, so he was somewhat prepared for the Emperor's cousin to supply the answer, which he did, although he closed his eyes then took a breath before admitting, "No. The General is instead insisting that he needs even more men to contain Zhizhi and his savages."

Hearing this piece of gossip he had learned from his father confirmed, Zhang turned back to the Emperor, who was ultimately the one man who mattered in this room; no matter how hard the others present tried to jockey for more power and influence, it was all aimed at one man, the otherwise normal-looking middle-aged man with a slight pot belly sitting unhappily on his throne.

"Bìxià," Zhang began, "given what I know of Caesar and his army, and with this new information about the state of affairs with Zhizhi, my counsel is that you do nothing."

For a long moment, Yuan continued staring at Zhang, clearly uncomprehending, but he managed to recover first, beating the others to repeat, "Nothing? What does that mean, nothing?"

Ignoring the trickle of sweat he could feel tracing down his spine, Zhang explained what that meant, but whenever one of the others, Shi and Xian most notably, opened their mouths to object or to pounce on something the young emissary said, it was Yuan who stopped them with the same sort of gesture the

Gwai Caesar used, a simple lifting of his hand in their direction. Therefore, Zhang was able to explain not only what he meant, but his reasons for it, and he was certain that he couldn't have elucidated it any better than he did at this moment. There was a long silence, as the other courtiers seemed to sense that it would be impolitic in the extreme to speak next, as all eyes went to the Emperor, who sat there, seemingly in no hurry as he stroked his beard, staring at the floor completely lost in thought.

Finally, he lifted his head, and without expression, asked Zhang, "How soon can you leave to return to Hanou and the *Gwai* to make this offer?"

"Caesar called their bluff," was Scribonius' judgement, shortly after the Ides of December.

While Pullus agreed, he still felt compelled to ask, in a general sense not aimed at any of the others gathered at the table, "But how did he know how much trouble Yuan is in with Zhizhi that he couldn't afford to do anything that might provoke us?"

"Because," Scribonius grinned, but he was only partially jesting, "he's Caesar, and Caesar knows all."

This provoked laughter from the others; as had become the habit, Gaius was now a regular guest along with Scribonius and Balbus, but whereas Diocles was always present, sitting at his own small table, he was now regularly joined by Barhinder, which had been the case ever since the night Karikala had made one last attempt to avenge his son's death. What none of them save one knew, Caesar's knowledge of the situation facing Emperor Yuan, specifically the setbacks in the form of military defeats at the hands of Zhizhi and his forces, had actually come from Barhinder, and it was Diocles' glance at his young assistant, one sending a silent message that the Bharuch youth understood, saying nothing.

"What are you grinning about?" Pullus growled, noticing Barhinder's smile. "You think that's funny?"

"No, Master Titus," Barhinder answered quickly.

For a long moment, Barhinder was afraid that Pullus was going to probe further, but after a long heartbeat, the Roman grunted and returned his attention to the topic under discussion.

"Bodroges told me that Pollio and his part of the army have their hands full with those *Li* bastards," Pullus commented. "Apparently, those mountains are full of caves, and it's a nightmare to operate in for us, and so far, those barbarians don't seem to have any interest in just hearing what Caesar is offering them."

It was, the others knew to varying degrees, indeed a thorny problem, and while the eastern part of the island was essentially pacified, it hadn't happened without difficulty, almost all of it stemming from the language barrier and the paucity of men attached to Caesar's army that spoke the Han tongue. That the *Li* spoke a distinctly different dialect had only exacerbated the problem, as one of the Tribunes had learned when, while under a flag of truce, Lucius Petronius Asellio, who had been remarkable for his complete lack of distinction for this entire campaign, was shot out of his saddle because of this difference by a *Li* crossbowman. He had survived, fortunately, but the incident had apparently hardened the resolve of the people who were native to this island, and they had spurned every attempt on Caesar's part to assure them that the Romans would be far more benevolent than even General Xao had proven to be. Additionally, Caesar had made the determination within a matter of a month that, whereas former Han soldiers were more amenable, the *Li* were far too undisciplined and unruly for future service in the ranks of the Legions. The current situation was that the ten Legions under Caesar's command were now distributed around the island, which had been made easier because of the presence of the Han infrastructure that had been abandoned a few years earlier. Men were no longer in tents, and while it was still warm and moist, it wasn't nearly as bad as India or the Via Hades; more than anything, the rankers appreciated the fact that they wouldn't be aboard ships for the foreseeable future. In fact, this had proven such a strong incentive that, when the rumors began that Caesar was considering staying even longer than what passed for the winter routine that had been a staple of warfare for centuries, to Pullus' surprise, the response on the part of his men had been a collective shrug of the shoulders. As he always did with such matters, Pullus relied on a select few men of the ranks who he trusted to give him an honest assessment on the collective state of mind of the men he led, and chief among them was his former tentmate, Publius Vellusius.

"I have to hand it to these Han barbarians, Primus Pilus," he had informed Pullus. "These are the best quarters we've seen since we were in Bharuch. Granted," he allowed, "they all lived in one big room, but they had eleven men per section to our ten."

Knowing better than to invite the Gregarius to his own quarters, which he would never know belonged to the officer who commanded one the *Tu-wei-fu* that had defended Hanou, instead, Pullus had arranged to meet at the Pearl Market, which, after a tense period of time where the inhabitants of the city waited to see what these *Gwai* would do to them, had begun to operate again, albeit on a smaller scale. Despite its name, the merchants of the Pearl Market specialized in silks of all styles, from plain fabric to highly decorated and embroidered pieces of clothing, although there were stalls selling a variety of other things. Pullus supposed it was inevitable that the men, of all Legions, loaded down with silver and gold coins from a variety of places, would look for a way to spend that money, and perhaps two months into their time in Hanou, men began showing up wearing clothing that, while cut in the Roman style of the simple tunic, were in a variety of colors. It took some time to discover the cause for the Han merchants' willingness to accept Roman business, which meant that the rankers who had been the most eager to show off their finery to their comrades paid an exorbitant price due to the fact that Han coinage, which were similar to the coins of other kingdoms in that they tended to be round, used bronze instead of the more valuable silver. Although it led to some hostility on the part of some rankers who felt they had been cheated, once the discrepancy had been noted, Caesar, working with the Han emissary Zhang, and surprisingly enough, the rebel General Lei, had established a rough exchange rate. Now, Pullus and Vellusius were just one of many Legionaries wandering about the large market on their off-duty time as the Primus Pilus questioned his comrade, both of them holding a bamboo skewer, upon which were chunks of roast pork and chicken.

"What do you think the boys will say if we stay here even longer?" Pullus asked Vellusius, who had just torn off a chunk of pork.

Chewing while they walked, Vellusius finally answered thoughtfully, "Honestly, Primus Pilus, I don't think they'd be all that upset." He laughed, then added, "Our biggest complaint is that their *tsu* isn't nearly as good as *sura*. You have to drink a whole jar of *tsu* to get the same effect as a cup of *sura*." The old ranker sighed. "I really wish we had some now. Otherwise," he shrugged, "I think they're enjoying having more than just Caesar's Centuries to choose from."

It was, Pullus thought wryly, not all that surprising to learn that the rankers based their happiness on the ability to debauch, and he had to admit that he himself had been captivated by the beauty of some of these Han women. He also knew that much of it came from their unique appearance, and the exotic nature of lying with a woman who was so different from those they had been accustomed to, even the Pandya women. Yes, they had been much, much darker than even the Parthian women, but when it came to facial features, they presented a familiar appearance to a man from Rome. Some had bigger noses than others, some had wider mouths, some had stronger jawlines, whereas to Pullus and his fellow Romans' eyes, Han women were completely different, from the shape of the eyes to their smaller noses and rounder faces; it went well beyond skin color. In fact, before he finally satisfied his curiosity with one of Caesar's Centuries, Balbus had been certain that the vagina of the Han women would be significantly different than any of the countless other women he had bedded, and it still made Pullus laugh when he thought about his scarred friend's bitter disappointment to learn that he had been wrong.

"Pullus, can I ask you a question?"

"I suppose," Pullus replied slowly, although he was almost certain what Vellusius wanted to know.

"It sounds like we're going to be here for longer than normal," Vellusius began carefully, glancing up at Pullus to read his expression. He also kept one eye on Pullus' *vitus*, the last one made of grapevine as his Centurion held it loosely; when he didn't get hit, he asked cautiously, "Do you have any idea how long it will be?"

"No," Pullus answered, being honest for the most part. After all, his suspicions that were based on what he had learned from Diocles through Apollodorus didn't exactly mean he knew. "I don't, Publius." Suddenly, something in the manner in which Vellusius had asked the question struck him, though he couldn't really say why, and he asked, "Why do you want to know?"

Pullus was rewarded when Vellusius suddenly looked away, although he answered readily enough, "It's just that I've...met someone." His eyes widened slightly as he added, "A woman, I mean to say, Primus Pilus."

"I assumed as much," Pullus answered in amusement. "I never took you for a Greek." This made Vellusius laugh, but Pullus was now intensely curious, because in all of their time together, now spanning more than two decades, Publius Vellusius had never exhibited the slightest interest in forming a more permanent attachment with a woman. This was what prompted him to comment lightly, "She must be something to snag someone like you, Publius."

"Oh, she is!" Vellusius nodded emphatically. "She's wonderful. She's very beautiful, and she's kind, and she's..." Suddenly remembering who he was talking to, Vellusius flushed, his voice trailing off. "...I just mean, she makes me happy."

Vellusius would never know the sharp stab of pain felt by his giant comrade, while it caught Pullus by surprise; he had managed to avoid thinking about Hyppolita for months now, but hearing Vellusius describe this unknown Han woman, using the kind of tone that he knew he would probably have used himself when describing the queen brought it all roaring back.

"What's her name?"

"Jiā," Vellusius answered, naming the young prostitute who had once been the object of affection of *Hou Chan* Bao, who still lived, but without his right arm had been reduced to begging in Xuwen after managing to smuggle himself across the strait by spending his life's savings that he had intended to purchase Jiā, a connection that neither Vellusius, Bao, nor Pullus would ever know.

"How do you two communicate?" Pullus asked curiously, and this earned him a grin that was notable for having fewer teeth than Pullus remembered seeing before.

"Oh, we have our ways." Vellusius winked, earning a chuckle from Pullus. More seriously, he continued, "I've learned a few bits of words from her, and she's learning a bit of Latin. When I have a question or want to say something that I don't know the words for, I just go to Gotra."

It was something Pullus was generally aware of, but just as he was ignorant that Caesar's more detailed knowledge had come from Barhinder, the giant Roman didn't know just how valuable Barhinder had become serving as a bridge between Caesar's army and the Han. Although Barhinder had cultivated a good relationship with the Han emissary, the information about the deteriorating situation facing Emperor Yuan hadn't come from Zhang but from Long, whose contacts among fellow merchants and traders enabled him to peddle the most precious commodity of all, especially to men like Caesar, information.

"I hope you pay him for that help," Pullus said gruffly, then felt a bit chagrined at Vellusius' look of indignation.

"Of course I do, Primus Pilus! How could you even ask that?"

"*Pax*, Publius," Pullus apologized. "I knew the instant I said it that I should have known better." Returning to the original subject, Pullus said thoughtfully, "So, you don't think the men would have much problem staying longer, so the question is...how long?"

"That," Vellusius admitted, "I don't know."

While their conversation had confirmed Pullus' sense of the situation, this was the most important question, and it was still unanswered; how long would Caesar keep them here on Zhuya?

The answer would turn out to be more than eighteen months, and the reason for the delay was precipitated by a number of factors, including complacency on part of his army, and what Caesar discovered was that, while there was some yearning on the part of his Legions for home, more than anything, the men—Roman, Parthian, and to a lesser extent, the

Pandyans—wanted stability that lasted longer than four or five months.

"The men are tired of thinking about what's coming next," was how Pullus had put it to Caesar, one of the four Primi Pili who had been selected, two from Yazhou in Balbinus and Cartufenus, and two from Hanou, Batius and Pullus, but to nobody's surprise, the other three insisted that it be Pullus who spoke for them. "We haven't spent a normal winter season since Muziris, and the men feel like the months we spent on the Ganges, the month we spent on the Mon peninsular waiting for the fleet, then the time we spent on the Via Hades isn't enough. Besides," he smiled as he spoke, "they've found a lot to like here on Zhuya."

Caesar was listening impassively, his face betraying none of his thoughts, but Pullus felt confident that their general was less than pleased, and it only partly had to do with the idea that the men were dictating the pace of events. In general, of all the enemies Caesar had faced over the course of his remarkable career, it was time who was his mortal foe, and it was hard for him to understand men who enjoyed idle time beyond a certain amount. What only his Legates knew was that the negotiations between Caesar and Emperor Yuan were at a delicate stage, although Pullus and the other Primi Pili weren't blind to Zhang's repeated absences as he traveled back and forth. What concerned Yuan also concerned Caesar, albeit for different reasons, that the complacency the Legions were displaying endangered the goals of both leaders. While Yuan had no intention of reestablishing a presence on Zhuya, it would be a tremendous loss of what the Han referred to as face and Caesar and his fellow Romans thought of as their *dignitas* if it turned out that the Emperor had essentially traded one rebel army for what he viewed as another in the form of Caesar and his men.

On Caesar's part, he was acutely aware that, whether the Han had abandoned Zhuya a few years earlier or not, that no Emperor would feel comfortable seeing the most formidable, veteran army in the history of both East and West establishing a foothold no more than twenty miles from the mainland at its narrowest point. Sooner or later, probably once the Han subdued Zhizhi and his *Xiongnu* in their attempt to carve out a territory of their own, the Han Emperor would turn his attention to the south. Now that they had faced the Han in the form of the rebels on Zhuya, Caesar was confident that they could repulse an attempt by Yuan to dislodge him and his army; the question was, how many times? While Caesar hadn't lied about the island being able to produce enough rice to feed his army, the issue was whether or not there was enough to feed the army and the civilian population. This was much less clear, but for Caesar, this wasn't his primary concern; the problem he confronted was that, if he had been pushed to divulge his thoughts, for all of his intellectual prowess and his rhetorical ability, he didn't actually know why he remained so restless, just that he was still determined to keep going east. It was something buried so deeply within him that Caesar, as introspective as he could be when he chose, was forced to confront this one reality here going into his sixty-third year, that he didn't know why he felt this driving need. It was no longer about outdoing Alexander; he had done that just by reaching the Ganges, although Palibothra remained unconquered, which was a sore in his mind, always lurking there to remind him that he hadn't actually fulfilled his personal goals. Only gradually had he become aware that this hadn't been enough, and what was ultimately his manipulation of the men of his army in endowing in them the idea of reaching the fabled Han Empire was fulfilled, and now, his men were giving the indication that, at least for the foreseeable future, they were content with this little island kingdom, even with the troublesome *Li*. Matters weren't helped by the fact that the distance between Zhuya and Chang'An was roughly the same as it had been from Muziris to the Ganges, or from Susa to Merv, meaning that, even on a road system that Caesar deduced rivaled the great *Viae* of their faraway Republic, the trip took more than three weeks in each direction. As much to keep himself busy as anything else during Zhang's absence, Caesar had taken it upon himself to make a tour of the island, but in force, taking part of his army with him and making a large circular route that began by heading east from Hanou, then following the contour of the island south before swinging west to Yazhou, where Pollio was still commanding.

His decision to leave both the 5th and 10th behind in Hanou met with a mixed reaction, but Caesar was disappointed to see that Pullus hadn't put up much of a protest, and what little he did seemed to be more a matter of form, his heart clearly not in it. It was a troubling sign for the general that his most veteran and reliable Legion seemed content to serve garrison duty, much as they had done in Bharuch, and the thought did cross his mind that perhaps his giant Primus Pilus was reluctant to leave the city for the same reason as last time. Although, he thought with a peevish amusement, if he impregnates a local woman this time, at least it won't be a queen. Troubled enough to use Apollodorus to make a discreet inquiry with Diocles, he was relieved to learn that, while the Primus Pilus was a regular visitor to the same brothel that Bao had once frequented, Pullus took particular pains to never see the same woman twice, which Caesar correctly assumed was his Primus Pilus' attempt to avoid the same kind of complications with an emotional attachment as what had taken place with a queen in Bharuch. Nevertheless, he took it as another troubling sign, and part of his reason for taking the 14th, 25th, and 30th Legions with him was to give him time with their respective Centurions to assess their morale and willingness to continue.

Accompanying him, under guard of course, was General Lei, in whom Caesar saw his former nemesis who had become, if not friends, then not enemies in Kambyses, the Parthian nobleman who had defended Ctesiphon and Seleucia, and in doing so, had introduced the Romans to the terrible yet powerful weapon of flaming naphtha. There was a larger problem with the Han prisoner, however; unlike Kambyses, who spoke Greek, while Lei was conversant in several tongues, they were all related to his native language of the Han. This was why, for another time, Caesar "requested" that Barhinder Gotra accompany this endeavor, along with the merchant Long, who had picked up more Tamil during his time with the army, as well as a smattering of camp Latin. Nevertheless, Caesar was surprised when, three days out of Hanou, as the army marched along the rough road that paralleled the coast as it curved south, Barhinder suddenly came trotting up to where Caesar was riding with Lei, Achaemenes, Gundomir, and Teispes. It was the young man's nervousness that Caesar noticed, and while this wasn't all that unusual, there was something in Barhinder's agitation that he sensed was important, prompting him to stop his cumbersome conversation with the Han general.

"What is it, Gotra?" Caesar asked over his shoulder, even before Barhinder drew alongside on the other side of Achaemenes. "You look upset."

"No, Caesar," Barhinder replied immediately, and almost as quickly realized that this wasn't true, so he added hurriedly, "it is just that Long told me something that I think might be important."

Even if he was prone to dismiss the excitement of young men under his command, Caesar had learned that Barhinder was vastly different; although it didn't happen often, whenever Gotra had approached him, it had been important.

"What is it, Gotra?" Caesar asked, but when Gotra's eyes cut to Lei, who was watching with undisguised interest, Caesar nudged his horse, the gray stallion that he alternated riding with the son of Toes, out of the marching column, saying curtly, "Follow me."

Naturally, Barhinder obeyed, following Caesar a few paces to the side. Drawing up, at Caesar's nod, he said, "We are about to reach Boon Siou, are we not, sir?"

"We are," Caesar replied. "I've already sent Decurion Darius and his *ala* ahead."

"Long just told me that he just now learned from one of the drovers there is a sizable garrison," Barhinder informed him, referring to the dozen peasants who, just as the other conquered kingdoms had learned, could improve their lot in life under these strange barbarians by taking their silver performing a variety of menial tasks.

"Sizable?" Caesar asked sharply. "What does that mean?"

"Long said that he was told there are more than three thousand of General Xao's troops. They are led by a man called Yin Zhao, and he is one of the men who refused to answer General Lei's call to come to Hanou and surrender."

"Come with me," Caesar snapped, spinning the stallion and moving to a quick trot to resume his spot. Waiting only long enough for Barhinder to reach his side, Caesar addressed Lei, although all he said was "Yin Zhao."

Lei didn't react...much, but there was a slight widening of his eyes that lasted less than a heartbeat that told Caesar what he needed to know, but rather than Achaemenes, it was Barhinder Caesar turned to. "Ask General Lei what is waiting for us at Boon Siou."

Put on the spot like this, it took Barhinder two attempts to put the correct words together to put to Lei, while Caesar studied the Han general intently as the exchange took place. His manner wasn't evasive to Caesar's eyes; if anything, he seemed amused, which was partially explained by Barhinder.

"He says that when he sent his out order to surrender, that if he had been able to, he would have wagered that it would be Yin Zhao who refused."

"How many men are under his command?"

Hiding his impatience at the laborious exchange, Caesar continued to watch Lei intently, until Barhinder finally answered, "On the day of our attack on Hanou, the Boon Siou garrison numbered two thousand, nine hundred eighty men, a thousand spearmen, a thousand crossbowmen, four hundred cavalry, and the rest using the *gladius*."

"What about artillery?"

Another exchange, then Barhinder replied, "Five of their version of our *ballista*, Caesar."

Lei began talking again, speaking at some length before Barhinder held up a hand in a silent signal, and he turned back to Caesar, admitting, "I am not certain I understand completely, Caesar, but General Lei said that he had issued orders for Yin to take two thousand of those men to Shishanzen..."

"Shishanzen," Caesar interrupted, his eyes narrowed as he tried to associate the location with one of the extremely confusing names. After a heartbeat, he said, "That's the small town a few miles south of Hanou."

"I believe so," Barhinder agreed, then continued, "General Lei says that Yin sent him a message the day we attacked that he was in position in Shishanzen."

"But we have already cleared the town," Caesar mused. "It was one of the first things we did, two days after the city fell." Realizing something, he told Gundomir, "I sent three Cohorts of the 14th to Shishanzen. Go find Primus Pilus Figulus and bring him here."

Returning his attention back to Barhinder, through him, Caesar pressed for more information, this time about the defenses of Boon Siou, and they were still involved in this exchange when Gundomir returned with Figulus next to him, riding the horse that had been assigned to all Primi Pili since their days in Parthia. Unlike Pullus, who actually enjoyed riding, though he pretended he didn't, the manner in which Figulus was bouncing up and down in the saddle sent the signal that he was still a man of the infantry, but Caesar had learned to hide his amusement at the sight, knowing that their backsides weren't the only tender thing when horses were involved. Very quickly, Caesar learned from Figulus that there had been no resistance in the town, nor had there been any sign of men who were clearly part of General Xao's army. As Figulus was explaining, the notes of a *cornu* sounded from the direction of the vanguard, the 30th on this day, playing the notes that informed Caesar of a returning patrol. Calling to his party to follow, Caesar went to the canter, reaching the lead Century at about the same time the riders coming from the opposite direction did, and he immediately saw that it was the young Decurion Darius himself. Although Caesar had been leery about the Parthian, the illegitimate son of Gobryas who had been part of the *drafsh* led by the *satrap*, although Gobryas had been completely unaware of his bastard or that Darius was part of the mounted archers, and the young lowborn Parthian had proven to be extremely resourceful and cunning, displaying a ruthlessness during his consolidation of power over his dead father's holdings that his father would have recognized in himself. However, he had also shown foresight; indeed, next to Bodroges, Artaxerxes, and a half-dozen other Parthians now in positions of command, Darius had been one of the first to recognize Caesar and his Legions for what they were, an unbeatable force that was smarter to join than fight. Although Caesar had sensed that Darius' oath of loyalty to the Roman cause had been one more out of convenience than anything else, it had turned out that it was the crown prince of the Elymais, Kamnaskires, who had proven untrustworthy, attempting to incite the Cohorts of auxiliaries composed of Parthians and his men from Elymais into an insurrection in Pattala. Darius had proven Caesar's doubts to be unfounded when, as Kamnaskires' second in command, he had slain the Elymais prince, ending the rebellion before it really got started, for which Caesar had promoted him to Decurion. While Hirtius had become the Legate who commanded the massive cavalry arm, and Decimus Silva was the senior Roman Decurion, Darius commanded one of the *alae* that was composed of mostly Parthians, developing into a fine officer. An officer who, Caesar could see by the grim set of his mouth, had some unwelcome news, which he quickly confirmed.

"There is a force holding that town," Darius began after offering a salute that would have gotten him smacked with the *vitus*, but Caesar had long since learned when to overlook such things, and he could see that the Parthian was genuinely upset. He learned why when Darius continued bitterly, "And they have artillery. I lost five men before we got out of range." Shaking his head, he added, "And I apologize, Caesar. We did not get close enough for me to get an idea of the number of men they have." He smiled then, flashing impossibly white teeth against his dark skin. "Although I should probably give thanks to Ahura Mazda that they did not wait for us to get within range of their scorpion bows before they launched their rocks."

"There's no need for apologies, Darius," Caesar assured him. "I have an idea of their numbers."

He stopped then, suddenly thinking of something.

Turning to address Barhinder, he said, "Ask General Lei where the nearest garrison to Boon Siou is located, and if he thinks they would have joined with this Yin."

Hiding his impatience, Caesar waited for the exchange to take place, but while he wasn't surprised, he wasn't happy at Barhinder's expression, who informed him, "General Lei says that, while there are no garrison commanders who are as..." he had to search for the word, "...militant as Yin, it is possible that some of the men at Ban Ning might desert to go to Boon Siou."

Caesar had to think for a moment, trying to recall where Ban Ning was. Remembering that it was east of the imaginary north/south line that bisected the island, with Pollio and the

Legions in Yazhou responsible for maintaining order and bringing the *Li* under control, he had to acknowledge the possibility that there could be a substantial force waiting for them in Boon Siou.

He didn't hesitate then, turning to his personal *Cornicen*, ordering, "Sound the call for Primi Pili to attend to me. It looks as if we'll have to take Boon Siou by assault."

In Yazhou, Pollio was operating under even more of a handicap in that, while he had found a merchant who spoke passable Tamil, he was the only one who could make sense of the gibberish the people spoke, using one of the Pandyan interpreters assigned to the 12th Legion. Another complication lay in the fact that Yazhou was closer to the small range of mountains that served as the base of operations for the *Li*, who saw in the arrival of the *Gwai*, the Romans now aware of the epithet and what it meant, an opportunity to regain control of at least part of the island. As time passed, through the merchant named Bang, Pollio had learned that, just as there was factionalism within the larger Han Empire, there were deep divisions among the *Li* that went back generations. In simple terms, the *Li* who occupied the eastern half of Yazhou had been more amenable to the dead rebel General Xao's offer of cooperation than their western cousins. Some of the tension stemmed from the fact that those *Li* of the mountains relied less on piracy than those of the east, therefore having less contact with the Han of the mainland, and after the abandonment ordered by Yuan, the mountain *Li* had been relying on banditry among their Han cousins who had chosen to remain. Caesar hadn't gone as far as ordering a census of Pollio's half of the island, but he had been insistent on at least knowing the rough proportions between Han and *Li*, which only increased Pollio's frustration. He was assisted by Ventidius, and Pollio's hope had been that the Muleteer's experience in governing Bharuch would prove to be valuable, but they had both been frustrated because of the huge language barrier; although they had become more accustomed to dealing with people from lands whose beliefs and culture were so vastly different from their own, but there had always been a common tongue between Romans and those of the kingdoms through which they had either conquered or traversed until reaching the Han. Pollio happily offered what was a huge amount of money for anyone who spoke one of the languages of India, yet despite this, and even after the residents of Yazhou determined that they weren't going to be slaughtered and for the most part allowed to conduct their business unimpeded, only Bang had come forward.

A month after the fall of Yazhou, the 12th and 28th were operating out of the city, and the town of Lingshui was now occupied by the 8th on the southern coast, while the 15th and the 21st were in the town of Qiongzhong, at the base of the Wuzhi mountains. However, despite Pollio's best efforts, the *Li* proved to be hopelessly intransigent, and while they weren't strong enough or organized enough to pose any kind of existential threat, the men of the 15th and 21st saw almost continuous action, albeit one Cohort at a time, which was the largest unit sent out into the countryside. Very early on, Pollio determined that his best strategy was to keep the *Li* from having free rein over the lowlands around the mountains, keeping them more concerned about protecting their mountain stronghold. What combat there was came in the form of sudden ambushes as a Cohort from one of the two Legions marched, where much like with the Khmer, the underbrush would seemingly disgorge dozens of lightly armed men, armed with a motley collection of weapons, while only their tribal leaders wore anything that could be called armor, and were also the only men using a sword. Unlike the men in Hanou, the men under Pollio's command, the two Qiongzhong Legions in particular, weren't enamored of the idea of staying put, which prompted the Legate to begin rotating the Legions, starting by bringing the 21st, who for whatever reason, had seen the most action with the *Li,* back to Yazhou, and sending Cartufenus and his 28th there, while swapping the 8th for the 12th. Once this rotation began, the restlessness among this part of the army died down, marked by Caesar's decision to release the women of Caesar's Centuries, a decision that would have caused an uproar if there hadn't been replacements, albeit with varying degrees of willingness, to take their place. Very quickly, the original women found themselves claimed by a man from the ranks who had developed feelings for a particular woman, which inevitably led to disagreements between men who believed their claim to be superior. The result was that, while it was slower than with the Legions in Hanou, Pollio's part of the army began settling into the idea of a longer stay. And, as Caesar and his Legates would learn, this would create its own set of challenges.

The assault on Boon Siou was a short but bloody affair, with Flaminius' 30th and Figulus' 14th assigned the main task, but with the fall of the town, the last effective resistance on the island was over, at least on the part of the Han who had served under General Xao. Caesar's circuit of his part of the island lasted a month before returning to Hanou to find a message waiting for him, from Zhang, sent by their courier system. The problem was, of course, that while Zhang spoke Tamil, he didn't write it, but as Caesar learned, in the capital there were men who had learned several written languages. It fell on Barhinder's shoulders to translate the written words, whereupon yet another challenge presented itself because, while Barhinder was literate in written Sanskrit, the unknown scholar in Chang'An wrote the dispatch in Tamil, and while, like with the spoken language there were many similarities, it was different enough that, aware of the probable import of the message, Barhinder was terrified of making a mistake, which he divulged to Diocles.

"I think that I am going to tell Caesar that I cannot read Tamil at all," he had confided to the Greek.

"Is that true, Barhinder?" Diocles asked gently, instead of scolding him.

"Yes!" Barhinder replied defensively. Then, under the Greek's steady gaze, he admitted, "At least, not very well." Sighing, he explained, "There are several differences, just as there are in the spoken language, but while I learned those differences from my grandfather when speaking, he could not write, so I never learned what they are."

It was, Diocles acknowledged to himself, a valid concern, particularly given the stakes involved. This prompted him to approach Pullus, explaining Barhinder's reluctance, which in turn got Pullus off his ass and heading to the *Praetorium* in the administrative center.

Once Pullus explained Barhinder's concern, to his surprise, instead of summoning Barhinder, Caesar stood up from behind his desk and said, "Let's go back to your office, Pullus."

As Caesar intended, this caught him by surprise, which in turn meant that Caesar caught his most trusted Centurion in a moment where what came out of his mouth would be the truth when Caesar posed the question that had been keeping him up at night.

"What if we stay in Hanou for at least a year?" Caesar opened, without preamble. "Do you think the men would object?"

More to stall for time, Pullus asked, "You said 'at least.' What does that mean? How much longer are you talking about?"

"That," Caesar admitted, "I can't tell you right now because I don't know." Since it wasn't a long walk to where the First Cohort of the Equestrians were quartered, Caesar wasted no time. "Matters with the Han emperor are...delicate right now, Pullus. And while I think it's a possibility, I can't completely guarantee that Yuan is going to respond the way I think he will to my last reply."

"Do I want to know?" Pullus asked lightly, although he was only partially jesting.

"Probably not," Caesar replied, and Pullus would never know that this was Caesar's repayment for some of the times his Primus Pilus had made a similar reply to one of Caesar's queries, although he hid his amusement at Pullus' obvious consternation. "Let me put it this way. The emperor was unhappy with my decision not to turn over General Lei and the other officers on the list Zhang presented to me. Although," he allowed, "the Emperor did agree that enlisting some of Xao's rankers into the Legions solved a problem, since none of Yuan's generals would have wanted men they considered rebels marching in their ranks."

Something occurred to Pullus, and he cursed himself for not thinking of it before, knowing himself well enough that he wasn't surprised when he heard his voice ask, "Are we going to be going to war on Emperor Yuan?"

"No," Caesar answered instantly, "not if I can avoid it."

Pullus made no attempt to hide his relief, but this led to another obvious question.

"What *are* we going to do, Caesar?"

"That," Caesar wasn't as quick to reply, "is what I'm thinking about now. My first goal is to gather as much information as I can about the mainland, but I don't have to tell you that's a problem. I can't just send Hirtius and the cavalry on a scouting mission in force without running the risk of provoking Yuan, but as you can imagine, it's proven to be damnably hard to learn much."

Their conversation was cut short by reaching the stone building housing the First Century, which by this time had been converted into a form recognizable to men under the standard. The Han's idea of quartering for the rankers consisted of one large room per floor, with tiers of bunks, presumably organized by what the Romans had learned was called the *Hou*, but without any kind of partitions between the Han version of the Roman section, although the Han's *Sui* consisted of eleven men. Walls had been constructed, creating a series of quarters large enough for a section, although it was a bit cramped, even for men who had become accustomed to living aboard a ship for extended periods of time. Pullus' private quarters, which had belonged to the *Hou Kuan* of the Leaping Dragons, weren't large enough for the Legion office as well, so it was on the opposite side of the long hallway that ran the length of the building. Fortunately, the door was open so that Diocles, Barhinder, and Lutatius, who happened to be there on a supply matter, all leapt to their feet, although only Lutatius went to *intente*. Without being told to by Caesar, Pullus indicated to Lutatius to leave, the Optio happy to comply, shutting the door behind him.

"I understand you have some concerns, young Gotra," Caesar began the instant he heard the door shut. "About your ability to decipher Tamil?"

"Yes, sir." Barhinder looked almost relieved...almost. "While it is similar to Sanskrit, there are several differences. It is," he said hesitantly, "difficult to explain, and I am not sure that my Greek is good enough to explain to your satisfaction. I know my Latin is not," he finished, with such a forlorn expression that Caesar, and the other two men present, had to hide their amusement.

"Why don't you try anyway?" Caesar prodded him, then gave Barhinder a cheerful grin that seemed to drop decades off of the older man. "Who knows? Maybe I'll understand it, bad Greek or not."

As intended, this made Barhinder relax slightly, his laugh not forced, and he spoke for the next several moments, using a wax tablet to write several words, while Caesar listened intently, stopping him only to ask a question every few moments. While Diocles seemed to understand the issues, Pullus could only listen and feel hopelessly lost about how the formation of characters used in both languages that, to him at least, looked identical, clearly had a different meaning.

When Barhinder finished, Caesar took control of the conversation. "If I understand you correctly, Gotra, your concern is based on the idea that whatever Han in their capital who reads our dispatches may misinterpret my intentions because of an error that you might make?"

There was no mistaking the relief on Barhinder's face, but he also added, "It also is the other way round, sir. Without knowing how fluent this Han scribe is, I am afraid that when we receive a reply, there may be some mistake on my part in translating it."

It was a valid point, Pullus knew, but it was an insight that would seem to come from an older, more mature man, and not for the first time, he was impressed that Barhinder had thought about this aspect. He could see that Caesar did as well, because he gave a thoughtful nod.

"That is true, Gotra. And," Caesar said solemnly, "it *is* a big responsibility. But," he took a step closer so that he could rest a hand on Barhinder's shoulder, "the fact that you're aware of the possible ramifications assure me that you're the best man for this task. And," he added, "I also swear to you that you wouldn't be held responsible for any kind of difficulty that arises because of a miscommunication."

There was no missing the slight sag of relief of Barhinder's body, but he didn't hesitate to say, "I swear to you, sir, I will do my utmost to make sure that the wording is clear, both in what I write and in what I translate for you."

"That is all that I ask, Gotra," Caesar replied.

And, as it turned out, Barhinder would be put to the test three days later, when a message arrived from Chang'An, with an offer that would serve as the prelude to what would become the final chapter of this extraordinary campaign.

"The province we're being offered is called Minyue," Caesar announced to the assembled officers. "It is four times the size of Zhuya, and it's about six hundred miles north of here, with a long coastline that supposedly has several large anchorages." He paused for the inevitable rumble of comment this created between his officers, knowing that this reaction was just the beginning, because what he was about to say next had a high potential for dramatic reaction. Once they understood that Caesar had no intention of continuing until it was quiet again, the room fell silent. Even so, Caesar had to take a deep breath, before he went on, "In exchange for this province, we would be at the service of Emperor Yuan for a period of five years, as part of his royal army. Although," he added unnecessarily, "I would retain full command."

For a bare moment, Caesar thought that perhaps he had miscalculated, because instead of an uproar, the room went even quieter, but it was destined to last for no more than a heartbeat before the eruption of noise, in the form of voices hardened by decades of bellowing at the top of their lungs.

"He wants us to be his *subjects*?"

"No Roman would ever bend the knee to a king, especially a barbarian!"

"And what about the savages already living there? What will they do? If they're like the *Li*, we'll spend all five years fighting those *cunni*!"

"If we accept this, that means that we won't even be able to return home for another *five years*?"

This and other challenges were hurled at Caesar, seemingly all at once so that those were the only ones Caesar could pick out amid the babble of voices, all of them angry. With, Caesar noticed, one exception; Pullus was sitting there, massive arms folded, behaving very much like this was a form of entertainment as he watched with obvious amusement. You *bastard*! Caesar shouted in his mind. You already knew! Instantly following that came a chiding; of *course* he knew, Gaius. You really think that young Gotra would have kept his mouth shut? And, he allowed, it was clear that Pullus hadn't divulged this to any of the other Primi Pili, all of whom were now present, a week after the message arrived, Pollio, Ventidius, and his Primi Pili arriving the day before.

"Pullus," Caesar had to speak louder than he would have liked over the others, "you've been silent. Why is that?"

Rather than look discomfited, the brawny Centurion replied without hesitation, "Because I know that you'd never accept that offer, because it's not an offer; it's a bribe."

Out of everyone present, it was Caesar's Legates who looked the most abashed, which Caesar assumed was because, once Pullus articulated it, Caesar's response to this was a foregone conclusion, one they should have immediately reached themselves.

"You're correct," Caesar acknowledged, his own arms folded now as he sat down on the front of his desk. "I have no intention of accepting the offer, but are you suggesting that I make that known to Emperor Yuan immediately?"

Pullus, suddenly looking not as smug, shifted a bit on his stool as he thought about it for a moment. Caesar saw the look of dawning understanding on the Primus Pilus' face, which was confirmed when Pullus answered, speaking slowly as he formed the thought, "No, you shouldn't. In fact, I think that you should tell him that you're thinking about it, but there are several issues that need to be discussed with us before you do tell him your final decision."

It was actually Figulus of the 14th who offered, "You can also tell that bast...the Emperor that you'll have to send a party out to survey this place he's offering, because you can bet that it's a *cac*hole. He wouldn't be offering up land that would be prime farm or pastureland."

Very quickly, a consensus developed; rather than an outright refusal, Caesar would make noises as if he was seriously considering Yuan's offer, and he would in fact dispatch an expedition to travel to this Minyue place to examine it, both because of their certainty that they were under observation at all times, and on the admittedly small chance that this Minyue was inhabitable. The only question left unanswered was who, besides Volusenus, Hirtius, and the cavalry would be making another voyage, while it was also decided that, as far as the rankers were concerned, they would be assured just like Yuan that he was sincere in considering this place as a final stopping place for all men who chose it. What was left unsaid was the recognition on the part of all of the officers, to one degree or another, that this was a risk; once the men determined that Caesar had no intention of accepting this offer, he and the senior officers might be facing another mutiny.

It was destined to be the Alaudae who accompanied Legates Volusenus and Hirtius, with half of the cavalry, with Silva as the senior Decurion, leaving on the Kalends of Februarius, a year after they landed on Zhuya. The cavalry had been whittled down to six thousand men by this point, and countless numbers of horses, although thanks to an aggressive breeding program overseen by the Galatian Decurion Arctosages, they hadn't been forced to rely on the smaller ponies native to this part of the world. Finding native horsemen, however, had proven to be more of a challenge; of the new Han recruits that were added to the army rolls, less than five percent had been deemed competent enough horsemen to join the cavalry, which by this point in time was led by a roughly equal number of Germans, Gauls, Galatians, and Parthians. Gundomir's brother Barvistus had been moved, at his request, from Caesar's personal bodyguard to the cavalry, which Caesar suspected was because of the younger brother's antipathy to the friendship Gundomir and Teispes had formed, which made Barvistus feel like the odd man out, all part and parcel of life in an army that had been together for almost seven years now. For the Legions and cavalry left behind, life continued as normal, with the addition of the speculation that quickly became the dominating topic in every section's quarters across the army; what was this Minyue place like? Pullus had learned through his Centurions that the consensus was that, if it was similar to

Zhuya, those men who were inclined to settle down to farm or raise some sort of livestock would be content, while the same couldn't be said for those men, like Vellusius, or at least the Vellusius before Jiā, whose idea of a place to settle down included a variety of brothels and the Han version of *tavernae*, which could only be found in a relatively large town or a city like Hanou. Otherwise, what was taking place with Caesar's army on Zhuya was a repetition of the same thing that had begun back in their first winter in Parthia. Relationships that may have started out as transactional evolved, some slowly, some more rapidly, although the pace of even the quickly developing romances between rankers and Han women was slower than they had been in places like Bharuch and Muziris, due to the vast differences in culture. In fact, it turned out to be the Pandyan rankers, now into the third year into their own enlistment, who were the first to begin forming more permanent partnerships, which, unsurprisingly, created problems of its own.

"It's because many Han women in Hanou have at least heard of Pandya before because it has a port city," Barhinder had explained, Pullus having pressed him to speak to Long about it in the aftermath of a brawl in the Jade Goddess brothel between a half-dozen Romans and an equal number of Pandyans. He paused, not as willing to relate the rest of what Long had said, but knowing that Master Titus wouldn't let it rest until he did, he went on, "And your coloring still scares many of them."

"The *Gwai* thing," Scribonius commented. "Juán said something about it," instantly regretting it because of what could only be called smirks on the faces of his friends.

"Did she?" Pullus teased. "I didn't realize that you spent so much time talking when you're with her."

"Oh, go piss on your boots," Scribonius muttered.

As surprised as Pullus and Balbus had been when they learned of the burgeoning relationship between Long's oldest daughter and their friend, it was nothing compared to the state of shock Scribonius still found himself in when he thought about it, which was several times a day. Setting aside the age difference, which as the Romans had learned in their travels, wasn't unusual with other cultures either because of the higher mortality rate of women, Scribonius considered it a minor miracle that Juán had even noticed the lanky *Gwai* Centurion. What was now a relationship had actually begun during their time at Ke Van, after Long's business and home was burned to the ground, forcing him and his family to seek refuge in the huge camp outside the town. Scribonius had been returning from the *Quaestorium*, checking on three of his men recovering from a fever when the unusual sound of a female weeping drew his attention, following the noise to find the girl he recognized as Long's daughter crouched behind the tent that had become her family home, head in hands and hair covering her face, her shoulders shaking as she sobbed. For a long moment, he seriously considered just walking past; unlike Pullus, Scribonius had never developed an attachment to a woman during his time under the standard, not because he didn't like women, but because his heart still belonged to Aurelia, to whom he had been betrothed until he followed his brother to join the ranks led by the demagogue Cataline. In the aftermath of what was essentially a slaughter, in which his older brother fell, Scribonius had been forced to flee, ending up in Hispania, where he had joined the 10th Legion, while his former betrothed married the surviving Scribonius brother. Since that time, Scribonius, while not nearly as prolific a debaucher as Balbus, had availed himself of the whores who were part of the tail of camp followers during the Gallic campaign and civil war, and whenever in winter quarters since Parthia.

Now, as he stood there debating what to do, he was as surprised as Juán when he squatted beside her and, without thinking, reached out to pat her awkwardly on the shoulder. In hindsight, he realized that her reaction, a shriek of terror as she leapt to her feet while babbling in Han, holding her hands out in supplication, making it clear that she thought Scribonius was about to rape her, was understandable. This mortified him, yet despite the language barrier, he managed to communicate that he had no such intention, mainly by simply dropping to the ground to sit there, saying nothing but just gazing at her steadily. To Juán, this behavior was so odd that she thought the tall *Gwai* might be touched in the head, yet for some reason, she found herself dropping back into her spot, and while there were still tears, she proceeded to tell this strange man everything, about how she and her family had lost the only place she had ever lived, all because her father had been so stupid to sell unwanted daughters to his *Gwai* barbarians. And, Scribonius just sat and listened, understanding none of it, yet knowing that something was troubling her and wishing he knew what it was. She quickly lost her self-consciousness, allowing her teeth to be shown, which was considered impolite in the extreme, as she unburdened herself, using her hands as much as her words, using one to brush her long black hair from her face as it flew about because of her emphatic gestures. By the time she took a breath, Sextus Scribonius was smitten; what he would only learn later was that Juán was every bit as intrigued by this tall soldier, and while it wasn't as important a role as he played in larger events, it was Barhinder to whom she went to learn more about this Scribonius. Under the guise of teaching Juán Latin, something that her father actually encouraged, although not for the same purpose as his daughter, he aided her in her quest. It took several weeks before the moment was right, Barhinder slipping out of the Legion office and hurrying to Long's pair of tents, one for his business scouring the countryside for rice and other consumables, where Juán worked keeping accounts using a strange-looking contraption called an abacus, letting her know the moment was at hand. As far Scribonius was concerned, it was just a regular meeting of the Pili Priores, and he was completely unaware that, once the meeting broke up, when Barhinder stopped him on his way out of the outer office to ask him about a report that he knew very well had already been turned in, allowing for the other Centurions to leave and return to their area, it was for a different purpose. Scribonius, assuring Barhinder that the report had been sent, exited the tent, shaking his head at yet another moment where the bureaucracy of the entity known as the army had fouled up.

"*Salve*, Sextus Scribonius. How are you today?"

That had been the true beginning of what was now the longest relationship with a woman Sextus Scribonius had ever had, and while he was happy, he was also aware that there would come a moment where he would have to make a decision, because Scribonius, who had been the first of anyone in the entire army to deduce that Caesar had no intention of stopping, knew they would be leaving Zhuya, marching once again to wherever Caesar took them.

"Caesar says that he is seriously considering our offer," Zhang announced, having hurried to the palace as soon as Ming, a merchant's son he had hired as a scribe who could read and write Tamil, had translated the message that had arrived by courier. "And he said that he was sending his exploring officer Volusenus to Minyue immediately to perform a survey."

It was now the Roman month of Februarius, five days after the Ides, or *xingyuè;* the "apricot month" to the Han, with bare trees and a bite to the air here in Chang'An, and Yuan was in a sour mood. Despite knowing how unlikely it was that the *Gwai* general would immediately agree to his offer, it was still a bitter blow, although he did acknowledge to himself that his disappointment had more to do with the war with Zhizhi than any expectation that Caesar would have been so foolish to snap at the bait he had offered.

"I don't suppose that Caesar offered a date by which we could expect an answer," Yuan grumbled.

Before he answered, Zhang turned to his scribe, who he had brought with him, but Ming, who was clearly petrified at being in the presence of the Emperor, peered down at the scroll that bore the red seal of the *Gwai* general Caesar, then gave a tiny shake of his head.

"No, Bìxià," Zhang replied regretfully, but before he could say anything else, Yuan snapped, "I know! I'm not blind. I saw him shake his head." Then, to Zhang's relieved surprise, the most powerful man in their world held up a hand in placation, saying, "That was unnecessary, Meng. I should not have chastised you in this manner."

It wasn't an apology, but Zhang didn't expect one; that Yuan actually went this far was extraordinary, and the fact that he used his familiar name was a moment that he would recall the rest of his life.

"Emissary Zhang," Xian spoke for the first time. "Do you believe that Caesar is sincere in his statement that he is seriously considering our Emperor's offer?"

By this time, Zhang had become experienced in the game played by courtiers to the Emperor, and he was certain that there was some form of trap in the eunuch's seemingly innocent question, so he didn't answer immediately, forcing himself to think carefully, even as he recognized that it was a valid question.

"I believe," he finally began, speaking slowly as he tried to think of all the ramifications his words might carry with them, and not just for himself, "that he is stalling for time, Counselor." Pausing to further gather his thoughts, he went on, "I also think that much depends on the mood of his army and whether they are determined to return to Roman lands, or whether they are willing to settle down."

"The mood of his army?" Shi scoffed from his chair in his usual spot off to the side of the Emperor's throne; Zhang had learned very quickly, thanks to Master Zhou, who was actually present for this hastily called meeting, that nothing Zhang saw in the audience chamber was random, that every piece of furniture, especially the specially made chairs for the Emperor's council, was placed in its spot for a reason. "If this *Gwai* is the kind of general that he supposedly is, his army will do whatever he tells them to do!" Suddenly assuming what Zhang had learned was Shi's sly expression, the Emperor's cousin suggested, "Perhaps it's time to start spreading gold among the *Gwai's* troops, Your Highness. If I'm understanding Emissary Zhang correctly, that Caesar is afraid of his own men, there might be an opportunity for us."

Zhang knew that he had to stop this before it got any further; through Master Zhou, he had learned that Yuan was growing increasingly worried about the possibility that the *Xiongnu* upstart Zhizhi might actually be successful in wresting control of the strategically important western provinces away from him, a tragedy that would reverberate throughout the entire Han Empire.

"I beg your forgiveness, Bìxià," Zhang said humbly. "Clearly, I gave Excellency Shi the impression that Caesar is not in control of his army, and that he fears his own men. Nothing I've seen supports that belief. All I meant to say is that, if Caesar's men are happy with this survey that he is ordering of Minyue, it's entirely possible that his men would be willing to settle down."

Zhang hid his relief when Yuan nodded his head, and experienced a sense of satisfaction at the scowl Shi gave him, but while this seemed to soothe the Emperor, it wasn't destined to last long, when Xian asked, "Even with His Highness' condition of five years of service, Emissary Zhang? Do you think that his men would be willing to exchange five years of their lives in his service in exchange for this land? Land," the eunuch turned to Yuan, and while his tone was deferential, the words weren't, "that His Highness himself said is worthless because it's too mountainous."

"It may be worthless to us," Master Zhou interjected from his spot on the opposite side of the room from Shi, rubbing his beads with the fingers of one hand, "but we don't know enough of these Romans to know whether or not they would view it as we do." Before Xian could reply, Zhou pointed out, "Remember, while they are subsisting on rice now, according to Emissary Zhang, they much prefer wheat as their staple crop. And," his brow furrowed, but he couldn't remember the funny name, and he turned to Zhang, who fortunately knew what his master was looking for, supplying the words, "chickpeas and lentils." There were some snickers at these ridiculous names, but Zhou pointed out, "For all that we know, these things may grow on mountainous terrain like Minyue."

While this certainly made sense, and was possibly true, Zhang didn't think it likely, and he was relieved to see that Yuan seemed to feel the same way, replying, "As usual, that is a wise observation, Master, but I don't know that we can rely on it as being the case. So," he turned his head to address Zhang, and while his tone was neither hostile nor accusing, it still made Zhang go weak in the knees, "if this alternative that *you* suggested isn't accepted by Caesar, what else do you suggest? After all," he pointed out, unnecessarily, "of all of us, you are the only man of the Han who has spent any time with these barbarians, and this was your proposal."

All of this was true, Zhang knew, not that it made him feel any better, but fortunately, Zhang had in fact been spending much of his time in the capital researching another alternative, so he was able to reply without hesitation, or at least much, "I do have another idea, Your Highness."

By the time Zhang was through, the mood in the room seemed to be evenly divided, with one group of the Emperor's councilors glowering at the young emissary and the other beaming with approval, unusual in itself in a culture where emotions were supposed to be kept hidden. Aiding Zhang's cause was that, of all the smiles, it was Emperor Yuan's that was the broadest.

"That, Meng, is a truly brilliant idea," Yuan had enthused, which of course forced the others to agree, with varying degrees of keenness, but they all knew that this kind of endorsement couldn't be gainsaid. "In fact," the Emperor chortled, "we need to make offerings that Caesar does turn down my offer of Minyue."

During his walk back to his quarters, Zhang felt as if he was floating, and he decided in the moment to hurry to his father's house to let him know that his idea had found such favor. After all, the elder Zhang had provided the catalyst for Zhang's proposal to the Emperor, based in one conversation.

"You know," Zhang's father had said as they sipped *chai* several weeks earlier, on the son's obligatory visit to his sire, "as much as your grandfather enjoyed exploring the barbarian lands to the west along the Silk Road, he always had one regret."

"Oh?" Zhang asked as he drank from his cup, though he wasn't all that interested. "What was that?"

"He always wanted to see the Islands of the Wa," Zhang's father replied. "It is the end of the world, after all. And," he set his cup down, "I don't know if you're aware, but we have tried in the past to claim the islands as our own and have never been successful. Apparently, the Wa are savages who are so fierce that they've been able to repel anyone landing on their shores."

Zhang had gone still, but his mind was racing, although he cautioned himself against getting too excited.

"What do we know about the Wa?" he asked, trying to sound casual.

"Not much," his father admitted. "Although what we do

know would be in the Imperial archives. You know," the elder Zhang commented, "I actually know *Zhubu* Zhi quite well," naming the Master of Documents for the Imperial government. "If you'd like, I can introduce you. I'm sure he would be happy to help and give you access to everything we have on the Wa."

That had been the beginning of what would become the one thing that Caesar couldn't resist, the allure of the only unconquerable kingdom left in their world. Despite the fact that Zhang Meng was the man who put it all in motion, not even he could have imagined what the next two-plus years would bring, nor the ramifications to his entire world.

"There's a reason Emperor Yuan offered us Minyue," Volusenus said, immediately after taking a seat in Caesar's office. "It's worse than Greece or Cisalpine Gaul in terms of the terrain." It was now late April, and Volusenus had come straight from the docks, having transferred from the *Philotemia* to the Liburnian three days earlier, leaving the part of the fleet carrying the Alaudae and the cavalry behind. Referring to one of the several tablets he had brought, Volusenus continued, "That said, it *is* lightly populated, and there's only one village of about three thousand people at the mouth of a river the locals call the Min that's the widest and most navigable inland, although it's nothing like the rivers in India. And," he looked up, "we didn't see any uniformed men, although the village does have a wall, and there were a handful of men with spears standing on the walls. They," he chuckled, "ran like scared rabbits when Primus Pilus Batius took his Century into the village."

Volusenus paused to take a sip from his cup, and Caesar mused, "So, as we suspected, what Yuan offered us is land that he's happy to be rid of because it holds no value to him."

"That would be my assessment, Caesar," Volusenus agreed. Holding up a hand, he continued, "That's not to say that there is *no* arable land, although during our time there, the weather is essentially the same as it is here, and it's too wet to grow wheat anyway."

"By the gods," Caesar groaned, "I *loathe* rice, I truly do."

"So do most of the men," Volusenus offered, although

there was no need, Caesar knowing very well that, of all the complaints about this strange land, it was the lack of wheat to make bread that was at the top of the list. Going back to his tablet, he continued, "Decurion Silva took five *alae* inland, following the Min almost to its source, which was about seventy-five miles, but that's where the real mountains start. The range runs north to south, but the terrain was too rugged for horses, at least for us who don't know of the passes and other trails."

"So the locals wouldn't tell you?" Caesar asked skeptically. "Even with Gotra and Long?"

"It wasn't that," Volusenus said, shaking his head. "It's just that we couldn't find any peasants who have ventured into those mountains. Apparently, there's a dragon or some such that devours anyone who ventures too far."

It had been yet another discovery on the part of Caesar and his army on their trek eastward; although Romans knew in a general sense about dragons, once they left India, the ubiquity of dragons in various forms, either as sculptures, engravings, carvings, and most commonly embroidered on flags and banners had ignited a fierce debate that permeated through every rank, which was roughly evenly split between men who believed they had to exist given how commonly they were depicted, and those, like Caesar, who believed it was just another thing conjured up by the imagination of men who needed some way to explain otherwise unexplainable events. Regardless of his disbelief, Caesar had also recognized that, especially for his newest recruits, the dragon was a powerful symbol, and he had adopted it in a limited way. For his role in assaulting Hanou, for example, Caesar had awarded Pullus an ornate ring made of solid gold, with a dragon engraved on its face, although the large Primus Pilus only wore it on special occasions with all of his other awards. At this moment, however, all that mattered was that the peasants of Minyue clearly believed these creatures existed if Volusenus was to be believed, and Caesar did, if only because he had seen how well Gotra and the Han merchant worked together to extract information from otherwise suspicious Han of all ranks.

Setting aside the presence of a dragon, Caesar asked

bluntly, "Based on what you've seen, is there enough arable land to support the men of the army who want to settle down?"

"That depends," Volusenus replied cautiously, "on how many of them there are." Before Caesar could say anything, he hurried to add, "There's also a large island two days sailing to the east. While Silva was on his scouting trip, I took five Cohorts of the Alaudae to survey it. If anything, it's even worse than Minyue, the mountains are less than twenty miles from the coast, and there's even less flat ground."

Caesar grimaced, unhappy not at Volusenus but with himself, knowing as soon as he said it what his Legate's answer would be.

"That," he sighed, "is what I'm trying to determine, how many men that would be. Right now, the only men who are even close to the end of their enlistment are the Alaudae, the 8th, and the 12th. They all had a *dilectus* two or three years before we left Brundisium, and the Equestrians was just the year before, and their terms were all sixteen years, so by law, none of them are close. But..."

It was unusual that Caesar didn't finish a thought, but Volusenus understood why, and he supplied, "...this isn't about the law, it's about what we've all been through."

"Exactly," Caesar nodded, relieved that he didn't have to articulate it himself, because he knew very well that what his army had been through had all been in support of *his* goals, not Rome's, not the Senate, not the plebs, but for Caesar's ambitions. There was a silence, which he broke by saying, "You said that the Alaudae and cavalry should be arriving in two days?"

"About that," Volusenus agreed, "depending on the weather of course. This isn't the wet season anymore, but we ran into heavy weather coming from the east almost every other day. We lost a *chuan* on the way there, but it was only carrying some of the cavalry horses, and Silva brought enough spares."

"Then I'm going to wait for the rest of your fleet to return to Hanou," Caesar decided. "Then I'm going to wait one or two days before I call an assembly." Seeing Volusenus' reaction, he explained, "If I called a meeting now, Gaius, and told them that Minyue isn't what Yuan told us it was and isn't suitable for habitation, how many men would think I was just telling them this because I wanted to continue this campaign?"

He didn't want to, but Volusenus was forced to admit, "A fair number."

"This way, once Publius from the Alaudae," Caesar went on, using the generic name for a ranker that had been in use for the gods only knew how long, "goes out into the city to the *tavernae* and tells all of his friends in the Equestrians that Minyue is the *cac*hole that I'm going to tell them it is, it makes my task easier."

While that was true, to Volusenus, it didn't address the larger issue, but he approached the topic cautiously.

"Are the men still happy to stay here in Hanou?"

"Yes," Caesar answered shortly then said nothing else, telling Volusenus what he needed to know.

He was about to ask the next, obvious question, then decided against it. Part of him didn't want to know what Caesar planned to do about the complacency that had settled on his army, although he also didn't know why Caesar intended to continue this campaign. Despite his absences, Volusenus was kept informed of Caesar's thinking by his fellow Legates, and he knew that Caesar wasn't going to march against the Han unless the Romans were provoked into it. The most likely provocation would be if the Han cut off the Roman supply line, tenuous as it was, that stretched back to Ke Van, where Long's oldest son had remained, scouring the countryside for every extra grain of rice, pig, and other consumables to augment what could be produced on Zhuya. When Caesar had informed Zhang that the island produced enough food to sustain his army and livestock, it hadn't been a lie, but the margin of error had been razor thin, and they had been on Zhuya long enough for the harvest in October, which had yielded less than expected. Why this had happened was a matter of debate, but it had brought home to Caesar something that his counterpart Emperor Yuan had discovered; the presence of a garrison of a size that allowed the Han government to maintain control of the island and pacify the fractious *Li* strained the resources on Zhuya, forcing Yuan to shift some of those needed resources from other parts of his vast empire. In short, staying on Zhuya wasn't a viable long-term option, if Caesar wanted his army to be self-sufficient, but neither was taking on the Han Empire.

When Volusenus left Caesar, this was the dilemma that the greatest general in history pondered, sitting in yet another office seized from yet another enemy, just as he had been doing for weeks, but had gotten no closer to a solution, and while he hadn't truly expected Minyue to be a paradise where his men would be happy to settle, he was still profoundly disappointed. Even with as prodigious a mind as Caesar's, he was no closer to a solution than when he first began contemplating what came next. He was proven correct in one regard; the arrival of the Alaudae and the cavalry back to Hanou meant that, just as he had predicted, within a day and once the rankers were allowed out into the city, the men of Pullus' Legion were aware of the unviability of Minyue as a place to settle. It took another few days for the cavalrymen who returned to their postings around the island to spread the word to the Legions in their garrisons in Soon Biou, Yazhou, Qinzhou and Chongzou, but while it reduced the immediate pressure about their future, Caesar knew that he was living on borrowed time. It was on the Ides of May when Zhang Meng arrived in Hanou, in person, with another proposal from Emperor Yuan.

"It's called the Isle of Wa," Caesar informed his assembled officers, eight days after the Ides of May on what would turn out to be the ninth year of a campaign that would last a decade. All of the Legates and Primi Pili were present, but since this had been a preplanned meeting, none of them had been aware of Zhang's return until they arrived and saw the Han emissary sitting to one side of the room. Once the rustling of comment died down, Caesar continued, "And, as you can see," he indicated the large map, of which a massive amount of space was empty, "even the Han know very little about it, other than its existence and what you see here."

Pullus, sitting in his usual spot in the second row just behind the Legates, examined the large map, made of pieces of vellum stitched together, and he was struck by a thought; *I wonder how many of these are rolled up somewhere by now?* What greeted his eyes now was, as had happened so many times before, maddeningly incomplete, with the outline of the Han coastline extending only about halfway up to the top of the map, and he could see the word "Minyue" to the left of the vertical line representing the eastern coastline farther north. By this time, he had heard about the results of the expedition and that what the Han emperor had offered was essentially a wasteland of mountains and very little flat ground. The vertical line terminated a couple of inches above Minyue, waiting to be filled out, and it made Pullus wonder whether Zhang was deliberately withholding information about what he did know was the heart of the Han empire.

He returned his attention to Caesar in time to hear him say, "Emissary Zhang has informed me that he's been instructed by Emperor Yuan to make another offer now that we've examined Minyue and determined it's not suitable for our purposes." Pullus was certain that he wasn't the only one who noticed the vague wording about what exactly Caesar had had in mind for the unwanted region, but he continued listening to his general. "While the Han say they don't know much about the people of Wa, they do know that it's a much, much larger island than Zhuya, and it has enough arable land to support a large population." Caesar, as was his habit, had been moving his head as he spoke, scanning the members of his audience to make eye contact with each and every man present, something that was unique to their general, but Pullus noticed how Caesar seemed to be pointedly ignoring Zhang, who was sitting there with his normal expression that the Romans found impossible to interpret. "It's also the case that more than one of the current emperor's predecessors mounted expeditions to take the island, but they were all unsuccessful. The emperor's emissary wasn't particularly forthcoming, but after some persuasion, what he told Achaemenes was that these previous campaigns hadn't just failed but had been extremely costly in lost lives." He offered his listeners a small smile. "From what I can gather, the Wa are to the Han what Carthage was to us, and my guess is that if it wasn't for the emperor's current problems on his western border, he would be extremely interested in taking Wa for himself." He's not mentioning names, Pullus thought, because he doesn't want Zhang to be aware that he's talking about what he believes is really going on, and as far as Pullus could tell, it appeared to be working. "The important thing," Caesar was continuing, "is that there is obviously something about this island that the emperor and his people covet."

He paused to take a sip, which Pollio took advantage of by asking, "Is the emperor offering us this island?"

Whereas it was normal for Caesar to prime one of his Legates, or occasionally Primi Pili to ask a question for which he was prepared, Pullus saw by his expression that Caesar hadn't set this up, a flash of irritation crossing his face.

Nevertheless, he didn't lash out at Pollio, answering evenly, "In simple terms, yes. But," he raised a hand, "there are conditions attached, and that's what we need to discuss."

Pullus didn't return to his quarters for a full watch, and when he entered the Legion office across the hall from his private quarters, it was only to beckon to Diocles, who leapt from his desk and followed Pullus into his quarters.

"Shut the door," Pullus said, unnecessarily, Diocles having long before learned to interpret the signs his large master gave and was already doing so. Dropping down onto his chair at the table where he and his friends took their meals, Pullus asked, "Did you know about this?"

"About what?" Diocles asked cautiously.

"About this business with the Isle of Wa," Pullus replied, and the Greek felt his master's eyes searching his face.

"Only that it exists," Diocles answered honestly. "Apollodorus told me something about it the day after Zhang arrived." Seeing Pullus' acceptance of this, he asked with a frown, "Why?"

"Because," Pullus sighed, "we're going to be leaving Hanou on the Kalends of Junius, and we're going to be going to this Isle of Wa and taking it."

Made in the USA
Monee, IL
10 July 2022